WITHDRAWN

Fantasy Voyages

Fantasy Voyages

Great Science Fiction from *The Saturday Evening Post*

with introductions by
Vincent Miranda, Science Fiction Editor

1979
The Curtis Publishing Company
Indianapolis, Indiana

All of the characters in this book are fictitious, and any resemblance to actual persons, living or dead, is purely coincidental.

Fantasy Voyages
Great Science Fiction from The Saturday Evening Post
Revised Edition
Art Associate: Caroline M. Capehart
Editorial Staff: Jacquelyn S. Sibert, Cathy L. Bergner
Stories Selected By The Editors of
The Saturday Evening Post

Library of Congress Catalog Number 79-55717
ISBN 0-89387-036-6

Contents

Doctor Hanray's Second Chance

by Conrad Richter

Conrad Richter's excursions into fantasy were unfortunately few. The Post *introduced two of these rare pieces. "Doctor Hanray's Second Chance" provided the central theme for his novel* The Waters of Kronos, *for which he received the 1960 National Book Award. The other piece, "Sinister Journey," is also contained in this volume. Richter's other novels include* The Fields, The Trees, The Light in the Forest *(which became a popular Disney film) and* The Town, *which gained him the 1950 Pulitzer Prize for fiction.*

Doctor Hanray's Second Chance

by Conrad Richter

If he had known it would be like this, he wouldn't have come, he told himself. Here he was, back in his native valley at last. He had driven more than a thousand miles to see it again, this triangle of river and long blue mountains that shut in the rich brown farming land. This was where he had been born and bred. Why, he used to know every field and patch of woods. Here if anywhere, he felt, he could find himself again.

And yet, now that he had come, it didn't mean anything. It seemed hollow and dead, like every other place he had been since these spells had come over him. It was true then, he told himself. Something must be seriously wrong with him, something different perhaps and yet quite as deadly in its way as the burns of atomic radiation he had at first suspected. But exactly what it could be, neither the doctors nor himself had as yet been able to find out.

He drove slowly along the black-top road. A large board announced: ROSE VALLEY MILITARY RESERVATION. U. S. ARMY. NO ADMISSION. Ahead to the right and left he could see the high steel fence topped with strands of barbed wire. At the little house in the center of the road, he obeyed the sign that said, STOP!

"I would like permission to go into Stone Church," he requested.

"What for?" the guard wanted to know.

"Just to look around. I was raised here."

"You can't do that. It's too late in the day. Besides, no civilians allowed. This is a restricted area. Very secret and highly dangerous."

"I know about that," the man in the car said. Then, after a moment, "I believe I have a right to visit the graves of my parents."

"You'll have to prove who you are." The guard went in for a moment and came back with a sheaf of dirty papers, evidently a list of the dead in the reservation. "What's the name?"

"My father's name was Doctor John Hanray. My name is Peter Hanray. Here are some identification papers."

The guard stared. His tanned face flushed. His lean, hard features altered with respect.

"I'm sorry I didn't know you, Doctor Hanray. I can see it's you now, sir, from your pictures. I'll phone Colonel Hollenbeck you're here. You'll find him in his office. He's in Building A."

"I didn't come to see Colonel Hollenbeck," Hanray declared quietly. "I just want permission to go in and look around. By myself."

The guard stirred uneasily. "Yes, sir. I'll speak to the colonel, sir." He hurried back into the little house, and the visitor thought he could make out an occasional phrase: "Yes, sir; it's him, sir . . . the one who made the A-bomb. . . . He don't want to come up. . . . No, alone; all alone! . . . Yes, sir, I'll tell him." The guard appeared. "The colonel's coming down," he said with satisfaction, as of a victory he had part in, and went on talking eagerly of the valley, as if his job in the reservation had made them fellow natives.

Outside a distant building, a flurry of dust suddenly rose and died. After a moment an olive-colored military car came flying up, and a tall, gentlemanly colonel got out.

"I'm sorry to keep you waiting, Doctor Hanray," he said,

shaking hands. "If you had let us know you were coming, we'd have been all ready for you. Just the same, if you can give me a few minutes, I'll take you around."

"Thank you," the scientist said bleakly, "but it's not an official visit. Just a personal one. I'm not working right now. In fact, I have been laid up a bit. You may know that I was raised here at Stone Church. I'd like to visit my parents' graves and look around. By myself. I'm sure you'll understand."

The colonel's face fell a little. "Certainly. If that's what you want, sir, I'll have my chauffeur drive you around."

"If you don't mind, I'd like to go in alone."

The colonel's face looked gravely unhappy. "I understand, sir. Unfortunately, the regulations are very strict, as you know. Visitors are required to have guides, even the most distinguished ones. Something might blow up or you might get lost. Even men who lived in the valley all their lives come back to work here and get confused. Everything's been changed around. I'm sure, though, that if I phoned Washington——"

"No, that's all right," the physicist said wearily. "I'll take a guide. But ask him to stay as far behind me as he can. If I can't go in that way, I don't want to go in at all. When I stop, tell him to stop behind me and wait. I hope you have a patient man. I may stand looking at nothing, so far as he's concerned, for a long time."

Well, he told himself, as he drove quietly through the steel fence, the valley had certainly changed. As the colonel had warned him, he hardly knew where he was any more. The rambling Army buildings, the absence of familiar landmarks confused him. Now whose barn had stood here at this pile of stones, and where was the house? A few of the old houses could still be seen, but surely that paintless, boarded-up box couldn't be the Foster house, where he had once enjoyed such good times.

He stopped, motioning for the jeep behind him to drive abreast of his car.

"I'm trying to find out where I am. Where's the road that used to come down over Penny Hill?"

"Oh, there's no road up there any more. The Government didn't want it. They bulldozed it out."

Hanray felt a sense of loss and bereavement. He had loved that Penny Hill road, used to walk it as a boy.

"Well," he said, "perhaps you can tell me whose house this used to be over here?"

But the guard did not know who had lived there. "Whoever they were," he added, " they kicked about getting out. You can bet on that."

"What did they kick about?"

"Anything and everything. First they said they didn't have enough time."

"How much time did they have?"

"Everybody on the reservation had the same notice. Three days to get their money from the Government and move out. But they weren't satisfied. They came back afterward and tried to buy back some of the stuff they'd sold with their property. Like their bathtubs, those that had them. Their sinks and corncribs and sheds. They claimed the new places they bought didn't have them and they couldn't buy any new plumbing or lumber on account of priorities."

"Well, the Government didn't need their old bathtubs and corncribs."

"No, they had to burn up the old lumber and throw the sinks and bathtubs on the junk pile. The colonel said it would cost twenty-five to fifty dollars in red tape to get every sink or bathtub through Washington. And it would take weeks besides. The colonel told them to forget it. They were just casualties of the war."

The scientist winced. "Here too," he murmured to himself.

"Oh, four or five of your neighbors here were tough babies. They stuck on their places and wouldn't get off. The last one to give up was an old woman. She stopped by the gate with her house goods and told the guard all her troubles, how her father and grandfather farmed the farm before her, and their folks before that, way back to the Revolution. The guard listened till he was tired. Then he said, 'Well, now you know how the Indians felt when you ran them off.'" The uniformed man in the jeep laughed, but the physicist didn't laugh.

"I'm afraid that old lady didn't run off any Indians," he said, very low.

"Well, maybe not. But the contractors had to come in. We had to start getting out things for the men at the front to fight with. Like your A-bomb. They made plenty stuff for it right here. I guess you know that."

The scientist winced again.

The guard went on admiringly, "I guess that was the greatest thing ever invented. Just think, something that wiped out a whole city and a hundred thousand of those rats at one crack. And I hear that's nothing to what you can do now."

Hanray sat at the wheel, very still. He felt the old nausea and shell-like feeling coming over him. Then he drove slowly on.

Well, he told himself after a little, they hadn't destroyed the road that ran down by Jarretts' farm anyway. This must be it he was passing, looking strangely narrower and shorter than it used to. How many times had he walked that road with one of the Jarrett girls after church or choir practice! But where were Jarretts' woods in which the preacher's boys had hidden one night to scare him?

How much faster you went in a car than he used to in a buggy. This was Stone Church already, or Deckertown as some called it, with half the houses gone and the rest reduced to windowless boxes. Tillbury's store had vanished, as had Hulsizer's blacksmith shop and red stable. And now suddenly, as he reached the corner where one road used to turn off to Maple Hill and the other to Alvira, he saw the old stone church before him, the doors, windows and belfry all blinded with boards.

Beyond this, he knew, lay his father's house. He got out of the car slowly and walked over. Sight of the place shook him a little. Could this be his boyhood home whose idyllic picture he had carried in his mind all these years? The paint was gone, the porches torn away, the picket fence vanished, the great sugar maples cut down. It was just a bare box, a two-and-a-half-story shack stripped of every vestige of ornament and comfort. The doors and windows he so well knew had been closed with rough lumber. Not a splinter was left of stable or orchard. From where he used to pick up Baldwin and Smokehouse apples, he could see the raw industrial strip of buildings of the XYT explosive line, and beyond, the reach of ugly stacks and tanks against the autumn-sunset sky.

He couldn't stand looking at it long, but retreated to the cemetery. Only here was it as it had always been; a few more graves perhaps, but otherwise as he remembered. He had heard reports how well the Army had taken care of the dead left in its reservations. The graves looked even better kept than formerly, the grass clipped, the black iron fence intact, the white stones erect and recently cleaned. He read again the line FAITHFUL PHYSICIAN carved on his father's stone—and in fine italics at the bottom, *He went about doing good.* His mother had done that. As a young scientist he had disliked to see it the next time he came home. But today the simple words filled him with emotion and curious envy. He had once thought, he told himself, that he had far outdistanced his father, but now he knew it was his father's life that had outdistanced his. Standing here by his parents' graves, his back turned on the boarded-up houses and church, on the scarred earth and ugly munitions buildings, he could almost believe that it was all a dream. The air blew from over South Mountain as it always had. Crows cawed in the old unused fields up on Penny Hill, whose huge rounded head looked golden in the setting sun.

It was as if vestiges of the peaceful life he knew as a boy still remained up there, and he found himself seeking them, stepping over the iron fence, passing through Kellys' little woods and climbing the strong flanks of Penny Hill.

Presently he came to a halt. In a little hollow high up on the slope, he had come on a vestige of the old Penny Hill road. Farther down around the bend, he knew, it had been completely destroyed. Farther up around the next bend or two, it must run futilely into the steel fence. But here for a short distance it lay untouched and utterly unchanged, the same yellow shale and curious narrowness, the same weathered rail fence and dried grasses. It even smelled as it used to. Since leaving here he had been over the entire country and most of the world besides. He had found no place with that certain sweet smell of Rose Valley. The three black cherry trees, now older and fatter, still stood by the fence, and he was glad to lean against one of them in the faintness that had come over him since the climb.

The longer he stood there in the growing dusk, the less it seemed that he had ever been away. Nothing here had changed. He could almost believe that he was still a boy and that the valley behind him still lay intact and unharmed. Why, this had been his favorite route from school in town. So often had he passed this spot, he thought there must remain in the road some faint impress of his feet. Just at this season, with darkness coming on, he used to tramp along here from town with his schoolbooks under his arm, the scent of life in his nostrils and the world his oyster. Standing here now, peering through the growing dusk, he could almost feel himself as a boy swinging along the road bound for the lamplit window at home.

His nerves tautened. Did he only imagine it or was something actually coming up there in the dusk? Yes, it was moving down the road. He could make it out now, straining his eyes through the early obscurity, a figure rounding the shale banks, a shadowy boy in knee breeches carrying a book satchel. The strangest feeling ran over him. He must be really ill, he told himself, for there was no road above for the boy to have come from and none below for him to pass over. Besides, boys today did not wear knee pants. Yet he could plainly hear the sound of the boy's shoes on the road. He told himself now that it must be a real boy, someone who lived today on the reservation, who knew this short cut and whom the guards let through. Then, as the boy came almost abreast, he recognized, with a feeling that made all adult sensations seem tame, the familiar red-ribbed sweater that had been his own, the certain look of its stout coarse weave. He even remembered the peculiar smell of warm dye when he used to pull it over his head.

The boy was shying to the farther side of the road at sight of a stranger. *Speak to him—speak to him before he is gone,* the man cried to himself. But when he did so, his voice sounded harsh and croaking, "Are you acquainted around here, boy?"

"Why, yes," the boy said, stopping, but he did not come any closer.

"Is there a doctor around?"

"There's two in town and one at the Stone Church."

"Do you know the doctor's name at the Stone Church?"

"It's Hanray—Dr. John Hanray."

"And your name?" he asked.

"Peter Hanray," the boy told him shortly, and started away.

"Wait, I want to go with you!" the man said, as soon as he was able.

They made a curious pair going down the shale road in the dimness, the boy hurrying tirelessly ahead, the man following heavily after. At every moment the latter looked for the road to peter out, expected to see, below, the cold hard electric lights of the Army barracks and XYT-line buildings. But all that lay around them was the soft dim blur of the unwired country dusk. There were the faint glow of a lantern in Bomboys' red barn as they passed, and early lights in the Peysher house and Hauser log cabin. At Shaffers' yellow house and Klines' unpainted one, children played and shouted in the yard. Here the Penny Hill road joined the other road as it always had, while ahead Jarretts' woods loomed up in its old, dark and mysterious way. Tramping down the village road he could smell the old-time aroma of wood smoke, raw-fried potatoes and valley-cured ham. Hulsizer's blacksmith shop still stood open. A flame of red fire glowed in the darkness, and a great hulking beast waited in the gloom outside.

And now the scientist breathed faster, for they were rounding the corner. He could glimpse late sky shining as usual through the open belfry and the white paling fence standing unbroken around his father's house. Soft golden lamplight came from a side window. That was the kitchen window, he knew, and a sudden fear touched him that those two he wanted most to see wouldn't be there.

The boy ran ahead of him through the side gate and up the steps. He burst in through the door, and the man behind him saw the kitchen as he had always remembered it, with the water bucket on the stand, the wood stove steaming with pots and pans, and hurrying in from the pump on the back porch his mother, more real than he had imagined her, in dress and apron that were part and parcel of his youth. Something in him wanted to run to her, but her smile and anxious scrutiny were all for the boy.

"He was up on Penny Hill," the boy said. "He wants to see papa."

His mother's smile left, and she put on the grave face she showed to the outside world. "Will you come in?" she bade him politely, as to a stranger.

Hardly could he control his emotion as he stepped into that well-known room. The table was set as always when he used to come home from town: the dishes he had long since forgotten, with pink flowers and which had come in cereal packages, the blue glass butter dish and the plated silverware worn softly black along the edges. He could smell the savor of baked beans from the oven, shot through with the scent of the stove.

He noticed that his mother watched him intently. For a moment his heart stood still, thinking she must know him. But she still spoke as to a visitor. "Do you want to come in the office? Or you can wait in the parlor if you'd rather. Peter will light the lamp for you. The doctor said he'd be back right away. He's just over on the ridge road."

Hanray dared not speak. He let himself be led into the parlor. He would get hold of himself in here, he told himself, once he was left alone. Why, he knew all these poor shabby furnishings better than any of the rich things in his fine Midwest home. The old green tassels still hung from the table cover; the haircloth sofa stood by the door; faded blue flowers bloomed in the wallpaper, and the same spots were still worn in the ingrain carpet. His Grandfather and Grandmother Ainsley hung on the wall, and a few photographs stood on organ and table, but none of his father, mother or self. That would have been unforgivable vanity or pride, to flaunt one of your immediate family in your own parlor. He heard the same old rings on the telephone from the exchange at Maple Hill. All that was missing now, besides his father, was Doxy, the stern, black-and-brown, long-haired shepherd dog.

He sat very still. The rattle of buggy wheels came

around the house, the steps of the boy sent out to unhitch, then the unmistakable sound of his father coming up to the side door. A minute more and he came forward, a man in a brown beard and clothes like a farmer, with a doctor's worn bag in his hand. He looked tired. Likely he had been up all last night with some shiftless mountain patient. Sight of him brought back the feeling he had had as a boy for his father, a kind of shame that he wasn't rich and successful like Doctors Grove and Hereward in town; that he seldom charged enough or collected what he did charge; and especially that he never carried himself with the professional dignity of the town doctors. They were men of science above such inferior things as humility and religion. His father, on the other hand, attended church like some simple, unlearned countryman, even acted as superintendent of the Sunday school when he could, greeting perfect strangers with the brotherly and overfriendly way of a preacher. That, as a boy, he used to resent the most—that his father showed the same warmth and affection for a stranger as for his own family. But today, now that he was only a stranger himself, an unspeakable gratitude welled up in him for his father's warm greeting and for the kind brown eyes that searched his face.

"How are you?" he said, grasping his hand and holding it in the manner he always did when he tried to recall a name. "I feel I should know you. I know your face, but I can't call your name. Do you live around here?"

"I used to," the visitor said.

"Has it been a long time?"

"A very long time."

"You have come far perhaps?"

"Farther than I can tell you."

"I'd have been here before," his father apologized, "but I was over at Berrys' on the ridge road. Maybe you remember them. Old Mr. Berry is pretty feeble. There is little a doctor can do for him any more except pray."

Into the scientist's mind came the memory of his father's prayers, so unlike a man of medicine and science, his friendly, hopeful voice, a voice that now seemed very near God. *Oh, father,* he thought, *if only you would pray for me.* But he said nothing of that, just followed his father into the familiar bare office, smelling of carbolic acid and iodoform.

His father closed the door. "Now you can sit down and tell me your trouble," he said kindly.

The scientist thought he would give a great deal if he could feel his father's gentle and skillful hands go over him. But what he had to say was something else.

"I've come to see you about your boy."

"About Peter!" His father was surprised.

"About him and his future. I understand he's only fourteen, he's already well along in high school and he's thinking of taking up physics and chemistry in college. I've come to you to beg him to change his mind. What he must do is prepare for a life like yours."

He saw that his father was staring at him.

"I don't know how you know this or who told you. I can talk to him again, but I'm afraid there isn't much use. I don't think I've been much of an example to him. He says he's seen too much doctoring from the inside. He doesn't want to starve and he doesn't want to have anything to do with death and dying."

The scientist shrank.

His father went on, "Peter's more interested in science. All he talks about is the great opportunity for public service in being a scientist. He says that he wants to do only good in the world."

The scientist winced again. He leaned forward desperately.

"You must change his mind for him then!" he begged. "Make him see the great opportunity in medicine, the salvation of going around doing good like you."

"Like me!" his father said in surprise. He looked up.

His wife was standing in the doorway. "Supper's ready, John. You better eat before more patients come. I don't have very much, but if the gentleman would care to sit down with us, he'll be welcome. Did you notice, John? He looks like someone we know." She turned. . . . "Are you by any chance related to the Ainsleys?"

"I am," he said unsteadily, "but please don't ask me how."

"I knew it," she said. "You remind me of my Uncle Harry."

His father turned to him as they went out for supper. "If you would only talk to him?" he asked. "We're just his parents, but perhaps he will listen to you!"

It was strange how the scientist felt an uneasiness to face the boy again. Young Peter was standing by his chair, impatient to sit down. He welcomed the supper guest coolly, looking the other way. They sat down at the familiar table. His father bent his forehead to his hand, resting the elbow on the table, gave the usual sign and started to pray. How often, the scientist thought, had he heard those familiar words, "The summer is over, the harvest is ended and we are not saved." But never had the words held such a new and terrible meaning as today.

All through the meal he could scarcely refrain from stealing glances at the boy across the table. Was it possible that he had once been as slender, light-hearted and fair-skinned as that, his blood vessels so new and pliable, his eyes clear as spring water? Could he ever have been so young, innocent and idealistic? Why, the boy's face was fresh as a girl's. Once when his mother wanted a clean handkerchief, he rose reluctantly enough, but, once up, bounded up the stairs so effortlessly on his long legs that the visitor felt a sudden awe, mingled with despair, for the boy he had once been.

Vainly he tried to win him. When he spoke, the boy

listened unwillingly and, if pressed, with veiled hostility. He made only short inscrutable replies, then looked the other way. It was plain, the man told himself, that the boy did not approve of him. Why, he was famous throughout the world, but the boy rejected him. There was something about him the boy did not relish. Yet this was the one he must make peace with, he knew. There was no mistaking that. All through the meal he talked, argued and begged, until he felt the sweat stand on his face. His father and mother had begun to look at him queerly. The boy resisted as hard as ever, until the man knew he was foiled and defeated; that never could he dissuade the boy from his dream.

It was when hope was at its lowest ebb that a scratching sound was heard at the door. The boy answered it, and a black-and-brown shepherd dog burst in. It was Doxy, keen and shaggy old Doxy. He jumped up at the boy in greeting; then, smelling on the floor, ran straight to the visitor, jumped up, barked and licked him. For a little while he ran back and forth between boy and man, smelling eagerly at one and then at the other, as if something puzzled him.

"That's singular," his father said. "Doxy doesn't go to many people. But he acts as though he knows you."

"And likes you," his mother added. She was always the one to encourage.

The scientist saw that now for the first time the boy was regarding him intently, with a kind of respect, as if his hostility was broken and he saw in him something he hadn't seen before. The man sat very still. He had received honors from a dozen sources, including the President of the United States, but never had he felt quite the gratitude as for this. Some inexplicable thing inside of him was released and began to melt, like that time long ago when, as a child, he had gone to Fourth Gap and later found himself back in the blessed peace and warmth of home.

"If you don't mind," he asked his mother, "may I stay here for a while this evening?"

That was his mistake, he knew. Hardly was it said and permission given before the dog began to growl. His hair bristled. Then a sudden knock rang from the door. The boy went to answer.

"It's somebody for you," he stammered.

"Is it the guard?" the visitor asked, and the boy nodded.

The scientist sat very quiet. It shook him a little. It had come sooner than he expected. But he should have known he couldn't stay in this blessed place forever.

"I'll have to go now," he said, and got to his feet. He saw that his parents looked frightened. He kissed his trembling mother and then his father's bearded mouth as he used to do when he was small. Last he shook the cold hand of the boy.

The rap came once more, demandingly. Again the dog growled deep in his throat.

"I'm coming!" the scientist called. Then to the others, "Good-by."

"Good-by," his father answered. "I'll pray for you."

"Remember you're an Ainsley. We'll both pray for you," his mother told him.

"God bless you," he said, and opened the door.

Not until he was clear of the house, with his foot reaching for the steps, did he remember there were no steps there.

When he came to himself he was lying on the ground. As his eyes grew accustomed to the darkness, he saw that the sugar maples and picket fence were gone. He picked himself up painfully. The house was dark. The door looked as if it had been boarded up for a long time. So did the windows. And yet so real and strong remained the memory of his father and mother and the lamplit table that he pounded on the boards.

"Papa!" he called.

Only silence from the decayed shell of a house answered him. Below he could see the cold glitter of electric lights on the tanks and buildings of the secret XYT explosive line. Nearer at hand were the cemetery and the guard waiting. Well, he told himself, he could face things a little better now. His father and mother had said they would pray for him. And the boy inside of him had made his first sign of peace to the man he had become.

Fallout Island
by Robert Murphy

Robert Murphy's "Fallout Island" echoed the contemporary concern for the effects of uncontrolled nuclear testing and the possibility of nuclear war, while being spiced with the grotesque mutations which enlivened the late 50s-early 60s science fiction-horror cinema such as Them!, The Amazing Colossal Man *and* It Came from Beneath the Sea. *Here Robert Murphy carried these cinematic horrors to the printed page.*

Fallout Island:
What Prehistoric Creature Ruled Here?
by Robert Murphy

They had raised the island just after dawn, and now, several hours later, were standing off the opening through the encircling coral reef until the tide was high enough to float them through. The indigo of the sea about them shattered to white on the reef, and beyond it the shallower waters of the atoll ran through the lovely shades of jade to emerald to aquamarine to another line of spray and the gleaming sands of the beach beneath a background of palms. The island, eight or ten miles long, higher in the south where an ancient, badly weathered dead volcanic cone thrust up above the jungle, looked undisturbed and serene beneath the clear sky.

There were five men on the schooner: the two Fijian sailors sitting quietly together before the foremast and the three white men standing together in the stern. Erickson, the schooner's owner, had the wheel; the two Americans, John Gilfillan and Alan Bransom, both taller and considerably less weathered than he, stood one on each side of him.

It was Bransom who had hired the schooner; Gilfillan had come along on his invitation, paying his own way to Hawaii, where they had picked up the schooner. Although Gilfillan had known Bransom for several years in San Francisco, where they both lived at the same club, the man was still rather mysterious to him. Bransom apparently had a business of some sort which paid him well and didn't make too great demands upon his time; and when he had asked Gilfillan to take a holiday with him, a sort of sentimental journey to one of the little-known Pacific islands, Gilfillan decided to go. He had inherited enough money to do what he liked and spent most of his time fishing, shooting, skiing and writing an occasional magazine piece. He had never been in that part of the world and had been at a loose end at the moment.

He looked at the island they had come so far to visit and then looked questioningly at Bransom, for he didn't believe now that it was a sentimental journey; he had decided during the long trip that Bransom hadn't any sentimentality whatever in his makeup.

"Like it?" Bransom asked.

"It looks like a paradise," Gilfillan said.

"It was, almost," Bransom said. . . . "Didn't you think so, Cap?"

"Yah, I t'ought so," Erickson said. "Fine people, pretty girls. I have t'em almost to myself, no ot'er trader come by much." He grinned.

"And they never brought them back for you?"

"No," Erickson said and pointed off over the sea to the southeast. "Americans took t'em all down t'ere. Made t'em stay t'ere. Was said, wind is bad for here, fallout came down."

"You must have missed them."

"Yah, I miss t'em. I have not been here for twenty year, maybe more. Now I am here again, I miss t'em more."

"Well," Gilfillan said, "it must have cooled off by now. . . . Don't you think so, Alan?"

"Hope so," Bransom said. "As Cap pointed out, there was an odd condition here. Wind seemed to be funneled in from all over, and with all the testing, the fallout just kept dropping in. We had to get out."

"Quick, huh?" Gilfillan said.

"Yes, quick," Bransom said and looked at Gilfillan. "You're beginning to put two and two together, I take it."

"I believe I am," Gilfillan said and grinned.

"Now that I think of it—not that I haven't thought of it before—it does seem that a trip here sounds like an expensive whim."

"I've enjoyed watching you trying to figure it out," Bransom said. "I'll tell you when we get ashore. . . . How much longer, Cap?"

"Soon, now," Erickson said and raised his voice. "Tommy, watch by the channel when we pass, yah?"

One of the Fijians stood up and moved closer to the bow. Erickson swung the schooner closer to the reef and ran parallel to it. The water shoaled and paled to starboard, showing the submerged coral heads rising from the depths and the brilliant colors of the life that grew upon it and swam about. The other Fijian came aft and climbed up on the cabin roof to get a little height. They passed the opening, in which the water deepened in color, and Erickson swung out again. The two Fijians joined him; the one who had been on the roof made a gesture showing an angle, and Erickson and Tommy nodded. "Been long time since I was here," Erickson said to Bransom. "Coral grow up, but Americans blast when t'ey come, make pretty deep. All right, I t'ink." He looked at the Fijians and jerked a thumb at the sails. They lowered and lashed them, Erickson started the engine, and with Tommy in the bow again and the other Fijian back on the cabin roof giving hand signals they eased their way slowly through the opening and dropped anchor a few hundred yards off the beach. Erickson stopped the engine.

"Back again," he said and then frowned slightly at Bransom. "Not many birds," he said in a rather surprised tone. "Not many birds, like before."

"No," Bransom said. "I didn't think there would be. I'll get the radiation meter, and we'll try a trip ashore."

Neither Erickson nor the Fijians were very enthusiastic about going ashore, so Bransom and Gilfillan went in in the dinghy, tied up to the wreck of an old wharf and managed to get ashore on it without having to go in through the surf. Bransom, with Gilfillan following, walked about on the beach with the radiation meter and went a little way into the palms before deciding to turn back. It was very quiet, except for the dry rattle of the palms in the light wind.

"Spotty," Bransom said. "Still a bit above industrial levels here and there, but that's all right. We're not going to spend a long vacation here anyhow."

"What was that bit about the birds?" Gilfillan asked. "Remember you told Cap when we anchored that you hadn't thought many of them would be here."

"An informed guess. Birds take radiation badly, not so well as insects and animals. The ones that were native here would have been wiped out, probably, and not many more would have come in. Even if they did, it must have been too high for them for a long time."

"Well, wouldn't they have—ah—mutations, or something? Or go back to what they were long ago? I've read a lot of stuff, speculation, maybe. . . ." His voice died away, and he made a gesture with one hand.

"They all died," Bransom said. "As for going back, they couldn't have done that. Nature never goes back, never repeats itself. It just progresses in one direction. Now that I think of it, there used to be lizards here, too, a couple of feet long. They ran all about. We used to eat one once in a while."

"The world's different nowadays," Gilfillan said. "These mutations, now——"

"We've always had mutations," Bransom said a little sententiously. "Radiation just speeds the mutations up, or perhaps increases the number of them. Well, let's get back. We've missed lunch, and I don't want to miss dinner too." He started to walk, and Gilfillan fell in beside him.

"Didn't you have a house here when you were watching for Japanese?" Gilfillan asked after a moment. "Don't you want to see it again?"

"No," Bransom said. "It was never much to look at, and there will be little of it left by now. It was south, on the old peak; anyhow, high enough to see something. I haven't any sentimental attachment to it."

"Then——" Gilfillan began and stopped. He looked a bit embarrassed.

"Then why did I come back—at great expense?" Bransom asked. "That was going to be your question, wasn't it? I'll tell you; I should have told you when I asked you to come along for company. It amused me to be mysterious, and I carried it too far. I was in the diamond business before I was called back into the service and sent out here. There was a man named Wolfe in Maiden Lane in New York who owed me about eighty thousand dollars' worth of stones. He got into trouble, and the cops were after him. But he'd always been honest with me; he heard that I'd been sent out here, and he wouldn't send the stones to anybody else, so he sent them to me."

He gave Gilfillan an oddly calculating look, for the story wasn't true. He had stolen the diamonds in Antwerp during the Nazi invasion, got them back to the States, been called into the Army and sent to the island as a coast watcher. He had hid the stones, deciding to leave them until he was sure all inquiry about them had ended. When the island had become radioactive, he had felt doubly sure of their safety; and now, having found out that the insurance companies had given them up, he was back to get them again.

Gilfillan noticed the look but thought little about it; he was rather fetched by the romantic tale. "Here?" he asked. "He sent them here? Good Lord, was he crazy?"

"Could be," Bransom said. "But he'd always been on the

level before, and maybe everybody gets a little crazy the first time his foot slips and the heat's on."

Gilfillan stared. "And you got them?"

"Yes," Bransom said. "Wolfe managed to get them into the hands of an Air Force guy I knew, and he got them here eventually."

Gilfillan stopped. "I'll be damned," he said. "And they're still here?"

"They're still here. I couldn't keep them around camp. There were two other men here, fairly honest types, but you can see— I hid them on the edge of a swamp half-way between here and the peak."

"And didn't have time to get them back," Gilfillan said.

"That's right."

"Well, I'll be damned all over again," Gilfillan said. "Did you ever tell this Wolfe this weird tale?"

"No," Bransom said. "Somebody talked too much, later, or something happened. They put him away, and he's still there," he said and started to walk.

They didn't speak further until they were back at the schooner, where Erickson gave them a hand over the rail.

"I am glad you come back so soon," he said. "You have been here, now we can go, yah?"

"Already?" Bransom asked. "You don't like it here?"

"No," Erickson said. "I do not like t'is fallout, t'is stuff I cannot see. I t'ink of t'ose Japanese fishermen in t'eir boat. I tell t'e boys, not catch fish here. No, I do not like it." He made a wide gesture toward the island, behind which the sun was setting now. "I do not know what is t'ere. It does not feel good to me any more."

"I want to go ashore for a couple of hours in the morning," Bransom said. "After that we can leave. Is that all right with you?"

Erickson shrugged. "You hire t'e schooner. I stay t'at long, t'en we go." He looked toward the island again, where the palms and the old peak looked flat and stiff against the evening sky as though they were hammered out of black iron. "What we have done to ourselves," he said and shook his head.

The Fijian sailor Tommy stuck his head out of the companionway hatch. "Chow," he said and ducked down again.

"You don't have to go, John," Bransom said as they started across the deck. "It's not your party. Why don't you wait on board here and be comfortable?"

"I'll go," Gilfillan said. "I've never been on one of these islands before, and you may need some help to find the stones."

Immediately after breakfast they went ashore in the dinghy again, Bransom carrying the radiation meter and Gilfillan a double-barreled shotgun they'd borrowed from Erickson. They walked south on the beach for a mile or so. The palms at the back of the beach began to give way to brush and pandanus and mangrove as the island grew lower and swampy, and a quarter of a mile ahead they could see the beach narrow; the sea came closer in, almost touching the jungle, and where it did this a stream apparently came out to meet it, and the beach was choked with vegetation.

"We'd better cut in here," Bransom said. "We couldn't get through that stuff up ahead, and there's a low ridge that runs along behind the beach and roughly parallel to it."

He changed course and consequently didn't see what Gilfillan, who was still looking down the beach, saw: a strange kangaroolike creature several feet high break out of the beach thicket and with several hops disappear into the jungle.

"Alan!" Gilfillan exclaimed. "Alan! What the devil was that?"

Bransom stopped. "What was what? What did you see?"

"It looked like a kangaroo. It hopped like one."

"We're a long way from kangaroos here," Bransom said. "A bird, maybe."

"No," Gilfillan said. "It was too far away to see well, and it vanished too fast, but it wasn't a bird."

"So. What color was it?"

"It looked gray against the thicket," Gilfillan said. "I couldn't be sure. It— Damn it, it was a queer-looking thing."

Bransom obviously wanted to get on, but controlled his impatience. "Well," he said reasonably, "if it was too far away to see well, how can you be sure? Maybe it was a rat, then."

"A rat two or three feet high?" Gilfillan asked. "It seemed that big to me."

"Keep a watch when we get into the brush," Bransom said, starting to walk again. "Maybe you'll see it again."

They entered the jungle. After the open beach it very quickly became gloomy and dense and difficult to get through. Pandanus sent down its snaky bunches of roots in all directions from a foot or two in the air, and the trunks twisted about; it was wet underfoot and, despite the thick carpet of fallen pandanus leaves, the mangroves had managed to grow and writhed about above their stiltlike roots. They were soon wet to the knees and sweating, for there was no breeze; they couldn't hear the surf any longer, and the silence soon became as oppressive as the heat. Gilfillan had never been in such a place before, and he didn't like it. He felt half suffocated.

Bransom seemed to know where he was going, and Gilfillan, who had lost his sense of direction completely, followed him. In places the stagnant water was above their knees now, and the bottom was slimy muck; as they slipped and cursed and splashed about, Gilfillan began to worry about what would happen if they both stepped into a hole where the water was above their heads. He was about to move up and tap Bransom on the shoulder and ask him about this when Bransom came upon the low ridge he had mentioned and scrambled onto it and stopped. The ridge was a foot or so above the water and two or three feet wide. Brush grew upon it, and it was crisscrossed by creepers and the trunks of leaning trees; they couldn't see very far ahead and would have to work their way along it through the cluttering growth, but at least the footing seemed solid. They stood together for a moment to get their breaths, muddy, sweating and scratched.

"Sorry I let you in for this," Bransom said. "I forgot it was this bad. Not too far to go now."

"What?" Gilfillan asked. He had heard the words, and in one part of his mind they made sense to him, but his attention was divided; he thought that he had also heard, somewhere ahead, in the steamy riot of greenery that was closing them in and holding off the air and the sky, a grunting, bubbling sigh, a stirring of water, an indefinable sound that was frightening and inimical.

"Not too far to——" Bransom began again and saw Gilfillan's expression. "What's the trouble?"

"A noise," Gilfillan said.

Bransom stared at him, and they both stood listening for several minutes, but the silence was profound and unbroken.

"It's certainly a place to give you the willies," Bransom said. "I don't think it was anything. You must still be thinking of that thing you saw on the beach. Let's go and get it over with."

They started their slow progress again, squirming around and through the vegetation, but now Gilfillan's mind was oppressed by a feeling of apprehension. He was sure that he had heard the noise and was on the alert to catch it again. The shotgun had been a nuisance, heavy and clumsy and always getting tangled in the brush, but now it was very important to him; he took pains to keep its muzzle forward and ready for instant use.

This readiness was probably what saved them, for they hadn't gone more than seventy-five yards when there was a great flurry of water, and from behind an eight-foot mangrove a little to the right of the ridge a huge reptilian head reared up into the air like something in an evil nightmare. The head hung above them, longer than a man, narrow and flat; its long, half-open jaws were lined with great gleaming teeth; the cold and lidless eyes fixed on them. As Gilfillan stared shocked and unbelieving at it, thinking that it couldn't be there, that it came from the dark beginning of the world before man could have survived, the terrible head slid back for the strike, and Gilfillan stopped thinking. He thrust the muzzle of the shotgun over Bransom's shoulder and pulled both triggers.

The recoil of the loosely held gun knocked him off the ridge and, as he fell, the heavens seemed to open and inundate him with sound. The shotgun's blast was followed immediately by a tremendous roaring and thrashing, the world seemed to be heaving under him, and foul water filled his nose and mouth. He struggled, half stunned in the slime; he was being thumped and pulled and yanked about and dimly realized that Bransom was shouting at him.

"Come on! Come on!" Bransom was shouting, dragging him up the side of the ridge. "There's another one coming!"

He staggered to his feet, and then Bransom was desperately shoving him along the ridge.

Exhausted, battered and in rage, they had been near collapse when they finally fell down on the sand near the old ruined wharf. After a long time Bransom sat up. His face was haggard, his eyes had sunk back into his skull, and his body was laced with lines of dried blood to which the sand adhered. He stared at the prostrate Gilfillan.

"You saved us both," he said. "You all right?"

"Ah," Gilfillan said, "I'll manage." The cold horror that

had been with him ever since the monstrous beast had appeared above him was leaving him now beneath the calm and open sky.

"What was it?" Bransom asked. "Good Lord, even in my worst nightmares—— What was it?"

"Some sort of marine lizard, I think," Gilfillan said. "A seagoing dinosaur. A branch of the dinosaur family went back to the sea. A Tylosaurus, maybe. They were twenty-five or thirty feet long. They probably crawl out where the beach is narrow and go in there to rest, or breed, or something." A hoarse and unexpected chuckle suddenly came out of him. "You'll have to bring your information up to date. You seemed pretty positive that nature never went back to the past."

"It couldn't go back a million years or more so fast," Bransom said.

"Couldn't it?" Gilfillan asked.

"It doesn't make any sense."

"No," Gilfillan said. "But then nobody knows what a certain level of radiation, held over a long period, a dozen years or more, would do. Those lizards you mentioned bred every year, maybe oftener, and there were a lot of breedings. Anyhow, there the things were. Don't ask me to explain it."

There was a long silence between them and then, as though talking to himself, Bransom said, "I've got to go back. I've got to."

Gilfillan sat up painfully and stared at him. "Go back?" he demanded, as though he hadn't heard correctly. "Go back in there? You can't do it. You don't know how many more of those things there are, or whether there are others even worse. Smaller, more maneuverable, more deadly. Remember the thing I saw on the beach. You might get bogged, lost, caught by darkness——" He shuddered. "You'd never get out," he said. "You can't count on killing those things with firearms. They've got several hearts, more than one brain. We were lucky. Lucky as hell. I doubt I did more than blind it."

"I've got to do it," Bransom said, as though he hadn't heard any of this. "I can hire an airplane and bomb it, or rent a gunboat in South America somewhere and stand off the island and work it over. Or bring some men with flame throwers here."

"Nonsense," Gilfillan said. "You'd have to saturate at least nine square miles, and you'd probably blow your package of diamonds to the devil. Even the flame throwers would need a small army and cost you more than you could afford. Besides that, the island's probably under a mandate. Even if you could get permission, which I doubt, there would be people, officials, scientists, the press."

This last objection brought Bransom to his feet. "No!" he almost shouted. "No! I can't do that, I can't have—" He stared at Gilfillan, and his voice died away. It was a reaction that caught Gilfillan by surprise; he would often speculate about it in the future and finally come near the truth. "It isn't any use," Bransom said after a moment. "I've spent so much money now that I couldn't afford it."

"I'm sorry, Alan," Gilfillan said. He didn't know what else to say.

Bransom stood there with his shoulders slumped, looking even more haggard now than he had when he first sat up. "Gone," he said. "All gone. Ah, the hell with it. The hell with it for good and all."

He turned and started to walk toward the dilapidated wharf, dragging his feet through the sand. After watching him for a moment Gilfillan got to his feet and started after him, somewhat confused and feeling that he'd been kicked and beaten by a gang of thugs. The reaction to the business in the swamp, the entire day, had taken hold of him, and he felt cold and a little nauseated. It would be a dreary trip home, he thought, and he hoped there would be a tide so they could get away from the lagoon before night.

The Green Hills of Earth

by Robert A. Heinlein

Robert Anson Heinlein began his career in 1939 when his first story, "Life-Line," appeared in Astounding. *Here, under the nurturing eye of editor John W. Campbell, he published 20 of his first 28 stories. Starting in 1947, four of his best stories appeared in the* Post: *"The Green Hills of Earth," "Space Jockey," "It's Great to be Back" and "The Black Pits of Luna." All four of these stories were later collected in* The Green Hills of Earth *in 1951 and in* The Past Through Tomorrow *in 1967. These* Post *stories were all* people *stories deeply concerned with the human condition. "The Green Hills of Earth" represents Heinlein at the peak of his ability—the saga of an average man turned poet-hero, a tale of honor, sacrifice and glory.*

The Green Hills of Earth

by Robert A. Heinlein

This is the story of Rhysling, the Blind Singer of the Spaceways—but not the official version. You sang his words in school:

I pray for one last landing
On the globe that gave me birth;
Let me rest my eyes on the fleecy skies
And the cool, green hills of Earth.

Or perhaps you sang in French or German. Or it might have been Esperanto, while Terra's rainbow banner rippled over your head.

The language does not matter—it was certainly an Earth tongue. No one has ever translated Green Hills into the lisping Venerean speech; no Martian ever croaked and whispered it in the dry corridors. This is ours. We of Earth have exported everything from Hollywood crawlies to synthetic radioactives, but this belongs solely to Terra, and to her sons and daughters wherever they may be.

We have all heard stories of Rhysling. You may even be one of the many who have sought degrees by scholarly evaluations of his published works—Songs of the Spaceways; The Grand Canal, and other Poems; High and Far; and Up Ship!

Nevertheless, although you have sung his songs and read his verses, in school and out, your whole life, it is at least an even-money bet—unless you are a spaceman yourself—

that you have never even heard of most of Rhysling's unpublished songs, such items as Since the Pusher Met My Cousin; That Red-Headed Venusberg Gal; Keep Your Pants On, Skipper; or A Space Suit Built for Two. Nor can we quote them in a family magazine.

Rhysling's reputation was protected by a careful literary executor and by the happy chance that he was never interviewed. Songs of the Spaceways appeared the week he died; when it became a best seller, the publicity stories about him were pieced together from what people remembered about him plus the highly colored handouts from his publishers. The resulting traditional picture of Rhysling is about as authentic as George Washington's hatchet or King Alfred's cakes.

In truth, you would not have wanted him in your parlor; he was not socially acceptable. He had a permanent case of sun itch, which he scratched continually, adding nothing to his negligible beauty.

Van der Voort's portrait of him for the Harriman Centennial edition of his works shows a figure of high tragedy, a solemn mouth, sightless eyes concealed by black silk bandage. He was never solemn! His mouth was always open, singing, grinning, drinking or eating. The bandage was any rag, usually dirty. After he lost his sight he became less and less neat about his person.

"Noisy" Rhysling was a jetman, second class, with eyes as good as yours, when he signed on for a loop trip to the Jovian asteroids in the R. S. Goshawk. The crew signed releases for everything in those days; a Lloyd's associate would have laughed in your face at the notion of insuring a spaceman. The Space Precautionary Act had never been heard of, and the company was responsible only for wages, if and when. Half the ships that went farther than Luna City never came back. Spacemen did not care; by preference they signed for shares, and any one of them would have bet you that he could jump from the two hundredth floor of Harriman Tower and ground safely, if you offered him three to two and allowed him rubber heels for the landing.

Jetmen were the most carefree of the lot and the meanest. Compared with them, the masters, the radarmen, and the astrogators (there were no supers or stewards in those days) were gentle vegetarians. Jetmen knew too much. The others trusted the skill of the captain to get them down safely; jetmen knew that skill was useless against the blind and fitful devils chained inside their rocket motors.

The Goshawk was the first of Harriman's ships to be converted from chemical fuel to atomic power piles—or rather the first that did not blow up. Rhysling knew her well; she was an old tub that had plied the Luna City run, Supra-New York space station to Leyport and back, before she was converted for deep space. He had worked the Luna run in her and had been along on the first deep-space trip, to Drywater, on Mars—and back, to everyone's surprise.

He should have made chief engineer by the time he signed for the Jovian loop trip, but, after the Drywater pioneer trip, he had been fired, blacklisted, and grounded at Luna City for having spent his time writing a chorus and several verses at a time when he should have been watching his gauges. The song was the infamous The Skipper is a Father to His Crew, with the uproariously unprintable final couplet.

The black list did not bother him. He won an accordion from a Chinese barkeep in Luna City by cheating at one-thumb and thereafter kept going by singing to miners for drinks and tips until the rapid attrition in spacemen caused the company agent there to give him another chance. He kept his nose clean on the Luna run for a year or two, got back into deep space, helped give Venusberg its original ripe reputation, strolled the banks of the Grand Canal when a second colony was established at the ancient Martian capital, and froze his toes and ears on the second trip to Titan.

Things moved fast in those days. Once the power-pile drive was accepted, the number of ships that put out from the Luna-Terra system was limited only by the availability of crews. Jetmen were scarce; the shielding was cut to a minimum to save weight, and few married men cared to risk possible exposure to radioactivity. Rhysling did not want to be a father, so jobs were always open to him during the golden days of the claiming boom. He crossed and recrossed the system, singing the doggerel that boiled up in his head and chording it out on his accordion.

The master of the Goshawk knew him; Captain Hicks had been astrogator on Rhysling's first trip in her. "Welcome home, Noisy," Hicks had greeted him. "Are you sober, or shall I sign the book for you?"

"You can't get drunk on the bugjuice they sell here, skipper." He signed and went below, lugging his accordion.

Ten minutes later he was back. "Captain," he stated darkly, "that Number Two jet ain't fit. The cadmium dampers are warped."

"Why tell me? Tell the chief."

"I did, but he says they will do. He's wrong."

The captain gestured at the book. "Scratch out your name and scram. We raise ship in thirty minutes."

Rhysling looked at him, shrugged, and went below again.

It is a long climb to the Jovian planetoids; a Hawk-class clunker had to blast for three watches before going into free flight. Rhysling had the second watch. Damping was done by hand then, with a multiplying vernier and a danger gauge. When the gauge showed red, he tried to correct it—no luck.

Jetmen don't wait; that's why they are jetmen. He slapped the emergency discover and fished at the hot stuff with the tongs. The lights went out, he went right ahead. A jetman has to know his power room the way your tongue knows the inside of your mouth.

He sneaked a quick look over the top of the lead baffle when the lights went out. The blue radioactive glow did not help him any; he jerked his head back and went on fishing by touch.

When he was done he called over the tube, "Number Two jet out. And for gosh sake get me some light down here!"

There was light—the emergency circuit—but not for him. The blue radioactive glow was the last thing his optic nerve ever responded to.

As Time and Space come bending back to shape this star-specked scene,
The tranquil tears of tragic joy still spread their silver sheen;
Along the Grand Canal still soar the fragile Towers of Truth;
Their fairy grace defends this place of Beauty, calm and couth.

Bone-tired the race that raised the Towers, forgotten are their lores;
Long gone the gods who shed the tears that lap these crystal shores.
Slow beats the time-worn heart of Mars beneath this icy sky;
The thin air whispers voicelessly that all who live must die—

Yet still the lacy Spires of Truth sing Beauty's madrigal
And she herself will ever dwell along the Grand Canal![1]

[1] From The Grand Canal, by permission of Lux Transcriptions, Ltd., London and Luna City.

On the swing back they set Rhysling down on Mars at Drywater; the boys passed the hat and the skipper kicked in a half month's pay. That was all—finis—just another space bum who had not had the good fortune to finish it off when his luck ran out. He holed up with the prospectors and archaeologists at How-Far? for a month or so, and could probably have stayed forever in exchange for his songs and his accordion playing. But spacemen die if they stay in one place; he hooked a crawler over to Drywater again and thence to Marsopolis.

The capital was well into its boom; the processing plants lined the Grand Canal on both sides and roiled the ancient waters with the filth of the runoff. This was before the Tri-Planet Treaty forbade disturbing cultural relics for commerce; half the slender, fairy-like towers had been torn down, and others were disfigured to adapt them as pressurized buildings for earthmen.

Now Rhysling had never seen any of these changes and no one described them to him; when he "saw" Marsopolis again, he visualized it as it had been before it was rationalized for trade. His memory was good. He stood on the riparian esplanade where the ancient great of Mars had taken their ease, and saw its beauty spreading out before his blinded eyes—ice-blue plain of water unmoved by tide, untouched by breeze, and reflecting serenely the sharp, bright stars of the Martian sky, and beyond the water the lacy buttresses and flying towers of an architecture too delicate for our rumbling, heavy planet. The result was Grand Canal.

The subtle change in his orientation which enabled him to see beauty at Marsopolis when beauty was not, now began to affect his whole life. All women became beautiful to him. He knew them by their voices and fitted their appearances to the sounds. It is a mean spirit indeed who will speak to a blind man other than in gentle friendliness;

scolds who had given their husbands no peace sweetened their voices to Rhysling.

It populated his world with beautiful women and gracious men. Dark Star Passing, Berenice's Hair, Death Song of a Wood's Colt, and his other love songs of the wanderers, the womenless men of space, were the direct result of the fact that his conceptions were unsullied by tawdry truths. It mellowed his approach, changed his doggerel to verse, and sometimes even to poetry.

He had plenty of time to think now, time to get all the lovely words just so, and to worry a verse until it sang true in his head. The monotonous beat of Jet Song–

When the field is clear, the reports all seen,
When the lock sighs shut, when the lights wink green,
When the check-off's done, when it's time to pray,
When the captain nods, when she blasts away––
Hear the jets!
Hear them snarl at your back
When you're stretched on the rack;
Feel your ribs clamp your chest,
Feel your neck grind its rest.
Feel the pain in your ship,
Feel her strain in their grip.
Feel her rise! Feel her drive!
Straining steel, come alive,
On her jets!

–came to him not while he himself was a jetman, but later while he was hitchhiking from Mars to Venus and sitting out a watch with an old shipmate.

At Venusberg he sang his new songs and some of the old, in the bars. Someone would start a hat around for him; it would come back with a minstrel's usual take doubled or tripled in recognition of the gallant spirit behind the bandaged eyes.

It was an easy life. Any space port was his home and any

ship his private carriage. No skipper cared to refuse to lift the extra mass of blind Rhysling and his squeeze box; he shuttled from Venusberg to Leyport to Drywater to New Shanghai, or back again, as the whim took him.

He never went closer to Earth than Supra-New York Space Station. Even when signing the contract for Songs of the Spaceways he made his mark in a cabin-class liner somewhere between Luna City and Ganymede. Horowitz, the original publisher, was aboard for a second honeymoon and heard Rhysling sing at a ship's party. Horowitz knew a good thing for the publishing trade when he heard it; the entire contents of Songs were sung directly into the tape in the communications room of that ship before he let Rhysling out of his sight. The next three volumes were squeezed out of Rhysling at Venusberg, where Horowitz had sent an agent to keep him liquored up until he had sung all he could remember.

Up Ship! is not certainly authentic Rhysling throughout. Much of it is Rhysling's, no doubt, and Jet Song is unquestionably his, but most of the verses were collected after his death, from people who had known him during his wanderings.

The Green Hills of Earth grew through twenty years. The earliest form we know about was composed before Rhysling was blinded, during a drinking bout with some of the indentured men on Venus. The verses were concerned mostly with the things the labor clients intended to do back on Earth if and when they ever managed to pay their bounties and thereby be allowed to go home. Some of the stanzas were vulgar, some were not, but the chorus was recognizably that of Green Hills.

We know exactly where the final form of Green Hills came from, and when.

There was a ship in at Venus Ellis Isle which was scheduled for the direct jump from there to Great Lakes, Illinois. She was the old Falcon, youngest of the Hawk class and the first ship to apply the Harriman Trust's new policy of extra-fare express service between Earth cities and any colony with scheduled stops.

Rhysling decided to ride her back to Earth. Perhaps his own song had got under his skin—or perhaps he just hankered to see his native Ozarks one more time.

The company no longer permitted deadheads. Rhysling knew this, but it never occurred to him that the ruling might apply to him. He was getting old, for a spaceman, and just a little matter-of-fact about his privileges. Not senile—he simply knew that he was one of the landmarks in space, along with Halley's Comet, the Rings, and Brewster's Ridge. He walked in the crew's port, went below, and made himself at home in the first empty acceleration couch.

The captain found him there while making a last-minute tour of his ship. "What are you doing here?" he demanded.

"Dragging it back to Earth, captain." Rhysling needed no eyes to see a skipper's four stripes.

"You can't drag in this ship: you know the rules. Shake a leg and get out of here. We raise ship at once." The captain was young; he had come up after Rhysling's active time, but Rysling knew the type—five years at Harriman Hall with only cadet practice trips instead of solid, deep-space experience. The two men did not touch in background or spirit; space was changing.

"Now, captain, you wouldn't begrudge an old man a trip home."

The officer hesitated—several of the crew had stopped to listen. "I can't do it. 'Space Precautionary Act, Clause Six: No one shall enter space save as a licensed member of a crew of a chartered vessel, or as a paying passenger of such a vessel under such regulations as may be issued pursuant to this act.' Up you get and out you go."

Rhysling lolled back, his hands under his head. "If I've got to go, I'm damned if I'll walk. Carry me."

The captain bit his lip and said, "Master-at-arms! Have this man removed."

The ship's policeman fixed his eyes on the overhead struts. "Can't rightly do it, captain. I've sprained my shoulder." The other crew members, present a moment before, had faded into the bulkhead paint.

"Well, get a working party!"

"Aye aye, sir." He, too, went away.

Rhysling spoke again. "Now look, skipper—let's not have any hard feelings about this. You've got an out to carry me if you want to—the 'distressed-spaceman' clause."

"Distressed spaceman, my eye! You're no distressed spaceman; you're a space lawyer. I know who you are; you've been bumming around the system for fifteen years. Well, you won't do it in my ship. That clause was intended to succor men who had missed their ships, not to let a man drag free all over space."

"Well, now, captain, can you properly say I haven't missed my ship? I've never been back home since my last trip as a signed-on crew member. The law says I can have a trip back."

"But that was years ago. You've used up your chance."

"Have I, now? The clause doesn't say a word about how soon a man has to take his trip back; it just says he's got it coming to him. Go look it up, skipper. If I'm wrong, I'll not only walk out on my two legs, I'll beg your humble pardon in front of your crew. Go on—look it up. Be a sport."

Rhysling could feel the man's glare, but he turned and stomped out of the compartment. Rhysling knew that he had used his blindness to place the captain in an impossible position, but this did not embarrass Rhysling—he rather enjoyed it.

Ten minutes later the siren sounded, he heard the orders on the bull horn for Up-Stations. When the soft sighing of the locks and the slight pressure change in his ears let him know that take-off was imminent, he got up and shuffled down to the power room, as he wanted to be near the jets when they blasted off. He needed no one to guide him in any ship of the Hawk class.

Trouble started during the first watch. Rhysling had been lounging in the inspector's chair, fiddling with the keys of his accordion and trying out a new version of Green Hills.

Let me breathe unrationed air again
Where there's no lack nor dearth

And something, something, something Earth.

It would not come out right. He tried again.

Let the sweet fresh breezes heal me
As they rove around the girth
Of our lovely mother planet,
Of the cool, green hills of Earth.

That was better, he thought. "How do you like that, Archie?" he asked over the muted roar.

"Pretty good. Give out with the whole thing." Archie Macdougal, chief jetman, was an old friend, both spaceside and in bars; he had been an apprentice under Rhysling many years and millions of miles back.

Rhysling obliged, then said, "You youngsters have got it soft. Everything automatic. When I was twisting her tail you had to stay awake."

"You still have to stay awake."

They fell to talking shop, and Macdougal showed him the new direct-response damping rig which had replaced the manual vernier control which Rhysling had used. Rhysling felt out the controls and asked questions until he was familiar with the new installation. It was his conceit that he was still a jetman and that his present occupation as a troubadour was simply an expedient during one of the fusses with the company that any man could get into.

"I see you still have the old hand-damping plates installed," he remarked, his agile fingers flitting over the equipment.

"All except the links. I unshipped them because they obscure the dials."

"You ought to have them shipped. You might need them."

"Oh, I don't know. I think——"

Rhysling never did find out what Macdougal thought, for it was at that moment the trouble tore loose. Macdougal caught it square, a blast of radioactivity that burned him down where he stood.

Rhysling sensed what had happened. Automatic reflexes of old habit came out. He slapped the discover and rang the alarm to the control room simultaneously. Then he remembered the unshipped links. He had to grope until he found them, while trying to keep as low as he could to get maximum benefit from the baffles. Nothing but the links bothered him as to location. The place was as light to him as any place could be; he knew every spot, every control, the way he knew the keys of his accordion.

"Power room! Power room! What's the alarm?"

"Stay out!" Rhysling shouted. "The place is 'hot.'" He could feel it on his face and in his bones, like desert sunshine.

The links he got into place, after cursing someone, anyone, for having failed to rack the wrench he needed. Then he commenced trying to reduce the trouble by hand. It was a long job and ticklish. Presently he decided that the jet would have to be spilled, pile and all.

First he reported. "Control!"

"Control aye aye!"

"Spilling Jet Three—emergency."

"Is this Macdougal?"

"Macdougal is dead. This is Rhysling, on watch. Stand by to record."

There was no answer; dumfounded the skipper may

have been, but he could not interfere in a power-room emergency. He had the ship to consider, and the passengers and crew. The doors had to stay closed.

The captain must have been still more surprised at what Rhysling sent for record. It was:

We rot in the molds of Venus,
We retch at her tainted breath.
Foul are her flooded jungles,
Crawling with unclean death.

Rhysling went on cataloguing the Solar System as he worked, "harsh bright soil of Luna," "Saturn's rainbow rings," "the frozen night of Titan," all the while opening and spilling the jet and fishing it clean. He finished with an alternate chorus:

We've tried each spinning space mote
And reckoned its true worth:
Take us back again to the homes of men
On the cool, green hills of Earth.

Then, almost absent-mindedly, he remembered to tack on his revised first verse:

The arching sky is calling
Spacemen back to their trade.
All hands! Stand by! Free falling!
And the lights below us fade.
Out ride the sons of Terra,
Far drives the thundering jet,
Up leaps the race of Earthmen
Out, far, and onward yet—

The ship was safe now and ready to limp home, shy one jet. As for himself, Rhysling was not so sure. That "sunburn" seemed pretty sharp, he thought. He was unable to see the bright, rosy fog in which he worked, but he knew it was there. He went on with the business of flushing the air out through the outer valve, repeating it several times to permit the level of radioaction to drop to something a man might stand under suitable armor. While he did this, he sent one more chorus, the last bit of authentic Rhysling that ever could be:

We pray for one last landing
On the globe that gave us birth;
Let us rest our eyes on the fleecy skies
And the cool, green hills of Earth.

Doomsday Deferred

by Will F. Jenkins

Will F. Jenkins is the real name of one of science fiction's first and greatest practitioners, Murray Leinster. His career extended to 1975 and began with "The Runaway Skyscraper" in the February 22, 1919, Argosy. *Most popular among his fans for his medical-service stories, he produced over a thousand stories and novels of all kinds. "Doomsday Deferred" is a frightening tale quite unlike much of Jenkins' work, and is closely related to stories like H.G. Wells' "The Empire of the Ants," Carl Stephenson's "Leiningen vs the Ants," Clifford Simak's* City *and the recent film* Phase Four; *all of which seem to point to the social insect as the eventual ruler of the Earth.*

Doomsday Deferred

by Will F. Jenkins

If I were sensible, I'd say that somebody else told me this story, and then cast doubts on his veracity. But I saw it all. I was part of it. I have an invoice of a shipment I made from Brazil, with a notation on it, "José Ribiera's stuff." The shipment went through. The invoice, I noticed only today, has a mashed *soldado* ant sticking to the page. There is nothing unusual about it as a specimen. On the face of things, every element is irritatingly commonplace. But if I were sensible, I wouldn't tell it this way.

It began in Milhao, where José Ribiera came to me. Milhao is in Brazil, but from it the Andes can be seen against the sky at sunset. It is a town the jungle unfortunately did not finish burying when the rubber boom collapsed. It is so far up the Amazon basin that its principal contacts with the outer world are smugglers and fugitives from Peruvian justice who come across the mountains, and nobody at all goes there except for his sins. I don't know what took José Ribiera there. I went because one of the three known specimens of *Morpho andiensis* was captured nearby by Böhler in 1911, and a lunatic millionaire in Chicago was willing to pay for a try at a fourth for his collection.

I got there after a river steamer refused to go any farther, and after four days more in a canoe with paddlers who had lived on or near river water all their lives without once taking a bath in it. When I got to Milhao, I wished myself back in the canoe. It's that sort of place.

But that's where José Ribiera was, and in back-country Brazil there is a remarkable superstition that *os Senhores*

Norteamericanos are honest men. I do not explain it. I simply record it. And just as I was getting settled in a particularly noisome inn, José knocked on my door and came in. He was a small brown man, and he was scared all the way down deep inside. He tried to hide that. The thing I noticed first was that he was clean. He was barefoot, but his tattered duck garments were immaculate, and the rest of him had been washed, and recently. In a town like Milhao, that was startling.

"*Senhor*," said José in a sort of apologetic desperation, "you are a *Senhor Norteamericano*. I—I beg your aid."

I grunted. Being an American is embarrassing, sometimes and in some places. José closed the door behind him and fumbled inside his garments. His eyes anxious, he pulled out a small cloth bundle. He opened it with shaking fingers. And I blinked. The lamplight glittered and glinted on the most amazing mass of tiny gold nuggets I'd ever seen. I hadn't a doubt it was gold, but even at first glance I wondered how on earth it had been gathered. There was no flour gold at all—that fine powder which is the largest part of any placer yield. Most of it was gravelly particles of pinhead size. There was no nugget larger than a half pea. There must have been five pounds of it altogether, though, and it was a rather remarkable spectacle.

"*Senhor*," said José tensely, "I beg that you will help me turn this into cattle! It is a matter of life or death."

I hardened my expression. Of course, in thick jungle like that around Milhao, a cow or a bull would be as much out of place as an Eskimo, but that wasn't the point. I had business of my own in Milhao. If I started gold buying or cattle dealing out of amiability, my own affairs would suffer. So I said in polite regret, "I am not a businessman, *senhor*, do not deal in gold or cattle either. To buy cattle, you should go down to São Pedro"—that was four days' paddle downstream, or considering the current perhaps three—"and take this gold to a banker. He will give you money for it if you can prove that it is yours. You can then buy cattle if you wish."

José looked at me desperately. Certainly half the population of Milhao—and positively the Peruvian-refugee half—would have cut his throat for a fraction of his hoard. He almost panted: "But, *senhor!* This would be enough to buy cattle in São Pedro and send them here, would it not?"

I agreed that at a guess it should buy all the cattle in São Pedro, twice over, and hire the town's wheezy steam launch to tow them upriver besides. José looked sick with relief. But, I said, one should buy his livestock himself, so he ought to go to São Pedro in person. And I could not see what good cattle would be in the jungle anyhow.

"Yet—it would buy cattle!" said José, gulping. "That is what I told—my friends. But I cannot go farther than Milhao, *senhor*. I cannot go to São Pedro. Yet I must—I need to buy cattle for—my friends! It is life and death! How can I do this, *senhor?*"

Naturally, I considered that he exaggerated the emergency.

"I am not a businessman," I repeated. "I would not be able to help you." Then at the terrified look in his eyes I explained, "I am here after butterflies."

He couldn't understand that. He began to stammer, pleading. So I explained.

"There is a rich man," I said wryly, "who wishes to possess a certain butterfly. I have pictures of it. I am sent to find it. I can pay one thousand milreis for one butterfly of a certain sort. But I have no authority to do other business, such as the purchase of gold or cattle."

José looked extraordinarily despairing. He looked numbed by the loss of hope. So, merely to say or do something, I showed him a color photograph of the specimen of *Morpho andiensis* which is in the Goriot collection in Paris. Bug collectors were in despair about it during the war.

They were sure the Nazis would manage to seize it. Then José's eyes lighted hopefully.

"*Senhor!*" he said urgently. "Perhaps my—friends can find you such a butterfly! Will you pay for such a butterfly in cattle sent here from São Pedro, *senhor?*"

I said rather blankly that I would, but—— Then I was talking to myself. José had bolted out of my room, leaving maybe five pounds of gravelly gold nuggets in my hands. That was not usual.

I went after him, but he'd disappeared. So I hid his small fortune in the bottom of my collection kit. A few drops of formaldehyde, spilled before closing up a kit of collection bottles and insects, is very effective in chasing away pilferers. I make use of it regularly.

Next morning I asked about José. My queries were greeted with shrugs. He was a very low person. He did not live in Milhao, but had a clearing, a homestead, some miles upstream, where he lived with his wife. They had one child. He was suspected of much evil. He had bought pigs, and taken them to his clearing and behold he had no pigs there! His wife was very pretty, and a Peruvian had gone swaggering to pay court to her, and he had never come back. It is notable, as I think of it, that up to this time no ant of any sort has come into my story. Butterflies, but no ants. Especially not *soldados*—army ants. It is queer.

I learned nothing useful about José, but I had come to Milhao on business, so I stated it publicly. I wished a certain butterfly, I said. I would pay one thousand milreis for a perfect specimen. I would show a picture of what I wanted to any interested person, and I would show how to make a butterfly net and how to use it, and how to handle butterflies without injuring them. But I wanted only one kind, and it must not be squashed.

The inhabitants of Milhao became happily convinced that I was insane, and that it might be profitable insanity for them. Each person leaped to the nearest butterfly and blandly brought it to me. I spent a whole day explaining to bright-eyed people that matching the picture of *Morpho andiensis* required more than that the number of legs and wings should be the same. But, I repeated, I would pay one thousand milreis for a butterfly exactly like the picture. I had plenty of margin for profit and loss, at that. The last time a *Morpho andiensis* was sold, it brought $25,000 at auction. I'd a lot rather have the money, myself.

José Ribiera came back. His expression was tense beyond belief. He plucked at my arm and said, "*Senhor,*" and I grabbed him and dragged him to my inn.

I hauled out his treasure. "Here!" I said angrily. "This is not mine! Take it!"

He paid no attention. He trembled. "*Senhor,*" he said, and swallowed. "My friends—my friends do not think they can catch the butterfly you seek. But if you will tell them ——" He wrinkled his brows. "*Senhor,* before a butterfly is born, is it a little soft nut with a worm in it?"

That could pass for a description of a cocoon. José's friends—he was said not to have any—were close observers. I said so. José seemed to grasp at hope as at a straw.

"My—friends will find you the nut which produces the butterfly," he said urgently, "if you tell them which kind it is and what it looks like."

I blinked. Just three specimens of *Morpho andiensis* had ever been captured, so far as was known. All were adult insects. Of course nobody knew what the cocoon was like. For that matter, any naturalist can name a hundred species—and in the Amazon valley alone—of which only the adult forms have been named. But who would hunt for cocoons in jungle like that outside of Milhao?

"My friend," I said skeptically, "there are thousands of different such things. I will buy five of each different kind you can discover, and I will pay one milreis apiece. But only five of each kind, remember!"

I didn't think he'd even try, of course. I meant to insist that he take back his gold nuggets. But again he was gone before I could stop him. I had an uncomfortable impression that when I made my offer, his face lighted as if he'd been given a reprieve from a death sentence. In the light of later events, I think he had.

I angrily made up my mind to take his gold back to him next day. It was a responsibility. Besides, one gets interested in a man—especially of the half-breed class—who can unfeignedly ignore five pounds of gold. I arranged to be paddled up to his clearing next morning.

It was on the river, of course. There are no footpaths in Amazon-basin jungle. The river flowing past Milhao is a broad deep stream perhaps two hundred yards wide. Its width seems less because of the jungle walls on either side. And the jungle is daunting. It is trees and vines and lianas as seen from the stream, but it is more than that. Smells come out, and you can't identify them. Sounds come out, and you can't interpret them. You cut your way into its mass, and you see nothing. You come out, and you have learned nothing. You cannot affect it. It ignores you. It made me feel insignificant.

My paddlers would have taken me right on past José's clearing without seeing it, if he hadn't been on the river bank. He shouted. He'd been fishing, and now that I think, there were no fish near him, but there were some picked-clean fish skeletons. And I think the ground was very dark about him when we first saw him, and quite normal when we approached. I know he was sweating, but he looked terribly hopeful at the sight of me.

I left my two paddlers to smoke and slumber in the canoe. I followed José into the jungle. It was like walking in a tunnel of lucent green light. Everywhere there were tree trunks and vines and leaves, but green light overlay everything. I saw a purple butterfly with crimson wing tips, floating abstractedly in the jungle as if in an undersea grotto.

Then the path widened, and there was José's dwelling.

It was a perfect proof that man does not need civilization to live in comfort. Save for cotton garments, an iron pot and a machete, there was literally nothing in the clearing or the house which was not of and from the jungle, to be replaced merely by stretching out one's hand. To a man who lives like this, gold has no value. While he keeps his wants at this level, he can have no temptations. My thoughts at the moment were almost sentimental.

I beamed politely at José's wife. She was a pretty young girl with beautifully regular features. But, disturbingly, her eyes were as panic-filled as José's. She spoke, but she seemed tremblingly absorbed in the contemplation of some crawling horror. The two of them seemed to live with terror. It was too odd to be quite believable. But their child—a brown-skinned three-year-old quite innocent of clothing—was unaffected. He stared at me, wide-eyed.

"*Senhor,*" said José in a trembling voice, "here are the things you desire, the small nuts with worms in them."

His wife had woven a basket of flat green strands. He put it before me. And I looked into it tolerantly, expecting nothing. But I saw the sort of thing that simply does not happen. I saw a half bushel of cocoons!

José had acquired them somehow in less than twenty-four hours. Some were miniature capsules of silk which would yield little butterflies of wing spread no greater than a mosquito's. Some were sturdy fat cocoons of stout brown silk. There were cocoons which cunningly mimicked the look of bird droppings, and cocoons cleverly concealed in twisted leaves. Some were green—I swear it—and would pass for buds upon some unnamed vine. And——

It was simply, starkly impossible. I was stupefied. The Amazon basin has been collected, after a fashion, but the pupa and cocoon of any reasonably rare species is at least twenty times more rare than the adult insect. And these cocoons were fresh! They were alive! I could not believe it, but I could not doubt it. My hands shook as I turned them over.

I said, "This is excellent, José! I will pay for all of them at the rate agreed on—one milreis each. I will send them to São Pedro today, and their price will be spent for cattle and the bringing of the cattle here. I promise it!"

José did not relax. I saw him wipe sweat off his face.

"I—beg you to command haste, *Senhor*," he said thinly.

I almost did not hear. I carried that basket of cocoons back to the riverbank. I practically crooned over it all the way back to Milhao. I forgot altogether about returning the gold pellets. And I began to work frenziedly at the inn.

I made sure, of course, that the men who would cart the parcel would know that it contained only valueless objects like cocoons. Then I slipped in the parcel of José's gold. I wrote a letter to the one man in São Pedro who, if God was good, might have sense enough to attend to the affair for me. And I was almost idiotically elated.

While I was making out the invoice that would carry my shipment by refrigerated air express from the nearest airport it could be got to, a large ant walked across my paper. One takes insects very casually in back-country Brazil. I mashed him, without noticing what he was. I went blissfully to start the parcel off. I had a shipment that would make history among bug collectors. It was something that simply could not be done!

The fact of the impossibility hit me after the canoe with the parcel started downstream. How the devil those cocoons had been gathered——

The problem loomed larger as I thought. In less than one day, José had collected a half bushel of cocoons, of at least one hundred different species of moths and butterflies. It could not be done! The information to make it possible did not exist! Yet it had happened. How?

The question would not down. I had to find out. I bought a pig for a present and had myself ferried up to the clearing again. My paddlers pulled me upstream with languid strokes. The pig made irritated noises in the bottom of the canoe. Now I am sorry about that pig. I would apologize to its ghost if opportunity offered. But I didn't know.

I landed on the narrow beach and shouted. Presently José came through the tunnel of foliage that led to his house. He thanked me, dry-throated, for the pig. I told him I had ordered cattle sent up from São Pedro. I told him humorously that every ounce of meat on the hoof the town contained would soon be on the way behind a wheezing steam launch. José swallowed and nodded numbly. He still looked like someone who contemplated pure horror.

We got the pig to the house. José's wife sat and rocked her child, her eyes sick with fear. I probably should have felt embarrassed in the presence of such tragedy, even if I could not guess at its cause. But instead, I thought about the questions I wanted to ask. José sat down dully beside me.

I was oblivious of the atmosphere of doom. I said blandly, "Your friends are capable naturalists, José. I am much pleased. Many of the 'little nuts' they gathered are quite new to me. I would like to meet such students of the ways of nature."

José's teeth clicked. His wife caught her breath. She looked at me with an oddly despairing irony. It puzzled me. I looked at José, sharply. And then the hair stood up on my head. My heart tried to stop. Because a large ant walked on José's shoulder, and I saw what kind of ant it was.

"My God!" I said shrilly. "*Soldados!* Army ants!"

I acted through pure instinct. I snatched up the baby from its mother's arms and raced for the river. One does not think at such times. The *soldado* ant, the army ant, the driver ant, is the absolute and undisputed monarch of all jungles everywhere. He travels by millions of millions, and nothing can stand against him. He is ravening ferocity and inexhaustible number. Even man abandons his settlements when the army ant marches in, and returns only after he has left—to find every bit of flesh devoured to the last morsel, from the earwigs in the thatch to a horse that may have been tethered too firmly to break away. The army ant on the march can and does kill anything alive, by tearing the flesh from it in tiny bites, regardless of defense. So—I grabbed the child and ran.

José Ribiera screamed at me, "*No! Senhor! No!*"

He sat still and he screamed. I'd never heard such undiluted horror in any man's voice.

I stopped. I don't know why. I was stunned to see José and his wife sitting frozen where I'd left them. I was more stunned, I think, to see the tiny clearing and the house unchanged. The army ant moves usually on a solid front. The ground is covered with a glistening, shifting horde. The air is filled with tiny clickings of limbs and mandibles. Ants swarm up every tree and shrub. Caterpillars, worms, bird nestlings, snakes, monkeys unable to flee—anything living becomes buried under a mass of ferociously rending small forms which tear off the living flesh in shreds until only white bones are left.

But José sat still, his throat working convulsively. I had seen *soldados* on him. But there were no *soldados*. After a moment José got to his feet and came stumbling toward me. He looked like a dead man. He could not speak.

"But look!" I cried. My voice was high-pitched. "I saw *soldado* ants! I saw them!"

José gulped by pure effort of will. I put down the child. He ran back to his mother.

"S-*si*. Yes," said José, as if his lips were very stiff and his throat without moisture. "But they are—special *soldados*. They are—pets. Yes. They are tame. They are my—friends. They—do tricks, *senhor*. I will show you!"

He held out his hand and made sucking noises with his mouth. What followed is not to be believed. An ant—a large ant, an inch or more long—walked calmly out of his sleeve and onto his outstretched hand. It perched there passively while the hand quivered like an aspen leaf.

"But yes!" said José hysterically. "He does tricks, *senhor!* Observe! He will stand on his head!"

Now, this I saw, but I do not believe it. The ant did something so that it seemed to stand on its head. Then it turned and crawled tranquilly over his hand and wrist and up his sleeve again.

There was silence, or as much silence as the jungle ever holds. My own throat went dry. And what I have said is insanity, but this is much worse. I felt Something waiting to see what I would do. It was, unquestionably, the most horrible sensation I had ever felt. I do not know how to describe it. What I felt was—not a personality, but a mind. I had a ghastly feeling that Something was looking at me from thousands of pairs of eyes, that it was all around me.

I shared, for an instant, what that Something saw and thought. I was surrounded by a mind which waited to see what I would do. It would act upon my action. But it was not a sophisticated mind. It was murderous, but innocent. It was merciless, but naïve.

That is what I felt. The feeling doubtless has a natural explanation which reduces it to nonsense, but at the moment I believed it. I acted on my belief. I am glad I did.

"Ah, I see!" I said in apparent amazement. "That is clever, José! It is remarkable to train an ant! I was absurd to be alarmed. But—your cattle will be on the way, José! They should get here very soon! There will be many of them!"

Then I felt that the mind would let me go. And I went.

My canoe was a quarter mile downstream when one of the paddlers lifted his blade from the water and held it there, listening. The other stopped and listened too. There was a noise in the jungle. It was mercifully far away, but it sounded like a pig. I have heard the squealing of pigs at slaughtering time, when instinct tells them of the deadly intent of men and they try punily to fight. This was not that sort of noise. It was worse; much worse.

I made a hopeless spectacle of myself in the canoe. Now, of course, I can see that, from this time on, my actions were not those of a reasoning human being. I did not think with proper scientific skepticism. It suddenly seemed to me that Norton's theory of mass consciousness among social insects was very plausible. Bees, says Norton, are not only units in an organization. They are units of an organism. The hive or the swarm is a creature—one creature—says Norton. Each insect is a body cell only, just as the corpuscles in our blood stream are individuals and yet only parts of us. We can destroy a part of our body if the welfare of the whole organism requires it, though we destroy many cells. The swarm or the hive can sacrifice its members for the hive's defense. Each bee is a mobile body cell. Its consciousness is a part of the whole intelligence, which is that of the group. The group is the actual creature. And ants, says Norton, show the fact more clearly still; the ability of the creature which is an ant colony to sacrifice a part of itself for the whole. . . . He gives illustrations of what he means. His book is not accepted by naturalists generally, but there in the canoe, going down-river from José's clearing, I believed it utterly.

I believed that an army-ant army was as much a single creature as a sponge. I believed that the Something in José's jungle clearing—its body cells were *soldado* ants—had discovered that other creatures perceived and thought as it did. Nothing more was needed to explain everything. An army-ant creature, without physical linkages, could know what its own members saw and knew and felt. It should need only to open its mind to perceive what other creatures saw and knew and felt.

The frightening thing was that when it could interpret

such unantish sensations, it could find its prey with a terrible infallibility. It could flow through the jungle in a streaming, crawling tide of billions of tiny stridulating bodies. It could know the whereabouts and thoughts of every living thing around it. Nothing could avoid it, as nothing could withstand it. And if it came upon a man, it could know his thoughts too. It could perceive in his mind vast horizons beyond its former ken. It could know of food —animal food—in quantities never before imagined. It could, intelligently, try to arrange to secure that food.

It had.

But if so much was true, there was something else it could do. The thought made the blood seem to cake in my veins. I began frantically to thrust away the idea. The Something in José's clearing hadn't discovered it yet. But pure terror of the discovery had me drenched in sweat when I got back to Milhao.

Test-Tube Terror

by Robert Standish

Robert Standish is a pseudonymn of English author Digby George Gerahty, a frequent contributor to the Post *in the 60s. This story is an example of what noted science fiction critic and author Damon Knight refers to as "anti-science fiction"—a theme more common to the science-horror film. There is some validity to such a cautionary theory. Science should provide a control for potential danger in new developments, and at times, as we see illustrated here, the realization of the danger comes too late. Eleven of the Standish* Post *stories were collected in England as* The Talking Dog and Other Stories.

Test-Tube Terror

by Robert Standish

The brief description of myself given here has little or nothing to do with my story. I give it in order to create a "climate of credibility." My name is Mark Harrowby. I am a bachelor, aged thirty-six, a patent lawyer by profession. You will find my name listed in the London telephone directory at 149, Woolpack Street, Westminster. Among my various clients are numbered several immensely rich, internationally known corporations, the kind which don't entrust their secrets to blabbermouths. In short, I am a responsible citizen. Just remember that, if, while reading this story, your credulity becomes strained.

Three days after the Russians launched Sputnik No. 1, I received a letter bearing a Geneva postmark. It was written by Giselle Duclos, who, I may say, is responsible for the fact that I am still a bachelor. Giselle is twenty-seven years of age, Swiss by nationality and a willowy, blue-eyed blonde by Nature's favor. I fell in love with her ten years ago. Her brother, Pierre, is my oldest and closest friend, two years younger than I am. Madame Duclos, their mother, widow of a minor Swiss civil servant, ran a boardinghouse in Geneva for students. I spent some months there in 1939, which is how my life became entangled with theirs.

Every summer since 1946, Giselle, Pierre and I have gone on long walking tours, in the Swiss and French Alps, in the Dolomites, the Pyrenees and, once, in the Snowdon region of North Wales. We like walking and, although not mountaineers in the accepted sense of the word, we like best to walk among mountains.

Briefly, Giselle's refusal to marry me is due to her belief that Pierre's work is more important than marriage. I find this strangely inconsistent, bearing in mind that Pierre is a biologist and geneticist and Giselle is his assistant. A biologist who shirks marriage!

Like most Swiss, Giselle and Pierre are sober-minded, down-to-earth people. That is why the tone of Giselle's letter shook me. Here it is:

> *Dear Mark: I know how busy you are and how difficult it will be for you to get away from London, but you may believe me when I say that nothing—nothing you are doing can be as important as your coming to Geneva at once. I dare not explain more in writing. Let me know very casually when and where to meet you.* DO NOT TELEPHONE. *Love,*
>
> *Giselle*

There it was, laid on the line. Had I not been sure that she would not have written in this strain without good cause, I would have put my own affairs first. As it was, I booked on a flight two days ahead, sending Giselle a post card to say when I arrived and, casually as requested, mentioning that I was passing through Geneva and hoped to see her.

Giselle's appearance shattered me when she met me at the airport. She was thin, haggard and—I know no other word—hunted. She talked a lot and said nothing, using a torrent of words as a kind of safety valve.

We took the lakeside road toward Nyon and Lausanne, after driving twice round a quiet city block to make sure that we were not being followed. I will confess to being somewhat irritated by all this; it seemed that Giselle was out of character.

"We've rented a small furnished chalet in the moun-

See p 57

CATALOGING IN PUBLICATION 03/93

Richardson, Barry A., 1937-
Wood preservation / Barry A. Richardson. — 2nd ed. —
London ; New York : E. & F.N. Spon, 1993.

p. cm.

Includes bibliographical references (p.) and index.
ISBN 0-419-17490-7 (alk. paper)

1. Wood—Preservation. I. Title.

TA422.R53 1993 674′.386—dc20 92-30664
AACR 2 MARC CIP 3/93

tains," she explained to me, "and so far, I'm almost sure, they haven't located us yet. But it's only a question of time."

"Who is They?" I asked bluntly.

"We don't know, Mark; that's what makes it all so frightening."

The chalet stood at one end of a vast alpine meadow at about five thousand feet above sea level. It took us three hours of hard driving to reach it. There was no other human habitation in sight. Even the cows had been taken down to lower pastures, for snow was imminent. Two huge, ferocious-looking Alsatians prowled round the chalet, creating an uproar as we approached. Then Pierre emerged to quieten them.

He had a bad case of the jitters—worse even than Giselle. He looked as though he had not slept for a week.

"Thanks for coming," he said with a warm handshake, leading the way into the warmth of the chalet, where the savory smells of a stew cooking reminded me that I was hungry. When dinner was served, Giselle and Pierre picked at theirs; I wolfed two large plates of the stew. I had a fair idea that I was about to hear unpleasant things, which, I find, sit better on a full stomach.

"Well, let's have it," I said at length, when we had done the washing up.

"What would you say, Mark," Pierre asked abruptly, "if I told you that it lies in my power now—today—to destroy every blade of grass in the world?"

"I would say, Pierre, that you were the most dangerous human being alive and the sooner you were put behind steel bars, the better. Are you suggesting that you could do this?"

He nodded sadly. "But I don't expect you to believe me, Mark. I intend to prove it to you. No, I know you don't doubt me," he said, cutting short my protestations. "Nevertheless, it is important that you should shed all doubt.

That way, don't you see, you will be able to feel the staggering weight of responsibility that Giselle and I have been carrying about. We don't know what to do, Mark, and we're counting on you to help us decide."

"Let's have it from the beginning," I urged him.

"It all dates from about four years ago, when Giselle told me something she had heard to the effect that a fortune was waiting for anyone who could produce a really effective weed killer—something far better than any at present in use. Well," Pierre said apologetically, "I was tempted. I make very little money. I'm not awfully interested in money, really. But I thought it would be nice if Giselle could buy some pretty clothes. I could do with a couple of new suits, too, and a car that isn't rattling to pieces. Mother left us a little money, as you know, but it went. I needed a lot of things for the laboratory and they were expensive. Then, after I had begun work on the weed killer, I sold my insurance policies to raise money for the trip to Australia."

"You didn't tell me you had been to Australia," I said in amazement.

"I didn't tell anyone—then."

"You sound as though you are ashamed of trying to make a little money, Pierre, but you don't have to be. With your brains and ability, why shouldn't you want to live decently? But go on," I urged him.

"Well, I found my weed killer," he went on. "I won't tell you any details about it, Mark. It's better for your own peace of mind, and your safety, that you know nothing. Suffice to say that it was successful beyond my wildest dreams. It was"—he fumbled for words—"like looking for a box of matches and finding—a volcano."

"But what took you to Australia?" I asked him.

"I had to find someplace where—it couldn't get out of hand. I knew that inside the Great Barrier Reef, off the coast of Queensland, there were uninhabited islands. By discreet inquiries, we learned of Kangaroo Island. Nobody lived there because there was no fresh water. It was about three miles along and a mile broad, large enough for my purpose. On an island, don't you see, it was possible to keep it within bounds. Well, to cut it short, we chartered a small interisland cutter for a few days.

"We first walked right round the island to make sure nobody was living there. Then, at six o'clock one morning, just before sunrise, we took some of It—the weed killer—to what we judged was the center of the island. We simply poured the contents of a small jar onto the grass and waited. Well, there wasn't long to wait. Because of the hot sun, I suppose, all the processes were speeded up, just as the processes of decay are accelerated in a warm climate. All I need tell you now is that before noon the entire island, which at dawn had been clothed from end to end with coarse grass, was black—just as black as if it had been burned."

"You are telling me, then, that three square miles of grass were completely destroyed in a matter of six hours?" I asked. "Is that it?"

"That's it, Mark," said Pierre soberly. "Think it over and in the morning we'll show you something that will end your doubts."

There were three rough bunks in the chalet. Giselle's was in a curtained alcove. We all went to bed. I hope the others slept better than I did.

We rose early, for the autumn days were short. Without waiting for breakfast, we walked across the wide expanse of alpine meadow, Giselle carrying a small glass jar with a screw top containing what looked like a bright green sludge. Pierre carried a bamboo cane about six feet long, to one end of which was tied a piece of white rag. This he planted firmly in the soil at a spot about one mile from the chalet. Giselle handed me the jar.

"What do I do with it?" I asked.

"Unscrew it," she told me, "and simply pour the contents on the grass. Then we'll go back and have breakfast."

The jar, when unscrewed, gave off a foul stench. It was unbelievably horrible and unlike anything I had smelled before. I poured the contents on the ground—it had the consistency of heavy engine oil—replaced the screw cap, and that was that. We walked back to breakfast.

Aside from attempted mayhem by the two Alsatians, the morning passed without incident. There were things I wanted to say to Giselle, but this was manifestly not the time to say them.

At eleven o'clock by my watch, Pierre put on his heavy coat and said curtly, "Let's go."

Halfway toward the white flag, the stench of corruption came to meet us. Twice I was on the point of vomiting. When we arrived at the spot where I had spilled the green sludge—I can't go on calling it It—there was a lengthening, winding ribbon of blackened grass. Had I not known otherwise, I would have said that it had been burned. Pierre kept on looking at his watch.

Pierre and Giselle each carried, slung across the back, a small apparatus such as fruitgrowers use to spray their trees. In France, where vines are all-important, they are used to spray vineyards with sulphate of copper, I think it is.

"What are they for?" I asked, more for the sake of hearing my own voice than anything else. I think I knew anyway.

"Call them fire extinguishers," replied Pierre, "and you won't be far wrong."

I lost count of time then. In my throat a pulse was beating heavily and I realized that I was scared. I was in the presence of something evil—something Absolute, something which I sensed was capable of setting up a chain of causation so vast and so horrifying that already my imagination was balking.

"Alongside this," I heard Pierre say as though from a long way away, "the atom bomb is a child's toy."

On the lips of most men such a statement would have sounded ridiculous. But uttered by this tough- and sober-minded little Swiss, it had the ring of stark truth.

"Look!" he said a few moments later.

I turned to the black patch of grass, which had begun to grow larger—more rapidly. It seemed to be alive at the edges, creeping in an ever-extending path, undulating as it went. Except for the fact that there were no visible flames, nor any heat being given off, the grass was being consumed by what was for all practical purposes a fire. In five minutes the blackened strip was too wide to leap.

When the destroyed area was almost an acre in extent, Pierre asked, "Seen enough?"

I nodded. He and Giselle, starting back to back, walked in opposite directions around the perimeter, spraying the outermost edge and, as it seemed, extinguishing the fire. Yes, I had seen enough.

We returned to the chalet in silence. I was conjuring up ugly visions of a world in which that black, creeping, undulating horror had got out of hand, a world filled with the bellowings of starving cows, the piteous bleating of sheep. Then I thought of the thin cries of infants, tugging vainly at empty breasts; of growing children, losing their boisterous high spirits for lack of the food which stoked their fires. No grass, no meat, no milk, or cheese, or butter—not just for a few days or weeks, but forever.

My work brings me in contact with a great many scientists, who seem to share an attitude, believing, or professing to believe, that a fidelity to what they are pleased to call "pure science" absolves them from a regard for the humanities. I am exaggerating for effect, but the attitude is there all right.

But Giselle and Pierre were not like that, which, I am convinced, was why I liked them so. Science had made them humble, not arrogant. Nevertheless, as I turned these thoughts over in my mind, I did not understand how they could have experienced ten seconds of doubt as to what to do with Pierre's discovery or why they needed advice from me. But then, I was being hasty in my judgments, for I did not know the whole story.

"I wish," I said, "that you would tell me how I fit into this picture. What do you want me to do?"

"You've seen the harm Pierre's discovery could do," replied Giselle. "Do you believe that it could be used in any way for the good of humanity?"

"What we mean, Mark, and we may as well say it plainly," said Pierre, "is could we, or anyone, using it as a threat, bring about disarmament and peace? And if so, to whom should we entrust the secret?"

"Offhand," I replied, "I would say that the sooner your discovery is suppressed and forgotten, the better for everyone—particularly you two. But that is a hasty reply and I'd like to ask you a question in turn. Why pick on me? I'm not very wise. In your eyes, how do I seem to qualify to advise you?"

"We know you well, Mark, and we trust you," replied Pierre simply. "You are our friend and we are satisfied that your advice, whatever it may be, will be honest."

"All right, I accept that," I told them. "Now tell me something else. You are both Swiss nationals. Your country has a long tradition of neutrality. Why didn't you just go to Bern, put your formula, or whatever it may be, into the hands of the proper authorities, and let them do the worrying? That, to me, seems the proper thing to have done."

"If it had been something which could be used as a defensive weapon, Mark, we would not have hesitated. But it can't be. It is of its essence offensive. Switzerland, therefore, would never extract any value from it—if there is any value."

"But Switzerland is your country, Pierre," I said, "and I would have thought——"

"England is your country, Mark," interposed Giselle sharply. "We will turn over the secret to you if you ask for it, although I pray for your sake you won't accept the offer. Would you, in turn, and as a matter of duty, hand over the secret to the British government?"

The question hit me between the eyes. It was fair enough. It was not until several minutes had passed that I replied, "No."

"Why?"

"Because I can envisage a set of circumstances in which a British government, stampeded by some terrific emergency, might be tempted to use it as a weapon and —well, I suppose I believe that nothing—nothing at all— could justify its use. In the present ideological struggle— the undeclared war—the bone of contention is, when you get down to facts, the richness of the earth. Some peoples are alleged to have too much of it. Others too little. Your invention, discovery, or whatever you care to call it, is purely destructive. It would remove the bone of contention by destroying it and the contenders, reducing the world to the nice neat mathematical zero you scientists bandy about so freely."

"Giselle and I agree with you there, Mark. That, roughly, has been our conclusion. Then, do you think, any good purpose could be served by handing it over simultaneously to the Americans and the Russians?"

"No."

"To either the Americans or the Russians?"

"No," I replied firmly. "It seems to me," I went on, "that we have reached an impasse in our thinking. We agree that it is useless giving the secret to Switzerland because of the certainty that Switzerland would not use it, while

I wouldn't care to pass it over to any other country because of the risk that it might be used. Surely, that points the way clearly to its suppression. You've asked me for advice. Here it is: Destroy any of the stinking stuff still in your possession. Destroy all documents relating to it and forget the whole thing. And now, if it's all the same to you, I'd like to phone the Geneva airport for a reservation and ask Giselle to drive me there."

"But, Mark—"

"Listen, Pierre," I interrupted. "We may chew this thing to death by talking about it until tomorrow, but you'll never get any other advice from me."

"But you don't know the whole story, Mark," said Giselle unhappily. "It isn't so simple as you seem to think it is. We came to your conclusions months ago. We have already destroyed all Pierre's notes, together with our stock of the stuff, except the small jar which you handled this morning. The only thing left now is about fifty liters of the liquid that we use in the spray gun—the fire extinguisher."

"Then there's nothing to worry about," I said brightly. "I can go home now and earn my living."

"We both memorized Pierre's formula, Mark," said Giselle.

"Then forget it," I retorted.

"Have you ever tried to wipe something off the slate of your memory?" asked Pierre. "It isn't so easy as you make it sound."

"So you can't forget the formula? The secret remains safe so long as neither of you chatters."

"But, Mark, the secret isn't safe," said Pierre glumly. "Someone knows about it or at least suspects it. Our house has been ransacked twice. Giselle and I have been followed. Letters have been intercepted. I'm not sure, but I think our phone was tapped. I don't think we have been traced here yet, but it is only a question of time. It began with offers of huge sums of money. Giselle answered the phone one morning and a voice said, 'I am speaking on behalf of friends who want me to tell you that you and your brother can have more money than you will ever be able to spend. They would like to meet you at a time and place of your choosing—any time, anywhere.' In a crowd one day someone thrust a hundred-franc note into my hand. On it was written: 'There are millions more where this one came from.' Then the tone of the telephone messages became nasty, sinister. There were threats. That was when we destroyed everything."

"You've never had any indication as to who these mysterious people are?" I asked.

"No. Your guess is as good as ours," replied Pierre. "I suspect that it is either the Russians or the Americans. Neither wants the secret in order to use it, so much as to prevent the other getting hold of it."

"Yes, what you say sounds reasonable enough," I was forced to agree. "But even if you are right, all you have to do is to tell them both to jump in the lake and keep your mouth shut."

"There are ways of making obstinate people talk," said Pierre. "It has become one of the modern fine arts. I don't think either Giselle or I would be able to resist pain very long. Then what?"

Now I began to understand the fears which haunted Giselle and Pierre. Indeed, their fears had begun to communicate themselves to me. I also knew too much for my own health's sake, and I wished fervently that I had not been dragged into the affair.

"That changes things," I said at length. "My advice to you now is to go to Geneva immediately, both of you, to tell some high-ranking police official of your predicament and ask him to give you asylum where you will be safe."

"Mark is right," said Giselle. "That is what we must do."

"Thanks, Mark; we'll do that," added Pierre. "Let's eat something and go on into town."

Having made the decision, it seemed as though a weight had been lifted from them. There was a bottle of whisky in the cupboard and we drank a toast in silence.

Then the telephone rang, loud and shrill.

"It can't be for us," said Giselle, "because nobody knows we are here."

In order to stop the nerve-shattering noise of the bell, because the others showed no inclination to answer it, I lifted the receiver.

"Is that Professor Duclos?" asked a voice, speaking in French.

"There is no Professor Duclos here," I replied. "You must have the wrong number."

"Will you tell the professor," continued the voice calmly, "that some friends are inquiring when the grass on Kangaroo Island will start to grow again."

I hung up.

The words uttered were harmless enough, but I find it impossible to exaggerate the sheer malignity they conveyed to me and to the others when I relayed the message.

"It's easy enough to talk of going to Geneva," said Pierre, "but how are we going to get there? They know we are here, and nothing is easier than to prevent us reaching the main road. There isn't a living soul for miles."

"I think," I said, "that Pierre should have a chat with the police, now. A police escort looks pretty good to me."

Pierre agreed. He went to the phone. It was dead.

There was nothing to say. The facts were too painfully obvious. Paradoxically, the phone was more eloquent dead than alive, for no words spoken over it could have so emphasized our isolation. We all wanted passionately to get back to the city, just as, tacitly, we agreed that it was highly improbable that we should be allowed to do so.

They—the mysterious agents who, by letting us know they were aware of the death of Kangaroo Island; the people who had been instrumental in cutting the phone; the people whose vague existence constituted a menace, who had reduced Giselle and Pierre to nervous wrecks and who had shattered some of my complacency—They would find means of intercepting us. Two miles of the road back to civilization lay through dense, dark pine forest, sinister enough in broad daylight, but in darkness terrifying to contemplate. Not even the two Alsatians or Pierre's shotgun made the journey more palatable.

"They wouldn't shoot or try to kill us," I said hopefully, "because if you are right, you would be no good to them dead."

Then I became selfish and personal. They would never get anything out of me because, thank God, I knew nothing, but I wondered all the same how they would assure themselves that I knew nothing.

Darkness had fallen more than an hour before we thought of lighting the lamps. The stove was getting low. When I went outside to fetch some wood, it had begun to snow. Big wet flakes were falling. A vast white blanket covered the alpine meadow.

"Giselle and I have had longer to think about all this than you have, Mark," said Pierre at length. "We are prepared—for anything."

I let it pass.

"But you will be all right. You know nothing," he continued. "All the same, old chap, I'm sorry we dragged you into this mess and, as things have turned out, all to no avail."

Sitting on either side of the dining table, each with a pen and a pad of paper, Giselle and her brother spent the next minutes writing at furious speed. When they had finished writing, they went outside to the woodshed.

"You'll find what we've written—afterward," said Pierre.

"It's underneath a pile of sawdust. I don't think They will look there."

"It isn't your blasted formula, I hope?" I heard myself say.

"No, Mark," he replied equably. "What we have written is merely to exonerate you, in case there should be any attempt made to hold you responsible for what may happen to us. That's all."

I believed I understood, and I felt mortally ashamed.

Then I went for a short walk. I felt that they might wish to be alone for a little time. I had turned the car when Giselle and I arrived. I had left it facing downhill, in case there might be difficulty starting it. The snow was several inches deep, but no more was falling. The darkness was intense. I switched on the car's headlights, which threw a beam of light about half a mile down the hill. Against the white background, four dark figures were plainly visible, plodding stolidly up the hill. I had the impression that they were men to whom snow was no novelty. They could, of course, have been Swiss. Why not? This was Switzerland. The Swiss were used to snow.

I went inside to tell the others what I had seen. My courage had returned. They, I believed, were no longer vague, ephemeral creatures, formless and terrifying. They were now real, for I had seen them.

The two Alsatians had heard the newcomers. They went mad with rage. Pierre turned them loose and, roaring defiance, they went out into the night to do battle. A few seconds later there came the sound of two shots, fired, I judged, from a small-caliber pistol. Silence followed. Imagination conjured up a picture of two faithful dogs lying dead, their life's blood staining the virgin whiteness of the snow. Two shots, two seconds apart. Result: two dead dogs. Expert work by someone trained to kill. It was so sudden, so ruthlessly efficient that, despite the warmth of the chalet, I felt chilled to the bone.

Once again, I was scared. I cracked a feeble joke to hide my fears. It fell flat. This was an ill-chosen moment for witticisms.

Someone tapped on the window. "Come outside!" a voice said. "We wish to speak with you!"

We had extinguished the lamp. The only light in the room came from the mica door of the stove. Quite calmly, Pierre rose from his seat and kissed Giselle on the forehead. I shook the hand he offered me.

"Good-by!" he said, putting his hand to his mouth, dying as he did so.

Giselle kissed me on the lips and said something I did not hear. Then her hand carried something to her mouth. I could have stopped her, but I did not do so. Then, still smiling sadly, she died.

"Come outside!" called the same voice.

Something crashed through the window, landing with a thud on the wooden floor. Choking and clawing at my throat, I went obediently to the door. Something was put over my face. The next thing I remember, and that dimly, was a voice saying, "He knows nothing. He is no use to us." The left sleeve of my jacket was slit. The shirt also. There was a dull ache in my arm, like that from a blunt hypodermic needle. The words echoed in my brain: "He knows nothing. He is no use to us." How were they so sure?

I heard the crunch of heavy boots in the snow. The sound grew fainter until it died away. I was lying in the snow outside the door of the chalet. When I went inside, the fumes had cleared. I mended the broken window with a sheet of paper and some adhesive tape. Then I relighted the lamp.

Pierre and Giselle were still at the table. They had died in order to save the world from the horrors of the creeping black death they had evolved. This story is their epitaph.

They will not have died in vain if the world understands the message of their deaths. Science has outrun morality. That, I believe, is the true meaning of the Biblical reference to new wine in old bottles. Men, all kinds of men—statesmen, soldiers and airmen, scientists and lesser people—are being confronted daily with decisions beyond their moral capacity. The new wine is too strong; the bottles too weak. Giselle and Pierre dared not go on living, because they would not usurp the prerogatives of God. I live because they did not share their knowledge with me.

Meanwhile, as their memorial, there is a blackened acre in an alpine meadow and a dead, sterile island in the Barrier Reef. When, if ever, will they be green again? When God, who does not have to fumble in a biochemical laboratory, wills it so. This, however clumsily delivered, is the message which my good friends left behind them. They died that we may live.

Island of Fear
by William Sambrot

"Island of Fear" is a classic tale of a contemporary man confronting the basic myths of his culture, a theme that was something of a staple of 19th-century gothic-horror fiction. Mr. Sambrot relates his tale with the brevity and chilling terror of past masters of the horror story like Poe, Lovecraft and Saki. William Sambrot wrote several fine stories for the Post *in the 50s and 60s, most of which were collected in a book called* Island of Fear and Other Science Fiction.

Island of Fear

by William Sambrot

Kyle Elliot clutched the smooth tight-fitting stones of the high wall, unmindful of the fierce direct rays of the Aegean sun on his neck, staring, staring through a chink.

He'd come to this tiny island, dropped into the middle of the Aegean like a pebble on a vast blue shield, just in the hope that something—something like what lay beyond that wall—might turn up. And it had. It had.

Beyond, in the garden behind the wall, was a fountain, plashing gently. And in the center of that fountain, two nudes, a mother and child.

A mother and child, marvelously intertwined, intricately wrought of some stone that almost might have been heliotrope, jasper or one of the other semiprecious chalcedonies—although that would have been manifestly impossible.

He took a small object like a pencil from his pocket and extended it. A miniature telescope. He gasped, looking once more through the chink. Heavens, the detail of the woman! Head slightly turned, eyes just widening with the infinitesimal beginning of an expression of surprise as she looked—at what? And half sliding, clutching with one hand at the smooth thigh, reaching mouth slightly rounded, plump other hand not quite touching the milk-swollen breast—the child.

His professional eye moved over the figures, his mind racing, trying to place the sculptor, and failing. It was of no known period. It might have been done yesterday; it might be millenniums old. Only one thing was certain—no catalogue on earth listed it.

Kyle had found this island by pure chance. He'd taken passage on a decrepit Greek caïque that plied the Aegean, nudging slowly and without schedule from island to island. From Lesbos to Chios to Samos, down through the myriad Cyclades, and so on about the fabled sea, touching the old, old lands where the gods had walked like men. The islands where occasionally some treasure, long buried, came to light, and if it pleased Kyle's eyes, and money obtained it, then he would add it to his small collection. But only rarely did anything please Kyle. Only rarely.

The battered caïque's engine had quit in the midst of a small storm which drove them south and west. By the time the storm had cleared, the asthmatic old engine was back in shape, coughing along. There was no radio, but the captain was undisturbed. Who could get lost in the Aegean?

They had been drifting along, a small water bug of a ship lost in the greenish-blue sea, when Kyle had seen the dim purple shadow that was a tiny island in the distance. The glasses brought the little blob of land closer and he sucked in his breath. An incredible wall, covering a good quarter of the miniature island, leaped into view, a great horseshoe of masonry that grew out of the sea, curved, embraced several acres of the land, then returned, sinking at last into the sea again, where white foam leaped high even as he watched.

He called the captain's attention to it. "There is a little island over there." And the captain, grinning, had squinted in the direction of Kyle's pointing finger.

"There is a wall on it," Kyle said, and instantly the grin vanished from the captain's face; his head snapped around and he stared rigidly ahead, away from the island.

"It is nothing," the captain said harshly. "Only a few goatherders live there. It has no name, even."

"There is a wall," Kyle had said gently. "Here"—handing him the glasses—"look."

"No." The captain's head didn't move an iota. His eyes remained straight ahead. "It is just another ruin. There is no harbor there; it is years since anyone has gone there. You would not like it. No electricity."

"I want to see the wall and what is behind it."

The captain flicked an eye at him. Kyle started. The eye seemed genuinely agitated. "There is nothing behind it. It is a very old place and everything is long since gone."

"I want to see the wall," Kyle said quietly.

They'd put him off, finally, the little caïque pointing its grizzled snout to sea, its engine turning over just enough to keep it under way, its muted throbbing the only sound. They'd rowed him over in a dinghy, and as he approached he'd noticed the strangely quiet single street of the village, the lone inn, the few dories with patched lateen sails, and on the low, worn-down hills the herds of drifting goats.

Almost, he might have believed the captain; that here was an old tired island, forgotten, out of the mainstream of the brilliant civilization that had flowered in this sea—almost, until he remembered that wall. Walls are built to protect, to keep out or keep in. He meant to see what.

After he'd settled in the primitive little inn, he'd immediately set out for the wall, surveying it from the low knoll, surprised again to note how much of this small island it encompassed.

He'd walked all around it, hoping to find a gate or a break in the smooth, unscalable wall that towered up. There had been none. The grounds within sprawled on a sort of peninsula that jutted out to where rock, barnacled, fanged, resisted the restless surf.

And coming back along the great wall, utterly baffled, he'd heard the faint musical sound of water dropping within, and, peering carefully at the wall, had seen the small aperture, no bigger than a walnut, just above his head.

And looked through the aperture, and so stood, dazed at so much beauty, staring at the woman and child, unable to tear away, knowing that here, at last, was the absolute perfection he'd sought throughout the world.

How was it that the catalogues failed to list this master work? These things were impossibly hard to keep quiet. And yet, not a whisper, not a rumor had drifted from this island to the others of what lay within those walls. Here on this remote pinprick of land, so insignificant as to go unnamed, here behind a huge wall which was itself a work of genius, here was this magic mother and child glowing all unseen.

He stared, throat dry, heart pumping with the fierce exultation of the avid connoisseur who has found something truly great—and unknown. He must have it—he would have it. It wasn't listed; possibly—just possibly—its true worth was unknown. Perhaps the owner of this estate had inherited it, and it remained there, in the center of the gently falling water, unnoticed, unappreciated.

He reluctantly turned away from the chink in the wall and walked slowly back toward the village, scuffling the deep, pale immemorial dust. Greece. Cradle of western culture. He thought again of the exquisite perfection of the mother and child back there. The sculptor of that little group deserved to walk on Olympus. Who was it?

Back in the village, he paused before the inn to take some of the dust off his shoes, thinking again how oddly incurious, for Greeks, these few villagers were.

"Permit me?"

A boy, eyes snapping, popped out of the inn with a rag in one hand and some primitive shoe blacking in the other, and began cleaning Kyle's shoes.

Kyle sat down on a bench and examined the boy. He was

about fifteen, wiry and strong, but small for his age. He might have, in an earlier era, been a model for one of Praxiteles' masterpieces: the same perfectly molded head, the tight curls, two ringlets falling over the brows, like Pan's snubbed horns, the classic Grecian profile. But no, a ridged scar ran from the boy's nose to the corner of the upper lip, lifting it ever so slightly, revealing a glimmer of white teeth.

No, Praxiteles would never have used him for a model—unless, of course, he had a slightly flawed Pan in mind.

"Who owns the large estate beyond the village?" he asked in his excellent Greek. The boy looked up quickly and it was as if a shutter came down over his dark eyes. He shook his head.

"You must know it," Kyle persisted. "It covers the whole south end of this island. A big wall, very high, all the way to the water."

The boy shook his head stubbornly. "It has always been there."

Kyle smiled at him. "Always is a long time," he said. "Perhaps your father might know?"

"I am alone," the boy said with dignity.

"I'm sorry to hear that." Kyle studied the small, expert movement of the boy. "You really don't know the name of the persons who live there?"

The boy muttered a single word.

"Gordon?" Kyle leaned forward. "Did you say 'The Gordons'? Is it an English family that owns that property?" He felt the hope dying within. If an English family owned it, the chances were slim indeed of obtaining that wonderful stone pair.

"They are not English," the boy said.

"I'd like very much to see them."

"There is no way."

"I know there's no way from the island," Kyle said, "but

I suppose they must have a dock or some facilities for landing from the sea."

The boy shook his head, keeping his eyes down. Some of the villagers had stopped, and now were clustered about him, watching and listening quietly. Kyle knew his Greeks, a happy boisterous people, intolerably curious sometimes; full of advice, quick to give it. These people merely stood, unsmiling, watching.

The boy finished and Kyle flipped him a fifty-lepta coin. The boy caught it and smiled, a flawed masterpiece.

"That wall," Kyle said to the spectators, singling out one old man, "I am interested in meeting the people who own that property."

The old man muttered something and walked away.

Kyle mentally kicked himself for the psychological error. In Greece, money talks first. "I will pay fifty—one hundred drachmas," he said loudly, "to anyone who will take me in his boat around to the seaward side of the wall."

It was a lot of money, he knew, to a poor people eking out a precarious existence on this rocky island, with their goats and scanty gardens. Most of them wouldn't see that much cash in a year's hard work. A lot of money—but they looked at one another, then turned and without a backward glance they walked away from him. All of them.

Throughout the village he met the same mysterious refusal, as difficult to overcome as that enigmatic wall that embraced the end of the island. They refused even to mention the wall or what it contained, who built it, and when. It was as though it didn't exist for them.

At dusk he went back to the inn, ate *dolmadakis*—minced meat, rice, egg and spices—surprisingly delicious; drank *retsina*, the resinated, astringent wine of the peasant; and wondered about the lovely mother and child, standing there behind that great wall with the purple night clothing them. A vast surge of sadness, of longing for the statues swept over him.

What a rotten break! He'd run into local taboos before. Most of them were the results of petty feuds, grudges going back to antiquity. They were cherished by the peasants, held tight, jealously guarded. What else was there of importance in their small lives? But this was something entirely different.

He was standing on the outskirts of the darkened village, gazing unhappily out to sea, when he heard a soft scuffling. He turned quickly. A small boy was approaching. It was the shoeshine boy, eyes gleaming in the starshine, shivering slightly, though the night was balmy.

The boy touched his arm. His fingers felt icy. "I—I will take you in my boat," he whispered.

Kyle smiled, relief exploding within him. Of course, he should have thought of the boy. A young fellow, alone, without family, could use a hundred drachmas, whatever the taboo.

"Thank you," he said warmly. "When can we leave?"

"Before the ebb tide—an hour before sunrise," the boy said. "Only"—his teeth were chattering—"I will take you, but I will not come any closer than the outer rocks between the walls. From there, you must wait until the ebb tide and walk—and walk——" He gasped, as though choking.

"What are you afraid of?" Kyle said. "I'll take all the responsibility for trespassing, although I don't think——"

The boy clutched his arm. "The others—tonight, when you go back to the inn, you will not tell the others that I am rowing you there?"

"Not if you don't want me to."

"Please do not!" he gasped. "They would not like it if they knew—after, that I——"

"I understand," Kyle said. "I won't tell anyone."

"An hour before sunrise," the boy whispered. "I will meet you at the wall where it goes into the water to the east."

The stars were still glowing, but faintly, when Kyle met

the boy, a dim figure sitting in a small rowboat that bobbed up and down, scraping against the kelp and barnacles that grew from the base of the monolithic wall. He realized suddenly that the boy must have rowed for hours to get the boat this far around the island. It had no sails.

He climbed in and they shoved off, the boy strangely silent. The sea was rough, a chill predawn wind blowing raggedly. The wall loomed up alongside, gigantic in the mist.

"Who built this wall?" he asked, once they were out onto the pitching water, heading slowly around the first of a series of jagged, barnacled rocks, thrusting wetly above the rapidly ebbing tide.

"The old ones," the boy said. His teeth were chattering, he kept his back steadfastly to the wall, glancing only seaward to measure his progress. "It has always been there."

Always. And yet, studying the long sweep of the wall beginning to emerge in the first light, Kyle knew that it was very old. Very old. It might well date back to the beginning of Greek civilization. And the statues—the mother and child. All of it an enigma no greater than the fact that they were unknown to the outside world.

As they drew slowly around until he was able to see the ends of the thick walls rising out of the swirling, sucking sea, he realized that most certainly he could not have been the first—not even one of the first hundred. This island was remote, not worth even being on a mail route, but surely, over the many, many years that wall had towered, it must have been visited by people as curious as he. Other collectors. And yet, not a rumor.

The boat rasped up against an enormous black rock, its tip, white with bird droppings, startlingly luminous in the half light. The boy shipped his oars.

"I will come back here at the next tide," he said, shaking as though with a fever. "Will you pay me now?"

"Of course." Kyle took out his billfold. "But aren't you at least going to take me farther in than this?"

"No," the boy said shrilly. "I cannot."

"How about the dock?" Kyle surveyed the considerable expanse of shallow, choppy surf between the rocks and the narrow sloping beach. "Why, there isn't a dock!"

There was nothing between the walls but sand, dotted with huge rocks, and inland, a tangled growth of underbrush with an occasional cypress rearing tall.

"I'll tell you what. I'll take the boat in and you wait here," Kyle said. "I won't be long. I just want to get a chance to meet whoever owns the place and arrange——"

"No!" There was sharp panic in the boy's voice. "If you take the boat——" He half rose, leaning forward to shove off from the rock. At that instant a swell raised the boat, then dropped it suddenly out from under the boy. Overbalanced, he swayed, arms waving wildly, then went over backwards, hitting his head on the rock. He slipped under the water like a stone.

Kyle made a quick lunge, and missing, immediately dived out of the rowboat after him, rasping his chest on the barnacled shelf of rock a few feet beneath the boat. He got a good handful of the boy's shirt, but it tore like paper. He grabbed again, got a firm grip on his hair and stroked for the surface. He held him easily, treading water, looking for the rowboat. It was gone, kicked away by his powerful dive, perhaps behind one of the other rocks. No time to waste looking for it now.

He swam to shore, pulling the boy easily. It was only a hundred yards or so to the smooth white beach, curving between the two arms of the wall that sloped out and down into the ocean. When he came out of the water the boy was coughing weakly, salt water dribbling from his nose.

Kyle carried him well above the tide mark and sat him down on the sand. The boy opened his eyes and peered at him, puzzled.

"You'll be all right," Kyle said. "I'd better get your boat before it drifts too far."

He walked back down to the surf line, kicked off his shoes and stroked off to where the boat rose and fell, nuzzling another of the large rocks that littered the space between the towering walls. He rowed the boat back, facing the sea and the swift-rising sun. The wind had dropped to a whisper.

He beached the boat and gathered up his shoes. The boy was leaning against a rock, looking inland over his shoulder in an attitude of rigid watchfulness.

"Feeling better now?" Kyle called cheerfully. It occurred to him that their little mishap was an excellent excuse for being here, on property belonging to someone who obviously valued his privacy highly.

The boy didn't move. He remained staring back into the tangle of trees, back to where the massive walls converged in the distance, stark, white, ancient.

Kyle touched him on the bare shoulder. He pulled his hand away, fists tightly clenched. He looked at the sand. Here were the marks where the boy had risen, here the dragging footsteps where he'd come to lean against this rock. And here he still stood, glancing over his shoulder toward the trees, lips barely parted, a look of faint surprise just starting on his face.

And there, coming out of the tangled trees, a delicate tracery of footsteps led toward this rock and behind. Footsteps, slender, high-arched, as though a woman, barefooted, scarcely touching the sand, had approached for just an instant. Looking at the strange footprints, Kyle understood completely what he should have guessed when first he'd peered through that chink in the wall, gasping at the unimaginable perfection of the woman and her child.

Kyle knew intimately all the ancient fables of early Greece. And now, looking at the footprints in the sand, one of the most terrible leaped into his mind: the Gorgons.

The Gorgons were three sisters, Medusa, Euryale and Stheno, with snakes writhing where their hair should have been. Three creatures so awful to look upon, the legend said, that whosoever dared gaze upon them instantly turned to stone.

Kyle stood on the warm sand, with the gull cries, the restless Aegean sea sounds all about him, and he knew, at last, who the old ones were who'd built the wall; why they'd built it to lead into the living waters—and whom—what—the walls were meant to contain.

Not an English family named the Gordons. A much more ancient family, named—the Gorgons. Perseus had slain Medusa, but her two hideous sisters, Euryale and Stheno, were immortal.

Immortal. Oh, God! It was impossible! A myth! And yet——

His connoisseur's eyes, even through the sweat of fear, noted the utter perfection of the small statue that leaned against the rock, head turned slightly, an expression of surprise on the face as it peered over one shoulder in the direction of the trees. The two tight ringlets, like snubbed horns above the brow, the perfect molding of the head, the classic Grecian profile. Salt water still flecked the smoothly gleaming shoulders, still dripped from the torn shirt that flapped about the stone waist.

Pan in chalcedony. But Pan had a flaw. From the nose to the corner of the upper lip ran a ridge, an onyx scar that lifted the edge of the onyx lip slightly, so that, faintly, a glimmer of onyx teeth showed. A flawed masterpiece.

He heard the rustle behind him, as of robes, smelled an indescribable scent, heard a sound that could only have been a multiple hissing—and though he knew he mustn't, he turned slowly. And looked.

Sinister Journey
by Conrad Richter

Conrad Richter was an old-fashioned American born in Pennsylvania of Scotch-Irish, German, French and English blood in 1890. He plied many of those trades that authors tend to drift through in their early years: clerk, lumberjack, bank teller, farmhand and subscription salesman, among others. He eventually drifted into reporting for small town papers and, after moving to the southwest, began to accumulate material which became the base for much of his work. It is easy to understand that a man such as Richter would have once described "Sinister Journey" to an acquaintance as "a nightmare set in type."

Sinister Journey

by Conrad Richter

It was the night I slept in Douglas Creel's bed that it happened. You may recall my friend's mysterious disappearance. It was a sensation at the time. A modern American composer and pianist, he was celebrated among artists and liberal thinkers for his fight toward the planned improvement of conditions for mankind. You may remember he disappeared from a mining town in New Mexico named Grantham. What you may not know is that he was born there, the son of a pioneer Southwestern doctor, and that he had kept up his father's house.

He usually came back once a year, as a rule in the fall or early winter. He thought the sun and altitude benefited him, and here he did a good deal of composing. The neighbors complained. They said that fortunately they couldn't hear him all the time because of the roar of trucks hauling ore to the mill. But when they did hear, his big black piano kept them awake far into the night. If it had been tuneful music, they said, it wouldn't have been so bad. But the kind of modern stuff he worked over, playing the same notes again and again, got on their nerves. They even brought out a petition against him, but the town officials squashed it.

This particular November, Doug had come back to the house from Paris. The neighbors muttered and groaned and resigned themselves. Then the night of November twenty-third, they slept like babes. The sheriff said Doug had returned to the house at ten after dining at the Copper

Queen Hotel. He had never come out of the house again. Or if he had, he hadn't been dressed. His clothing was still intact next day, old Apolonia, his Mexican housekeeper, testified. His money remained untouched in the pocket of his trousers folded over a chair; his familiar green-leather music memorandum book was found in his coat in the closet. Only a pair of blue pajamas, his red slippers and a purple dressing gown were missing.

Doug had never married, was blessed with neither brother nor sister. His parents had died some years before, but there was no satisfying the public clamor that he be found. Some of his friends in New York and London hinted that enemies of liberalism had done away with him. This came out in the newspapers and made his disappearance an international affair.

I was East at the time and didn't come West until the excitement had died down. More than once when Doug was in Europe I had stayed and worked in his house, and now I drove straight to Grantham. The town was greatly changed since I had been there last. Lately uranium had been found in the hills and a mill revamped to handle the new ore. Trucks brought it in day and night. This fact together with the typical raw appearance of the town, the scarred hills with piles of dirt and tailings all around gave a modernistic atomic air to the place. It was the kind of environment that Doug loved. He felt completely at home in it, and I felt sure he would never have left it of his own volition.

When I knocked on the door, Apolonia, with her niece, Felicitas, standing behind her, greeted me like a long-lost brother. She said Judge Connover had been paying her out of the estate to stay at the house, but she hadn't been alone a single night since Mr. Creel had disappeared. Nor would she. Even with Felicitas she was nervous. She hoped I would stay for a while. With a man in the house they would feel safe.

It seemed perfectly natural to find myself in Douglas' studio again as night closed down. Clouds came with it and rain fell, a very welcome circumstance in the Southwest. The house had been built on one floor. Doug's studio where he both worked and slept was in a wing at the rear of the house. I found the records of his own Concerto in G Minor, the Utopia Concerto, on the turntable. Evidently he had played it not too long before he disappeared. On impulse I lifted the disks to the arm of the record changer and started them off. Then I sat down and leaned back. The sense of Doug's presence was still strong in the room, but if there were any vibrations of his thought still around, they were unintelligible to me. All that reached me besides the music was the fierce roar of ore trucks on the street in front of the house.

Grantham lies some six thousand feet above sea level. As a rule, coming up to this altitude from the east or west coast, I can sleep like a top. Tonight something kept me awake. How long I lay there sleepless I am unsure, but I remember thinking that a bit of food or drink in my stomach might help me to drop off. I resolved to get a drink of water from the bathroom.

Sitting on the edge of the bed, I put my bathrobe around me and felt for my slippers with my feet.

It had not occurred to me until now how extraordinarily dark Doug's studio seemed. "It's the rain," I told myself and started for the bathroom without turning on the light. Sleep experts claimed that a light woke you up too completely. So I used Doug's bed as a launching pier and took off in the blackness for where I knew the bathroom to be.

At first I thought nothing of it, but presently I realized that it had never taken me so long to reach the bathroom door. I kept on. My hands were stretched before me. When they found nothing but empty air, the queerest feeling came into my fingers. Why, I knew every foot of this room as I did my own at home! But when I had taken a dozen more steps, I knew at last I was irretrievably lost. And now suddenly I grew aware that the sound of ore trucks from the street had ceased. All was silence. At a considerable distance I thought I detected the faintest glow of pale light, but although I hurried toward it, for a long time it grew appreciably no closer. As a level road often appears to have a grade at night, so it seemed that I was going downhill.

When I came out at last, there was no sense of getting into fresh air. It had stopped raining. Unusually large and brilliant stars were out, and a quarter moon shone. By their light and some other unidentified glow, I looked on a place I had never seen before. The raw, mine-scarred hills, the rocks, the piles of tailings and rude Western houses were gone. All was level or gently rolling land dotted with the most curious small houses I had ever seen, many of them without walls, some without roofs, the ground cultivated closely around them, while streets no wider than walks wound through like narrow ornamental parkways. The whole effect was like one gigantic landscaped park swarming with tiny houses evidently planned for outdoor living. There was something of the charm of a Japanese landscape although obviously it was more modernistic than that.

"This is certainly not Grantham," I said to myself aloud.

"I believe it used to be called that many years ago," a voice answered me. It was in curious, slurred English that I could barely understand.

I looked around to see a man standing behind me. He was small and again I had the feeling of Japan. Then I saw it was not a Japanese, but an American face, although strangely different.

"Are you an officer?" I asked.

"I'm an observer of peace and plenty," he said.

"I don't know what that means," I confessed. "But perhaps you can tell me what I want to know?"

"We don't say or even think the word 'want' any more," he corrected me. "We have freedom from want here."

I stared at him, not understanding at first.

"You mean nobody wants for anything?"

He watched me in mild surprise.

"Nothing. It's all supplied. Of course, everyone has his own work to do. But we tolerate no hunger, ugliness or shabbiness, no poverty or housing shortage, no illiteracy or ignorance, certainly no medical or other lack that interferes with the peace, contentment and security of our people."

His words spoken so matter-of-factly, together with the evidences of this brave new world before my eyes, moved me. So Doug's great dream, the perfectly planned state he had always preached about, was actually realized.

"I've been looking for a friend," I began, but he interrupted me politely.

"We don't look for anyone or anything here. No one is ever out of his place and nothing is ever stolen or permanently lost, because everyone here has his wants supplied and therefore has no desire to be anywhere else than where he is. What you may have meant was to ask about another fugitive from your time era. Creel is his name."

"You know Douglas!" I exclaimed in delight.

"He's creating musical master works for our people. He lives, as most everybody knows, at GHK 2. I'll have someone take you there."

"Oh, I don't mind walking," I said. "In fact I'd like to get a look at your city."

"That would be impossible. Someone will have to take you," he insisted courteously. "Even a visitor must not want for anything."

"Not even for a little privacy and freedom?" I murmured.

"Privacy isn't freedom," he said gently. "Freedom from want is the only freedom and it's possible alone through general harmony with one's fellows and the public weal."

He pulled something from under his coat and spoke into it in a kind of shorthand English. After a remarkably short time a second observer appeared. He was very civil and took me down into a little dale where we horizontally entered a tube underground. The door was closed. I did not think we had moved. There was no sensation of starting or stopping, but presently the door opened and I found myself already within a marble-lined building where a higher observer welcomed me. The room into which he took me was furnished with comfortable elegance. We sat together on a form of sofa that moved slowly about as we talked. It was this official who kept telling me how perfect their existence was.

"You don't consider rain or drought an imperfection?" I asked.

"It never rains here," he smiled. "And there's never any drought." He took me out on a balcony. "You can well see how green everything is. Ample moisture is supplied by underground irrigation."

"How about sandstorms?" I persisted.

"Sandstorms are obsolete and unknown," he answered.

"Well, it still must get pretty hot in the summer and cold in winter," I insisted.

"The temperature never varies more than a degree or two, day or night, summer or winter," he assured me. "Our food crops are raised the year round. I'm not too well versed on that, but an observer from the food division can give you the exact figures."

All he had said staggered me. I began to wonder now if I hadn't perhaps fallen asleep in Doug's bed after all. I felt my eyes. They were wide open. I squeezed the skin of my cheek between thumb and forefinger till it hurt. But if I was asleep, I didn't wake up.

After a moment something gave me an idea. Looking up from the balcony I noted that a slightly different moon hung overhead from the one when I first came.

The heavens looked blue as any night sky in New Mexico and yet now as I examined them I thought they resembled less the open firmament than a high, vast, cerulean ceiling dotted with starry illuminations.

"Don't tell me we're in a cave!" I exclaimed.

"We have no such word in our language," he informed. "I believe in your time the word meant something dark and disagreeable. Here you can see for yourself that it is all very light and pleasant."

"But you're underground!" I stammered.

"We are simply under earth cover," he corrected me. "To most of us our earth cover is more beautiful and desirable than the fickle and dangerous sky. First it protects us against missiles that would vaporize us all. Then it permits control of climate for increased plant and human welfare. The unruly ball called the sun is a very coarse and unmanageable source of energy and power. Our light rays are refined and far superior. There are many other advantages too technical to discuss with someone from your backward era. One thing you will soon notice for yourself, that our days and nights are always clear, the earth cover never obscured by clouds as in the case of nature's ordinary firmament."

I had to admit when they took me to find Doug that I had never seen a more beautiful day. The sky looked blue and flawless. I could almost imagine it a gorgeous New Mexican morning in May. In other ways it was even superior. This was the early hour when Grantham would be filled with the roar of rushing trucks and cars. Here the streets were incredibly peaceful. I heard no passing blare of radio or television. The only sounds were those of restrained human voices and, under all, a soft persistent music, although where it came from I couldn't tell. It seemed to permeate everywhere we went. At first I imagined it discordant, a most unusual and modern sort of thing, composed of strange new unpleasant repetitions.

Fortunately it was low and I could put it out of my mind. After a while it came to me that to hear such dissonance and then look upon the beauty and relaxation around me made everything more enjoyable.

The disposition of all the small, almost dwarflike people I saw was especially agreeable. I witnessed no hurrying on the streets, no striving to be ahead at a crosswalk. Their orderly behavior together with the planned loveliness of the suburban landscape greatly impressed me, and I felt that Doug, when I actually found him, would be beside himself with pride at the vindication of his thesis.

GHK 2 turned out to be a felicitous-looking small house, with several rooms completely enclosed. One of the most attractive of small Millennia women came to the door. She seemed to understand my archaic American speech at once.

"Yes, my husband is here," she assured me as if fully prepared for a visitor from another time era.

I could scarcely believe my ears. The inveterate bachelor married at last and to such a delectable creature! I entered with hearty and jovial words of congratulation on my lips, but when I saw him they died in my throat.

Ever since I knew him, Douglas Creel had been a plump and vigorous figure with glasses, a dash of red in his cheeks and in his eye ever-renewed enthusiasm for his projects. Now in this land of actual fulfillment of his dreams, he looked extraordinarily haggard and ill. His eyes lighted on me with an almost desperate gleam.

"Michael! How did you get here?" he cried and wrung my hand like a drowning man. All the time he kept looking into my face as if he couldn't get enough of something he hungered for. I had almost to nudge him to get an introduction to his wife, whose name proved to be Kultura. She took no affront at the delay, but bade me welcome as if nothing could move her from her accustomed unexcitement.

"I hope you'll be permitted to live in our vicinity," she said.

"Thank you, but I won't be able to stay very long."

She gave me a faintly amused look.

"I'm sure you will. Nobody who comes from your and Douglas' time dimension ever wants to go back to that poor age of want and rivalry."

"I've never been in a more perfect and artistic world," I said gallantly, and she smiled her quiet approval.

Not till she had excused herself and gone to what she called a concurrence did he become himself. Then he grasped my arm so that it hurt.

"Michael, you must get me out of here!"

I looked at him with astonishment. "Out of what?"

"Out of this whole damnable era of freedom from fear and want."

"But I thought this was what you always wanted."

His face worked for a moment.

"I thought I knew better than God."

"This era, as you call it, was made by God, too," I reminded him.

"No!" he shouted in revulsion. "By man. By the empty, fatuous, conceited head of man."

"Are you well, Doug? It looks wonderful to me."

"You think it's wonderful to see man-made dwarfs!" he shouted. "All around me I see familiar faces, Grantham family faces. When I knew their ancestors they were big, independent people. Nobody could boss them. Now generation by generation that vigorous miner stock's been shrunken in head and body like the head hunters shrink their enemies' heads. Only this is worse because the heads and bodies are still alive."

"You're joking, Douglas. How could they do that?"

"First they control the air these cave people breathe, the light rays that regulate their growth and hunger. It takes less to feed them. It also controls their temper and disposition. Otherwise they'd never submit to living like grubs under a log, never laying eyes on the real sun and constellations of the world, but only these miserable overshiny Millennia imitations. They go from birth to death without seeing a rainbow or Mt. Taylor a hundred miles across the globe in the clear, New Mexican air. But that isn't the real tragedy of their lives."

He took me to the window by his piano.

"Look out. Do you notice anything?" he asked.

I told him I could see houses, shrubbery, flowers in bloom and, beyond, what I supposed were factories, the most idealistic I had ever looked upon, smokeless, noiseless.

"Do you see a church?" he barked.

"Well, no, not from here," I said.

"You can't see any because there's none here. Where nobody wants for anything, there's no need of God. His name and idea are neglected, forgotten. In all Millennia, I'm probably the only person who prays."

"You, Doug!" I exclaimed, for I had never known him to go to church.

"Oh, I've learned a lot of respect for God from His absence. Back home as a boy I was told that everything good came from God. They didn't tell me that the lack of good may be God too. I mean what makes you work and pray for something you don't have. Now I believe that's more of God than the other because it lifts you up and develops you while monotonous goodness makes you stagnate like a frog in a swamp."

"If this is stagnating, I'm for it, Doug," I protested.

"So was I at first. When I first came I had lack and want and strain still left from my American existence. Relief from those things was sweet. I thought it would last forever. But once relief becomes permanent, it's nothing. It becomes dull, cloying, pure animal existence. I found I was a human cow, to be kept in my stall and never frightened or disturbed, but to stay calm and cowlike and go on producing milk as my sole end and purpose in life."

"You said once that when all want was supplied to man, then arts and sciences would flourish," I reminded.

"I was a blind fool," he said. "It's the wildness and freedom of the Bible and Shakespeare that made them great literature, and Beethoven great music. The same things helped to make early America great as we knew it."

"Somebody here has to be more than cows to plan and control Millennia," I pointed out.

"Ah, the Giant Guardians, or Great Hearts, as they're sometimes called. The ones who provide all. We're told many wonderful stories. But we really know only one thing about them—that they don't live in docile security like we do or they'd never be big enough to run Millennia. They've had problems aplenty to overcome, and that's what's made them our masters. They even found out that human slaves must have some sort of lack to keep up their tone. A history official told me that sometime after the regime was established, the people sank back to nothing.

"They simply lived and ate and breathed. So the Giant Guardians had to give them some sort of obstruction and inharmony—not enough to arouse their manhood. Just enough to keep them from going to pieces altogether. One of these things is dissonance in music. Have you noticed? Listen. It's piped into every square foot of Millennia so nobody, day or night, can ever be without it. It stirs up subconscious unpleasantness, lack of security. Not too much. Just enough to keep the inner energies aroused to overcome this uneasy sense of inharmony inside of them. Listen. Do you hear it?"

"What kind of music do you play now?" I asked, remembering that his great pet had been dissonance.

"The Cacophony of the Cave," he said bitterly. "I'm given a piano by the state and asked to compose. But can I compose what I wish? No. Only variations of the same monotonous and repetitious phrases that back in our era originated among primitive slave peoples."

He paced up and down, a wild light in his eyes.

"What I have suffered here, nobody knows. Never did I catch the spirit of my American era till I left it. Its phrases kept ringing in my head. I had to put it to music. But they heard me as they hear everything, and stopped me. Such longing and moving and passionate sounds are contrary to order here. They interfere with tranquillity. I was forbidden to touch the piano for such purpose. They gave me what they call a Concurrer to see that I co-operated."

He gave the piano a sharp thump as he passed, turned to me and went on.

"But they couldn't stop me. I needed no piano. All those magnificent sounds and harmonies rang in my ears night and day. There was no time to lose. I saw ahead of me the time when they would no longer come to me, when I'd be only half alive like these kept people. So I set down my song of America secretly. It's a concerto for the piano, although the orchestration isn't finished yet." He took from some secret place in the piano a handwritten manuscript of music paper. Just sight of it seemed to exert great influence on him. A light shone in his eyes. For a minute he was the man I used to know in New Mexico. Then a step sounded on the walk outside.

"Kultura!" he whispered. "The Concurrer." Quickly he replaced the manuscript. "She'll try to get you out of here, Michael, but never leave me. And never rest till you go back again to our time."

"I'll go back. And you'll go back with me!"

"You, perhaps, but never me." His face looked pitiable. "Those who once pander to tyranny are never free from it. They've committed the unpardonable sin. Sooner or later they must pay for it with their lives."

His voice was so filled with anguish that I can hear it yet. Then the door opened and his wife came in, sweet and calm as if there was nothing but security and light in the world.

"I've been allotted a place for your friend, Michael, to live. Down in RLD 146. I'll show him there."

Douglas exchanged a look with me.

"Let him stay one day, Kultura. I want him to hear me play at the Concert of Abundance tonight. Just to have him there will give me something I need."

Not a sign of displeasure or unwillingness crossed her face. It seemed only interest in my well-being that made her keep proposing objection after objection, including my lack of suitable clothes which could not be supplied me for several days. Finally my willingness to attend the concert in bathrobe and slippers appeared to disarm her. It did not require as much courage on my part as it sounded. Most Millennia dress was so bright and extreme that pajamas and bathrobe looked rather fitting, indeed on the conservative side.

Just the same, I wondered if she did not suspect some collusion between us. At dinner she spoke to me kindly yet pointedly of what she called the Benevolent Instruction given enemies of Millennia, transgressors of the spirit of freedom from want. Only the contented and co-operating citizens of Millennia, she reminded me, enjoyed the good and abundant life I saw around me. A state like Millennia required extensive servicing by unseen co-ordinators. Beneath us lay an immense labyrinth of tunnels and caverns where the water, power, disposal and other systems were based, and it was here that those lacking in proper appreciation for their blessings were trained in what she called Benign Common Weal. She spoke of them temperately, but it was not lost upon me that they were doomed inmates of the bowels of the earth, breathers of what air could be pumped down to them, spending their lives there never to see the synthetic light of Millennia again.

If her purpose was to frighten me, she succeeded admirably. Before we left for the concert that evening, I imagined I saw Douglas take something from beneath the sounding board of the piano and slip it into his music case. Then the three of us went to the tube underground.

We came out of the tube into the greatest outdoor bowl —if it can be called outdoor—that I had ever seen. It lay cradled between the rolling subterranean hills and was already nearly filled with an audience of staggering size. Looking across the vast sea of Millennia faces drawn here by the promise of music, I had the feeling of being in a land of advanced enlightenment and culture.

But that feeling vanished, once I heard the music. It was a very large and impressive orchestra. It played with great skill and dexterity. But when the music with great volume and precision started, I found it the same dissonance and repetition I had heard piped into the streets and houses of Millennia. Even Douglas, when his time came, performed in the common monotonous manner. Just the same, at the end of the number, they clapped Douglas back with a unanimity that could not be denied.

That was when it happened. I saw him lift a hand to the orchestra to be silent, that this time he would play alone. Again he seated himself at the shimmering blue piano. A change had come over him. Up to this time he had seemed weary, mechanical, almost drugged. Now just the way he sat at his instrument stirred me. When he reached out and with strength unknown among these pygmies pulled with his own hands the piano closer to him, the crowd murmured and I felt the hair at the back of my head rise. So far he had played from the usual Millennia music, printed in a kind of glowing colored type read without a light at a distance and so arranged that it rolled on and on. But now he set up a quarto of ordinary music paper scrawled in black. To my consternation it looked very much like the manuscript of his secret American concerto.

For a long moment he sat silent and motionless. Then his hands lifted over the keys.

I have heard in my not inconsiderable lifetime a great many compositions, symphonies, tone poems and suites that purport to convey the spirit of America to the listener, but never anything that succeeded like this. Perhaps part of its powerful effect on me came from hearing it in what Douglas called this desert of the hopes of mankind. From the very first there sounded a ringing call to life and freedom. The dissonances and monotonous repetitions of slave-people existence were gone. In their stead blew a breath of fresh air from the mountains and sea, neither of which these kept-people had ever seen.

As it went on, I could see the early ships tossing on the ocean bringing lovers of freedom to our shores, the strong bodies of pioneers cutting down the dark forests and breaking up the darker prairie soil. I could picture the mills and factories springing up along the streams, first with foaming water for power, then with the pound and hiss of steam and finally the smooth hum of electrical might. I could hear the hoofs of oxen and horses, the iron tires of wagons and carriages, the rush of train, automobile, boat and plane, with the indescribable stir that was the vast fluidic emancipation of people traveling east and west, north and south, wherever they wanted. Not in childish and mechanical imitation were these given, but infused with a magnificent harmony, wildness and even ferocity of spirit that opened my eyes to my own country and era as nothing had ever done before. I realized it must have been Douglas' exile and hunger for it here that had led him to catch its secret as he never could have done in New York or at his father's house in Grantham.

In a fierce and powerful climax that returned again and again with its passionate and majestic chords, Douglas finished. Then something happened I would not have believed possible. The thousands of docile kept-people went crazy in their bright October colors. It was as if racial memory was not yet dead at the pit of their brains and Douglas had reached deep to stir up their ancient passion. They stood up, shouting and waving, grabbing at and striking one another. I stared, amazed. So long had their natural emotions been repressed that they didn't know how to react to them. Sight of their fellows breaking into madness only multiplied the violence in themselves. They began surging over the seats toward the platform and the man who had aroused them.

At first I thought they meant to lionize Douglas, show him their admiration and affection. But I was to learn that the emotions of liberty are a dangerous thing in persons unprepared for it and unable to tell the difference between liberation and mob rule. The hordes of hysterical little people swarmed over the platform, knocking down this man bigger and more gifted than they, striking him and one another. I saw Douglas with a bloody face struggle to rise and go down a second time with the pygmies jumping on him. I remembered then his tragic and bitter prediction, and knew that he would never rise again.

Now one of the bloody little men started singing in triumph the main and recurring air that had run through Douglas' concerto. Others took it up and soon the entire bowl was a shrill and fearful chorus. The observers-of-freedom-from-want who so far had been helpless, seized the opportunity to try to regain control. One of them shouted orders through the relay system, but no one heard him. Others reached Douglas and dragged his body out. Meantime another snatched the offending music from the piano and tore the manuscript to pieces, scattering it to the crowd. A ribbon of paper with a bar or two written in Douglas' hand came fluttering toward me. I caught it and put it into my bathrobe pocket.

But that act betrayed me. In a moment the mob on the platform recognized my unconforming height and dress.

It started toward me. Thanks to my superior size and strength, I was able to force my way through those nearest me. But a greater mob remained between me and escape. I remembered that on entering I had noticed occasional doorways in the descending aisles. They were for exit, I thought. Now I managed to reach one of the doors and wrench it open. Inside, it was pitch dark. Hardly had I forced the door shut and shot the bolt before I heard the mob rattling the handle.

Where the passageway led to, I didn't know. But the door was starting to give and I hurried along, feeling my way. Meantime the fiercely sung chorus from the concerto rose and penetrated the darkness like the hands of Douglas himself at the piano. It lifted me up and urged me on and this, I suspect, was the time catalyst.

The first thing I thought strange was that I blundered against no wall while I ran. As on the night before, my outstretched hands found utterly nothing. And yet there was a kind of floor beneath me which seemed to pitch upgrade. Far ahead and still much higher, faint light seemed to hang in the blackness. Behind me I heard the door shatter and tremendous echoing of voices in the passageway.

Then abruptly, pandemonium ceased. In utter silence I ran on. Just as I reached the faint light an unseen object tripped me and I fell. Fortunately it was into something soft and springy. Feeling it with my hands, I thought it most resembled a bed. The conviction grew that it was Douglas' bed. In a moment I made out across the dim room the black bulk of his grand piano. Then I heard a sound more beautiful than music to my ears. It was the roar of an ore truck passing the house.

The rest of the night I slept like a log. When I awoke in the common light of day and with Doug's familiar furnishings around me, I told myself it had all been an illusion, a dream. I got up and shaved and dressed as if nothing had happened. When I left the room, I found Apolonia and Felicitas waiting in the front hall.

"Where were you yesterday?" Apolonia's eyes were big on me.

"I just came yesterday," I reminded her.

"You came the day before," she accused. "Yesterday you never came out. I knocked, but you didn't answer. All day and last night I am nervous like a cat. I am afraid to come in that I find your clothes on the chair like Mr. Creel's and nobody here."

"I guess I was pretty tired from my trip and slept right through," I told her.

Just the same, I didn't care to spend another night in Douglas' house, and found a room for myself at the Copper Queen. My bathrobe was soiled and torn. I had a bellboy send it out to be cleaned and mended. Not until evening did I remember what I thought I had put into the pocket. In the morning I asked the bellboy where he had sent the bathrobe and went over.

"I wonder if you found anything in the pocket?" I asked, feeling a bit foolish.

They brought out the cleaner who had worked on it, a Mexican girl who looked at me with a calmness that reminded me of Millennia when I had first come.

"There was nothing important in the pocket, sir," she said. "Nothing but a torn piece of paper with marks like music on it. It was just a scrap and I threw it in the trash. Last night Pedro burned it."

The Place of the Gods

by Stephen Vincent Benét

Stephen Vincent Benét was a poet and author of great renown. Some of his very best work was as a fantasist and folklorist, and his most famed tale was the oft-filmed "The Devil and Daniel Webster," which has also been presented as a play and even an opera. Among his other works are the narrative poem "John Brown's Body" and an operetta based on "The Legend of Sleepy Hollow." In his later years Benét developed a great concern for the dangers he felt America faced from the rest of the world. "The Place of the Gods," with its view of a post-holocaust America, certainly echoes that concern.

The Place of the Gods

by Stephen Vincent Benét

The north and the west and the south are good hunting ground, but it is forbidden to go east. It is forbidden to go to any of the Dead Places except to search for metal, and then he who touches the metal must be a priest or the son of a priest. Afterward, both the man and the metal must be purified. These are the rules and the laws; they are well made. It is forbidden to cross the great river and look upon the place that was the Place of the Gods; this is most strictly forbidden. We do not even say its name, though we know its name. It is there that spirits live, and demons; it is there that there are the ashes of the Great Burning. These things are forbidden; they have been forbidden since the beginning of time.

My father is a priest; I am the son of a priest. I have been in the Dead Places near us with my father. At first I was afraid. When my father went into the house to search for the metal, I stood by the door, and my heart felt small and weak. It was a dead man's house, a spirit house. It did not have the smell of man, though there were old bones in a corner. But it is not fitting that a priest's son should show fear. I looked at the bones in the shadow and kept my voice still.

Then my father came out with the metal—a good, strong piece. He looked at me with both eyes, but I had not run away. He gave me the metal to hold. I took it and did not die. So he knew that I was truly his son and would be a priest in my time. That was when I was very young. Nevertheless, my brothers would not have done it, though they are good hunters. After that, they gave me the good piece of meat and the warm corner by the fire. My father watched over me; he was glad that I should be a priest. But when I boasted or wept without reason, he punished me more strictly than my brothers. That was right.

After a time, I myself was allowed to go into the dead houses and search for metal. So I learned the ways of those houses, and if I saw bones, I was no longer afraid. The bones are light and old; sometimes they will fall into dust if you touch them. But that is a great sin.

I was taught the chants and the spells. I was taught how to stop the running of blood from a wound, and many secrets. A priest must know many secrets—that was what my father said. If the hunters think we know all things by chants and spells, they may believe so; it does not hurt them. I was taught how to read in the old books and how to make the old writings; that was hard and took a long time. My knowledge made me happy; it was like a fire in my heart. Most of all, I liked to hear of the Old Days and the stories of the gods. I asked myself many questions that I could not answer, but it was good to ask them. At night, I would like awake and listen to the wind; it seemed to me that it was the voice of the gods as they flew through the air.

We are not ignorant like the Forest People; our women spin wool on the wheel, our priests wear a white robe. We do not eat grubs from the tree, we have not forgotten the old writings, although they are hard to understand. Nevertheless, my knowledge and my lack of knowledge burned in me; I wished to know more. When I was a man at last, I came to my father and said, "It is time for me to go on my journey. Give me leave."

He looked at me for a long time, stroking his beard, then he said at last, "Yes. It is time."

That night, in the house of priesthood, I asked for and received purification. My body hurt, but my spirit was a cool stone. It was my father himself who questioned me about my dreams.

He bade me look into the smoke of the fire and see. I saw and told what I saw. It was what I have always seen—a river and, beyond it, a great Dead Place, and in it the gods walking. I have always thought about that. His eyes were stern when I told him; he was no longer my father but a priest. He said, "This is a strong dream."

"It is mine," I said, while the smoke waved and my head felt light. They were singing the Star song in the outer chamber, and it was like the buzzing of bees in my head.

He asked me how the gods were dressed, and I told him how they were dressed. We know how they were dressed from the book, but I saw them as if they were before me. When I had finished, he threw the sticks three times and studied them as they fell.

"This is a very strong dream," he said. "It may eat you up."

"I am not afraid," I said, and looked at him with both eyes. My voice sounded thin in my ears, but that was because of the smoke.

He touched me on the breast and the forehead. He gave me the bow and the three arrows.

"Take them," he said. "It is forbidden to travel east. It is forbidden to cross the great river. It is forbidden to go to the Place of the Gods. All these things are forbidden."

"All these things are forbidden," I said, but it was my voice that spoke, and not my spirit. He looked at me again.

"My son," he said, "once I had young dreams. If your dream does not eat you up, you may be a great priest. If it eats you, you are still my son. Now go on your journey."

I went fasting, as is the law. My body hurt, but not my

heart. When the dawn came, I was out of sight of the village. I prayed and purified myself, waiting for a sign. The sign was an eagle. It flew east.

Sometimes signs are sent by bad spirits. I waited again on the flat rock, fasting, taking no food. I was very still; I could feel the sky above me and the earth beneath. I waited till the sun was beginning to sink. Then three deer passed in the valley, going east; they did not wind me or see me. There was a white fawn with them—a very great sign.

I followed them at a distance, waiting for what would happen. My heart was troubled about going east, yet I knew that I must go. My head hummed with my fasting; I did not even see the panther spring upon the white fawn. But before I knew it, the bow was in my hand. I shouted and the panther lifted his head from the fawn. It is not easy to kill a panther with one arrow, but the arrow went through his eye and into his brain. He died as he tried to spring; he rolled over, tearing at the ground. Then I knew I was meant to go east; I knew that was my journey. When the night came, I made my fire and roasted meat.

It is eight suns' journey to the east and a man passes by many Dead Places. The Forest People are afraid of them, but I am not. Once I made my fire on the edge of a Dead Place at night and, next morning, in the dead house, I found a good knife, little rusted. That was small to what came afterward, but it made my heart feel big. Always when I looked for game, it was in front of my arrow, and twice I passed hunting parties of the Forest People without their knowing. So I knew my magic was strong and my journey clean, in spite of the law.

Toward the setting of the eighth sun, I came to the banks of the great river. It was half a day's journey after I had left the god road; we do not use the god roads now, for they are falling apart into great blocks of stone, and the forest is safer going. A long way off, I had seen the water through trees, but the trees were thick. At last I came out upon an open place at the top of a cliff. There was the great river below, like a giant in the sun. It is very long, very wide. It could eat all the streams we know and still be thirsty. Its name is Ou-dis-sun, the Sacred, the Long. No man of my tribe has seen it; not even my father, the priest. It was magic and I prayed.

Then I raised my eyes and looked south. It was there—the Place of the Gods.

How can I tell what it was like? You do not know. It was there, in the red light, and they were too big to be houses. It was there, with the red light upon it, mighty and ruined. I knew that in another moment the gods would see me. I covered my eyes with my hands and crept back into the forest.

Surely, that was enough to do, and live. Surely, it was enough to spend the night upon the cliff. The Forest People themselves do not come near. Yet, all through the night, I knew that I should have to cross the river and walk in the Place of the Gods, although the gods ate me up. My magic did not help me at all, and yet there was a fire in my bowels, a fire in my mind. When the sun rose, I thought, "My journey has been clean. Now I will go home from my journey." But even as I thought so, I knew I could not. If I went to the Place of the Gods, I would surely die, but if I did not go, I could never be at peace with my spirit again. It is better to lose one's life than one's spirit, if one is a priest and the son of a priest.

Nevertheless, as I made the raft, the tears ran out of my eyes. The Forest People could have killed me without fight, if they had come upon me then, but they did not come. When the raft was made, I said the sayings for the dead and painted myself for death. My heart was cold as a frog and my knees like water, but the burning in my mind would not let me have peace. As I pushed the raft from the shore, I began my death song; I had the right. It was a fine song. I sang:

"I am John, son of John. My people are the Hill People. They are the men.
I go into the Dead Places, but I am not slain.
I take the metal from the Dead Places, but I am not blasted.
I travel upon the god roads and am not afraid. E-yah! I have killed the panther, I have killed the fawn!
E-yah! I have come to the great river. No man has come there before.
It is forbidden to go east, but I have gone; forbidden to go on the great river, but I am there.
Open your hearts, you spirits, and hear my song.
Now I go to the Place of the Gods; I shall not return.
My body is painted for death and my limbs weak, but my heart is big as I go to the Place of the Gods!"

All the same, when I came to the Place of the Gods, I was afraid, afraid. The current of the great river is very strong; it gripped my raft with its hands. That was magic, for the river itself is wide and calm. I could feel evil spirits about me in the bright morning; I could feel their breath on my neck as I was swept down the stream. Never have I been so much alone. I tried to think of my knowledge, but it was a squirrel's heap of winter nuts. There was no strength in my knowledge any more and I felt small and naked as a new-hatched bird—alone upon the great river, the servant of the gods.

Yet, after a while, my eyes were opened and I saw. I saw both banks of the river; I saw that once there had been god roads across it, though now they were broken and fallen like broken vines. Very great they were, and wonderful and broken—broken in the time of the Great Burning, when the fire fell out of the sky. And always the current took me nearer to the Place of the Gods, and the huge ruins rose higher before my eyes.

I do not know the customs of rivers; we are the People of the Hills. I tried to guide my raft with the pole, but it spun about. I thought the river meant to take me past the Place of the Gods and out into the Bitter Water of the legends.

I grew angry then; my heart felt strong. I said aloud, "I am a priest and the son of a priest!" The gods heard me; they showed me how to paddle with the pole on one side of the raft. The current changed itself; I drew near to the Place of the Gods.

When I was very near, my raft struck and turned over. I can swim in our lakes; I swam to the shore. There was a great spike of rusted metal sticking out into the river; I hauled myself up upon it and sat there, panting. I had saved my bow and two arrows and the knife I found in the Dead Place, but that was all. My raft went whirling downstream toward the Bitter Water. I looked after it, and thought if it had trod me under, at least I would be safely dead. Nevertheless, when I had dried my bowstring and restrung it, I walked forward to the Place of the Gods.

It felt like ground underfoot; it did not burn me. It is not true—what some of the tales say—that the ground there burns forever, for I have been there. Here and there were the marks and stains of the Great Burning on the ruins, that is true. But they were old marks and old stains. It is not true, either—what some of our priests say—that it is an island covered with fogs and enchantments. It is not. It is a great Dead Place—greater than any Dead Place we know. Everywhere in it there are god roads; though most are cracked and broken. Everywhere there are the ruins of the high towers of the gods.

How shall I tell what I saw? I went carefully, my strung bow in my hand, my skin ready for danger. There should have been the wailings of spirits and the shrieks of demons, but there were not. It was very silent and sunny where I had landed; the wind and the rain and the birds that drop seeds had done their work; the grass grew in the cracks of the broken stone. It is a fair island; no wonder the gods built there. If I had come there a god, I also would have built.

How shall I tell what I saw? The towers are not all broken; here and there one still stands, like a great tree in a forest, and the birds nest high. But the towers themselves look blind, for the gods are gone. I saw a fish hawk, catching fish in the river. I saw a little dance of white butterflies over a great heap of broken stones and columns. I went there and looked about me; there was a carved stone with cut letters, broken in half. I can read letters, but I could not understand these. They said UBTREAS. There was also the shattered image of a man or a god. It had been made of white stone and he wore his hair tied back like a woman's. His name was ASHING, as I read on the cracked half of a stone. I thought it wise to pray to ASHING, though I do not know that god.

How shall I tell what I saw? There was no smell of man left on stone or metal. Nor were there many trees in that wilderness of stone. There are many pigeons, nesting and dropping in the towers; the gods must have loved them, or, perhaps, they used them for sacrifice. There are wild cats that roam the god roads, green-eyed, unafraid of man. At night they wail like demons, but they are not demons. The wild dogs are more dangerous, for they hunt in a pack, but them I did not meet till later. Everywhere there are the carved stones, carved with magical numbers and words.

I went north; I did not try to hide myself. When a god or a demon saw me, then I would die, but meanwhile I was no longer afraid. My hunger for knowledge burned in me; there was so much that I could not understand. After a while, I knew that my belly was hungry. I could have hunted for my meat, but I did not hunt. It is known that the gods did not hunt as we do; they got their food from enchanted boxes and jars. Sometimes these are still found in the Dead Places. Once, when I was a child and foolish, I opened such a jar and tasted it and found the food sweet. But my father found out and punished me for it strictly; for, often, that food is death. Now, though, I had long gone past what was forbidden, and I entered the likeliest towers, looking for the food of the gods.

I found it at last in the ruins of a great temple in the mid-city. A mighty temple it must have been, for the roof was painted like the sky at night with its stars—that much I could see, though the colors were faint and dim. It went down into great caves and tunnels—perhaps they kept their slaves there. But when I started to climb down, I heard the squeaking of rats, so I did not go. Rats are unclean, and there must have been many tribes of them, from the squeaking. But near there I found food, in the heart of a ruin, behind a door that still opened. I ate only the fruits from the jars; they had a very sweet taste. There was drink, too, in bottles of glass; the drink of the gods is strong and made my head swim. After I had eaten and drunk, I slept on the top of a stone, my bow at my side.

When I woke, the sun was low. Looking down from where I lay, I saw a dog sitting on his haunches. His tongue hung out of his mouth; he looked as if he were laughing. He was a big dog with a gray-brown coat, as big as a wolf. I sprang up and shouted at him, but he did not move; he just sat there as if he were laughing. I did not like that. When I reached for a stone to throw, he moved swiftly out of the way of the stone. He was not afraid of me; he looked at me as if I were meat. No doubt I could have killed him with an arrow, but I did not know if there were others. Moreover, night was falling.

I looked about me. Not far away there was a great, broken god road, leading north. The towers were high enough, but not so high, and while many of the dead houses were wrecked, there were some that stood. I went toward this god road, keeping to the heights of the ruins, while the dog followed. When I had reached the god road, I saw that there were others behind him. If I had slept later, they would have come upon me asleep and torn out my throat. As it was, they were sure enough of me; they did not hurry. When I went into the dead house, they kept watch at the entrance; doubtless they thought they would have a fine hunt. But a dog cannot open a door, and I knew, from the books, that the gods did not like to live on the ground but on high.

I had just found a door I could open when the dogs decided to rush. Ha! They were surprised when I shut the door in their faces; it was a good door, of strong metal. I could hear their foolish baying beyond it, but I did not stop to answer them. I was in darkness; I found stairs and climbed. There were many stairs, turning around till my head was dizzy. At the top was another door; I found the knob and opened it. I was in a long small chamber. On one side of it was a bronze door that could not be opened, for it had no handle. Perhaps there was a magic word to open it, but I did not have the word. I turned to the door in the opposite side of the wall. The lock of it was broken and I opened it and went in.

Within, there was a place of great riches. The god who lived there must have been a powerful god. The first room was a small anteroom. I waited there for some time, telling the spirits of the place that I came in peace and not as a robber. When it seemed to me that they had had time to hear me, I went on. Ah, what riches! Few, even, of the windows had been broken; it was all as it had been. The great windows that looked over the city had not been broken at all, though they were dusty and streaked with many years. There were coverings on the floors, the colors not greatly faded, and the chairs were soft and deep.

There were pictures upon the walls, very strange, very wonderful. I remember one of a bunch of flowers in a jar; if you came close to it, you could see nothing but bits of color, but if you stood away from it, the flowers might have been picked yesterday. It made my heart feel strange to look at this picture, and to look at the figure of a bird, in some hard clay, on a table and see it so like our birds. Everywhere there were books and writings, many in tongues that I could not read. The god who lived there must have been a wise god, and full of knowledge. I felt I had right there, as I sought knowledge also.

Nevertheless, it was strange. There was a washing place, but no water; perhaps the gods washed in air. There was a cooking place, but no wood, and though there was a machine to cook food, there was no place to put fire in it. Nor were there candles or lamps. There were things that looked like lamps, but they had neither oil nor wick. All these things were magic, but I touched them and lived; the magic had gone out of them. Let me tell one thing to show. In the washing place, a thing said "Hot," but it was not hot to the touch; another thing said "Cold," but it was not cold. This must have been a strong magic, but the magic was gone. I do not understand—they had ways—I wish that I knew.

It was close and dry and dusty in the house of the god. I have said the magic was gone, but that is not true; it had gone from the magic things, but it had not gone from the place. I felt the spirits about me, weighing upon me. Nor had I ever slept in a Dead Place before, and yet, to-night, I must sleep there. When I thought of it, my tongue felt dry in my throat, in spite of my wish for knowledge. Almost I would have gone down again and faced the dogs, but I did not.

I had not gone through all the rooms when the darkness fell. When it fell, I went back to the big room looking over the city and made fire. There was a place to make fire and a box with wood in it, though I do not think they cooked there. I wrapped myself in a floor covering and slept in front of the fire.

Now I tell what is very strong magic. I woke in the midst of the night. When I woke, the fire had gone out and I was cold. It seemed to me that all around me there were whisperings and voices. I closed my eyes to shut them out. Some will say that I slept again, but I do not think that I slept. I could feel the spirits drawing my spirit out of my body as a fish is drawn on a line.

Why should I lie about it? I am a priest and the son of a priest. If there are spirits, as they say, in the small Dead Places near us, what spirits must there not be in that great Place of the Gods? And would not they wish to speak after such long years? I know that I felt myself drawn as a fish is drawn on a line. I had stepped out of my body; I could see my body asleep in front of the cold fire, but it was not I. I was drawn to look out upon the city of the gods.

It should have been dark, for it was night, but it was not dark. Everywhere there were lights—lines of light, circles and blurs of light—ten thousand torches would not have been the same. The sky itself was alight; you could barely see the stars for the glow in the sky. I thought to myself, "This is strong magic," and trembled. There was a roaring in my ears like the rushing of rivers. Then my eyes grew used to the light and my ears to the sound. I knew that I was seeing the city as it had been when the gods were alive.

That was a sight indeed! Yes, that was a sight! I could not have seen it in the body—my body would have died. Everywhere went the gods, on foot and in chariots; there were gods beyond number and counting, and their chariots blocked the streets. They had turned night to day for their pleasure; they did not sleep with the sun. The noise of their coming and going was the noise of many waters.

It was magic what they could do; it was magic what they did.

I looked out of another window; the great vines of their bridges were mended and the god roads went east and west. Restless, restless were the gods, and always in motion! They burrowed tunnels under rivers; they flew in the air. With unbelievable tools they did giant works; no part of the earth was safe from them, for, if they wished for a thing, they summoned it from the other side of the world. And always, as they labored and rested, as they feasted and made love, there was a drum in their ears—the pulse of the giant city, beating and beating like a man's heart.

Were they happy? What is happiness to the gods? They were great, they were mighty, they were wonderful and terrible. As I looked upon them and their magic, I felt like a child; but a little more, it seemed to me, and they would lay their hands upon the stars. I saw them with wisdom beyond wisdom and knowledge beyond knowledge. And yet not all they did was well done, and yet their wisdom could not but grow until all was peace.

Then I saw their fate come upon them, and that was terrible past speech. It came upon them as they walked the streets of their city. I have been in the fights with the Forest People; I have seen men die. But this was not like that. When gods war with gods, they use weapons we do not know. It was fire falling out of the sky and a mist that poisoned. It was the time of the Great Burning and the Destruction. They ran about like ants in the streets—poor gods, poor gods! Then the towers began to fall. A few escaped—yes, a few. The legends tell it. But even after the city had become a Dead Place, for many years the poison was still in the ground. I saw it happen; I saw the last of them die. It was darkness over the broken city and I wept.

All this, I saw. I saw it as I have told it; though not in the body. When I woke in the morning, I was hungry, but I did not think first of my hunger, for my heart was perplexed and confused. I knew the reason for the Dead Places, but I did not see why it had happened. It seemed to me it should not have happened, with all the magic they had. I went through the house looking for an answer. There was so much in the house I could not understand, and yet I am a priest and the son of a priest. It was like being on the side of the great river at night, with no light to show the way.

Then I saw the dead god. He was sitting in his chair by the window, in a room I had not entered before, and, for the first moment, I thought that he was alive. Then I saw the skin on the back of his hand—it was like dry leather. The room was shut, hot and dry; no doubt that had kept him as he was. At first I was afraid to approach him; then the fear left me. He was sitting, looking out over his city; he was dressed in the clothes of the gods. His age was neither young nor old; I could not tell his age. But there was wisdom in his face, and great sadness. You could see that he would not run away. He had sat at his window, watching his city die; then he himself had died. But it is better to lose one's life than one's spirit; and you could see from the face that his spirit had not been lost. I knew that, if I touched him, he would fall into dust; and yet, there was something unconquered in the face.

That is all of my story, for then I knew he was a man. I knew then that they had been men, neither gods nor demons. It is a great knowledge, hard to tell and believe. They were men; they went a dark road, but they were men. I had no fear after that. I had no fear going home, though twice I fought off the dogs and once I was hunted for two days by the Forest People. When I saw my father again, I prayed and was purified.

He touched my lips and my breast; he said, "You went away a boy. You come back a man and a priest."

I said, "Father, they were men! I have been in the Place

of the Gods and seen it! Now slay me if it is the law, but still I know they were men."

He looked at me out of both eyes. He said, "The law is not always the same shape. You have done what you have done. I could not have done it in my time, but you come after me. Tell!"

I told and he listened. After that, I wished to tell all the people, but he showed me otherwise. He said, "Truth is a hard deer to hunt. If you eat too much truth at once, you may die of the truth. It was not idly that our fathers forbade the Dead Places." He was right; it is better the truth should come little by little. I have learned that, being a priest. Perhaps, in the old days they ate knowledge too fast.

Nevertheless, we make a beginning. It is not for the metal alone we go to the Dead Places now; there are the books and the writings. They are hard to learn. And the magic tools are broken, but we can look at them and wonder. At least, we make a beginning, And, when I am chief priest we shall go beyond the great river. We shall go to the Place of the Gods—the place Newyork—not one man but a company. We shall walk in the broken streets and say its name aloud, without fear. We shall look for the images of gods and find the god ASHING and the others—the gods LICOLN and BILTMORE and MOSES. But they were men who built the city; they were not gods or demons. They were men. I remember the dead man's face. They were men who were here before us. We must build again.

The Phantom Setter
by Robert Murphy

The ghost story is a difficult medium for a modern writer for it would seem that all that there is to say had already been written in that great flood of ghostly tales which peaked in Victorian times. "The Phantom Setter" is a tale that ranks with the best in its evocation of an eerie vengeance repeated again and again in a setting so natural that it can only emphasize that slight twinge of terror that Murphy evokes. Of all the tales in this volume, this is the one best to be read late at night as the wind howls outside.

The Phantom Setter

by Robert Murphy

Not long after Jack Barlow rented a small house and moved into the pretty, little mountain village to run a timbering operation, he was standing at his back door late one afternoon when a big, gaunt blue-ticked setter trotted through the yard. He wondered to whom it belonged and whether it would be any good on grouse. He had always loved grouse shooting and hadn't been able to do any of it for five or six years; now that he was back in grouse country and hadn't a dog, he wanted to meet someone who did have one with whom he could shoot until he could get one of his own.

It was the first setter he had seen in the village, and he called to it. The dog stopped, turned its head toward him, looked at him for a long moment in an oddly speculative way, wagged its tail slightly and went on.

This piqued him a little, for he had a way with dogs. They liked him at sight, and any dog which didn't hate the human race always came to him when he called it. This was the first one within his recollection that hadn't, and certainly the first one that had seemed to sum him up, make a gesture of friendliness and then dismiss him. It had seemed to say that it had more important things to do than pause for a pat on the head, no matter how pleasant this might be.

He was still thinking about the setter when he walked down the street to the little hotel where he had most of his meals, for he hadn't found a housekeeper yet. After he finished his dessert, he went into the living room, sat down and waited until the proprietor—a tall, middle-aged man named Gibney—had finished his dinner and joined him. They talked a little about the weather and the lumbering, and then Barlow asked, "The grouse season opens pretty soon, doesn't it?"

Gibney gave him a rather odd look. "Grouse?" he asked. "Oh, yes, it starts in about a week. You a grouse hunter?"

"I've been one since I could carry a gun," Barlow said, "but I've been in the wrong kind of country for the past five years. I'd like to start in again. There was a big setter in my yard a while ago, and I thought I'd ask you——"

Gibney interrupted him. "Is that why you came here?" he asked.

This seemed like a strange question to Barlow. "Here?" he asked. "What do you mean?"

"I mean, is that why you came to town? Grouse?"

"I came to town for the lumbering. Surely you know that."

"Why"—Gibney said and blinked—"why, yes, so I do." He got up, gave Barlow another odd look and said, "Well, make yourself comfortable. I've got to write some letters."

He turned to go out of the room, but Barlow wasn't through with him yet. "I wanted to ask you who owned the setter," he said, "and if it was any good on grouse."

Gibney took a few steps, stopped and half turned. "Nobody owns him," he said, "and nobody ever will. From all I hear he's as good a grouse dog as you're liable to find. But if I were you I'd let him alone."

Gibney started to walk again. He went out of the room, his footfalls fading down the hall, and Barlow stared after him. He couldn't imagine what had got into the man, who had always seemed friendly and sensible enough before. He was apparently still friendly; his tone hadn't been hostile or unpleasant; but it was hard to find him sensible. Why would a sensible man warn him against a dog that was both ownerless and good at his work? Was there some rivalry over the beast in the village, with trouble in the offing for anyone—any stranger, especially—who got interested in him? Barlow was well aware that there were occasionally some strange characters in out-of-the-way mountain villages, but what did that have to do with Gibney's question as to why he, Barlow, had come there? Gibney knew—and had known all along—that he was getting out timber. Gibney had even advised him, when he had first started, what local men to hire and what men to leave alone.

None of it made sense. Barlow shook his head and went out of the hotel. When he was on the street he paused for a moment, looking about, wondering what to do with himself. He didn't want to return to his house; it was too early to go to bed, and he didn't feel like sitting in the little old-fashioned living room wondering what Gibney had meant. There was a fog now, and the few lights along the street were haloed and dim. The eaves along the porch roof of the hotel dripped in a melancholy way, and the village—which was only a few scattered houses, the hotel and a store—seemed to have withdrawn into the mist and partially disappeared. Half a block away there was a diffused reddish glow, and Barlow remembered then that he previously had noticed a bar sign in that direction. He had stayed away from it, not being much of a drinker, but tonight he thought it would be better than his empty house; he walked down the street and went in.

It was not much of a place, made by knocking down the wall between two rooms in an old house. There was a homemade bar with a dirty mirror and a few bottles behind it, several battered tables and an old jukebox; the light was dim. He had met the man behind the bar, so he nodded to him, moved to the bar and asked for a beer. When it came he picked it up and looked around. At the other end of the room three men were seated around one of the tables, and Barlow was surprised to see that they didn't look like most of the natives he had seen around the village. Their clothes were better; they looked more like retired city men, and not poor ones either. Each one had a drink in front of him, and they were talking in a desultory way. He was so bemused at seeing them there, in that dingy place, that he stared at them. They looked back at him uninterestedly, and after a moment he remembered his manners and turned away.

"Do those men live here?" he asked the bartender in a low voice.

"Them?" the bartender asked, inclining his head slightly. "No. They all got little houses—fancy cabins, sort of—outside of town and come up about this time of year."

"What for?" Barlow asked. "What could they do here?"

"They say they hunt them grouse," the bartender said. "But nobody sees them doing it very often."

"Ah," Barlow said and walked over to their table. "Gentlemen," he said, "my name is Barlow. I don't want to intrude, but I'm a grouse hunter, and Jerry tells me that all of you are too. Would you mind if I sat down?"

The three of them seemed to withdraw into themselves. They looked at him somewhat stonily, with an obvious lack of enthusiasm, for a long moment; then the tallest of them spoke up. "Ah," he said in a grudging tone. "Yes. Do sit down. My name is Roberts. This is Charley Deakyne, and that's Bill Farley to your right."

Deakyne was a chunky, sandy-haired man, and Farley had a square, ruddy face; all three of them wore good tweeds and had an executive look about them. They nodded to him with no change of expression, with no warmth whatever, and Barlow was suddenly thoroughly fed up with them.

"I'm sorry," he said. "I seem to have come along at an inopportune time." He turned away, went back to the bar, swallowed his beer, paid for it and with a nod at the bartender walked out of the place. As he went out the door he glanced quickly back at the three men; none of them had moved.

The fog was, if anything, thicker than when he had gone in and, as he walked through it back to his house, he began to simmer with an anger that was half bafflement. What the devil, he wondered, was wrong with everybody? The three deadpan executive types, he was sure, had manners if they felt like using them; the hotel proprietor didn't make sense. It seemed to happen when he mentioned grouse—which, in his previous experience, had always brought men together for lively and pleasant talk; for grouse hunters were a dedicated lot and had much to say to one another. It was certainly different in this place.

The rest of the week he was busy, running about in his jeep to the four places where he had men working in the bright autumn woods and seeing to the sawing up of his logs after they were trucked to the sawmill. He kept a sharp eye out for grouse as he moved around or bumped over the logging roads, but saw only two or three of them. It looked as though the shooting was going to be very poor, and he began to feel discouraged about it; in the old days, moving about as he had been moving, he would have seen dozens of birds. A good dog would have been a god-send to him, and he saw no chance of getting one.

On Sunday afternoon, at loose ends and still feeling discouraged, he got his gun out of its case and took it out on the back porch to clean the grease out of it. He was working with rags and cleaning rod when he looked up and was startled to see the big setter sitting ten feet away in the grass with its head cocked to one side, looking at him. It waved its tail gently. It was rather old and ribby, bigger than people want setters any more, and there was a ring around its neck where the hair was very thin, as though a collar had chafed it badly. Barlow stopped rub-bing the gun; he almost stopped breathing. His head was instantly filled with wild schemes to get the beast into the house or the garage, and he frantically cast about in his mind to remember where there was something he could use for a leash. The dog somehow seemed to sense what he was thinking, moved off several steps and, as some dogs do, raised its upper lip slightly and grinned at him.

This manifestation, at once sardonic and as plain as words would have been, brought Barlow back to earth again. It indicated to him that the dog knew perfectly what he had been thinking, that such things had been tried on it many times before and that it didn't intend to be taken in. Barlow stood the gun in the corner of the porch and grinned.

"All right," he said. "We won't try to fence you in. All grouse hunters are crazy, but this one isn't as crazy as all that." He stepped off the porch. "Come on," he said, "let's take a walk."

The dog watched until he reached the back of his lot, where the woods began. There he stopped and waved an arm, calling it on. It came past him at a run and, as they got into the woods and moved on, it began to hunt, quartering back and forth in front of him, never too far away. It was a delight to Barlow to be in the woods again, moving through the crimson and gold of maple and beech and the somber gloom of the hemlock thickets with a dog working in front of him.

It was like the one or two really good dogs he had owned years ago, covering an extraordinary amount of ground at a fast and steady pace, never beyond his view. It made him feel, as he had felt with those fine dogs of the past, as though there was a sort of empathy between them. No word need be said; the dog acted as a part of the hunter, a more sensitive extention of the man, never out of touch.

Presently he saw how good it really was; at the edge of a witch-hopple thicket it suddenly stopped, crept forward with its belly low for a few steps and stopped again.

Barlow stopped himself, for the dog was not pointing yet; either the bird was still stirring a little or the dog wasn't quite sure of its location. Suddenly, with great caution, the dog moved off to the right and, taking a wide half circle, faced Barlow again from the other side of the thicket and froze. The bird had been running in front of them, and the dog had swung around it, headed it off and stopped it. It had been a beautiful performance.

Barlow began to walk in, tingling with expectation. When he reached the middle of the thicket, a big, old grouse rose from under his feet with its booming thunder of wings, angled up through an opening in the trees with its tail spread wide and disappeared. To see a grouse rise again in the autumn woods, after the dog had handled it so well, brought a lump to Barlow's throat. With the curious dichotomy of the hunter he loved both the bird and the hunting of it; and he had neither seen the bird nor hunted it for a long time.

He called the dog; it came without hesitation and sat down beside him. As he gently stroked its head, he knew that he wanted it more than he had wanted anything for years, and that he couldn't have it. There was no way to bind it to him; its actions in his yard had shown him plainly enough—even if Gibney, the hotelkeeper, hadn't told him—that it would go its own way and come to him when it wanted to. He wondered if that was why he had been warned against it. Had Gibney seen people make fools of themselves over it before and warned him out of kindness, or was there more? He had a sudden, inexplicable feeling that there was, that he had been seduced by a strange, masterless dog into an experience that he would be sorry for. He put his hand under the dog's jaw to raise its head and look into its eyes, but it broke away from him and started to hunt again. He watched it for a moment, rather disturbed but unable to leave it, and followed.

They found no other grouse, which didn't surprise Barlow; he hadn't expected that they would find any so close to the village. He was beginning to think of turning back when they came out onto a road, which Barlow recognized as the one which wound around the hills and finally went through the village. There was a car parked 700 or 800 yards away, and it started toward them. When it reached them it stopped, and Barlow recognized the driver as the man named Roberts, whom he had seen in the bar.

"Good afternoon, Barlow," Roberts said. "I thought I'd find you about here. Someone saw you leave the village with the dog, and from your direction I guessed your course." He smiled slightly at Barlow and then switched his attention to the dog, which turned its back on him and sat down.

"Ah, yes," Barlow said. "Kind of you to go to all the trouble. I suppose there's a phone call at the hotel, or someone wants me."

"Not that I know of," Roberts said. "I wanted to talk to you."

Barlow looked at him in surprise. He was still looking at the dog, and there wasn't any more warmth or friendliness in his voice than there had been in the bar. "Talk to me at home then," Barlow said in irritation. "I'm usually there in the evenings."

"I want to talk to you here," Roberts said, and his glance swung to Barlow, cold with hostility. "Before—" He caught himself. "I don't want you around here, Barlow. I'll buy you out and give you a very good profit."

Barlow stared at him. "Will you, now?" he asked, checking his rising temper. "Good. Bring a hundred and fifty thousand dollars in cash to my house tonight at eight, and I'll go. Otherwise, stay out of my way. I don't like you."

He turned away, climbed the bank beside the road and started into the woods. The dog stood up and followed him. He had gone about fifty feet when Roberts shouted,

"It's as much for your good as mine, you fool! Go while you can! Go before that accursed beast— Go! Go!"

Barlow increased his pace and didn't turn around; the dog moved out, and the shouting from the road diminished behind him and finally ceased.

The dog left him shortly before he got back to his house. One moment it was quartering about in front of him and the next it had vanished completely. He didn't whistle or call; he knew it wouldn't be back that day and wondered with a pang whether it would ever be back again. The shooting season started on the morrow and, now that he had seen what the dog could do with an old grouse smart enough to make a fool of an ordinary bird dog and live for a long time so close to the village, a feeling of depression descended upon him. This depression deepened when he thought of Roberts, who had acted almost like a madman. Roberts, with his ridiculous offer—to which he had got an equally ridiculous reply—and his shouting, was certainly a disturbed character; but the more Barlow thought over what Roberts had said, the more it seemed as though the dog was the cause of it. It seemed obvious that he wanted Barlow out of the village because of the dog and had met him on the road to get ahead of the two others with an offer, but why had he called the dog an accursed beast?

Barlow was so engrossed in his puzzled thoughts when he entered the back door that at first he didn't see Farley, he of the square, ruddy face in the bar, and jumped when Farley said "Hello!" from the door of the living room. "I didn't mean to startle you," Farley went on. "I thought you saw me. I say, I'm sorry I acted such an ass the other night."

Barlow had gathered himself and prepared to give Farley the same treatment he had given Roberts, but this approach disarmed him. "It's all right," he said. "Won't you sit down?" Farley took a chair, and Barlow studied him.

He was still wary, despite Farley's belated politeness, and said, "Have you come to buy me out too?"

"Buy you out?" Farley asked. "Why would I try to buy you out?"

"Roberts offered to," Barlow said. "He waylaid me on the road."

Farley showed some signs of agitation; he half stood up and then sat down again. His face hardened. "Why, that—" he began and stopped. Then he smiled, a painful, unhappy grimace. "He obviously didn't succeed," he said. "He was always too jumpy, too gruff, not diplomatic enough. He probably meant, at first, to ask you what I'm going to ask you and somehow got put off it."

"And what is that?"

"To let me shoot with you."

Barlow simply stared at him; it was the second one of them he'd stared at. "Let you shoot with me?" he asked. "Why?"

"The dog likes you," Farley said. "He went for a walk with you. Believe me, Barlow, I'd give almost anything. It might work. Just once, just once more." He was almost pleading now; he leaned forward in his chair, and his hands twitched on the arms of it. "Just once. Please."

Barlow was astounded; maybe this one was mad too. "Look," he said, "all of you treated me as though I had cholera, and I've got to like the people I shoot with. You all begin to show up after I'd been seen walking the dog. I don't know what this dog's got that any really fine dog hasn't—"

"You don't?" Farley almost shouted at him. "You don't? You're lying! When you came in here, you were so bemused that you didn't even see me, and that's proof enough. Barlow, it's worth a thousand dollars to me, I tell you!" He came out of his chair and started for Barlow, but Barlow put up one hand and stopped him.

"That's enough," he said. "I want no part of any of you.

Go get yourselves dogs with your thousand dollars and let me alone. Now, if you'll excuse me——"

Farley got a pleading look on his face and held up his hands. "No!" he exclaimed. "You've got to listen to me, Barlow. I'll give you two thousand. What other use do I have for money any more? I loved grouse shooting, and it's been thirty years since I've had any like that. There isn't any like it any more. I've come back and come back, it won't look at me and——"

His voice had been rising; he was like a man pleading for an extension of a loan or something else he needed very badly, and Barlow turned away from him, went out through the kitchen and headed for the woods. As he entered the edge of them he turned and saw Farley at the back door. He pointed his finger at the man and said, "Go away. I won't talk to you. And find that other one, Deakyne, and tell him to stay away from here."

He turned again and walked rapidly on, considerably upset by the scene and even more confused.

The next day the grouse season opened, and Barlow was up early. He had bought a supply of meat, and he put a big pan of it out by the back porch. As he cooked his breakfast he made a number of trips to the back door to look out and see if the dog had come, but there was no sign of it; it still hadn't appeared by the time he finished his breakfast. Feeling like a fool, he took his gun and coat out on the back porch and sat there, hoping it would come, but it didn't. He waited for an hour, feeling more foolish all the time; then he swore, got into the jeep and drove off to where he had seen a bird or two in the past.

He hunted until the middle of the afternoon and didn't see a grouse. Like most men who are accustomed to hunt with a good dog, he had the feeling that he was possibly passing birds that froze at his approach and that a dog would have found, or that there were birds which had run on ahead of him like the one the setter had stopped. Having seen the dog work, he missed it all the more.

It was a day of mounting frustration, and the day following was just like it except that he heard a grouse fly off and never saw it; he began to wish that he had never seen the dog. On the third morning, discouraged and glum, he slept an extra hour and finally got up as grumpy as a bear fresh out of hibernation; when he looked out the back door, more out of habit than of hope, the dog was sitting on the back porch. His grumpiness evaporated; he ran about and got the pan of meat and took it out. The dog grinned at him before it began to eat.

"Ah, you devil," he said to it, half in delight and half in exasperation, "you should have lived in the days of the Spanish Inquisition. You'd have been the chief torturer."

The dog had finished eating by that time; it sat down and looked at him. For a moment its eyes held an odd, cool expression of satisfaction. *Just as though it has me exactly where it wants me,* he thought. He had never seen a dog look quite that way before, and a little shiver went up his spine. He shook it off, went into the house and came back with his gunning coat and gun. The dog followed him to the jeep, and they drove off.

Barlow drove six miles to a very wild stretch of country he had marked long before as a likely spot, parked the jeep off the road and started into the woods. The dog began to quarter back and forth in front of him, its pale body flashing through the sunlight patches of the autumn woods, and Barlow followed happily. They went deeper into the woods, crossed a rocky, swift stream and got into a high, golden beech woods dotted with somber patches of hemlock. It was a good place for grouse, and Barlow began to feel the fine anticipation again.

Suddenly he realized that the dog was not in front of him, that it had disappeared. He stopped to listen for it, disturbed. As he stood there a cloud covered the sun, and the woods darkened; a mean, cold little wind sprang up, rattling the dry leaves and sighing in the hemlocks. The darkness increased, and Barlow heard a distant rolling like thunder, and then suddenly the sun came out again and the wind fell. The woods were sunny and still once more, and off to his left he saw the dog again.

He followed on. Presently it was borne in upon him that he had got into an area which had never been timbered, a thing he had never expected to see. The trees were huge, towering up around him; he had never seen their like except in one or two small parks where the primitive growth had been carefully preserved. Here, all around him, as far as he could see, there was not a sign that man had ever been this way. He was so amazed by this, to find such an area in a country which he knew had been thoroughly cut over forty or fifty years ago, that he forgot for a time to watch the dog. He recalled it with a start and looked around. Forty yards in front of him, in an opening piled with a tangle of deadfall timber, he saw it standing on point.

He moved in. As he stopped a little behind the dog, a grouse got up and, although it flew straight away, he missed it. The dog didn't move, and he took another step. A second grouse rose from the deadfall, half climbing and half flying, with its tail spread wide. As it straightened and began to fly off, he knocked it down. The dog still held steady and, as he stood there, staring, with an empty gun, twelve more birds came up in singles and twos and threes and boomed away.

He was still standing there in disbelief when the dog brought in the dead grouse and laid it in front of him. He picked it up, the bird he would rather hunt than any other, soft and beautiful, big, of a gray cast, with the wide, banded tail and the black ruffs on the neck. He held it for a moment, still unbelieving, for no one had seen fourteen grouse together in that country for thirty years. He looked at the dog, which had turned away to hunt again. It seemed younger, somehow; its coat seemed shinier in the sun; it moved more smoothly, and the worn ring around its neck was harder to see.

A queer feeling of unreality took hold of Barlow as he moved off after it through the great, ancient trees, a feeling that didn't seem to have validity, because he could feel the weight of the dead grouse in his game pocket and the fading warmth of it against his back. He didn't have much time to think about it, for the dog soon pointed again. This time he took the first bird out of a flock of ten and watched, with the sheer pleasure of a dedicated grouse hunter who loves to see birds fly, while the remaining birds took off as the first flock had done.

The rest of the morning was like that; there were grouse everywhere, in flocks and by twos and threes and occasionally a single. It was like a grouse hunter's dream of heaven, like the remembered days of his youth when there were still plenty of birds. Sometimes he watched them go for the pleasure of watching; occasionally he shot at a difficult single, passing up the easier ones. When he had six birds he took the shells out of his gun and stopped shooting, whistled to the dog and turned back. The dog came in and followed behind him, as though it, too, was satisfied.

It had been—with the birds, the shooting, the perfect work of the dog and the wild beauty of the country—the happiest day he had spent for many years; he had long since forgotten the feeling of unreality that had descended upon him at first. It was recalled to him suddenly, with a sense of shock, when he found a cougar's tracks in the sand along a small stream. He had never seen the track of a cougar, the catamount of the early settlers; the beast had been gone from the country before he was born, but there was no question in his mind, from the size of the footprints, that that was what it was. He stood looking at the tracks for a long time, trying to believe that he saw the actual evidence of a living creature that he knew for sure had been exterminated in that country by the turn of the century. All around him grew the great trees that had been long gone, too, and, thinking confusedly of these things, he suddenly realized that he hadn't got into a section that had somehow been spared the attentions of white men, but that they hadn't got there yet. He had gone back in time.

The cold little shiver once more ran up his spine, and he looked quickly about. The woods were still, dreaming quietly in the sun, and the dog was gone. He whistled and called; a wild turkey gobbled from far away, and that was all.

And then there was a rising roar all about him, and the sunlight was dimmed; a dark and flickering shadow fell all around him, and he looked up to see a wide, dark river of birds, seemingly without limit or beginning or end, between him and the sky. He could pick out, here and there against the great river of bodies, some pigeonlike shapes and the swift, pigeonlike beat of their wings and knew that he was seeing what no man of his generation had ever seen: one of the great flights of the passenger pigeons that were gone from the earth.

Any remaining doubt that he may have had was wiped from his mind; a sudden fear that he would never get back again, that he was lost and alone in a world that was now gone, a fear that turned him cold all over, suddenly came upon him and he started to run. He struggled up the steep side of the stream bed under the roaring torrent of pigeons and ran up toward the crest of the mountain that he had been descending a short time before, desperately fighting his way through deadfalls and stumbling over rotting, fallen timber. When he reached the top, scratched and bruised and dripping with sweat, he had to stop; there was a pain like a knife in his side, and his heart sounded like a drum.

He leaned against a tree until his breathing returned nearly to normal and his sight cleared and saw the second-growth timber all around him; as far as he could see, back over the way that he had come, there were no more of the great ancient trees, and the pigeons had gone as if they had never existed. His sigh of relief was more like a sob, and he started to walk again. In ten minutes he came out on the road and saw the jeep parked where he had left it. He went up to it, thumped it to make sure that it was real and got in. His bulky game pocket pushed him forward in the seat, and he got out again. He took the six grouse out of his coat one by one and laid them carefully and unbelievingly on the floor. Only then, as he looked at them, did he recall that the limit was two a day now and wondered what he would say if a game warden stopped him. He shook his head, got in and started the engine.

He was a good deal calmer by evening, but he had no desire to eat anything; after the dinner hour he walked to the hotel and found Gibney in the living room by himself. Gibney glanced at him. "You look shaken up," Gibney said, "so I guess you did it."

"Yes," he said, "I did it. Maybe you can tell me now why you warned me."

"Sit down," Gibney said. "You won't believe what I'm about to say; witchcraft isn't very popular any more."

"Witchcraft? I don't—"

"I don't know what else to call it," Gibney said. "That's why I never talk about it when another grouse hunter comes along. I don't enjoy being called a fool."

"Another grouse hunter?" Barlow said. "You mean they hear about it and come here—come here—" He realized he was repeating himself and stopped. "I didn't hear about it," he said. "I wanted to hunt grouse again, and then the dog came into my yard, and then Roberts and Farley——"

"They've been there," Gibney said. "And they want to get back. They'll do anything, almost anything, to get back again."

Barlow stared at him. "You mean the dog takes them?" he asked. He was beginning to see now.

"The dog took them," Gibney said. "He takes everybody once. Listen now. Ten years ago that dog belonged to a man named Micheals. He was a perfectionist, a strange man, mad about grouse hunting. He trained the dog, and one day the dog did something that put him in a rage. So he hanged the beast."

"Hanged him!" Barlow exclaimed, aghast. "Good heavens, man, whoever hangs a dog?"

"Micheals had spent some time among the Eskimos, hunting polar bear, and Eskimos hang dogs they don't want. So Micheals hanged him. Didn't you see that ring around his neck? By the time somebody cut him down he was, to all intents, dead. But he wasn't dead, as a matter of fact. He came around again, and six months later it was Micheals who was dead. His gun went off accidentally and killed him."

Barlow didn't say anything.

"Pure accident maybe. But after that the dog waited for grouse hunters. He'd appear and get into their good graces, take a walk with them and show them how good he was and then——"

"Yes," Barlow said.

"Did the dog disappear for a while, and the sky darken and all that?"

"Yes," Barlow said again.

"And then after it had taken them into the past somewhere, on the best hunt of their lives, it would never have anything to do with them again."

"Never?" Barlow asked. "Never? There isn't any way to——"

"Do you want to be like Roberts and Farley and Deakyne? Coming back and back, hoping, waiting? There's no future in it, Barlow. Believe me, I know. I've heard it all."

Barlow was silent for a long time, staring at the floor, remembering the impossible flocks of grouse, the great trees, the pigeons, the day. He wasn't frightened of that place now; he wanted, more than he had ever wanted anything, to go back.

"'Sorrow's crown of sorrow,'" Gibney said softly, quoting Tennyson, "'is remembering happier things.'"

"Yes," Barlow said once more. By a great effort of will he dispelled his longing and his hopes. "Thank you," he said and stood up and walked out of the hotel. The mist had come again, giving what he could see of the village an eerie and ghostlike air. He could see the diffused glow of the neon sign on the bar, where Farley and Roberts and Deakyne were doubtless sitting together, and he shivered and turned from it and walked on.

The Big Wheel

by Fred McMorrow

Tales of souls being gathered either for heaven or hell have long been popular. Deals with the Devil are so many in number that they constitute a sub-genre of their own. Benēt's "The Devil and Daniel Webster" would be a prime example here and the recent immensely popular film "Heaven Can Wait" represents the other side of the coin. The key to the popularity of such stories is that the protagonist has a chance to bargain and deal with his sacred or demonic opposite and perhaps evade his fate for a while. McMorrow, however, offers no such respite. His Diana IV M is a special kind of demon.

The Big Wheel

by Fred McMorrow

The little man did not look up from his book of poems when the sound of the engine came through the window of his office, a sound that had no more business being on Mechanic Street than what it belonged to, a Jupiter Custom 12, or the kind of man or woman a Jupiter Custom 12 would belong to, whoever was behind the wheel.

"Sammy," the little man said, "go out and tell the man in the Jupiter Custom 12 to come in here. Then take his car and put it inside in the back."

Sammy looked out the window. "Now, how in hell did you know that was a Jupiter Custom 12, Mr. Deels?" Sammy asked. "You got eyes in your ears or something?"

"You get used to them," Mr. Deels said. "You'll catch on when you've been with us a little longer. Go on now, before he starts blowing his horn."

Mr. Deels went on reading his poems until, his eye jumping to the left side of a page, he saw the hem of a camel's-hair coat just beyond. He looked up. "Welcome," Mr. Deels said. "My name is Mr. Deels. Hell on wheels with Mr. Deels."

"Hello, how are you," said the big man in the camel's-hair. "I heard you had a Diana IV M around here, and I'd like to see it."

"That's a beautiful car you've got there," said Mr. Deels.

"Yes, I know," the man said. "About the Diana IV M—"

"I can imagine the time and money it must have cost just to find that car of yours," Mr. Deels said.

"Yes. If you don't mind, I'm interested in buying your Diana IV M, if you've got one, and I'm willing to pay cash."

"I know, I know," said Mr. Deels. "Cash." He sighed and arose and closed his book and put it in a desk drawer and locked it. "I'm just curious," he said. "Do you know how many Diana IV M's there are in the world, Mr. Carmody?"

"I thought you'd recognize me," said Mr. Carmody.

"I suppose you're used to it," Mr. Deels said.

"Everybody goes to the movies," said Mr. Carmody.

"Movies?" Mr. Deels said. "Oh, yes. But I believe I asked you a question."

"All right," Mr. Carmody said impatiently, "if it makes you happy, I suppose there are fifty Diana IV M's in the world."

Mr. Deels smiled and wiped his hands, surprisingly small, clean and uncalloused for the owner of a garage on Mechanic Street, on a piece of cheesecloth and dropped it in a trash basket. "Well, Mr. Carmody," he said, "there are less than half as many Diana IV M's in the world today as there are Jupiter Custom 12's. What's the matter? Didn't you know that?"

"Why, no," Mr. Carmody said.

"I'm surprised at you," Mr. Deels said. "I'm shocked."

"What?" Mr. Carmody said.

"Yes," Mr. Deels said, "I'm shocked that a man who drives a Jupiter Custom 12 doesn't know how many Diana IV M's there are in the world."

"Well—" said Mr. Carmody.

"Why do you want the Diana, Mr. Carmody?"

"Why?" Mr. Carmody said. "Because it's a great car and I've got the money to own it, that's why. Look, you ask a lot of questions."

"I'm interested in people who go to so much trouble just

to buy an automobile, coming down here and all," Mr. Deels said. "It's a little game with me. I like to find out what their motives are."

"Motives?" Mr. Carmody said, and the famous features began to flush and the nostrils quivered and grew taut. "What are you, some kind of a nut? I mean, where the devil do you get off, acting the way you do in a crazy little dump like this? I mean, this is no way to treat a customer who's willing to give you your price. I mean, you don't get customers like me every day, do you? I mean—"

"No offense," Mr. Deels said. "Really, no offense. Let's take a look at your car."

Mr. Carmody laughed. "My car?" he said. "What are you going to do, offer me a trade-in? Don't you know who you're talking to?"

"You want a Diana IV M, don't you?" Mr. Deels said. "Then let's take a look at your car. This way."

He led the way through the garage, through and between and over and past incredible piles of leaf springs and mufflers and tires and carburetors and engine blocks, and desiccated corpses of terrible old cars and trucks, to the back wall where the Jupiter Custom 12 was. Off to one side some mechanics were working on a Torquemada, apparently reconditioning it.

"Oh, I get it!" Mr. Carmody said suddenly. "Of course! Say, Mr. Deels, I'm awfully sorry. I should have realized."

"You should have realized what, Mr. Carmody?" Mr. Deels said, his eyes traveling over the Jupiter.

"Well," Mr. Carmody said, "maybe my car isn't as rare as a Diana, but it's pretty close, and you probably want it as a piece of merchandise."

"A piece of what?" Mr. Deels said, walking around the Jupiter, his hands gliding over the paint and chrome, feeling the nicks and dents.

"Merchandise," Mr. Carmody said. "You know, goods, buy and sell!"

"Oh, yes," Mr. Deels said. "Merchandise." He leaned over into the cockpit and tried an inside door handle, and it jiggled loosely, and his hand drew back as if he had touched a snake. He stepped back and looked along the right side of the car, tracing the long scar of a side-swipe or a drunken attempt to back up in a tight space.

"Get in and start the motor, will you, Mr. Carmody," Mr. Deels said, folding his arms.

Mr. Carmody jumped in and slammed the door and yanked the choke out all the way and stamped on the self-starter. The car urr-urr-urred, but would not start. "Don't worry about that, Mr. Deels," Mr. Carmody said. "She's just a little sluggish waking up, like all old girls her age." He assaulted the starter again, but the engine would not kick over. "Come on, you! Come on, damn you!" Urr-urr-urr-urr-urr. Urr-urr-urr-urr-urr. Zzzzzzzzz. "Oh, hell!" Mr. Carmody kicked at the fire wall and pounded the wheel with his fist, nostrils flaring.

"Please," Mr. Deels said. "Permit me." Mr. Carmody shrugged and got out, and Mr. Deels slid behind the wheel. He moved his hands and feet about the controls like an organist, and the Jupiter cleared her congested throat and spat and went into a rhythmic purr. Mr. Deels touched the accelerator gently, watching the tachometer and wincing as he listened to the palpitations and pings of metal fatigue and owner neglect in the engine's heartbeat. He shut off the ignition.

"I understand that you own several horses, Mr. Carmody," Mr. Deels said.

"I've got a few nags on the coast, I guess," Mr. Carmody said.

"What are their names, Mr. Carmody?"

"Their names? What's that got to do with anything?"

"And how many times have you been married, Mr. Carmody?"

"Six, though I don't see what my horses or my marriages —I mean, I don't see how it's any of your business."

Mr. Deels smiled. "You're absolutely right, Mr. Carmody," he said.

"Some of the nuts you got to put up with in this world," Mr. Carmody said. "Reading poems in a lousy little body-and-fender shop! Say, since we're getting personal, and I'm in one of the arts, you might say, and I might know something about poetry, maybe you wouldn't mind telling me what kind of poems a kooky grease monkey reads? Who wrote it? Anybody I know?"

"Not very well," Mr. Deels said.

"Well, who?"

"I did," Mr. Deels said.

"You did? I'll be damned. What's it about, the romance of grinding valves or getting crankcase oil squirted in your face or something like that?"

"Some of it," Mr. Deels said. "And about speed and touch and movement and texture. But we were getting down to business."

"It's about time."

"Let me show you the Diana," Mr. Deels said. "It's over there, through that door."

"Wait a minute," Mr. Carmody said. "What about my car?"

"What about it?" Mr. Deels said.

"Well, don't you want to drive it? Don't you want to look it over a little more? Don't you want to know what it's like, what you're getting?"

"I know what it's like," Mr. Deels said. "I know exactly what it's like. The Diana. This way."

"Some businessman," Mr. Carmody said, following the silent Mr. Deels. "Boy, you found a home on Mechanic Street!"

Mr. Deels led Mr. Carmody into a little, one-car garage as like the main garage as a hospital operating room is like a slaughterhouse. The floor was holy-stone clean, the walls a subdued shade of green, indirectly lighted; along one wall hung racks of tools and spare parts that glistened like silver. In the center, her nose pointing at the street door, the Diana IV M, long, sleek, poised, waiting, alive, tensed, all of her lovely, all of her thrilling to Mr. Carmody's eyes and to his heart, her chrome seeming to blend into the ultimate midnight black of her body paint without definition as if she were, like an animal, all of a piece rather than the creation of so many components of metal, rubber and glass.

Mr. Carmody tried to say something, but he was a dreamer who tries to scream and finds his throat full of cotton. He swallowed hard and found his voice. "She's like a woman," Mr. Carmody said.

"The huntress of the night," Mr. Deels said. "The moon herself."

"My Lord," Mr. Carmody said. "Where'd *you* get her? What's she doing here? Who owned her? Have you got records on her? Papers?"

"Papers?" Mr. Deels said. "This isn't a horse or a dog, Mr. Carmody, this is a Diana IV M. This isn't something that has to be proved. She speaks for herself."

"Well, how will I know who owned the car?"

"Why should you want to know?"

"Well, I want to be able to tell people, sure, this is a Diana IV M, there's less than fifty cars like it in the whole world, a maharaja owned her, handful of diamonds, weight in gold, you know."

"That's the most important thing, isn't it, Mr. Carmody?" Mr. Deels said. "You want to *own* her. Like you own the Jupiter."

"She's a Diana," Mr. Carmody said. "Now, look, Mr. Deels. Let's knock off all this frick-frack, frick-frack. I want the car, I've got the money, I'll pay whatever you ask and you don't have to bargain with me. Now who owned her?"

"There's only been one owner," Mr. Deels said, his hand caressing the Diana's fender as if it were the flank of a sleek black animal. "An impatient, unkind sort of man with no real appreciation or understanding of cars like this. A man who would pay thousands of dollars for a blooded horse and then shoot her if he could not break her spirit the first time he rode her."

"Why'd he get rid of the car?"

"There was an accident," Mr. Deels said. "Oh, don't worry, we repaired what damage there was. Yes, there was an accident, and her owner had no further use for her after that. He just couldn't handle a Diana. Tell me something, Mr. Carmody: How did you know about the Diana?"

"Why, I was—I mean, I heard about—wait a minute," Mr. Carmody said, and frowned. "Funny. I can't for the life of me tell you just who told me about the car—or even how to get here! Now, what do you think of that? But somehow I knew where to go, and I knew it'd be here."

Mr. Deels nodded slowly. "You've come to the right place," he said.

"How could I forget something like that?" Mr. Carmody said. "Well, never mind. I've got a checkbook here, Mr. Deels. You name the figure."

"Nothing."

"I didn't get that."

"I said the figure is nothing. Let's say it will be a simple trade. Your car for mine."

"Brother," Mr. Carmody said, "you've got yourself a deal! Except I'm not half as much of a nut as you are."

"I don't understand."

"I mean I don't buy cars just by listening to the motor. For all I know, you've got a busted-down old Model-T motor under that hood, and I'm going to see this car move before I sign anything. Now let's get in and take a little ride around the block, shall we?"

"Certainly," Mr. Deels said. He fished a set of keys out of his pocket. "Would you like to drive?"

"Later," Mr. Carmody said. "You know the neighborhood."

"You do *know* how to drive a Diana, don't you?" Mr. Deels said.

"Listen, buster," Mr. Carmody said, "I've smashed up more boats like this than you ever laid a monkey wrench to."

"I'm sure you have," Mr. Deels said. "Get in."

"I'll open the garage door for you," Mr. Carmody said.

"That won't be necessary. Get in."

"Oh, I get it. Electric eye. Pretty fancy for Mechanic Street," Mr. Carmody said. He climbed in beside Mr. Deels, and the seat seemed to come in and grip him fast, as if it had been made for his hips alone.

Mr. Carmody had never heard an engine start as the Diana's did. There was really nothing like sound, like ignition kicking off. Like an animal rising from sleep, the Diana suddenly started to vibrate, to stretch and to come to life. Mr. Deels touched the accelerator and they seemed to evaporate through the garage door into Mechanic Street.

Night had fallen and there was no traffic. The buildings were unfamiliar blurs of black, like the Diana herself. Mr. Deels wound the Diana around curves and corners of strange streets without touching the brake or gearing down, so it seemed, and she did not turn like a car but like a snake, and she kept going faster.

They turned onto a highway Mr. Carmody had never seen before, beyond whose lanes there was only limitless dark, a highway traveled by Diana IV M's and Jupiter Custom 12's and Zenobias and Arcturuses, all hurtling along without sound, their headlights fierce as feral eyes, and never bumping or passing one another.

The speed became so great that Mr. Carmody could not

speak, and he fought to breathe as his back was pushed farther and farther into the clasp of the Diana's seat, and he seized Mr. Deels's arm and tried to communicate that he had had enough. "She's all yours now, Mr. Carmody," said Mr. Deels, his voice as clear as it had been in the garage, and he opened the driver's door. "Take the wheel. Try her," he said, and stepped into the moving dark.

Mr. Carmody managed to get behind the wheel. He tried to control the hurtling fury around and under him, but it seemed to enrage the Diana. There was a new burst of speed, and the curve which her headlights suddenly picked up, and over which she shot into a well of hopeless, bottomless black, was the last sight the mortal eyes of Mr. Carmody would ever see or need to see.

Mr. Deels did not look up from his book when the sound of the engine came through the window. "Sammy," Mr. Deels said, "go out and tell the man in the Arcturus to come in here." Mr. Deels went on reading until the stranger stood before him.

"Welcome," Mr. Deels said. "My name is Mr. Deels. Hell on wheels with Mr. Deels."

"Hello yourself," the stranger said. "I heard you had a Jupiter Custom 12 around here, and I'd like to take a look at it."

"That's a beautiful car you've got there," Mr. Deels said.

"Yes, I know," the man said. "About the Jupiter Custom 12. . . ."

The Death Dust
by Frank Harvey

Frank Harvey's tale is dated now by the events of the past few years, but it is still an example of a good story well told. Harvey wrote several stories of the U.S. Air Force on the verge of space. Eight of these were collected as Air Force, *a 1959 Ballantine paperback. The problem his characters face here was a real one for our first moon crew. We can well remember the elaborate quarantine set up for their return. We can also be thankful that we did not encounter "The Death Dust."*

The Death Dust

by Frank Harvey

The United States Air Force had named our moon vehicle *Super Nova,* which means "exploding star." We weren't going to explode—we hoped—but we were certainly going to produce one of the loudest roaring sounds heard by anyone in the world up to now.

Now it was four o'clock in the morning at Cape Canaveral, Florida. There were three of us: Maj. Dick Rivero, copilot and astrogator; Dr. Charles Ferris, our medical and human-factors specialist; and myself, Maj. Jim Casey, aircraft commander. I say aircraft commander advisedly. The *Super Nova* was a gleaming metal skyscraper as it stood on the launching pad at the cape. It had five stages, weighed fifteen hundred tons and its rocket engines added up to seventeen million pounds of thrust. But the payload—the top of the skyscraper in which we would ride—was an airplane. It was a bigger and much more sophisticated version of the X-15 rocket plane which Scott Crossfield and Bob White had tested so thoroughly in the Mojave Desert. Major Rivero and I would sit side by side in front. Doctor Ferris would ride in the small cabin behind us—certainly not an ideal arrangement for a five-hundred-thousand-mile round trip, but let me say this for the *Super Nova:* It was designed to send three men to the moon and back—not for a rest-and-relaxation junket—and none of us was complaining. Returning from outer space, our X-15F would circle the earth three times, dipping a little deeper into the air blanket each time, before committing itself to a landing at Edwards Flight Test Center, in California. So, in a true sense, the X-15F was an aircraft, and I was its commander.

It was a rigid requirement that each of us be small. You wouldn't think the engineers would quibble about a pound or two after designing a space ship as high as an office building, but they had. It took twenty pounds of fuel, for example, to carry a fountain pen to the moon and back—so every ounce, even flesh and blood, had to pay its way.

I couldn't have asked for a better crew. Colonel Burns, of the Aeromedical Laboratory, had wanted very much to go himself, but he was too old and too heavy. He sent Dr, Charles Ferris, a thin-faced, solemn little guy with a dry sense of humor, full of terms like "mean diurnal cycle" and "uncompensated respiratory acidosis." Don't let it fool you. Chuck was what the USAF calls a "quiet tiger." When the heat was on, he just wouldn't quit. Once he had slit the chest of a man whose heart had stopped beating, reached in and massaged the heart—and saved the man's life. I didn't hear it from Chuck. I read it in the records.

If you follow the doing of the Strategic Air Command at all, you know Major Rivero. He's a jet-bombardment expert—one of the slickest boys in SAC when it comes to handling a K-system. He flew jet fighters, too, in Korea, which was where I met him first. We had a nice little group out there: Rivero, Dad Smith, Smoke Hunter, Pete De Flores—you know the roster. I'm an ex-fighter jock myself, and I suppose I'm partial to the breed.

Now, on the launch pad at Canaveral, I looked through the double-paned windscreen at our target, a ghostly lemon-colored disk which hung over the Atlantic in the lilac haze. My mouth was too dry to spit. I was scared. Certainly I was. So were the other guys, even though they weren't showing it. Doctor Ferris was the coolest, I guess, but he could afford to be. The only person who'd miss Doc, if our bird wandered off toward the sun, was a certain lovely brunette who owned a smelly great Dane and drove a sports car a hundred miles an hour. She'd grieve for Doc at least a week. Then there'd be a new third party in the sports car, and it wouldn't be the lovely brunette's mother. She admitted that her favorite toy was boys, and nobody challenged the statement.

With Major Rivero it was different. Dick was married to one of the cutest little gals—and one of the best cooks—in the whole USAF. I'd eaten Jinny Rivero's Caesar salad and her enchiladas. Angels, sitting down to dinner, should be so lucky! Dick must be thinking of Jinny now, the way I was thinking of Hank. Hank's my boy. He's eleven. Since his mother died, we've been living out of the same barracks bag, and we kind of like each other.

"Launch Control to *Super Nova,*" a voice said in my headset. "Final check. You ready for lift-off, Major Casey?"

I glanced sideways. Rivero's thumb was up. I twisted slightly in my contour seat, hampered by the full-pressure suit, and looked at Ferris. He grinned through his face plate. "O.K., Launch Control," I radioed. "This is Major Casey. We are ready for lift-off."

"Roger, Major Casey. We are ninety seconds and counting. . . ."

Our contour seats had been adjusted so that all of us bent forward at the waist in the attitude which Colonel Burns' tests had indicated was best in violent forward acceleration. Every inch of our bodies was supported. We did not need that support at once. The cluster of seven rocket F-1 engines that gave ten million five hundred thousand pounds of thrust to our first stage lighted off together with a sound that dug through the insulation and twisted in my ears like broken glass. Outside the windscreen, the palmettos and blockhouses on the cape were so blindingly bright in the reflected glare that it hurt to look at them. We seemed to be nailed down. Then our streamlined skyscraper began to lift, as if it were on hydraulic jacks.

"Go, baby, go," the launch controller's voice said, a whisper in the storm of sound. The cape fell away. Our tail flames turned the scattered clouds a furnace white. Still we moved slowly, like a freight elevator. The lilac haze slipped below us. Through the air blanket outer space was a delicate lettuce green and the stars winked peacefully.

"We in a balloon?" Rivero's voice said, sounding brittle and tiny. "Or are we in a moon rocket?" Then, at last, the speed began to build.

I am not too clear about the stage firings. They were automatic, of course. There were short periods of weightless coasting in between. Each stage fired harder as we grew lighter. Even in our contour seats the G loads got brutal. I blacked out in the middle of the fourth-stage firing. Stage five stayed with us. We would have to use it to escape from the moon on our return trip. A voice was speaking as I came out of the black-out.

"Hello, *Super Nova*. This is Central Control. We have taken over from Launch. Do you read us, Major Casey?"

"Loud and clear," I said. "Go ahead."

"You all right?"

"Fine," I said. "How do we look on the scopes?"

"Green," the voice said, excited and happy. "Green as a cotton-picking emerald—straight across the board. You've got escape velocity now. You can't possibly fall back. If your moon homer works, you're in."

I looked out. We were in the near-horizontal part of our flight path, very high, headed due east. As I watched we shot out of the earth's shadow into bright sunlight. I did not want to take my eyes from the scene, even for a moment. Over the intercom I asked Dick Rivero to read off our primary-panel indications. Dick's voice said, "Altitude: nine hundred miles. Speed: thirty-five thousand feet per second. Cabin pressure: normal. Everything's in the green, skipper."

I thanked him. The continent of Africa was rising slowly

out of the sea and spreading out under us on the curve of the world. As we lifted I could see the whole massive sprawl of the Sahara, like a beige rug beside the swimming-pool glitter of the Mediterranean. My throat ached and there was a prickling hotness behind my eyes. This was a sight no man had seen before. Maybe this was a sight that should be reserved for God. The horizon was no longer flat—or even curved. It was gone altogether, and I was looking at the whole planet earth, a giant cloud-streaked ball of dark ocean and glowing land, floating there, like a dream, against the star blaze of deep space. Out ahead of us, across two hundred forty thousand miles of emptiness, hung our destination, incredibly clean and white, like a globe of glowing ice.

"Brother," Dick Rivero said softly on the intercom, and it sounded like a prayer. I glanced over at him. "How are you doing Dick?"

He snapped back instantly, and was his old kidding self. "Skipper—you know what the paratrooper said before his first jump?"

"No. What did the paratrooper say?"

"He said, 'I wish the folks back on the farm could see me now—*back on the farm!*'"

It was good for a laugh. We all had to laugh or cry, and laughing was a lot better. Doctor Ferris said, "I hope Dr. Wernher von Braun is right."

"Right about what?"

"He wrote a science-fiction story about the moon. Said there was no dust. Not a speck. People ran around with wheelbarrows, gathering rocks. It was a ball."

"In two and three-tenths days," Dick Rivero said, "we will know if the good doctor is right. If our moon homer works, that is. If it doesn't—we are in for a good long trip around the sun."

"Like eternity?" Ferris said.

"Yeah," Dick Rivero said. "Like eternity."

We passed through the Van Allen belt too rapidly for the deadly radiation, trapped by the earth's magnetic field, to get through our shielding. We were weightless, of course. It was an unpleasant feeling—and dangerous. If any of us became violently nauseated, we could drown in our own stomach fluids, there being no gravity to empty our throats. We'd brought special pumps for this contingency, but we didn't need them. We were too busy to be sick, and after a while we built up a tolerance to weightlessness, and the queasiness went away.

The X-15F was fitted with a meteor bumper designed to vaporize anything up to the size of a pea and prevent it from reaching our pressure hull, but no impacts were really expected, and none occurred. We did hit very fine space dust about eighty thousand miles out. It eroded the observation windows slightly, destroying the lens-bright surface, but did not threaten our cabin integrity at all. The radar and radio reception was good except for bursts of solar static at times. Those monster antenna dishes on earth were following us with focused beams, and it was working very well. They even sent us hi-fi recordings of Nat King Cole, and at one point we heard a rebroadcast of a Yankee baseball game. Actually, after the excitement of the blast-off wore away, the trip became pretty humdrum. We had our helmets off, but we kept our pressure suits on. We'd need them if and when we reached the moon, and they were the very devil to get into in cramped quarters. Even our meals were no treat. Because of our weightless condition, we had to squeeze our food into our throats out of big plastic tubes—like eating tooth paste.

However, as we left the earth behind and the moon got larger ahead of us, the tension grew steadily. We had all studied the flight profile, and we knew that just a few hundred feet per second in burnout velocity, back near the earth, could make a disastrous difference in our chances of reaching the moon. We also knew that a degree or two of error in path angle could throw us off the target by thousands of miles. We were placing our faith in the infrared homing equipment. I won't go into detail except to say that the homer was supposed to work somewhat like a magnet. It was supposed to seek out the moon for us, lock onto it and bring us down automatically, firing short bursts of rocket power to correct for deviations.

When we were many hours out, I called earth and checked on our profile. "You're doing just fine," they told me. "According to our radar indications, you're right on the button. No sweat."

"Thanks," I said. If I'd been sitting in some air-conditioned radar room on earth, I'm sure I wouldn't have been sweating either.

"You should transfer from earth gravity to moon gravity very soon now," the earth radio said. "Watch for it."

"What's the guy think we're doing?" Major Rivero said on the intercom, not taking his eyes off the homer. "Playing tiddlywinks?"

We watched the moon in silence. It was half full. The sunlight, coming in from the side, made furry-looking shadows in the craters. Even the dark side glowed with reflected earthshine. The place looked very beat up, as if a peevish giant had worked on it with a sledge hammer. Rivero said, "Oh, oh—looks like——"

I felt my body sag in the seat.

"There goes a guidance rocket!" Rivero yelled. "We got it made, you guys! Our homer just locked onto the moon!"

We didn't have it made. We had a chance to make it. There's a difference. I looked through the windshield. I had made a study of the moon's surface. We were coming down in one corner of a flat area which the astronomers call Mare Imbrium. It looked like a mud flat after a crowd of kids has tossed a bunch of junk into it. There were strings of tiny holes, such as water droplets would make. There were cozy cups, like the imprints of pebbles. And there were wide pie-crust craters. The whole area was baked hard and white by the sun.

"Let's get into our helmets," I said. "I don't look for any emergency on the landing, but we have to be ready, just in case."

When we were all fully suited, I turned the X-15F around, using the hydrogen-peroxide jets in the nose and wings, and we began to drop toward the moon tail-first. There was a large booster stage still fastened to our tail. It would serve two purposes: reverse rocket power for the moon landing and enough solid-fuel energy to blast us back to earth on the return trip. The homer had swiveled automatically as I reversed our heading. It was now firing at intervals to reduce our speed and to keep us on course.

I was now very tense. The homer would carry us close to the moon. Then I would take over manually for the landing. I watched the backdown mirror. The moon's surface now looked a great deal like the California desert, except that there were no gullies or bushes. The sun's rays were horizontal, as in late afternoon on earth, and every rock and hummock had a knife-sharp shadow stripe. Those pits which had seemed like water droplets were now half a mile wide. The piecrust rings were cliffs reaching up toward us.

I said, "Extend landing gear!"

Rivero said, "Gear coming out, sir!"

I saw the steel tripod sprout from its streamlined nest in the booster hull.

"Landing gear down and locked!" Rivero said.

"Very well," I said. "Now stand by for an emergency lift-off if we strike a hole and start to tilt dangerously."

As we approached the surface, I saw the white floor of the Mare Imbrium begin to stir nervously, as if it were alive, under the downthrust of the landing rockets. It was white dust. It boiled and churned wildly, and then we settled into it as into an arctic white-out, and I cut the power.

There was a bump, a tilting as the tripod legs automatically positioned themselves to keep the moon rocket vertical, pointed back toward earth. The sink meter slowed to zero and stopped, and Dick Rivero's voice said, "Don't look now—because you can't see a thing—but I think we just landed on the moon!"

It was cut and dried from here on out. We were programed to spend exactly fourteen hours on the moon, and every moment of that time was covered on our check list. First we had to preflight the space vehicle for blast-off. We did not anticipate any difficulties, but it was only sensible to have the back door open and the hinges oiled. We had flipped coins, back on earth, to see who would be the first man to set foot on the moon—in case we reached it—and I had been lucky. I'd go down the ladder first, followed by Doctor Ferris, and Major Rivero would stay inside the ship and monitor the temperatures and pressures on its instruments. It was our home away from home, and we didn't want anything to go wrong with it while we were outside working. Dick would have his chance to walk around on the moon as soon as we returned.

Getting out of the cramped space lock and positioning the descent ladder in the blinding fog of dust was a slow, irritating job. The stuff was as fine as talcum powder and, since there was no atmosphere and very little gravity as compared to earth, it merely hung there, glowing and opaque in the brilliant sunlight. I made a Geiger-counter test on top of the ladder and again at the bottom, standing in what felt like eider down, and there was no dangerous radioactivity. "O.K., Doctor Ferris," I said on my helmet radio. "Come on down. The coast is clear."

"Clear?" Chuck Ferris' voice said. "You call this clear?"

"Of course it's clear," Dick Rivero's voice said from inside the ship. "There's no dust out there. It's your imagination."

Several moments later Ferris loomed dimly beside me, a talcum-powdered ghost in the glowing mist. We joined hands and began moving cautiously out into the fog. We staggered like a couple of drunks at first, being unused to the reduced gravity. But as we left the vicinity of the rocket ship, the dust thinned—there was no wind to scatter it—and walking became easier.

"Hey, you guys," Dick Rivero said, and I couldn't miss the excitement and impatience in his voice, even on the radio. "Seen any little polka-dotted men yet?"

"None," I said.

"Any green cheese lying around?"

"All right," I said. "You watch the gauges. We'll take care of the local sight-seeing. Your turn is coming."

In perhaps ten minutes we were out of the dust fog altogether, standing on the floor of a snow-white lunar valley. It was completely silent, of course, as there was no air to transmit sound, and I have never seen anything so eerie or so lonely. The peaks that rose into the black-velvet sky were like molten bronze in the level sunlight. The stars were like tiny clusters of diamonds. Over the rim of the bronze mountains the earth shone so brightly I had to squint when I looked at it. North America was now in sunlight.

"It's afternoon at Yankee Stadium," Doctor Ferris said on the radio at my elbow. "Wonder how Mickey Mantle's doing at bat?"

"Mantle should hit one here," I said. "He'd probably drive it into lunar orbit."

I heard a muffled exclamation—pain and irritation mixed—and looked quickly to see if Doctor Ferris had fallen. He had not. He was looking with concern at me. I said, "Rivero—that you?"

"Yeah, dammit!" Dick Rivero's voice snapped.

"What's wrong?"

"Nothing—I just tore a little hole in my glove in the space lock."

"Space lock!" I said, suddenly angry. "What the devil are you doing in the space lock?"

For a moment Rivero did not answer. Then his voice sounded sheepish, like a kid caught with his hand in the cooky jar. "It's nothing, skipper. I just stuck my hand out to get a sample of this white dust. I'm back inside now."

"You're inside now," I said. "And you are staying inside until we get back. Is that clear?"

"Yes, sir!"

"We'll be back in less than an hour."

"Yes, sir!"

Doctor Ferris and I got down to business. We dug through the cushion of white dust and brought up some rock samples which looked like limestone. We stowed them in our back packs. We unstoppered our gas-collector bags and left them open while we checked lunar temperatures, both sun and shade. Earth scientists had been close in their predictions. In the sun the thermometer registered one hundred and ten degrees Fahrenheit. We were in the twilight zone, near the dark half of the moon, and hence relatively cool. I was glad we had not landed in the glowing heart of the bright side. It might have been too hot to leave the ship. The shadows behind rocks were ink black and very cold; almost two hundred degrees below zero Fahrenheit.

Personally, my big moment came when Doctor Ferris took a color movie of me banging an American flag through the lunar crust, with the planet earth hanging beside me as a sort of incidental decoration. Too bad Columbus hadn't been equipped with color cameras. He'd have had quite a laugh on the boys who were predicting he'd go over the brink of the flat world in a giant waterfall.

"I've got a feeling I have to hurry before the sun goes

down," Doctor Ferris said. "I keep forgetting the lunar day is fourteen earth days long."

Then suddenly I heard Dick Rivero's voice. "Skipper—this is Rivero. Do you read me?"

"Roger, Dick," I said. "Go ahead."

"You guys about through out there?"

"Pretty near. Why?"

"Hurry it up, will you? I—I don't feel so good."

"What's wrong?"

"I took off my helmet and gloves. I felt stuffy, couldn't seem to breathe right. Now—well—I feel like I might be going to throw up, and there's a funny rash on my hands."

"Hold tight, Dick," I said. "We're coming in! Right now!"

I didn't even wait to fool with the gas collector. I began to run. I was scared. I realized now how close to the panic point we all were. We were living on the razor edge of death, and had been ever since we lifted off the pad at Cape Canaveral. We'd done a lot of kidding. We'd put up a good front. But the fear was in every one of us: We took it in and breathed it out with every breath we drew. One slip, one mistake, one miscalculation, that's all it took on a space mission.

It took us fifteen terrible minutes to get back to the spaceship and another five to get through the space lock into the cabin. When I saw Dick Rivero, sprawled in his contour seat with his helmet off, I knew instantly that it was very bad. His face was bright red, as if he'd spent the day in the broiling sun. His eyes were already hollow, and they burned feverishly. I had on my space helmet and I could not hear his voice, but I could tell by his lips what he was saying. "Dust," those lips whispered. "Dust—dust. . . ."

I saw the white stuff then. It was all over the cabin, as if somebody had broken open a sack of flour. Doctor Ferris and I were coated with it. Doctor Ferris pushed past me and lifted one of Dick's hands from below the edge of the contour chair. I had to bite my lips to keep from yelling. That hand was horrible to look at. It was swollen and blackened like the paw of some animal. It looked as if it had been held in a raging fire.

I said, on my helmet radio, "Doc—what is it?"

"I don't know," Ferris replied. "Some anaerobic bacteria, possibly. The symptoms are like hemorrhagic fever. I saw it in Korea. Miserable stuff. Broke the blood vessels under the skin."

"Is there an antidote?"

"I've got some serum that might help," Doctor Ferris said. "There's one way to find out. Try it."

"The dust," I said. "It's all over the place."

"Yeah," Chuck Ferris said. "The place is a bit messy. But we have no choice, have we?" Then he did one of the bravest things I've ever seen a man do. He took off his space gloves and began hunting swiftly in his medical locker for his hypodermic and his serum.

I'm inbound now for earth. I was able to blast off alone. Dick Rivero couldn't help because he was dead. The serum which had relieved hemorrhagic fever in Korea had done him no good at all. Doctor Ferris had given his own life for nothing. A few hours after we left the moon, Chuck's hands got pink, got red, then blistered, and he knew that he, too, was doomed. On his helmet radio, Chuck told me about the bacteria, or virus, or whatever it was that filled the white dust. It must be almost impossible to kill, Chuck said, or it could never have survived the savage heat and bitter cold of the lunar crust. Obviously it attacked human tissue with frightening and lethal speed. Perhaps it killed animals, too, and plants—any living thing. If it reached the earth— Chuck stared at me through his space helmet. "If you take it in," he whispered, "you may turn our earth as white and barren as the moon." Then he pulled the helmet off—I guess he didn't want to die with his head in a bottle —and when I looked at his face I had to shut my eyes. . . .

I am the only living person in the X-15F now. I have been in radio contact with the earth for some time. I have explained the danger of the white dust. At first they suggested burning the X-15F immediately after landing. But while they talked, I looked out and saw the dust clinging to the ship in the vacuum of space. If I used reverse rockets to slow down and entered the earth's atmosphere at a moderate speed, some of that white death might blow off and sift down on the green continents as the X-15F wheeled around in orbit, prior to landing.

The earth is growing fast now. It fills the sky. I have not fired my retrorockets. I have not turned the X-15F around, so they could not reduce my speed. I am coming in nose first, and the Gulf of Mexico is dead ahead. I have removed the safety cover from the retrorocket firing switch, and now I press it firmly and feel my body sag heavily back in the contour chair as the rockets fire. They do not act as a brake. They increase my speed rapidly: twenty-six thousand miles an hour . . . twenty-eight thousand . . . thirty-three thousand. . . .

It will be quick. A sudden smear of meteor fire—then nothing. But I have beaten the deadly stuff in the white dust of Luna. None of it—not an atom—will reach the planet earth. Now I am thinking of Hank, my son. I brace myself. I lean forward. I do not shut my eyes. . . .

The Lost Continent
by Geoffrey Household

Geoffrey Household has long been known as a writer of romantic novels of high adventure and intrigue. This story belongs primarily to the adventure-mystery genre, but its central subject has also long been the target of a great number of science fiction and fantasy writers, including H. Rider Haggard, A. A. Merritt, Jane Gaskell and Robert E. Howard. "The Lost Continent" is a clever variation on a classic subject.

The Lost Continent

by Geoffrey Household

Atlantis? It's of more interest to poets and mystics than to archaeologists. The lost continent is only a fable. We have no proof; you're looking at the best there is. No, not me. In the case behind my desk.

A puma, you think? Have you just been to the zoo? Well, then, why do you call it a puma rather than a lion or a leopard? Yes, you're quite right. One could swear it was dug up in Peru or Ecuador. But an ivory puma is impossible. No pumas in the Old World. No elephants in the New World.

I'll tell you its history, though I warn you it is very unsatisfactory. It has no ending. You go out where you came in. You'll just say to hell with me and Jim Hawkes and all those visionary swordsmen who conquered the Americas and carefully destroyed or displaced every blessed thing they ought to have preserved for us.

But like all good stories it is really that of a man's character—a grubby little man with bad teeth and no education, who cared as little for money and as much for truth as any dedicated scholar rediscovering the past for the wages of a manual worker.

At first Jim Hawkes was not allowed in when he turned up at the side door of the museum and asked to see me. They thought he had samples in his little bag. That was what he looked like—a salesman peddling cheap pens on commission. Yet there was something honest and earthy about him which was hard to distrust. He was a real Cockney too—with the Londoner's genius for summing up doormen and minor officials and getting his own way in spite of them.

While he remembered to be on his best behavior he addressed me as "sir." When he got excited he called me "guv'nor." At that first interview he sensibly gave a thumbnail sketch of his background before coming to business, but I can't distinguish between what he said then and all I learned about him later. It's enough that he had passed twenty years of peace and war as steward on a tramp steamer, married a Portuguese wife and settled down on her little farm in the Azores. He was one of those Englishmen who consciously loathe industrial civilization. Most of them haven't the enterprise to get out until they are tied to it. But Jim Hawkes knew an opportunity when he saw one. And the sea had already accustomed him to exile.

Introductions over, he asked me if I believed in Atlantis. He used the right word. It's a matter of belief, not scholarship. I told him gently that we believed in nothing without proof.

"Here it is," he said.

He opened his bag, scattering straw all over the room, and put that ivory puma on my desk.

It was like nothing I had ever seen. So far as technique and material went it might have been a superb Persian ivory of the sixth or fifth century B.C., possibly brought to the Azores by the Carthaginians. But the style was wrong. Too realistic.

I remember thinking it odd that such a marvelous craftsman at carving ivory in the round had been unable to reproduce the strength and majesty of the lion. I know lions. In art, that is. Remind me to give you a copy of my monograph, *Treatment of the Conventional Mane.*

"It's not a lion," Jim Hawkes said. "I think it's a puma."

I made no comment. I took him across to the American Section and put his ivory alongside our two pre-Inca pumas

—one in stone and one in pottery. Jim Hawkes had a case.

When we were sitting down again in my office I asked him how he had got hold of such a curiosity, rather suspecting that he would tell me some unbelievable yarn to cover up the fact that he hadn't any right to it. But, no. He was eager, falling over himself to invite questions. That was why he had come.

He told me that on the island of Graciosa he had discovered a shallow cave with its entrance nearly hidden beneath subtropical vegetation. The floor—part earth, part fine, dry dust—was completely undisturbed. On a rock ledge at the back of the cave was standing the ivory puma.

He thought at first that it was a child's toy. For all I know, it may have been—though an ivory as large as a half-grown kitten argues a very high level of civilization in the nursery. Then he realized that it did not belong to our day at all, and his mind at once jumped to Atlantis.

But it would be wrong to think of him as just one of those lost-continent-cum-flying-saucer sort of cranks. His hobby—and I can't think of a better for anyone living in the Azores—was Atlantis. He knew all the usual arguments for and against. Like so many seamen he was a great reader, though he had left school at the age of twelve. And he had a passion for facts. I tell you; he saw the difference between fact and conjecture much more clearly than some of my colleagues.

"What I want, Mr. Penkivel, sir," he said, "is to 'ave that cave excavated proper like. Not treasure 'unting! Every cupful of soil sifted by them as knows what's what. And I don't want nothink out of it for meself—and I'll pay the labor."

I asked him why me. Simple. He had turned up at the museum and demanded the bloke who knew most about ivories. Just possibly I am. But I also happened to be the bloke whom the porter was most annoyed with at the moment.

Now I really must repeat that there is no conclusive evidence for the existence of Atlantis. But as well as a so-called expert in ancient art, I am also a Cornishman. Part of us always dips into the ocean with the sun. So when I had taken Jim out to lunch next day and again convinced myself that he was dead straight, I decided I might as well spend the six weeks' holiday, which was coming to me, in running a trial trench through that cave. I did not tell my colleagues what I intended. They would have thought I needed a holiday even more than I really did.

Like all islanders Jim knew how to travel cheaply. When he returned to the Azores on a Portuguese cargo boat, I went with him—feeling self-consciously precious and wondering to what sort of society I had condemned myself.

I needn't have worried. Jim's background was in keeping with the man—simple and satisfying. He had a white, single-storied, peasant house, three acres of wheat and pasture and some terraces of fruit and vine, which wandered up the hillside. It was one of the highest farms on Graciosa, blazing with sun or hidden under blowing mist half a dozen times a day and looking out over a full semicircle of empty, secretive Atlantic.

All this he had married, together with *Senhora* Hawkes. It was certainly a love match, though it wouldn't have been possible without her inheritance. Maria Hawkes was a peasant poppet, with the face of an angel and the body of Humpty Dumpty. She, too, had got a bargain by her marriage. Her energetic little ex-steward, always wanting to know why, had doubled the value of her land. They had as yet no children. That allowed Jim his luxury of Atlantis. His excuse for the journey to London had been a visit to his brother, but the *senhora* knew as well as I did that his true motive was to explain the ivory.

His cave was on a steep, overgrown hillside, high above

their land. The entrance was a horizontal cleft under an overhang of rock, so that it could be seen only by a man climbing up from below, and even then he might not spot it through the bushes for what it was. Beyond the cleft was a roomy, low-roofed chamber which ran back into the hill for seventy feet, narrowing all the way, until the passage ended at a fallen boulder.

It was just the sort of place to have sheltered early man. But the islands were uninhabited when the Portuguese discovered them; so I could not expect to fine traces of anything larger than a rabbit. If I did, the historians and geographers would have a good deal of rewriting to do. That was a fascinating thought for a holiday, let alone the fact that I might come across another inexplicable ivory.

I don't normally dig; it's my job to give my opinion of what others have dug. But the cave would have been easy even for an amateur. Right inside, where Jim had made his find, there was only a layer of dust over the bedrock. We sifted all of this. It was quite sterile. I could trust him absolutely with the sieve. When I tell you that he managed to spot a rat's tooth you can imagine how keen he was.

Over the rock at the entrance were eight feet of soil, shallowing rapidly, of course, as one got farther into the cave. Through this we drove our trench with the help of two laborers whom Jim had hired. Meanwhile Maria Hawkes brought up enormous meals of fish and wine on a donkey and loaded the panniers with earth from our dig to put on her pineapples. She couldn't understand our professionally slow, patient progress. But if that was how her man wished to amuse himself she did not complain. Other wives had to put up with drink or gambling.

For the first week I was as happy as any fellow let out of an office can be. At the end of the second week I began to get bored. So did the onlookers, who left us for good. We found not a trace of man. The authorities are always right. A pity—except when I am the authority myself.

The only excitement came when one of our cross trenches hit charcoal only two feet above the bedrock. Jim Hawkes was bursting with expectancy and quite silent. He saw what it could mean. So did the laborers. But I had to tell them there was no evidence of a human hearth; it was undoubtedly blown debris from a forest fire. I think I shall go out and look at it again.

Jim wouldn't let me pay for anything, and I knew he could not afford to go on. The farm was being neglected; ready money was short after his trip to London; and dear Maria Hawkes had added to the expense by considering it her duty to feed the spectators as well as us. At the end of the third week I persuaded Jim to give up and dismiss the laborers. I felt like—well, like a doctor telling him he must lose his leg. But it had become quite obvious that excavation was not going to tell us anything of the ivory puma.

When the first idle day was over—idle for me—I scrambled up to the cave and, of course, found Jim already there. He had been up before dawn and hoeing ever since, but now he was chipping away with a cold chisel at the boulder which blocked the end of the passage.

"Know anything about explosives, guv'?" he asked.

I said I did. Not a very likely trade for an antiquarian. But in the war I was a sapper.

"Then 'ow about it? Think we'd be muckin' up the evidence?"

Yes. That was what he said. He had the instincts of a born archaeologist.

I told him I was sure there was no evidence to muck up, but that the boulder would take some smashing. It had fallen from the roof recently. Say, two or three hundred years ago. To judge by the narrowing of the cave walls, I decided nothing much could be behind it, except a cleft or vent. That had to be there, for an occasional draft of warmish air could be felt at floor level. The air had removed my last, faint doubt of Jim's story. It accounted for the preservation of the ivory—otherwise rather unlikely in the moist climate of the Azores.

There was a wide crack down the middle of the boulder and a useful cavity below it. Doubtfully I told Jim my requirements. They didn't bother him. He spoke very serviceable Portuguese and was popular everywhere. He was back the next evening with a keg of old-fashioned gunpowder—excellent stuff for shifting rock—from the island's general stores, this time on my bill, and had got fuse and detonators free from the whalers.

He did not mention what we were doing, even to Maria—most women are inclined to be excitable in the presence of explosives—so we had complete privacy. I made a good job of it, although my main length of fuse turned out to be a lot faster than the sample I had cut. I'm not sure whether I shot out of that cave together with the blast or just before it.

When the smoke had cleared Jim and I opened up the passage. Fortunately, as it turned out, the whole force of the explosion had been directed outward, showering debris onto our working floor, cracking the rock, but disturbing nothing beyond it. We had still a couple of hours of work with pick and crowbar before we could reduce it to rubble and climb over.

To my surprise the cave had done all the narrowing it was going to do and continued as a very rough v-shaped passage. I am not enough of a geologist to be sure of its origin. A combination of earthquake and steam pressure, I think.

Keeping the beams of our flashlights as much on the untrustworthy roof as on the ground, we cautiously followed the tunnel until it ended at an appalling abyss in the volcanic rock. That was where the warm air came from. A steam-heated hell fed by the tricklings-in at sea level or below. We threw down boulders and heard not the faintest sound. The gap was too wide to jump but fairly easy to bridge.

While I was wondering if I could ever pluck up enough courage to cross the homemade bridge which Jim—I knew it—was going to insist on constructing, he gave a shout. He was lying on his stomach examining from a respectful distance the sheer edge of that terrifying drop. He pointed to what he had found. Two shallow grooves for the beams of a bridge had been chiseled out of the rock. Our flashlights showed two corresponding grooves on the opposite side of the chasm.

I have never been nearer to believing in a drowned continent. Who wouldn't in a place like that? I had quite unjustifiable visions of the very last of the inhabitants clinging to a barren peak which later became the green island of Graciosa and using the cave as their temple or treasure house. Nothing impossible about the rock cutting. Atlanteans, if they existed, presumably had chisels of bronze or obsidian.

Oh, yes, I thought of that! I took some scrapings and dust home in an envelope. No trace of bronze or any metal at all. Not conclusive, but in favor of steel. Particles so tiny as those from a steel chisel would have been oxidized and blown away on a breath. The microscope did show a glassy dust like a form of obsidian, but even my Cornish blood refuses to build on that. A thousand to one that it was a natural component of the rock.

Farm work went overboard again. Serious, this time. There was a sudden squall from the south which laid the heavy, overripe wheat. Maria wept, but Jim damned the weather and continued to square the ends of two twenty-foot lengths of pine sapling with a ship-builder's adz so that they would fit the channels. On to these spars we nailed planks from the bottom of an old farm cart. The donkey was busy all day hauling timber up the slope.

By the next evening our bridge was ready. I don't believe we would ever have thrown it across the gap if not for Maria. She had a marvelous head for heights and just laughed at her husband, whose distaste for this beastly brink of nothingness was just as great as mine. But he was far more determined.

The roof of the passage was not high enough for us to stand the spars of the bridge in the grooves and lower the far end by ropes. So we mounted the near end on a pair of wheels and kept up the far end at an angle of forty-five degrees by pulling on a rope. Maria pushed this contraption forward, or acted as brake if we raised it too high. When we finally dropped the bridge into position, axle and wheels went over the edge. We never heard a sound after the first bounce.

Maria greeted the accident with a merry laugh. She was perfectly happy standing a foot from the edge—and after all, the old wheels weren't worth anything. She strolled about on the bridge with plump unconcern. Jim and I went over it on our hands and knees.

After a few yards the passage opened out into an irregular rock chamber too large for the beams of our flashlights to explore. The *senhora*, becoming the weaker sex again, remained at the entrance with a flashlight of her own. She didn't like that place at all.

Working our way round the walls, we had just decided that this was the end of the cave with no way out of it, when Maria let out a piercing scream. She had sat down with her back against the rock and a pool of light in front of her to keep off the bogeys. She stretched out her left hand to make herself more comfortable and placed it on the face of a corpse.

We rushed across to her. The dead man was a Spaniard or Portuguese of the early sixteenth century. Body, clothes and weapons were well preserved in the still, dry air. He was on his back, with arms crossed on his chest. He knew he had had it and laid himself down to die with dignity, trusting in the mercy of God. And there in the dust, undisturbed since his last unsteady steps, were the marks of his loose boots.

He had taken a sword or dagger thrust low down on the side of the throat. I should not have noticed the perforation of the mummified skin if the linen of his shirt had not been dark with dried blood.

It wasn't the expert, the scholar trained to facts and nothing but facts, who saw the vital bearing of a four-hundred-year-old murder on the problem of the ivory puma. It was Jim, of course—Jim with his passion for never destroying the record of the past through avoidable carelessness.

"We can find aht what 'appened, Mr. Penkivel, guv'," he said. "Spend a bit of time on it and we don't 'ave to be Sherlock 'Olmeses."

He was right. The pointed, rather feminine tracks, though the edges were blurred, were utterly unlike our own and told the story. Two men had crossed the chasm. Side by side they walked to the far right-hand corner of the cave. There the dust was thoroughly trampled and disturbed as if they had been removing something which they carried away. On their way back to the bridge the man walking a little behind had stabbed the other.

The murderer's footprints had been overlaid by ours, and were muddled anyway; but a set of clean impressions which we found pointing to the gap seemed unexpectedly deep and firm. My astonishing collaborator was not content with a "seemed." He measured the depth of the heel prints. No doubt about it at all. The murderer when he left the inner cave was weighed down by his comrade's burden as well as his own.

The movements of the other were equally clear. When he fell forward he left impressions of his knees and body. About where his neck would have been, a patch of dust was caked by blood. Badly wounded or dying, he had then risen to his feet, staggered to where Maria nearly sat on him and crossed his hands on his breast.

You see why. Because the trusted companion who had stabbed him from behind made doubly sure of him by destroying the bridge. So he lay down to wait for the end. No weeping and cursing on the edge of that uncrossable abyss for him. His simple act made me understand the contemporaries of Cortes and Pizarro as no books could. Probably he had the sense to see that the sword had been merciful, that he hadn't long to live. Even so I think that if the corpse had been mine it would have been found on the brink of the chasm with arms outstretched and mouth open.

I could now make a plausible guess at how the ivory puma came to be in the outer cave. The murderer, repacking his loot, had got rid of it as an object of no value and inconvenient bulk. But it pleased him. He was a man of the Renaissance. I like to think of him as an Italian. So he stood it on the rock ledge instead of just throwing it away.

We found no concrete evidence of what the valuables had been. Maria with her quick fingers helped us to sift the dust. Nothing. Not even a spilt coin. But there was no need to drag in Atlantis. Boxes of gold and silver must often have gone astray in those days when the treasure fleets called at the Azores on their homeward voyage from the Spanish Main. The two adventurers, I suggested, could have been removing from the cave a hoard of stolen loot.

Jim did not deny it. He didn't stick to his lost continent. He merely pointed out, as modestly as the more courteous type of Oxford don, that I was ignoring inconvenient facts without explaining them.

"'Ow about the footprints of the blokes what put it there?" he asked.

I hadn't thought of that. Obviously the prints of the blokes who put it there—whatever "it" was—were not visible at the time of the murder or they would be visible still. So in the sixteenth century they had already been obliterated by slow time. In that case the treasure had been put in the cave long before the Azores were discovered.

By now I was unconsciously treating Jim as an authority. I suspect that my voice echoed through the darkness in a genuine academic falsetto as I tried to answer his question by complicated theories involving drafts of air cut off by the fallen boulder. But I had to admit that the case for Atlantis could not be finally dismissed.

You would have thought he'd have jumped at it and driven home another point, too—that the chiseled footings we had found suggested a permanent bridge, not the casual construction which would have been thrown across the abyss by two fearless conquistadors hiding or seeking a hoard of loot.

Jim stuck to the evidence, however, and nothing but the evidence. He squatted on the floor sucking his teeth—and then he blew his own beloved Atlantis sky high.

"Them two was puttin' somethink in," he said, "not takin' it aht!"

And he fiddled around some more in the marks of the heels with flashlight and foot ruler.

He was on to the truth. The tracks which led from the entrance to the disturbed corner were deeper than the tracks which led back to the site of the murder. So there it was. The two men *were* putting something in. They did not find a treasure in the inner cave at all. They carried it in across their bridge and dumped it.

So far, so good—but if that was what really happened, the murderer had to return from his victim to the corner in order to pick up the two loads and make off with them. And his tracks must still be there.

They were. Along the wall all the way. That's why we had missed them. Reconstruction was easy. Torch or candle had gone out in the struggle, so the murderer felt his way back to the treasure round the wall. Wounded man also had a pistol—a very fine one for its date—which may have influenced the cautious movements of the other.

"Not what you wanted, Jim," I said. "I'm sorry. But you're a lot better off."

"Fifty-fifty, Mr. Penkivel, sir," he answered sternly.

I knew he must have noticed it. There was nothing his eyes missed, though, of course, he could not know the value of the emerald set in the pommel of the dead man's sword. Nor could I in the beam of a flashlight. But it was worth a lot for its extraordinary size even if flawed, as it almost certainly had to be.

I turned his offer down flat. In proportion to his resources, Jim had contributed to an archaeological expedition more than any millionaire's fund ever dreamed of. He was entitled to the finds, if any.

And then that amazing man reflected doubtfully, "Would yer say we 'ad the right to take it aht, guv'? We're 'ere for knowledge, not treasure 'unting."

I assured him that there were plenty of sixteenth-century swords in the world and that this was of no special value except for the emerald set roughly and strongly into the hilt. Safest place to keep it, I suppose.

Well, yes, I must admit it was a superb weapon. But I wanted Jim to have the emerald; and I didn't know enough about the Portuguese law of treasure trove to be sure that if he produced sword and emerald as they were he would be allowed the value. Take it from me—state museums don't like paying out when they can get something for nothing.

"O.K., guv'nor," he said. "Sell it for me when yer gets 'ome because I wouldn't know 'ow. And you 'ave the ivory puma for the museum."

Why isn't it on exhibition? I've told you. Because the blasted thing is impossible! It asks us to assume a lost culture with affinities to both Old World and New. Yes, naturally, I had it dated by the radiocarbon method. The very large elephant which supplied the ivory died not later than 2000 B.C.

Origin unknown. All we can say. Nothing surprising in

that. Every great museum has some lovely thing in the basement waiting for the day when our successors will know enough to be able to label it.

There was nothing else in the cave worth recording. Jim and I decided to leave the body where it was and remove our bridge. Like a couple of idiots we talked of cementing a ring bolt into the roof so that we could support the far end while we pulled it back. Maria's feminine common sense soon dealt with that.

"But why not drop it down the hole?" she asked in her lilting Portuguese. "We can always make another."

It's the end of the story. Unsatisfactory, as I told you, except for Jim. I got him six thousand pounds for the emerald.

The chiseled bridge footings? Oh, those! Well, the romanticist—that's me—finds them so inexplicable that he is re-examining (please keep it to yourself!) the case for Atlantis. The cold-blooded authority—that's Jim—suggested that our two adventurers made a solid bridge because they intended at some later date to bring over a heavy mule train of stuff which they did not want to risk losing.

Possible, but odd. Remember they only entered the inner cavern once. They never explored it at all while they were building their bridge or afterward. They carried in their mysterious loot straightway and dumped it. Doesn't that look as if the bridge was already there?

And doesn't it suggest a sudden, hasty decision, not the behavior of men stacking away valuables in a carefully chosen hiding place? My own guess is that they found the cave and the treasure at the same time. They didn't know what to do with such wealth, how to ship it and dispose of it. So they agreed to carry it into the inner cave for the moment and perhaps break down the bridge.

Where did they find it? In the outer cave, of course, where it had remained untouched ever since it was abandoned by desperate refugees from the sunken cities of the plain on the lost continent of Atlantis.

The Trap
by Kem Bennett

Kem Bennett is a British author and translator who only occasionally indulges in fantasy and science fiction. Among his works are "The Devil's Current," "Fabulous Wink" and "Passport for a Renegade." In this story Bennett gives us a first contact story with a light touch. His aliens from Zinfandel look like the standard horrors of the 50s science fiction film, but act more like Vonnegut's "Trafalmadorians" as they gleefully rush about gathering people in "The Trap."

The Trap

by Kem Bennett

Early one May morning a flying saucer hovered over the small town of Walker, California. Nobody was about to see it, and without attracting the slightest attention, it came quietly to earth on the outskirts of the town on Highway 399. Having settled itself, it then changed—that is to say, it lost the well-known shape of a flying saucer and acquired instead that of a roadside eating house, complete with neon signs saying, CHARLIE'S LUNCH—Steaks, Dogs, Burgers. SOUTHERN FRIED CHICKEN A SPECIALITY.

At six a trucker called Ollie Lindberg, new to the route and therefore lacking the habit of eating anyplace in particular, pulled his rig into the forecourt of CHARLIE'S LUNCH, got out, tried the door, found it open and walked inside. He never came out.

Not far away, a man in pajamas stood at his bedroom window, yawning. When he saw CHARLIE'S LUNCH in the distance, he blinked and frowned; turned away from the window, shaking his head and wondering if his eyes deceived him. Taking a second look, he was just in time to see a flying saucer take off from an empty lot on Highway 399. The police were at first cynical, but after they had examined Ollie Lindberg's deserted rig, they changed their tune slightly.

Two days later, a restaurant landed near Greenway, Virginia, where it abducted a colored girl called Esmeralda Dingle, who dropped in for a soda on her way to work.

These events made happy times for the press. The newspapers went to town with banner headlines like SABRE JETS

STAND BY, DON'T USE STRANGE EATERIES, PHYSICISTS SAY IT CAN'T HAPPEN, and IS THIS THE PRELUDE TO INVASION? Then reports from France, where a saucer simulated a roadside bistro; and from England, where another displayed the versatility to turn itself into a mock-Tudor public house, complete with phony oak beams and plasterwork, spread the publicity over the face of the world. The only element of the world's population who failed to enjoy the sensation were the proprietors of the remoter eating places, whose trade fell off considerably.

The farmer stopped his station wagon on the main highway before turning into the dirt-road entrance to his farm. "This is as far as I go, friend. There's an intersection a mile up the road. Ain't nothing there but a gas station, but you should be able to thumb a ride into Gallup easy enough."

Jeremy thanked him, got out, fished his rucksack out of the back of the wagon, waved as the farmer drove down the dirt road, and then trudged off in the direction of the intersection. The vastness of America's Southwest stretched away for mile after mile on every side. Now for the first time this vastness pressed in on Jeremy, reminding him of his loneliness, his poverty and his utter lack of prospects. While he trudged he thought of Los Angeles, where he had been a writer until the panic impact of three-dimensional pictures had caused his studio to drop his option like a hot brick. Los Angeles meant the following things to Jeremy; success, three pictures, three years with money dripping out of his trousers pockets, marriage to an actress with plenty of shape, no scruples and a ratlike disdain for sinking ships, an imported car, and a house off Beverly Glen Boulevard in the Santa Monica Mountains. It had also meant two years with no pictures, less and less money, less and less house, car and actress.

Had he had the wit, he told himself as his tattered boots

scuffed up the dust of the roadside, he would have got out quickly—while there was still enough money in the bank to buy him a ticket back to England. In England the 3-D scare was over before it ever arrived. In England, with Hollywood glamour and three credits to help him, he could hardly have failed to dig a living out of the picture business.

In England he might even have been able to go back to writing the sort of thing writers ought to write—novels, for example, or anyway short stories. Mug!

Five minutes later, Jeremy lifted his gaze from the dusty black surface of the highway, already warming up as the morning sun got into its stride, and looked ahead with narrowed eyes. In the distance he could see the intersection, marked by a transverse line of telegraph poles and two low, shacklike buildings. One of these he readily identified by its pumps as the gas station that the farmer had mentioned, and the other had the look of a roadside café.

He put his hand into his trousers pocket, feeling the shape and pleasant solidity of the silver quarter, which was all the money he possessed. Coffee? Or maybe a sandwich? Or a pack of cigarettes? His mouth watered. Forget the cigarettes.

Jeremy's pace increased. Head bent, rucksack pushing him forward and downward as he leaned into his stride, he drove his lankiness toward the intersection.

Then, sometime later, he stopped. "Ain't nothing there but a gas station," the farmer had said. Jeremy stared, frowning, toward the intersection. Two buildings—one of them, by now, unmistakably a gas station, and the other, equally unmistakably, an eating place. Recent headlines leaped into his mind's eye. Then he shrugged. *Don't be a fool, Jeremy, my boy; the farmer must have forgotten.*

But the farmer hadn't forgotten. At the roadside two hundred yards from the intersection, a woman and two children cowered in the ditch while a man in greasy mechanic's overalls stood above them, staring toward the café. He had a shotgun in his hands.

"Good morning," Jeremy said.

The man turned. His eyes were bright with panic. "It's one of Them! I tell you it's one of Them!"

"How do you know?"

"Last night when we went to bed, it ain't there. This morning it is. It's one of Them, bud! It's got to be!"

"Well," Jeremy said, "fancy that."

"Come again?" The gas-station proprietor was looking at Jeremy as if he suspected he were a Martian. "Who are you, anyway?"

"I'm an Englishman. Flat broke. Trying to get home. I was a writer in Hollywood until the roof fell in."

"Oh." Part of the suspicion died out of the eyes of the man in overalls. "What are you gonna do?" he said.

Jeremy had his rucksack on the ground. He opened it and took out a pencil and a notebook. He was smiling. "I'm going to have a look at it."

"You must be crazy! You don't know what the thing'll do. You stay away from it, bud. Maybe it'll go away if we leave it alone."

Jeremy shook his head. "No. I don't think it'll do me any harm so long as I don't go in. I'm going to take a look."

The woman whispered, "Don't go, mister. Those things ain't natural."

Jeremy smiled at her. Then he walked away.

A pulse beat—thud, thud, thud,—inside his head and in the soles of his feet. He hadn't felt anything like it since Anzio in 1944.

This is it, an inward voice was saying. *This is your chance, Jeremy boy. Eyewitness account—syndicated all over the world. Why did I sell my camera? My heaven, this is it.* He started to wonder how much a first-class suite on the Queen Elizabeth would cost him.

REST-A-WHILE CAFÉ, the sign said over the door. COME

IN AND EAT! COFFEE, FRANKS, HOT DOGS. OUR BEER IS COLD!

Jeremy stopped at a safe distance—thirty yards. Was it safe? It felt safe. He propped his notebook on his knee, leaning with his back against a telegraph pole, and sketched the place with careful attention to detail. Then he scribbled down his thoughts. The windows revealed no movement. He waited.

Nothing happened. Jeremy took a few paces forward. A few more. Reluctantly, suspiciously, a few more again. He came to the porch and stopped. Could this—this monument of American ordinariness—be a flying saucer in disguise, a visitation, a creation of nonhuman beings? For heaven's sake!

In a moment of careless disbelief, he put his foot on the step of the porch. Nothing happened. He advanced. Nothing happened. He reached out his arm and gently opened the door. Inside there was a service counter, tables with plastic tops, peeling chromium fittings, behind the counter, a cash register, and a Man.

The Man was as tall as Jeremy—six feet and a little more. He had a brown face and graying hair, well-kept brown hands resting gently on the counter, and a warm welcoming smile. He wore a white apron with a name embroidered over the breast pocket—Charlie Smith.

"Good morning," he said in English. "What can I get you, friend?"

"Good morning. I—I don't know. I can't make up my mind whether to eat or not."

"I should if I were you," the Man said. "Got to eat to live, you know."

"The trouble is I'm pretty broke. What can you give me for twenty-five cents?"

"Are you an American?" the Man behind the bar asked.

"No. English."

"Down on your luck?"

"A bit."

The Man nodded sympathetically. "Can happen to anybody. Do you like roast beef and Yorkshire pudding?"

"Ye-es."

"I thought you would, being an Englishman." The Man turned, slid open a hatch and reached for a plate of roast beef and Yorkshire pudding. "There you are—roast beef and Yorkshire pudding—ten cents, since you're broke."

Jeremy had taken a pace backward. With a very dry mouth, he said huskily, "Look! I know! I know what you are—or at least I know you aren't what you seem to be."

"Don't you want your roast beef?" the Man said.

"Not likely!"

"Oh." The Man was disappointed. He took the plate off the counter.

"Where do you come from?" Jeremy asked.

Silence. The Man wiped the counter with a dishcloth. He looked up. "You wouldn't know if I told you."

"Not Mars?"

"No, not Mars."

"What happened to the other people who walked into one of your—your traps?"

"They were taken back to our World."

Jeremy laughed. "Well, you're not going to get me, chum," he said. "I'm going to write up every word of this fantastic conversation and it'll be printed in every newspaper in the world. After that you'll not find it so easy to get people to walk into your filthy traps."

"I'm afraid," the Man said, pressing a button, "that we've got you already."

There were more vistations. Reports came in from the Argentine, Australia, Japan, France again, Germany, Scotland, Switzerland and Sweden. In the States, one of the traps caught a mentally deficient boy of fifteen when it landed on a vacant lot in a suburban-development area near Detroit. But in the States by now, and in Europe, too, for that matter, the pickings were less easy for the saucers.

In a town in England, housing mostly miners working in nearby coal fields, a man threw a bundle of five pounds of gelignite through the window of a suspect roadhouse, but before the fuse had burned through, the restaurant changed back into a saucer and was off.

In the States again, near Fort Benning, an Army tank crept into range and pumped a high-velocity three-inch shell into one of the traps. Again it instantly changed shape and flew away, and nobody was near enough to say whether it had a hole in it or not. After that there were no more visitations in England or the United States of America and the newspapers chortled their triumph for weeks, until their readers were bored to death with the subject.

The visitations in remoter parts of the world declined in number and the day came when no human being had seen a flying saucer land for more than a year. Then, early one chilly November morning, when the smog was lying thick over Los Angeles, a police prowl car at La Canada spotted a saucer landing in the valley below, somewhere in the vicinity of Montrose. Radios yakked and chattered. Police cars like swarming bees flocked to Montrose to prowl the streets in search of an unfamiliar restaurant. By half past seven they had found it, a squat, California sort of eating place, ranch style, calling itself THE GAUCHO GRILL.

The National Guard turned out. Reporters gathered. Three television trucks arrived and half a dozen mobile radio transmitters. While the commander of the National Guard detachment was waiting for the word to open fire in his command vehicle, parked in a side street behind

THE GAUCHO GRILL, the restaurant door opened and Jeremy walked out.

In the street outside, he paused indecisively, looking right and left at the police cordons. Then, with a shrug, he walked slowly toward the cordon on the right, holding his hands at shoulder level and eying the battery of pistols and Tommy guns which were covering him with an expression of apprehensive distaste. He was wearing a gray suit, as well cut and conventional as one that his London tailor might have made for him, and he looked very well indeed.

When Jeremy was a few paces away from the cordon, a police captain snarled, "Hold it! One false move and you get the lot, buster!"

Jeremy stopped. He swallowed, finding it difficult to know what to say.

"I'm human."

"Yeah?"

"I'm called Jeremy Standing. I'm an Englishman. I'd been living in the States for five years when I walked into —into one of those places at an intersection on Highway 66 near Gallup, New Mexico, on the fifth of May the year before last."

A woman in the crowd shouted, "Don't you believe him, officer! He's a monster in disguise! Whyn't you shoot? You never know what he'll do!"

"I'm not a monster in disguise," Jeremy said huskily. "Please believe me. I'm an Englishman. My name's Jeremy Standing. I told you—"

"Funny name," the police captain said. "Where've you been, mister?"

"On a planet outside our galaxy, hundreds of millions of miles from the earth. I—"

"What's it called?"

"They call it Zinfandel."

"Never heard of it."

"I don't expect you have. It exists, though. I'm not lying. Why should I lie? I——"

"What do you want?" the police captain growled.

Jeremy shrugged. "I've come back, that's all. I don't know what I want, really. I want to write about it, I suppose. I've got ideas for a film, and I thought maybe——"

A man with a microphone was pushing his way through the crowd, trailing cable behind him. "Make way there! Make way, please! . . . I bet you got ideas, Mr. Standing! I bet you have, yes, sir! Now, what about telling the people of America what it was like on—on Zin—— What'd you say the planet was called?"

"It was called Zinfandel!"

"No need to shout, Mr. Standing. Now what was it like? Just tell the nation everything you know about this far-flung planet. You're the first man alive——"

"It was beautiful," Jeremy interrupted. "Green. Mountainous—at any rate in the place where I spent most of my time. That was a city called Arryl. The houses are built of a crystalline material which lets in the sunlight. There are strange trees everywhere, and flowers—just like the earth, but different in that much of the vegetation is different. They have daffodils, though, and narcissi that you couldn't tell from terrestrial ones. There must be a lot of other things that are the same there, but it depends upon a coincidence of evolution, you see—I don't know. I couldn't see everything, after all. Zinfandel is a planet slightly bigger than Earth."

"What did you do?" a voice shouted from the crowd.

"I—I lived," Jeremy answered. "I told my friends all that I could about Earth."

"Friends! You mean the inhabitants of Zinfandel, Mr. Standing?" the radio reporter queried.

"Of course—and my other friends, too, the people who had walked into one of the eating places as I did; there were about ten of them in Arryl and others in other cities.

There were three Americans in Arryl. I have their names, if you'd like me to broadcast them."

"Sure, sure. Carry on, Mr. Standing."

"Well, there was a James Minden from New York; and a Miss Esmeralda Dingle, a colored lady from Greenway, Virginia; and an Ollie Lindberg, of Santa Monica, California. I'd like their relatives to know that they're well and happy."

The police captain rubbed his cheek with the barrel of his police positive. "Why were you taken, Standing? What's the reason behind all these abductions?"

"Curiosity," Jeremy said simply. "The scientists on Zinfandel wanted to know how human beings worked."

A woman standing up in the back seat of a convertible shrieked, "Oh, my heaven! He means vivisection!"

"No!" Jeremy was angry. "No," he shouted, "nothing like that! Some of us volunteered for physical examinations, but mostly we just talked, and answered questions. All about our life on Earth, and wars, and politics, and things like that."

The police captain nodded slowly. "O.K. That may be true. But now tell me this: You're back, why aren't the others?"

"Because they didn't want to come."

"Didn't want to come! Don't give me that stuff! You mean to say—"

For almost the first time now, Jeremy smiled. There was an air of knowledge about him, an almost professorial assurance. The threat of dying under the impact of police bullets seemed to have gone. He was holding himself easily, and he looked like a man without a worry in the world.

"Life on Zinfandel is pleasant to live," he interrupted quietly.

"Better than here on Earth?" the radio reporter queried.

"Better than life in the United States of America? That's mighty hard to believe, Mr. Standing."

"I'm sorry if I seemed not to appreciate the American way of life," Jeremy said. "But believe me, life on Zinfandel is far and away happier than anything we have ever known."

"How come it's so good?" the police captain wanted to know.

"There is no poverty, hunger or disease," Jeremy answered. "What one needs is there for—for the making. One works if one wants to, not unless. One just lives. And the air on Zinfandel contains a higher proportion of oxygen than terrestrial air. One's brain is marvelously alive, like a child's brain—curious, seeking, unworried, infinitely free to be used. Do you see what I mean?"

"More or less," the police captain said. "Sounds to me like the mountains. I go to the mountains every summer with my kids. Got a shack up there."

Silence. A fat man behind the police captain said suddenly, "What did you eat, mister?"

"Anything," Jeremy answered. "Broiled steak and fried potatoes, Chesapeake Bay oysters, fried fish and chips, roast beef and Yorkshire pudding."

"Do you mean to say their food's just like ours, for Pete's sake?"

"Oh, no. Their food is so much better than anything we know that most of us stopped making things like steak and oysters after a while. We ate Zinfandel food because we liked it better."

"What's this 'making things,' Mr. Standing?" the radio reporter cut in. "You keep on talking about making things. Would you care to explain?"

Jeremy looked at the crowd. His expression became a little doubtful. Then he shrugged. In for a penny, in for a pound. "It's very simple," he said. "One can make things by thinking them into existence."

Silence. The crowd took the information, chewed on it, said nothing.

Then, raucously, from the back, a voice shouted, "How's about making me a blonde, buster? Make her like Marilyn Monroe."

Jeremy said, "You can't make anything with a soul—that is, you can make the body, but it wouldn't be inhabited, if you see what I mean."

"Inhabited, hell! Just make the body, that's all!"

"You wouldn't like it if I did!" Jeremy shouted.

A quiet, pinched little woman ducked beneath a policeman's arm. "Make something," she said. "Go on, sir. Show us. Make something we can see."

"What?"

"A—a diamond bracelet."

Jeremy held out his hand. The bracelet glinted and glittered in the pale November sunshine.

"What are we waiting for?" shouted the man beside the police captain.

From the windows of THE GAUCHO GRILL the Man who liked to call himself Charlie Smith on his visits to Earth saw the crowd stampeding down the street. He hesitated no longer than a split second. Too many. Dangerous. If they overflowed from the restaurant out into the street many might be injured during the time of the metamorphosis. Then there was accommodation on the journey to be considered; he could expand the saucer up to certain limits, but not beyond. Poor creatures.

Standing in the road outside the restaurant, he let ten people past him—the police captain and the man beside him, because they had a flying start and were first, several younger people who could run faster than the majority and, last of the ten, the quiet little woman who had asked Jeremy to make something. Behind her there was a gap in the crowd.

Charlie Smith held up his arms—and they changed into

tentacles. His body became insectlike, scaly; it thickened; it took on a greenish-yellow color and a metallic sheen. His eyes increased in diameter, became multilensed, like the eyes of a housefly and shone dully and terrifyingly red. Four more tentacles grew from his thorax, and his legs took on the shape of a beetle's. His gross metallic body canted forward until it was on all fours, more or less, supported by his beetle legs and two of the tentacles. The terrible eyes shone redly at the leading members of the crowd, and the remaining four tentacles waved slowly in the air—in readiness, it seemed, to grasp or to flicker out like striking snakes.

The crowd came to a standstill. The ones in front pressed backward and the ones behind readily gave way. There was a deathly silence and a stillness that was as brittle as ice.

Jeremy worked his way through the crowd. He held up his arms. "I'm sorry!" he shouted. "I'm afraid you've frightened him!"

Silence.

A woman's voice shrieked, "He's afraid we've frightened him!" Her hysterical laughter shattered the stillness.

Jeremy held up his arms again. "There are too many of you, that's the trouble. I expect they'll be back for more, but they can't take everybody, don't you see?"

A man said, "My heaven, look at it! Horrible! Just like a beetle!"

Jeremy turned. He went up to the beetle. Tentacles wavered, feeling his face. A sensitive man at the back of the crowd frowned as it dawned upon him that this was affection—a parting.

The beetlelike creature scuttled into the restaurant. The building shimmered, dissolved, became a silver saucer-shaped machine, rose a hundred feet vertically from the ground and was gone.

In the road, Jeremy stood still, looking up in the air,

following the flight of the saucer until it was no longer even a speck in the sky.

After a while, as their confidence returned, the people advanced again. When Jeremy tore his eyes from the blueness of the sky and looked at the crowd gathered around him, a burly individual in the uniform of an ice-cream peddler said, "O.K., mister. How about making me a gold brick for a start?"

Jeremy saw greed entering the faces of the crowd. He waited for a moment; then shrugged and held out his hand. A small block of gold materialized in the palm—yellow, yellow as sunlight! A great gasp of awed delight rose from two hundred throats.

Jeremy threw back his right arm. With the powerful round-arm swing of the grenade-throwing infantryman, he hurled the gold block far over the crowd's heads onto the open space the saucer had just vacated. For a split second the people in the crowd were paralyzed. Then they moved. The gold block disappeared beneath a heap of struggling, cursing human beings.

A police car nearby had its door open. A gruff voice said, "Better get in, Mr. Standing. Looks as though you're going to need a bodyguard from now on."

"Yes," Jeremy said. "Thank you."

He got in. The door slammed shut. The car edged forward. One of the two cops in the front seat sucked his teeth and said, "You shouldn't have let on you could make things, Mr. Standing. You'll never get any peace, now that folk know about it."

A thought was coming to Jeremy across a thousand miles of sky. It was coming from the Man who called himself Charlie Smith. "When you are ready, Jeremy."

Jeremy opened his eyes. "Yes," he said to the cop on the front seat. "But, then, I can always go back. . . . Now, what can I make for you two boys?"

Space Secret
by William Sambrot

In "Space Secret" William Sambrot gave us the contact story which anticipated the work of Enrich Von Daniken and the premise of Clarke and Kubricks' "2001." Man is probably not alone in the universe and a motive of hostility as a main objective of an alien race visiting earth is absurd in the face of logic. Organic life is likely to be quite rare in the universe. The idea of cooperation or cultural manipulation by a more advanced space-faring race would seem far more reasonable in the face of a sterile universe in which life has but a tenuous hold.

Space Secret

by William Sambrot

I am sending this report by special courier. I am personally unable to deliver it because I wish to be on hand to forestall any possible repercussions which might yet arise from the charges made by Dr. John Lassiter, of the Rand Corporation. Lassiter insists that the original video tape taken by the successful American moon rocket yesterday was stolen during the night and a substitute put in its place.

As you know, the successful moon shot was made with a rocket that carried an electronic camera, operating with photoelectric cells which transmitted pictures onto electronically sensitized tape. The rocket made the run to the moon and swung around, photographing the far side, which has never been seen from earth. Then continuing on around, executing a vast figure 8, the rocket shot back toward earth, circled it and finally made a successful reentry in the Pacific Ocean.

Although it was anticipated that the far side of the moon was in no way different from the near side, the prestige of being the first to have taken pictures of it was enormous. And quite naturally the Air Force made every effort, once the nose cone was recovered, to keep the video tape secret. It was rushed by special jet to the Air Force's Research and Development building in Santa Monica, known as Rand Corporation. There it was to be processed by Doctor Lassiter.

After the tape was processed, apparently Lassiter had

viewed it privately—a breach of security. What he saw caused him to send urgent summonses to all the top echelon of the Air Force and Rand Corporation. I was able, because of my position at Rand, to be among the four or five who were permitted to view the second showing.

John Lassiter, Ph.D., a theoretical physicist, topflight mathematician and electronics expert, is in his early forties, tall, rather thin, with penetrating eyes. He is a standout, intellectually, in a building full of geniuses. Rand Corporation, in Santa Monica, consists of about eight hundred brilliant people: scientists, economists, mathematicians, physicists, cybernetics and electronics experts, and the like. Also, they have a list of another two hundred fifty consultants on the outside, on whom they draw from time to time for expert advice.

For the record, the business of Rand Corporation is that of evaluating any given idea and projecting its inherent possibilities into the future. They have been correct on a great many occasions. For example, working from known data concerning the U.S.S.R.'s rocket potential, they accurately forecast the first Sputnik—an event of some importance, you will agree.

We assembled in the viewing room in the Rand building, with Air Police outside the door and scattered throughout the entire building and grounds. Security was complete.

Before he showed the tape, Lassiter made an impromptu speech which I consider well worth repeating:

"Gentlemen," he said quietly, "history has always interested me. Not the history of the textbooks, but the history of legends, of primitive peoples; the stories handed down through the millenniums. And among these, without fail, in any civilization, we come across a strangely similar belief—a legend of gods who descended from the sky to walk the earth like men."

He held up a hand, ticking off on his fingers as he talked.

"On the American continent we have the Mayans, the Incas, with their beliefs that bearded white gods would once more come back—gods who taught them their science, their mathematics, how to smelt ore, cut rock; gods who came from the sky. And there are the Polynesians, surrounded by the vast Pacific, who worship the red-headed bearded white god, who landed on Easter Island—the Eye to Heaven, as they call it. Everywhere throughout the world primitive men lifted their eyes to the skies for salvation, longing for the return of those kindly brilliant far-travelers, whose science so far outstripped their own."

He paused. "The pattern continues down to our time. Only, now, it appears to be one of watching—and waiting. But I won't bore you with flying saucers or Fortian proofs of visitors from other worlds. We have here"—he touched the kinescope—"our own proof. Proof that our planetary system teems with life, with science that is to our atomic piles what our atomic piles are to bonfires. Proof that we are not alone, not lost in the immensity of the infinite universe. We are not alone—and here's the proof, in color."

He switched on the kinescope. Instantly the screen came alive, showing the brilliant blue-black velvet of outer space, the stars, glowing in colors seen only outside the earth's atmosphere—greens, yellows, fiery reds, icy blues, burning steadily, without a flicker. The men in the room gasped. The rocket was approaching the moon closer and closer, the chilling whites and dead blacks looming closer and clearer.

"Now," Lassiter whispered. "Now you'll see. It's going to the far side—the side never before seen by man."

The scene on the screen moved along. Formidable mountains—sheer, fantastic slender needle spires, defying even the faint gravity of the moon. Immense pits, filled with the rubble of ancient disasters. More pits, more mountains, slashing crazy patterns of eye-hurting light and utter black of shadow without depth—and slowly, slowly the moon moved under the rocket until, visible faintly, the swollen greenish-blue rim of earth appeared, off in space. The rocket began leaving the moon and approaching the earth again. The tape came to an end. The lights came up. We turned, as one, and looked at Lassiter.

He was seated, motionless, eyes unblinking, only his large sensitive hands tightly clenched before him. He stared at the screen.

"It's beautiful," I said, "but no more so than we'd expected. Other than the prestige of having been first—well, really, Lassiter, the far side is no different from the side we've seen since the beginning of time."

"It's not the same!" He stood up, and his voice was a terrible broken shout in the soundproofed room. "That's not the tape I saw last night!"

There was an immediate stir in the room, and some of the Air Force people looked alarmed.

"Listen to me! Please!" He stood up, his face gray, his eyes stricken, like a man who has seen glory suddenly leave him forever. "Listen!"

We quieted. Already I heard one of the Air Force officers muttering something about, "Crazy as a hoot owl."

"Last night"—Lassiter began, pointing to the screen—"last night, on that screen——" His voice trembled slightly, as though in despair at ever being able to convey what he'd seen. "How can I begin to explain what I saw?" he whispered. We sat tensely, watching, listening. "How can I tell of the buildings there? The colors, the smoothly flowing lines of architecture? Slim, airy, yet full of strength. Serene, mature. Yes, that's it—mature. Water, trees, parks. And the spaceships——"

He paused, and when he repeated it, it was more a groan than a phrase. "The spaceships. One of them was taking off. Rising straight up, gently, swiftly, like a huge iridescent bubble. Light, incomparably lovely." His voice was suddenly subdued. "They have a source of power so far beyond us. So far beyond us——"

An Air Force man came to his feet. "Are you telling us that someone has had access to this room during the night and switched tapes on us?"

Lassiter turned and looked at him, his eyes peculiarly inward-looking. "Yes," he said.

"And the—the original tape showed a—a civilization on the other side of the moon?" There was frank disbelief in the officer's voice.

"A civilization compared to which we're still savages, crouching over a fire in a cave," he said.

The room was a hubbub of noise. I stood up and shouted for silence. When I got it, I looked at Lassiter. "Isn't the manufacture of that electronic tape a Rand Corporation top-secret process?"

He nodded. His mind was obviously far away.

"Who could possibly duplicate that process, then use the tape to take these obviously authentic shots of the moon approach—steal the original and substitute the duplicate—and all in one night?" I asked.

There was a murmur in the room—subdued laughter even.

Lassiter looked at me, and suddenly his eyes became keen, blazing with that truly great intelligence of his. "The same ones who are living on the other side of our moon."

There was a sudden silence in the room.

His glance swept us. "They're here—in this building. They switched the tapes. I repeat—the tape you saw just now is not the one I saw last night. And yet this substitute is authentic. It shows an actual moon-rocket approach."

"Whom do you suspect—Martians?" I said gently, giving the others in the room a significant look. They looked back, nodding slightly. One of the officers scribbled a hasty note and went to the door.

"Call them Martians, if you wish," Lassiter said softly. "Those ancient ones who visited here so many millenniums ago; who, out of pity or kindness—or maturity—taught the savages they found here the rudiments of civilization. Those far-travelers who still watch—and wait."

"You can't be serious, Lassiter," one of the Rand men said unhappily. "Even if there were such—such space people—why would they try to keep us in ignorance?"

"Because we're still savages!" he shouted. "Clever, murderous children, developing our brains, our skills, but never our emotions. How could they permit us to join them, the society of other worlds, until we achieve adulthood—genuine maturity? That's why they switched these films—so we couldn't really know."

He said more—much more. He pointed out the consistent pattern of failures that had harassed man's burgeoning space hopes. Failures he now understood to be deliberate stumbling blocks placed in mankind's path as it clawed—prematurely—for the stars. An altogether remarkable synthesis.

After exhaustive chemical analysis of the tape, it was proved to be of the same composition as stock still on the lab's shelves, which of a necessity, ruled out its being a substitute. After a few more reruns of the tape, the Air Force announced itself as well pleased with the brilliant success of the moon shot.

Lassiter, it was decided, had suffered a mental collapse because of overwork and the disappointment at discovering that the other side of the moon was no different from the side the earth has always seen. He is, as of this writing undergoing a series of psychiatric examinations which ought to disclose—but in all likelihood won't—that he is more sane than most of mankind. He is a remarkable individual, and I suggest that he be placed on the list of those to be watched most closely in the future.

Also, I recommend that steps be taken hereafter to intercept all camera-bearing rockets from earth while in flight, and prepared films or tapes substituted, thus avoiding another untoward incident, such as developed here.

For the Archives: Enclosed herewith is the original video tape which the U.S. Moon Rocket took of our lunar base.

Though I've made the journey from earth to moon and back innumerable times, I found Lassiter's description of this tape strangely moving. Especially his remark concerning the rather good shot of my own ship rising from the moon as I left with the substitute tape last night. He is right—it does indeed resemble an iridescent bubble.

The Unsafe Deposit Box
by Gerald Kersh

Gerald Kersh was a prolific and fascinating author: the writer of thousands of articles and short stories, novelist, playwright, screenwriter and a consummate master of the horror story. Among his best-known works were The Brighton Monster, Nightshade and Damnations *and the classic collection* Men Without Bones. *"The Unsafe Deposit Box" is a good example of his skill as a fantasist.*

The Unsafe Deposit Box

by Gerald Kersh

You have a sharp eye, sir, a very sharp eye indeed, if you recognize me by those photographs that used to appear in the newspapers and the sensational magazines about 1947. I fancy I must have changed somewhat since then; but yes, I am Peter Perfrement, and they did make a knight of me for some work I did in nuclear physics. I am glad, for once, to be recognized. You might otherwise mistake me for an escaped convict, or a lunatic at large, or something of that sort; for I am going to beg you to have the goodness to sit in this shadowy corner and keep your broad back between me and the door. Have an eye on the mirror over my head and you will in due course see the reflections of a couple of fellows who will come into this cozy little bar. Those men will be looking for me. You will perceive, by the complete vacuity of their expressions, that they are from Intelligence.

They'll spot me, of course, and then it will be, "Why, Sir Peter, how lucky to find you here!" Then, pleading business, they'll carry me off. And evading those two young men is one of the few pleasures left me in my old age. Once I got out in a laundry basket. Tonight I put on a workman's suit of overalls over my dinner suit and went to a concert. I intend to go back home to the Center after I've had my evening, but I want to be left alone a bit. Of course, I have nobody but myself to blame for any slight discomfort I may at present suffer. I retired once and for all, as I thought, in 1950. By then the inwardness of such atom bombs as we let off over, say, Hiroshima was public property. My work, as it seemed, was done.

So I withdrew to a pleasant little villa at the Cap des Fesses just outside that awful holiday resort Les Sables des Fesses in the south of France. Fully intended to end my days there, as a matter of fact—set up library and study there, and a compact but middling-comprehensive laboratory. I went to all the music festivals, drank my glass of wine on the *terrasse* of whatever café happened to take my fancy, and continued my academic battle with Doctor Frankenburg. This battle, which was in point of fact far less acrimonious than the average game of chess, had to do with the nature of the element fluorine. I take it that esoteric mathematics are, mercifully, beyond your comprehension; but perhaps you were told at school something of the nature of fluorine. This is the *enfant terrible* of the elements.

Fluorine, in temperament, is a prima donna and, in character, a born delinquent. You cannot keep it pure; it has such an affinity for practically everything else on earth, and what it has an affinity for, it tends to destroy. Now I had a theory involving what I can only describe to a layman as tame fluorine—fluorine housebroken and in harness. Doctor Frankenburg, whose leisure is devoted to reading the comic papers, used to say concerning this, "You might as well imagine Dennis the Menace as a breadwinner." However, I worked away not under pressure nor under observation, completely at my leisure, having access to the great computer at Assigny. And one day I found that I had evolved a substance which, for convenience, I will call fluorine 80+.

I do not mean that I made it merely in formula. The nature of the stuff, once comprehended, made the physical production of it really absurdly simple. So I made some —about six ounces of it, and it looked rather like a sheet of hard, lime-colored gelatin. And potentially this bit of gelatinous-looking stuff was somewhat more potent than a cosmic collision. Potentially, mark you—only potentially. As it lay in my hand, fluorine 80+ was, by all possible calculations, inert. You could beat it with a sledge hammer or burn it with a blowlamp, and nothing would happen. But under certain conditions—conditions which seemed to me at that time quite impossible of achievement—this morsel of matter could be unbelievably terrible. By unbelievably, I mean immeasurably. Quite beyond calculation.

The notebook containing my formula I wrapped in paper with the intention of putting it in the vault of the Banque Maritime des Sables des Fesses. The sheet of fluorine 80+ I placed between two pieces of cardboard, wrapped it likewise, and put it in my pocket. You see, I had a friend in the town with whom I often had tea, and he had a liking for the weird and the wonderful. Like the fool that I am, I proposed to amuse myself by showing him my sample and telling him that this inoffensive little thing, in a suitable environment, might cause our earth to go *pssst!*—in about as long as it takes for a pinch of gunpowder to flash in a match flame. So in high spirits I went into town, paid my visit to the bank, first having got a pot of Gentlemen's Relish and a jar of Oxford Marmalade for tea, and so called on Doctor Raisin.

He was another old boy who had outlived his usefulness, although time was when he had some reputation as an architect specializing in steel construction. "Something special for tea," I said and tossed my little package of fluorine 80+ on the table.

"Smoked salmon?" he asked.

Then I brought out the marmalade and the relish, and said, "No," chuckling like an idiot.

He growled, "Evidently you have just paid a visit to the Café de la Guerre Froide," and sniffed at me.

"No, I've just come from the bank."

"So," he said, "that's a parcel of money, I suppose. What's it to me? Let's have tea."

I said, "I didn't go to the bank to take something out, Raisin. I put something in."

"Make me no mystifications, if you please. What's that?"

"That," I said, "is proof positive that Frankenburg is wrong and I am right, Raisin. What you see there is half a dozen ounces of absolutely stable fluorine eighty-plus and a critical mass, at that!"

Dry as an old bone, he said, "Jargon me no jargons. As I understand it, an atomic explosion takes place when certain quantities of radioactive material arrive, in certain circumstances, at what you call 'critical mass.' This being the case, that little packet may, I take it, be considered dangerous?"

I said, "Rather so. There's about enough fluorine eighty-plus there to vaporize a medium-sized planet."

Raisin said, "A fluorine bomb, an ounce of nitroglycerin—it's all the same to me." Pouring tea, he asked nonchalantly, "How do you make it go off? Not, I gather, by chucking it about on tables?"

I said, "You can't explode it—as you understand an explosion—except under conditions difficult to create and useless once created; although, perhaps, while valueless as a weapon, it could be put to peaceful uses."

"Perhaps me no perhapses. A fighting cock *could* be used to make chicken broth. What did you want to bring it here for, anyway?"

I was a little put out. Raisin was unimpressible. I told him, rather lamely, "Well, neither you nor anyone else will ever see fluorine eighty-plus again. In about fourteen hours that piece there will—as you would put it—have evaporated."

"Why as *I* would put it? How do you put it?"

"Why, you see," I explained, "in point of actual fact, that stuff is exploding now. Only it's exploding very, very gradually. Now, for this explosion to be effectual as an explosion, we should have to let that mass expand at a temperature of anything over sixty degrees Fahrenheit in a hermetically sealed bomb case of at least ten thousand cubic feet in capacity. At this point, given suitable pressure, up she'd go. But when I tell you that before we could get such a pressure under which my fluorine eighty-plus would undergo certain atomic alterations, the casing of our ten-thousand-cubic-foot bomb would need to be at least two or three feet thick."

Being a Russian, Raisin stirred marmalade into his tea and interrupted. "It is a chimera. So let it evaporate. Burn your formula. Pay no further attention to it. . . . Still, since you have brought it, let's have a look at it." He undid the little parcel, and said, "I knew all along it was a joke." The paper pulled away, there lay nothing but a notebook.

I cried, "Good heavens—that ought to be safe in the bank! That's the formula!"

"And the bomb?"

"Not a bomb, Raisin—I've just told you that fluorine eighty-plus can't possibly be a bomb of its own accord. Confound it! I must have left it at the grocer's shop."

He said, "Is it poisonous?"

"Toxic? I don't think so. . . . Now wait a minute, wait a minute! I distinctly remember—when I left the house I put the formula in my right-hand coat pocket and the fluorine eighty-plus in the left. Now first of all I went to the Epicerie Internationale to get this marmalade and stuff, and so as not to crowd my left pocket I transferred. . . . Oh, it's quite all right, Raisin. There's nothing to worry about, except that this is not the kind of notebook I like to carry about with me. The sample is safe and sound in the bank. It was a natural mistake—the packages are very much alike in shape and weight. No cause for anxiety. Pass the Gentlemen's Relish, will you?"

But Raisin said, "This horrible little bit of fluorine—you left it in the bank, did you?"

"Fluorine eighty-plus. Well?"

"You bank at the Maritime?"

"Yes, why?"

"So do I. It is the safest bank in France. Its vaults—now follow me carefully, Perfrement—its vaults are burglar-proof, bombproof, fireproof, and absolutely airtight. The safe deposit vault is forty feet long, thirty feet wide and ten feet high. This gives it a capacity of twelve thousand cubic feet. It is maintained at a low humidity and a constant temperature of sixty-five degrees Fahrenheit. The walls of this vault are of hard steel and reinforced concrete three feet thick. The door alone weighs thirty tons, but fits like a glass stopper in a medicine bottle. Does the significance of all this sink in?"

"Why," I said, "why——"

"Yes, why? You can say that again. What you have done, my irresponsible friend," said Doctor Raisin, "is put your mass of fluorine eighty-plus in its impossible casing. That's the way with the likes of you. It would never dawn on you that a bomb might be an oblong thing as big as a bank. Congratulations!"

I said, "I know the manager, M. le Queux, and he knows me. I'll go and see him at once."

"It's Saturday. The bank's closed."

"Yes, I know, but I'll ask him to come over with his keys."

Raisin said, "I wish you luck."

A telephone call to M. le Queux's house got me only the information that he was gone for the weekend to Laffert, about eighty miles inland, up the mountain, where he had a bungalow. So I looked about for a taxi. But it was carnival weekend, and there was nothing to be got except one of those essentially French machines that have run on coal gas and kerosene, and have practically no works left inside them, and yet, like certain extremely cheap alarm clocks, somehow continue to go, without accuracy, but with a tremendous noise. And the driver was a most objectionable man in a beret, who chewed whole cloves of raw garlic all the time and shouted into one's face as if one were a hundred yards distant.

After a disruptive and malodorous journey, during which the car had twice to be mended with bits of wire, we reached Laffert, and with some difficulty found M. le Queux.

He said to me, "For you—anything. But to open the bank? No, I cannot oblige you."

"You had better," I said to him, in a minatory tone.

"But Sir Peter," said he, "this is not merely a matter of turning a key and opening a door. I don't believe you can have read our brochure. The door of the vault is on a time lock. This means that after the lock is set and the door closed, nothing can open it until a certain period of time has elapsed. So, precisely at 7:45 on Monday morning—but not one instant before—I can open the vault for you."

I said, "Then as I see it, you had better send for the locksmith and have the lock picked."

M. le Queux laughed. He said, "You couldn't open our vault without taking the door down." He spoke with a certain pride.

"Then I'm afraid I'll have to trouble you to have the door taken down," I told him.

"That would necessitate practically taking down the bank," M. le Queux said; and evidently he thought that I was out of my mind.

"Then," I said, "there's nothing for it *but* to take down the bank. Of course, there'll be compensation, I suppose. Still, the fact remains that, by the sheerest inadvertence, for which I hold myself greatly at fault, I have turned your bank-vault into a colossal bomb—a bomb compared with which your Russian multimegaton bombs are milk-and-water. Indeed, you would no more weigh or measure my fluorine eighty-plus in terms of mere megatons than you'd buy coal by the milligram or wine by the cubic centimeter."

"One of us is going crazy," said M. le Queux.

"Call a Hiroshima bomb a megaton," I said. "Dealing with my fluorine eighty-plus we have to make new tables. So a million megatons equal one tyrrannoton. A million tyrrannotons equal one chasmaton. A million chasmatons make one brahmaton. And after a million brahmatons we come to something I call an ultimon, because it is beyond even the scope of mathematical conjecture. In a certain number of hours from now—and we are wasting time talking, M. le Queux—if you don't get that vault of yours open, the universe will experience the shock of half a chasmaton. Please let me use your telephone."

So I called a certain branch of Security, and after that told a minister, who shall be nameless, to be so kind as to get a move on—referring him, of course, to several other nuclear experts, in case my own name was not enough for him. Thus I was able, within twenty minutes, to tell M. le Queux, "It's all arranged. Army and police are on the way. So are some colleagues of mine. The Custodia Safe Company, who installed your vault, are flying their best technicians into Fesses. We'll have your vault open in a couple of hours or so. I'm sorry if this inconveniences you, but it's got to be done, and you must put up with it."

He could only say, "Inconveniences me!" Then he shouted, "After this, Sir Peter Perfrement, you will kindly take your banking business elsewhere!"

I was sorry for him, but there was no time for sentiment just now, for I found myself caught in a sort of whirlpool of giddy activity. Accompanied by the usual quota of secret police from Security, four highly regarded nuclear physicists were rushed to Fesses. I was pleased to see among them my dear old enemy Frankenburg, who would have to admit that in the matter of fluorine he was totally confuted. There was also, of course, a swarm of policemen, both uniformed and in plain-clothes, and, goodness knows why, two doctors, one of whom kept talking and talking without rhyme or reason about fluorine being found in relatively high concentration in the human embryo and how good it was for children's teeth. An expert from the quiet old days of the high-explosive blitzes said that since one invariably evacuated the area surrounding an unexploded bomb until it was defused, it would be wise to evacuate Sables des Fesses.

At this the *maire* went into ecstasies of Gallicism. To evacuate this place at carnival weekend would be to ruin it—death rather than dishonor, and so forth. I said that if my fluorine 80+ blew, the problem of evacuation need not arise; for nobody anywhere, ever, would be any the wiser. The chief of police, giving me a suspicious look, said that the present danger was only hypothetical; but the panic that must attend a mass alarm would be inevitably disastrous. It would be necessary only to surround the block in which the bank was situated. This being in the business district of the town, and most of the offices shut up for the weekend, the matter might be accomplished—a hairsbreadth this side of impossibility.

So said the chief of police, filling a pipe as a pioneer fills his muzzle-loader with his last hard-bitten cartridge, and pointing it right at me. He made it clear, without speaking, that he thought this was all a put-up job, to get that bank vault open.

M. le Queux said, "But the armored car has been and gone, and the bank is just about empty of cash until Monday." Still the chief of police wasn't satisfied. Watching him tamp down the charge in his pipe, I could not help reciting a hunting proverb of my grandfather's: *Ram tight the powder, leave loose the lead, if you want to kill dead.* He made a note of that. Meanwhile, Frankenburg and the others were poring over my notes, which I had been compelled to hand over.

Frankenburg growled, "I want to check, and double-check. I want a computer. I want five days."

But little Doctor Imhof said, "Come, we must grant the possibility that what we read here is valid. Even for the sake of argument we must grant it."

"Well, for the sake of argument," said Frankenburg. "So?"

"So," said Imhof, "*any* relaxation of pressure must render Perfrement's so-called fluorine eighty-plus harmless, must it not? This being the case, a hole drilled in the vault door should be an ample measure of precaution. This hole made, why, let the matter wait until Monday."

"So be it," said I. "He talks sense."

So now the engineers from the Custodia Company, having come in by plane, unloaded their massive paraphernalia in the bank. And among the cylinders and eye shields and other gear I noticed a number of gas masks. "What are they for?" I asked le Queux.

Frankenburg, unwilling to be convinced, was complaining, "Yes, yes, bore holes—leave Perfrement's thing until Monday. But unless I misread this formula, his so-called fluorine eighty-plus will by that time have ceased to exist."

A certain Doctor Chiappe said in a glum voice, "Metaphysics: If we leave it, it ceases to exist; if we don't leave it, it ceases to exist; but, as I read Perfrement's notes, if we leave fluorine eighty-plus, we shall be involved with it in a state of co-nonexistence. Better bore holes."

I said, "I asked you, M. le Queux, what are those gas masks for?"

He said, "Why, when the door is in any way interfered with, the alarm automatically goes off. We omit no precautions, none whatsoever. As soon as the alarm goes off, the vault fills with tear gas from built-in containers."

"Did you say tear gas?" I asked.

"In a high concentration."

"Then," I cried, "get away from that door at once!" I appealed to Frankenburg. "You hate every word I say, old fellow, but you're an honest man. Conceding that my notes are right—and I swear they are—you'll see that my fluorine eighty-plus has one affinity. One only. That is with C_8H_7ClO—chloroacetophenone. And that, damme, is the stuff tear gas is made of!"

Frankenburg nodded. Chiappe said, "Slice it as you like—we've had it!"

And old Raisin grumbled, "This, I believe, is what the dramatists call a perfectly damnable impasse. Correct me if I'm wrong."

It was little Imhof who asked, "Is there no part of this place at all that's not guarded by alarms, and what not?"

Le Queux said, "Technically, there is only one part of our vault that's reachable from the outside—if you can call it the outside. The back of our vault abuts on the back of the jeweler's, Monnickendam's, next door. His vault, you see, is itself two feet thick. Hence——"

"Aha!" said the chief of police.

"Get Monnickendam," said the minister of Security, and that famous jeweler and pawnbroker was duly produced.

He said, "I'd open my vault with pleasure, but I have a partner, Warmerdam. Our vault opens by two combination locks which must be operated simultaneously. These locks are so placed that no one can operate both at the same time. I have my own secret combination and Warmerdam has his. We must both be present to open the vault."

"That's how one gets rich," old Raisin muttered.

Monnickendam corrected him, "That is how one *stays* rich."

"Where's Warmerdam?" they asked.

"In London."

London was telephoned, and Secret Service agents

dragged poor Warmerdam shrieking from a dinner table and rushed him to a jetport and fired him over to Sables des Fesses with such dispatch that he arrived in a state of semiobfuscation, with a napkin still tucked under his chin.

But now, by the chief of police's expression, it was evident that the whole matter was an open-and-shut case to him. I was some sort of master criminal, a Moriarty, and my real objective was the jewelers' strong room. He strengthened the police cordon, and Monnickendam and Warmerdam opened their vault.

The men from Custodia went to work—but not before the two jewelers had got a signed and witnessed indemnity from the president of the bank; they wouldn't trust the minister—and so the heavy steel and concrete of the strong room cut through, we began to bite into the back of the bank.

"Time runs out," I said.

Raisin irritated everybody by saying, "Imagination, my friends, and nothing but imagination, is making us all sweat. All things considered, do you think that a megaton, a tyrrannoton, or an ultimon could do us—us personally—more harm than, let us say, a pound of dynamite?"

The chief of police said, "Ha! You know a lot about dynamite, it seems."

"I should hope so," said Raisin. "I was sabotaging Nazis, my friend, when you were swinging a truncheon for the *Deuxième Bureau.*"

I had better be brief, however. At about five in the morning we broke through.

I said, "Fine. You can take it easy now. Fluorine eighty-plus can't blow." And when I then suggested a hot cup of tea, M. le Queux tried to strangle me.

But the men worked on, until the hole was about two feet in diameter; and then one of the smallest of them took my key, wriggled through, and came back with the contents of my safe-deposit box—the little paper package of fluorine 80+.

I pointed out to Frankenburg how greatly it had diminished. "By George, we had a close call then!" I said.

And that, as you might think, was that. Ah, but you'd be wrong. For you see in the course of that mad night, when every policeman in Sables des Fesses and its environs was mounting guard at the bank and at Monnickendam's, a gang of thieves broke into the Prince of Mamluk's Galleries, said to contain one of the four finest art collections in the world.

They stripped the place at their leisure. They took a priceless collection of antique jewels, three Rembrandts, four Holbeins, two Raphaels, a Titian, two El Grecos, a Vermeer, three Botticellis, a Goya and a Greuze. Greatest art burglary of all time, I'm told. They say that Lloyds would rather have lost a fleet of transatlantic liners than what they underwrote those pictures and things for.

Taking it by and large, I suppose it's for my own good that I was shipped back to England and put under guard.

If I'd had any sense, of course, I'd have kept quiet about that confounded fluorine 80+. As it is, I've made a prisoner of myself. They regard me—of all people!—as a compulsive chatterbox. As if fluorine 80+ is anything to chatter about. Why, you could make it yourself. Take 500 grams of fluorspar——

Oh-oh! Here come my two friends, I'm afraid. I will take my leave of you now, sir. . . . Good night to you.

Good evening, gentlemen!

The Second Trip To Mars

by Ward Moore

Ward Moore is well known for his small but select output in the science fiction field. His novels Greener Than You Think *and* Joyleg *(in collaboration with Avram Davidson) are wise and funny. His* Bring the Jubilee, *in which the South has won the Civil War, is perhaps the finest alternate-history novel ever written. His short story, "Lot's Wife," was filmed as* Panic in the Year Zero. *In "The Second Trip to Mars" he displays the humor and pathos that make him special to modern science fiction.*

The Second Trip To Mars

by Ward Moore

Until its report was known, the Murphy-Gobiniev-Langois-Alemeda-Mutsuhara expedition to Mars in 2002 was thought to be the first successful one. Truth is, the first flight was achieved, quite accidentally, by a Humphrey Beachy-Cumberland in 1887, the year of Queen Victoria's Golden Jubilee.

His full name was Humphrey Howard Clarence Beachy-Cumberland, and he was a distant—very distant—connection of the Churchills. Humphrey rather considered the Churchills pushing; he had no handle in front of his name, and held a low idea of peerages.

There had been Beachys at Agincourt and Crécy; Beachy-Cumberland was a good name at Naseby and Ramillies, Prestonpans and Salamanca; he didn't propose to change it for Lord Whatsis or the Earl of Nowhere. Even at twenty-five—he'd been born a twelvemonth after the Prince Consort died—he had solid principles. He had a lively interest in progress (improved housing for tenants; free lectures for the laboring classes); and a sense of responsibility (inspection of drains; pensions for superannuated servants).

Progress accounted for his interest in Giles Pundershot. Certainly not compatibility. Pundershot was a cad in every sense: he was base-born, he misplaced the letter *h*, he borrowed money without meaning to repay, he read other people's mail, he seduced housemaids, he wore the tie of a school he had not attended. Given the opportunity, he would probably have shot foxes. He was also a genius of the first magnitude, a physicist so far ahead of his time no university tolerated mention of his name, no scholar of standing bothered to refute him. Humphrey gave him a pound a week, rooms in the servants' wing, and a reasonable charge account at an ironworks of which he was a director. He also allowed him an undergardener and a half acre of ground for the construction of a flying machine. Both Humphrey and Pundershot were sure heavier-than-air flight would come before 1900.

Pundershot's flying machine was along revolutionary lines. It was, in fact, a projectile—a projectile without a cannon. "Megnetism," explained Pundershot; "ettrection and repulsion. Enti-grevity in a word. Spurns the earth."

"Rilly?" asked Humphrey politely.

"Trouble so far is it spurns it too bloody"—Humphrey winced—"too bloody much. If I'm right, it will go three hundred miles a second."

"Too much," commented Humphrey. "Too fast altogether."

"Eighteen thousand miles a minute," said Pundershot. "Million miles in an hour. Speed like thet is worthless."

"Rah-ther," agreed Humphrey.

"Well," said Pundershot, gloomily cheerful, "expect I'll have to tear it down and put it together eggayne."

Humphrey looked faintly dubious. He knew to a farthing what the projectile had cost him; experience taught that a second one would be at least four times as expensive.

"Er—what's it like inside?" he asked, putting off the moment of approving Pundershot's revised experiment.

"Nothing an emeteur'd understend. False 'ull, suspended and padded, oxygen tenk—machine's airtight—megnetic controls: 'on' and 'off.' Bit crowded because of the shock-ebsorbing mechanism between inner and outer 'ulls. Barely room for one, and dark. Want to 'ave a look round?"

Humphrey didn't particularly, but tact (mightn't Pundershot be offended if he showed no interest?) and shrewdness (after all, with a fellow like that the whole thing might be papier-mâché) made him peer through the open hatch.

"Get in if you want," invited Pundershot. "Can't see much, but you can morrerless feel things."

"Well," said Humphrey doubtfully, "well. All right."

Pundershot's description of the interior was understatement. Humphrey saw nothing, felt only a foretaste of the coffin, tried to squirm back.

"'Ere!" exclaimed Pundershot. "Watch what you're doing. Ottermatic 'atch closer's right next to your arm."

Naturally, Humphrey jerked his arm. It hit a button; the hatch cover snapped shut. "I say!" he cried, struggling to open the cylinder again.

Instead he connected with the unseen "on" button. The projectile rejected the gravity of earth with utter repulsion. Forty-eight million miles off, give or take a few furlongs, the planet Mars winked redly. The nose of the machine pointed precisely for it.

Humphrey Beachy-Cumberland's last thought as he tore through the earth's gaseous envelope was that he had provided a pension for Pundershot in his will. He wished he hadn't.

The Martians who surrounded him forty-eight hours later had reverted to barbarism a thousand generations before. The great cities had eroded into dust, knowledge had faded into fable and incantation; the delicate balances of a completely free, egalitarian, nonviolent society had collapsed. Small tribes, so barbarous that leadership was not inherited, but assumed by the strongest or most cunning, warred perpetually on one another, eager for new victims. Even so, Humphrey was lucky; practically all Martians had abandoned cannibalism.

He looked up into the impassive faces—the Martians all topped him by at least a head—noting the coarsely woven garments, the pale skins, wide chests, loosely held iron knives and hatchets.

"Water—please!" he gasped.

A Martian uttered some sharp syllables. *Bother,* thought Humphrey; *I shall have to teach them English. What a nuisance.*

The unintelligible sounds must have been humorous; the others laughed briefly. Ominously. Humphrey raised an imaginary glass to his lips. When there was no sign of comprehension, he cupped his hands and made exaggerated drinking noises. The joking Martian drew an ugly iron knife.

"Here!" said Humphrey sharply. "Put that down. You might hurt someone." He never enjoyed crude humor. He turned half away, repeating his pantomime. The knife wielder paused.

"Water," repeated Humphrey, raising his voice despite his dry throat, knowing foreigners always managed to understand sooner or later, if spoken to loudly and slowly enough.

Much later, after being threatened with mutilation or death in many ingenious ways—avoided by staring at the would-be assassin and assuring him coldly that this was no way to behave—Humphrey was on his knees at the edge of an unbelievably wide canal, assuaging his thirst with the dark, brackish water. His captors stood behind him, by no means intimidated by this stunted creature who seemed without normal fear—without normal sense either—and who did not speak as everyone else spoke. Not intimidated, but certainly puzzled.

Humphrey gazed across the canal and peered up and down to where it disappeared in the horizons. "No real rivers, I suppose. Well, have to make a start somewhere; call this the Thames. Thames Canal."

He turned to the Martians. "Thames," he said distinctly, "Teh-mmms. Cah-nal." He pointed to the engineering work built by their ancestors sixty thousand years earlier.

"*Fenutch goobra,*" muttered a Martian.

"No, no," insisted Humphrey. "Thames. Thames Canal." He moved back to the water to wash his face and hands. "Have to do something about a decent bathe. The beggars have iron; ought to be easy enough to make some sort of tub."

Daily tubs were a necessity, but other necessities took immediate precedence. He judged his hosts primitive enough to sleep in the open—a course he did not propose to follow. Discomfort hardened a chap, made him fit, but privacy was the basis of civilization. And Humphrey wasn't giving up civilization, even under the present trying circumstances.

"Well," he said briskly, "can't stand about all day. What about a spot of food now? Food, you know. Foo-ood."

Humphrey was distressed to discover just how backward the Martians were. After the childishness of threatening a stranger with beastly tortures, he hardly expected the culture of Manchester or Birmingham. He did not look for niceties like umbrellas or *Punch.* But they didn't even have the institution of the family. Tribes were divided along the lines of—h'm—gender. Boys remained with the women till they were old enough to join in the endless war with other tribes, returning only for—for carnal purposes. It was all thoroughly immoral.

Worse, there was no inheritance, primogeniture or entail. Humphrey could not stand by while this sort of thing went on without seeming to give it his approval.

His captors still strove to nerve themselves to kill him, but merely trying was a little harder every day. It was quite absurd and a trifle indecent to violate custom and the fundamental code—you shall not let a stranger live—this way, but never before had a stranger been so completely un-co-operative. He refused to shrink from a down-chopping ax or thrusting knife. He could not even be properly finished off in his sleep; attempts at stealthy approach to the rough shelter he had made were always met by an alert and disconcerting questioner.

Well, so long as convention had been flouted by failing to bash his brains or cut his throat instantly, Mister—this was as much of "Mr. Beachy-Cumberland" as they found it convenient to pronounce—could just as well be dispatched next month. Or even the month after. Meanwhile, now that they understood some of his words, possibly they could learn a few tricks to overcome the neighboring tribes.

Humphrey had no intention of being useful that way. To fight for Queen and country was an occasional disagreeable—and glorious—necessity. There was neither necessity nor glory in these aboriginal clashes. They were merely nasty.

Nevertheless, he inadvertently increased the power of the tribe and his own prestige. In these regions, at least, there were neither trees nor animals—as a lover of roast beef with Yorkshire pudding, he regretted the absence of animal life—only abundant variety of annual vegetable growth by the canal banks. So weapons which at a similar stage of development would have been of wood or bone were crudely forged from the oxidized iron lying so abundantly on the sands. Coal, too, was plentiful, cropping up in ridges.

Humphrey, as a stockholder and director, had conscientiously studied the ironworks. Though no metallurgist, he could make coke from coal for a stronger, lighter metal than the Martians used for their clumsy tools. Working at first alone, then with a few who thought it amusing to imitate him, he produced knives which cut rather than sawed, hoes to cultivate with, for heavier food crops and stronger fibers for weaving, shovels and picks to dig the less common ores.

The Martians saw the advantages of his methods and made themselves better battle-axes. Humphrey considered battle-axes contrary to progress.

"Look here," he said to a young Martian who had been among the first to copy his manner of smelting and forging. "This won't do, you know."

"*Squirrup chedges,*" murmured the young Martian.

"Nonsense," said Humphrey. "You can talk properly enough if you put your mind to it. Now then, why do you people want to fight among yourselves all the time?"

"*Kerestheme,*" said the Martian.

"Speak up," ordered Humphrey. "None of your gibberish."

"Foo-wud," tried the Martian haltingly. "Wo-min."

"Yes," reflected Humphrey. "To be sure. Of course." He pondered. "Your name's Tom Smith, isn't it?"

"Mogolum Tu."

"That's not a name, it's a whatyamacallit for a slide trombone. Believe me, you're much better off as Tom Smith. Now then, about food and—er—women. You see how easy it is to grow bigger plants by using better hoes. Now we can rig up a plow—no animals, nuisance—and by planting instead of trusting to luck, there will be more than this tribe can eat, even if all feast every day. Food enough for all the tribes.

"As for—uh—women, that can be managed better, too." Delicately he explained the advantages of monogamous marriage.

The problem on Humphrey's mind had nothing to do with the iron water wheel now creaking and clanking in the Thames Canal to bring irrigating water to sands uncultivated for millennia, nor the improved looms for finer weaving, nor negotiations with still another tribe considering joining the peaceful and prosperous federation. It did not even concern the group of dissidents around Henry Green—formerly Thotcho Gor—who protested that Tom Smith and Mister were going too far and too fast.

Humphrey's problem was holy orders. Broad Church himself, he knew little theology, always having left such matters to the vicar. The phrase, "apostolic succession," floated through his mind: one could not instruct selected natives in the gist of the Book of Common Prayer—he could remember long passages—and set them up to administer the sacraments. To think of it smacked of nonconformity. Yet how were the marriages he had arranged to be regularized? True, even irregular monogamy was preferable to the old conditions, but it was still irregular. And what of baptism and burial? When he himself was committed to the earth—Mars, then—he wanted the prescribed service read decently over his body.

Meanwhile he kept a growing group of assistants vastly busy. Tom Smith remained his closest disciple, but Tom had his hands full carrying out the projects Humphrey originated, explaining, placating, persuading. For new reforms and inventions, Humphrey depended on men who only recently stalked human game. He was amazed at how quickly they grasped ideas or theories, often hazy in his own mind, and translated them into practice. He knew paper could be made by pulping woody fibers; they found the plant best suited and devised means of production. He outlined the principles of type cutting and setting; they contrived a press. He had rough notions about glass and cement; they formed panes and bowls which were at least translucent; mixed concrete and mortar which promised to remain hard.

Reluctantly he compromised on holy orders. A ship's captain, he argued, performed valid marriages and committed bodies to the deep. Why not the captain of a planet beyond the seas of earth? He knew his logic grew shakier the further he extended it, but something had to be done. He soothed his conscience by telling himself he was not ordaining clergy, merely delegating functions; he had his students call themselves "deputy vicar" or "acting curate." Now, whatever happened to him—and he was aware that Henry Green's anti-Mister faction had grown dangerously since the extension of civilization to the tribes beyond the Serpentine and Avon canals—there would be men to teach the young and instill decorum into those whose behavior might otherwise become scandalous.

In 1897 they launched the first steamship on the Thames Canal. Humphrey had worked out a Martian calendar using earth years; its defect lay in his uncertainty of the exact date of his arrival, so he was never entirely easy about celebrating the Queen's Birthday, and Boxing Day was distinctly a hit-or-miss affair. But the launching unquestionably occurred in 1897, ten years after the projectile landed. The ship was small, shallow draft and cranky, with an unpredictable boiler and inefficient paddle wheels, but it carried Humphrey's emissaries to strange places where exotic plants grew and copper and tungsten were plentiful as iron, where Mister was only a name in a vague legend, and they were met with missiles as often as listeners to the message of progress.

This was the year bank notes were engraved and the Martians taught the fine points of property and to sell things for eight shillings sixpence ha'penny instead of giving them away. Wages and real estate and commerce, profits, dividends and unemployment—what a blessing civilization was.

The issue of Henry Green and the grumblings of his followers could be put off no longer. Humphrey had broadsides printed explaining the parliamentary system, responsible government and constitutional rule. At the first election, Tom Smith was returned for New Brighton on the Tweed Canal. Enough supporters were elected for him to form a government with himself as Prime Minister and Chancellor of the Exchequer, and Robert Jones—born Poromby Lusu—as First Lord of the Admiralty. Henry Green was, of course, Leader of the Opposition. Tactfully, the adjective Loyal was not insisted upon.

One of the first acts of the new House was to forbid marriage with a deceased wife's sister, another provided a postal service, a third decreed that judges and barristers wear wigs. A Defence of the Realm bill was vigorously fought by Green, who protested it would stamp out the last vestige of ancient liberties ("Shall we yield our own customs to the airy theories of an alien from an inferior planet?" Cries of "Hear! Hear!" from the Opposition, and "Shame! Savage! Slander!" from the Treasury Bench). Parliament was prorogued and the Prime Minister appealed to the country.

New Brighton on Tweed again returned Tom Smith, but Green's party won a majority of seats. During the polling this possibility had fathered dark prophecies, yet the new Conservative—for so Green called his party—government took office without friction and immediately passed a Defence of the Realm Act over the bitter outcries of Smith's Liberals.

The political situation settled, economic and religious conditions flourishing, Humphrey turned to culture. A weekly Times foreshadowed a daily; a public school was begun, an Encyclopædia Martiana projected. A Philosophical Society and an Art Academy were discussed and steps taken to form a Philharmonic Orchestra. Humphrey had the alloyed pleasure of turning the first telescope earthward and the pure joy of eating the first Martian crumpet.

He was only fifty-five in 1917, when the last wild tribes gave up their independence. That was the year Tom Smith finally resigned the Liberal leadership to Herbert Noro.

Humphrey's influence in the matter of name changing was weakening; the clergy buttressed it so far as first names went, but the tendency to retain the old Martian surnames grew. It was also the year Humphrey started building Cumberland House and landscaping the flower gardens leading from it down to the Severn Canal.

Though fifty-five was a ridiculously early age to consider retirement, he found less and less to do. Everything was in good hands. If he looked askance at some of the doings of his protégés he would not deny the Martians had taken hold. There was good stuff in them.

He did not travel much; when you've seen one Martian canal you've seen them all. He revised and enlarged the plans for Cumberland House; he supervised the masons and glaziers; he kept gardeners busy. He gave some time to compiling an edition of Landed Martian Gentry.

But largely he spent his days talking over old times, often with those who had once plotted to kill him. Cumberland House was staffed with men who had not adapted well to the new ways or backslid from them. Humphrey and they re-created the past, and both, for different reasons, felt better for it.

One Guy Fawkes Day he sat down, dressed for dinner, in excellent spirits. His butler served a plate of lichen broth and was withdrawing when Humphrey called, "Wait! I––"

The man rushed to catch his collapsing form, but, himself an old campaigner, he knew death when he saw it.

He was buried in his gardens; a stone he had designed was put up over his grave.

HUMPHREY HOWARD CLARENCE
BEACHY-CUMBERLAND
ESQUIRE
Formerly of Buckinghamshire
Who always remembered the land of
his birth.

Sean McDairmuid Murphy, an American, led the United Nations Interplanetary Expedition of 2002, so far as the other nationals in it—Yasu Matsuhara excepted—acknowledged any leadership. More accurately, Doctor Murphy was the senior scientist of the WAC Field Marshal, and its anthropologist.

Sergei Goviniev, the ethnologist, carried on a cold feud with the philologist, Hyacinthe Langois, on whether Martian civilization would have terrestrial analogies. Luis Alemeda, the geologist, was convinced neither humans nor any history of them would be found.

Doctor Matsuhara felt that Alemeda was biased by his vocation; he himself had an open mind on all subjects but botany and baseball. He was as sure he would find bamboo, or something very like it, as he was that San Francisco would win the pennant and series in '03. Anyway, '04.

The expedition was to have included a sixth member, Sir David Rabinovits. But since the United Kingdom withdrew from the Canadian-Australian-New Zealand-African-West Indian Commonwealth in 1990, Westminster had shown little interest in new horizons. Sir David had been dropped and the expedition left without a biologist.

"As well," said Langois. "Who can tell what comes from perfidious Albion?"

"'Perfidious,' yes," muttered Gobiniev. "A rootless cosmopolitan, gilded by a corrupt, imperialist Labor government; undoubtedly he was ordered to work against the People's Democracies. Like the toadies of the so-called Fifth Republic."

"Don't be silly," said Sean Murphy. "There's much to be laid at the door of Johnny Bull—Ireland is still divided—but using Dave Rabinovits as an agent wouldn't be part of it. They wouldn't pay Dave's way because they don't care about Mars or the UN or anything else but some silly celebration they're having this year."

The WAC Field Marshal made a beautiful landing not ten miles from where Humphrey's projectile had plowed up the sands. It was now a Planetary Park, kept primitively intact.

"Desert," crowed Doctor Alemeda. "Sterile desert."

Langois shook his head obstinately, scanning the sands through field glasses. A dust cloud appeared, resolving into a crowd of people. "What did I tell you? Men! And, I hope, women also."

"Those bits of color seem to be flags," said Matsuhara.

"Impossible," said Murphy. "Some evolutionary quirk."

"Union Jacks," identified Alemeda.

"A plot!" cried Gobiniev. "A trick to discredit the U.S.S.R.!"

An engine on wide iron wheels puffed black smoke ahead of a multi-doored, enclosed car. It stopped short of the WAC Field Marshal; the crowd on foot pressed close behind. The carriage doors opened and Martians came forward, dressed in tubular trousers and double-breasted coats. One of them, high hat in left hand, extended his right.

"From earth, what?" asked the Martian. "Good show."

"Oh, no," said Murphy. "Oh, no."

"How is it you don't speak Russian?" growled Gobiniev.

"Are you Russians?" inquired the Martian coldly. "Crimea and Turkestan? The bear that walks like a man?"

"Only one," explained Alemeda; "I am myself of Uruguay."

"Ah, the Banda Oriental—'the land we lost.' I presume there is also a Frenchman? Possibly an American?"

Matsuhara said diffidently, "We are surprised to find that your language is English."

"Really? Yet we aren't surprised to find you using it. But let bygones be bygones. I'm Austen Aboxu, Prime Minister and Secretary of State for Defence. Welcome—officially this time—to Mars. Since we first sighted you we've been getting up a reception at the New Oxford Guildhall. Come as you are—heh-heh—I don't suppose you're prepared to dress anyway."

A slightly dazed expedition heard his apologetic offer of a lift in his railway carriage. "It's a bit primitive; we're not much on land vehicles. Ships now—well, we rather pride ourselves there. Rules the waves and so on, you know."

Martian Coldstream Guards with imitation-bearskin busbies being placed around the WAC Field Marshal, they entered the carriage. "Naturally, we were disappointed this wasn't a British go," said the Prime Minister. "But I expect there'll be one along any day or so. Muddling through, of course; England loses every battle but the last one."

"So they say," mumbled Murphy.

"Now let me give you an idea of what will be going on at the Guildhall. The Acting Archbishop of Mars first; afraid you'll find him a bore. The Dean's worse. However, we must respect the cloth. I hope now they send us out some proper chaps, ordained and all that sort of thing."

"No doubt," said Murphy numbly.

"Then the Leader of the Opposition will have a few well-chosen. He'll pitch into me properly for not welcoming you as he would if the last by-elections had gone the other way. You mustn't mind; it's all in the way of business and I should do the same if he were the right honorable and I only the member for New Basingstoke. Then there'll be the Gentleman Ushers of the Black Rod, the Warden of the Cinque Ports, the Lord Leftenant of the Martian Poles——"

There were indeed. All these and many more, all with exceedingly long speeches of welcome to the intrepid explorers from "our foster-mother planet." Between speeches they nibbled at filet of pressed Martian grass, Mars sprouts à la Gladstone, and Canalgae au pommes de Mars. At length Sean Murphy asked permission to speak. This being granted—to the discomfiture of the leader writer for the Times, who had been about to make a very witty speech—Murphy began doubtfully, "I was commissioned by the United Nations to take possession of this planet in the name of the UN for all——"

Prime Minister Aboxu stopped him with a wave of the hand. "I'm afraid you can't do that, you know."

"Well," said Murphy, "I can see you're civilized; it's not like taking over an empty world. Perhaps you'll want to join the UN yourselves?"

"I'm afraid you don't understand," said the Prime Minister gently. "We're not a nation. At least not as you use the word. We owe our first and full allegiance to the Crown. After all, this is Her Majesty's Dominion of Mars and it is entirely up to Her Majesty—acting upon my advice—whether we join this—uh—United Nations thing."

"The fourth British Empire," muttered Sean Murphy brokenly. "Kathleen ni Houlihan, is there no justice?"

"Tomorrow," said the Prime Minister, suavely forestalling the Times' leader writer, "we've rather a treat. There'll be a march past of bobbies in the morning; a cricket match before tea; and a reconstruction—we've all the songs, but the words are a bit sketchy—of Pinafore in the evening. I hope you'll overlook our colonial shortcomings. But there are things we're most anxious to hear about. First, the Queen, Her Majesty. She is—dead?"

"Not as far as I know," answered Murphy carelessly.

"But—— It hardly seems possible. She is so old."

"Old? Oh, not so very, the way they look at age now."

Mr. Aboxu was puzzled. The Crown was immortal—but the Queen? No, no; he remembered his history too well. Still alive? He understood the difference between earth and Martian years, even with the confusion of a Martian calendar based on terrestrial rotation, and could usually translate them in his head, but the exciting day and his brief but telling defense of the dignity of the Crown confused him. It did seem that Her Majesty must be nearly two hundred, but perhaps there were new ways of reckoning since Mister's day. No, that would hardly— Ah, but science; Mister always regretted not knowing more of science and spoke of the time when life would be greatly lengthened through its discoveries.

"Ah, yes. Quite."

Langois dredged his memory to please his hosts, "They rejoice in England this year. It is the Queen's Jubilee."

The Jubilee? But that was the year Mister had arrived. The Golden Jubilee, the fiftieth anniversary of her reign. This must be—the hundred and sixty-fifth. No doubt of some special significance Mister had neglected to mention. "The Jubilee. Naturally. We're celebrating here too."

The master of ceremonies tapped impatiently. "Port, if you please. I know we all wish to drink to our visitors."

"Ah," sighed Gobiniev.

"So, first, our customary toast. . . . Mr. Prime Minister."

Mr. Aboxu rose and held his wineglass. Everyone at the table, including the explorers, followed his example.

"Gentlemen," said the Right Honorable Austen Aboxu, PC, MP; Member, Royal Martian Society for the Diffusion of Knowledge, his voice trembling slightly, "the Queen!"

They drank, and all snapped the stems of their glasses so no lesser toasts might ever be drunk from them again. In this, as in so much else, they did as Humphrey had taught them. It had new meaning now, now that, for the first time since Mister's day, Home seemed so close.

The Voice in the Earphones

by Wilbur Schramm

In "The Voice in the Earphones" Wilbur Schramm exhibits the skills that have long made him a myth-spinner of sterling reputation. His creation Windwagon Smith *was made into a classic Disney cartoon short. To read one of his comic tales one would hardly guess that Schramm is an academic and a leading expert on mass communication.*

The Voice in the Earphones

by Wilbur Schramm

It had never happened before in the history of aviation. The chances of its happening again are one in a number that has zeros stacked across the page like eggs in cold storage. And yet the fact remains that it happened. For a long time, people who saw it will tell their children and grandchildren how Shorty Frooze, who had never flown an airplane, found himself suddenly at the controls of an airliner 8000 feet up in the blue air over Kansas, and how, like a farm boy breaking the new colt, he calmly decided to ride the big ship in to a landing.

But to appreciate what really happened that July afternoon you have to know something about Shorty. His real name wasn't Frooze, of course. It was Habib el Something or Other, one of those Asia Minor names that are like nothing in English. They began to call him Frooze in the years when he was a fruit peddler in a little town near Kansas City. I can still remember him driving his donkey cart through the streets, jingling a bell and singing his wares in a high voice that penetrated every kitchen in town. "Can'aloupe!" he would call. "Wa'ermelon! Fresh frooze!" And the name stuck, even when he learned to say "fruits" and retired the patient little donkey and set up a sidewalk stand in Kansas City—Shorty Frooze.

The most important thing about Shorty was his son. Had you ever guessed Bill James was his boy? Bill dropped his last name when he went to the University of Kansas. He was as different from his father as could be. He was big and handsome and popular, and a great athlete. Shorty told me once that Bill resembled his mother, who died when Bill was born. And inevitably Shorty's boy grew away from nervous little Shorty, who couldn't even talk plain English. Bill wasn't exactly ashamed of his father, but when he took him to father-and-son banquets in high school, Shorty didn't enjoy it, and other people were ill at ease, too, and thereafter Shorty faded into the background. He stayed away from Bill's fraternity house in Lawrence. Whenever Bill played ball, I would see Shorty there, with a happy mist in his eyes, but always in some inconspicuous corner, and I could never find him when the game was over.

One big area of Bill's world was closed to Shorty. That was aviation. Bill was a natural flier. He soloed at seventeen. By the time he was eighteen, they said, he could fly a barn door if anyone would put an electric fan on it. He went to the airlines before he finished Kansas. When the shooting started in Europe, he wanted to go right into the RAF, but Shorty said no. He said Bill was all he had left. Wait at least long enough to finish out the year with the airlines, he pleaded. Because Bill wasn't quite twenty-one, Shorty had to give consent. They said some pretty bitter words before Bill stomped out of the house, back to his job. And then came the accident, barely a week later, with Shorty watching.

Shorty grieved unnaturally over Bill's death. He kept blaming himself, torturing himself. I always passed his little stand on my way to work, and for days at a time it would be closed, while Shorty sat at home, grieving. Then he took to hanging around the airport, talking to the mechanics and the pilots, and watching the ships slide in from every point on the compass. They knew why he did it; he felt closer to Bill there. But after a while he became a nuisance, and they had to ask him to stay away.

Then he went back to work again, frantically. I could find him at the stand any hour of the day or evening. To save money, he went often without food as he had when he was helping put Bill through Lawrence. And whenever he had a few dollars saved up he took an airplane trip. He would come to the airport hours before flight time. People stared at him and smirked behind their hands. The first time I saw him there, I stared too. I didn't know him. He had got out his Sunday suit, and it must have been the suit he was married in. It had tight trousers and a long coat, and made him look like something out of a musical comedy. But when the plane was announced, Shorty was always first in line, and he would scurry out to be sure of the front seat. That was as near as possible to the place where Bill had sat when he was pilot; there Shorty could see as nearly as possible what Bill must have seen from the pilot's cockpit. It would have seemed pitiful, his trying so hard to get closer to the boy in death than he could in life, if it hadn't been laughable. And that was how Shorty happened to be on the front seat of an airliner bound from Denver to Kansas City on the July day when it happened.

The other passengers confirm Shorty's story of what happened. They were well out of Denver toward Kansas City when the stewardess opened the door of the pilot's compartment and stepped into the passengers' part of the ship. She was as white as her blouse, they said. She sat down unsteadily beside Shorty in the front seat. Apparently only Shorty heard what she said. She pointed to the front compartment. "My God, see what's in there!" she gasped, and fainted dead away.

Shorty himself didn't know exactly why he did what he did in the next few minutes. Why he took the stewardess' keys and went into the pilots' compartment, instead of giving the stewardess first aid, is something that could be explained only in terms of some larger pattern of which that act was a part. The important thing is that he did go through the door forbidden to passengers. He locked the door behind him and looked along the passageway, which he had never seen, but which Bill had seen so often, past the radio equipment, past the baggage compartment, to the cockpit where pilot and copilot sit surrounded by windows and instruments.

At first he comprehended only that there was something vaguely wrong with what he saw. It came to him slowly that there was no pilot and no copilot, and no hand was on the controls, and no eye was watching where the ship flew.

Still slowly, like a man lifting an unknown weight, he mastered other details. One pilot stretched out on the floor. The other slumped down behind his seat. Shorty touched them, fearing he might be touching dead men. He listened to their hearts. He propped them up, then stretched them out and poured water from a vacuum bottle on their faces. You have read the story in the newspapers, of course, and you know that pilots and stewardess were suffering from a violent attack of food poisoning, from a lunch they had eaten before flight. But Shorty did not know that. He knew only that both pilots were unconscious, and he could not revive them, and he was alone with the controls of a transport plane high above Kansas.

The sensible thing, he admitted to himself, would be to go back and see whether a doctor or a pilot was among the passengers. He tried to weigh the possibility of there being a doctor or a pilot against the possibility of panic if there was none. And partly because of that judgment, partly because he was at last where Bill had sat on so many flights, he decided not to go back to the passengers —not for a little while.

He sat down in the pilot's seat, trembling, but not with fright. This thing with the little steering wheel on the end must be the "stick" Bill had mentioned so often. There was one for each pilot, and two pedals like clutch and brake in front of each stick. He tried to see how many of the dials and switches on the instrument panel he could identify from hearing Bill talk about them. One he was sure of—down at the lower left center, a handle marked AUTOMATIC PILOT. He judged that was what was keeping the plane level and straight. Things would be all right until the gas gave out. Here was the radio headset. Acting on a sentimental little impulse, he put on the earphones and picked up the microphone Bill must have addressed so often.

Bill would have said something professional like "Pilot to tower," he knew, and given the flight number and position. But the only thing Shorty could think of to say, in a high, embarrassed voice was "Hello there. Hello, Kansas City."

Nothing happened for a minute, and then a voice came into his earphones. He felt like a boy caught playing with forbidden toys. But the voice was calm and matter-of-fact. "Hello, old fellow," it said. "Been wondering where you were. Anything wrong?"

Shorty thought at the time that the voice would be engraved in his memory like chisel cuts in stone, but later he had trouble describing it for me. The radio didn't leave much color in it, of course, and it was like any other airways voice—flat, calm, sparing of words, the kind of rhythm men develop from dealing much with elements and refusing to get excited over mere man-made things. All afternoon Shorty kept trying to identify it with some person he knew, but not quite succeeding. It was a friendly voice, for all its impersonal quality. It invited confidence. And before Shorty really thought about what he was doing, he was pouring the whole story of his situation into the microphone.

When he stopped, there was a long, low whistle from the earphones.

"My kid Bill ought to be here," said Shorty. "He was a flier."

"Yes, I know," said the voice. Then it was silent so long that Shorty said anxiously, "Hello?"

"Well," said the voice thoughtfully. It took a long time to say, "Well."

"What shall I do?" asked Shorty.

"If I were you," said the voice, "I'd fly her into Kansas City."

"But I don't know how," said Shorty.

"I'll teach you," said the voice.

"You'll do what?" gasped Shorty.

"Put your hands on the stick and your feet on the pedals," said the voice. "Don't be afraid. They won't bite."

Shorty swore to me that is what happened up in the plane. That is how he came to do what he did. He says he didn't feel frightened at first; he felt foolish, like a man on a quiz program. Then he wondered how soon he would wake up. It took a long time, Shorty said, before the reality of the situation swung around in his mind and hit him like a fist.

And by that time the voice in his earphones had taken over, and wasn't giving him a chance to be frightened.

"Don't be scared of the instrument board, either," said the voice. "You won't need most of the things on it. They're luxuries. See if you can find a dial marked Altimeter and tell me what it says."

"Eight," said Shorty.

"That means eight thousand feet," said the voice. "Now look for a handle marked Automatic Pilot."

"Here it is," said Shorty.

"Turn it to OFF."

"Take off the Automatic Pilot?" gasped Shorty.

"Sure," said the voice. "You're going to learn to fly this crate, aren't you?"

Shorty's hand shook as he took off the Automatic Pilot. The left wing dropped slightly.

"Keep the stick center."

The wing went up.

"How did you know?" asked Shorty incredulously.

"Everybody does it the first time," chuckled the voice. "Now let's try a few things. Landing's simple, but you'll have to know how to bank. Let's try a left bank first. Put the stick a little left and a little forward. Push the left pedal a little. Just a little."

Bill had talked about that, Shorty remembered. He had said that the pedals worked just the opposite of a bobsled crossbar.

The big ship came around grandly. Shorty took one hand off the stick and wiped something wet out of his eyes. In that instant he understood more of what flying had meant to Bill than ever before. The thrill is the same—your first jump on a horse, your first racing turn in a sailboat, the first time you do a good bank in your plane.

"Level it off," said the voice. "Press the right pedal a little. Stick back to center. Pull it back a little to put the nose up. How was it?"

"A little jerky," said Shorty.

"You probably lost some altitude too," said the voice. "That's because you didn't keep your nose on the horizon."

"My nose?" asked Shorty.

"The plane's nose. Now let's try another left bank." The voice seemed to hypnotize him into it, Shorty said. "Now another," it said. "Better? . . . You know," said the voice, "you might fool me and come in on the other side. Let's try a right bank. Just the opposite. Right pedal, and so on. Come on, now; let's do it."

"That was pretty bad," said Shorty. "I remember, Bill said a right bank seemed harder than a left one at first."

"That's right. Now let's practice another one."

"What do you suppose the passengers think?" asked Shorty.

"What they don't know won't hurt them. Are you flying along the railroad tracks now?"

"Pretty close."

"East or west? Look at your compass. Top of the instrument board."

"East."

"Good. How are you at glides?"

"I never tried one," said Shorty.

"Better try two or three. About all there is to landing is a good long glide. Push the wheel a little forward and try one. Not too far forward. What does the altimeter say now?"

"Seven and a half. Does that mean seventy-five hundred?"

"Yes," said the voice. "Now look around and find the switch that lowers the wheels. You'll need that."

Shorty said he surrendered himself to the voice like a man floating downstream. What it told him to practice, he practiced. What it told him to push and pull and press, he did. Once there was a prolonged pounding on the door behind him. "Shall I open the door?" he asked the microphone.

"I wouldn't," said the voice in the earphones. "Why take a chance? You can fly this job, pappy. You don't need help."

That was one of the sweetest moments in Shorty's life.

"They told me I was too old to learn to fly," he confessed. "They even kicked me out of the Kansas City airport."

"They won't today," said the voice.

Shorty said he wished he had a fifty-cent cigar. That was the first moment in his life when he had felt like smoking one. He felt like leaning back in a big chair with his thumbs hooked in his vest.

As they flew on across Kansas, Shorty said he got a kind of physical pleasure out of living he hadn't experienced for thirty years. His senses seemed peculiarly alert to the blueness of the air above him, the sweep of the Kansas plain, the wind waves in the wheat and prairie grass below him. He saw another plane, headed southwest along the distant horizon, and felt the warm sense of brotherhood that ships feel at sea. Bill had told him about that feeling, but he hadn't understood it.

He even began to feel like talking—more so than he had ever felt with anyone except Bill, when Bill was a boy. With his customers, with the few neighbors he knew, he always tried to say as little as possible and to cover up his awkward English and his funny accent. This fellow talking into his earphones actually seemed to want to hear him talk. Shorty told him about himself, and about Bill, and about some of the things he could see from the plane. When he saw what looked like wheel tracks curving across the prairie, it was the most natural thing on earth to ask the voice what they were.

"That's the old Santa Fe Trail," Shorty's earphones said. "That's the road they took before there were railroads. They went to the old Spanish cities in Mexico and brought wagon-loads of goods home to sell. That's one of the most famous roads in America."

"Why, that's what I do," said Shorty, becoming excited. "That's how I do it. I get the stuff down south and bring it up here to sell. I used to sell it in wagons too. Can'aloupes and wa'ermelons and frooze." Unconsciously he dropped back into the old immigrant English.

"Sure," said the voice.

Shorty tried to imagine prairie schooners and caravans creeping along the ruts in the brown plain. And he fancied he could see another vehicle in the parade. It was pulled by a patient little donkey, and the driver jangled a bell and sang his wares in a high, loud voice. It was the first time he had ever thought of it that way.

Impulsively, he told about the quarrel with Bill, and how sorry he was that Bill's last words had been spoken in anger.

"I don't think Bill held any anger at you," said the voice.

"How well did you know Bill?" asked Shorty.

"Pretty well." There was a little silence, and then the voice asked, "How do you feel, old fellow?"

Over to the north was the yellow River Kaw, and the Lawrence hill was rising out of the endless plain. The hill, crowned by shining university buildings, had always seemed very high and insurmountable to Shorty. From this angle it looked different.

"You're going to take her down now, old fellow," said the voice. "You're going to make a good landing. Your kid Bill would be proud of you."

Shorty said that was the last time he felt any indecision about it.

"Better start to lose altitude now. Take her down to two thousand. Slow. Plenty of time. Slow. . . . Slow."

Shorty pushed the stick forward . . . slow . . . slow.

The smoke of Kansas City was on the sky and the taller buildings were beginning to separate from the horizon. When Shorty first saw the field he wondered how a plane could hit anything so small, but when he approached it a second time with motors throttled down as far as they would go, landing flaps down, wheels reaching for the ground, he felt a great surge of strength and knew he could do it. He banked around, feeling all the firmness and power of the ship as it turned into the wind. A sea captain's phrase went through his memory—"a taut ship"—and he knew suddenly what that meant.

In that instant, too, he understood something else about flying: you fly, the plane doesn't. Or at least there is a time of merger when you and the plane become one and fly. He wondered how often Bill had felt this same oneness with his plane. He felt very near to Bill at that moment, perhaps closer than ever in life. It was almost as though he and Bill were one.

Then he was steering into the white stripe of the runway, pulling back the stick little by little as the voice in the earphones told him to, cutting the airspeed, trying to bring the tail down level with the nose, trying to hold the wings level, knowing that the next ten seconds would tell whether it was a good landing or a crash.

Even in those seconds he remembered a plane he had once seen overrun a field and stand awkwardly, with nose buried in a swamp and tail high in the air, until everything above the ground burned away. Bill's plane.

Then the wheels hit the ground. The left one hit first—left wing low, he guessed—and the plane gave a great awkward bounce, turned a little off the runway and settled down. Shorty cut the ignition and let the ship roll. He didn't feel up to taxiing it. After it stopped rolling, he put his head down on the stick and closed his eyes.

When the field attendants rushed out in their little cars to bawl him out for not taxiing to the landing apron, his first impulse was to crouch down, so they wouldn't see him, or try to vanish in the crowd before anybody saw who he was. Then he remembered some things that had happened during the afternoon, and he sat up straight.

The attendants saw his civilian coat in the window, and stopped growling and were silent in astonishment. And then he had his little moment of triumph. Little Shorty Frooze who sold cantaloupes. Little Shorty who was kicked off the airport because he was a nuisance. He sat up as straight and tall as he could. He leaned out the window and spoke to them in what he imagined to be the authoritative voice of an airlines captain.

"We have sick men aboard," he said. "Take care of them before you touch anything else in the plane."

And that is all of Shorty's story except one very important incident. When they had shaken his hand and snapped his picture, he said he wanted to go to the tower to thank the person who had helped him bring in the ship. They laughed at the joke, and then saw he was in earnest.

The airport manager took him aside a moment. "Mr. —er—Frooze," he said, "you know, don't you, that we've been trying to contact your plane all afternoon? Nobody in the tower has been talking to you."

Well, you explain it. What happened in the blue air over Kansas I have told you just as Shorty told me. It doesn't seem possible that he could have imagined it all. On the other hand, it doesn't seem possible that he could have remembered enough from Bill's old aviation chatter to bring in that plane without help. Shorty swears someone was talking to him, and he thinks he knows who it was. I don't for a moment believe it was who he thinks it was, but strange things happen. And the important thing, after all, is what Shorty thinks, because he has stopped grieving over Bill now, and walks with his head up, and doesn't hide from people, and looks at the sky with the squint of a flier.

Moon Crazy
by William Roy Shelton

William Roy Shelton is not primarily a writer of fantasy. He began his writing career as a scenario writer for the Air Force. He became a bureau chief for Time *and then became a contributing editor for* The Saturday Evening Post *from 1962 to 1963. Shelton was the first writer of a national publication to cover Cape Canaveral and through the 70s has reported on dozens of important launches. In 1975 he scripted "Stowaway to the Moon" for television from his own short story of the same title. In "Moon Crazy" he explores a world of dream and nightmare often familiar to many of us, only here it's a world that became a tragic reality for Ralph Teeler.*

Moon Crazy

by William Roy Shelton

This was the third night that Ralph had watched the moon. He kicked off his shoes at the base of the cypress, then reached up to the lowest board he had nailed to the tree and began the long climb. A few boards behind him followed a seven-weeks-old opossum which paused and searched at each rung like a puppy climbing his first stairs.

Ralph climbed slowly, holding his body just far enough from the trunk so that the hair on his chest did not catch in the bark. When he reached the eighteenth rung, at the halfway mark, the moonlight struck in a diagonal line across his bare, freckled shoulders and glinted off the watch on his outstretched wrist. He hugged the trunk for a moment, hearing only his breathing in the forest, watching the moon. Then he felt the nose of the opossum nuzzle his feet and he began to climb again, pulling himself, finally, upon the slab-pine platform he had built at the top. Without pausing to catch his breath, he reached down, gripped the nape of the trembling opossum and hoisted him gently to the platform.

"There you are, Whiteface," he said, stroking the coarse fur. "Now you're the highest 'possum in the swamp and maybe in the whole state of Florida, and you're sure the scaredest. Just look round you. Don't you wisht you was an eagle, boy?"

A moment later, Ralph got to his feet and struck his palm solidly against the crude shack which covered most of the platform. He gave a low laugh at the sturdiness of his work; then, as the sound of his blow fell away through the trees, he placed his hands on his hips and looked about him. The bald crown of the cypress did not begin to flare until it had cleared the rest of the trees, and to the south he could see three quarters of a mile straight down the silvered path of the St. Johns River. To the north he could see a large island whose palisades of cypress and water oak gave it the almost exact shape of a diamond. In all other directions he could see far over the tops of trees. And he could see the moon clearly.

He stood thus till he was breathing easily again, then he smiled down at Whiteface, already curled on the platform, and opened the door of the shack. Inside, he paused, listening. A tripod made from bay saplings stood in the center of the floor directly beneath a rectangular slit in the roof. Underneath the tripod, and covered with a worn army comforter, was a homemade reclining chair with slabs of pine bark still clinging to its sides. When he was certain he could hear no mosquitoes, he reached up and removed the canvas from a short, squat telescope aimed at the sky. Then, removing his trousers, he placed himself on the chair, propping his head with the comforter until his eye was directly beneath the small end of the telescope. When he had made himself thoroughly comfortable, he raised his arms and focused the telescope upon the face of the moon.

What had been, only a few moments before, a flat and indistinct disk, loomed now as a huge, gleaming orb dazzling with light. It appeared as unevenly rounded as a peeled orange, and so nearly filled the inside of the telescope that only a thin band of aureate mist encircled it.

Already, with only three nights' watching, there were mountains and even entire land masses which were becoming familiar. His eye searched the depths of the large crater in the lower right quadrant, then darted upward to the series of low, twisted ridges near the receding top of the moon. Ralph's lips parted in smileless wonder. There were mysteries in its shadowed craters, and an unearthly stillness about its bright, flat plains which quickened his pulse and started his fingers, which had been relaxed at his side, to drumming gently against the comforter.

He smiled to think how people called this or that pattern the man or the woman in the moon, when there were so many other and far more interesting pictures. Here was a suckling pig resting on its side, and, there above, a leaping porpoise with a hunk bitten out of its tail by a shark. Near the bottom was a claw hammer and, beside it, a drifting parachute with a hole in the silk.

When he tired of his images, he placed his hands behind his head and stared fixedly at the moon. He could almost imagine that he felt a slight, not unpleasant tickling sensation well behind his eye, and he laughed to think of his head as a camera taking a picture of the moon. He remembered that his father used to say that "lunatic" came from the word "lunar," and that moonlight could sometimes affect a person in strange ways, but Ralph laughed again at this, because the moon was only a cold mass with neither light nor life of its own. . . . And here was another picture of the head of a cow with one of its horns disappearing around the side of the moon.

At first, so absorbed was he in his images, he did not clearly perceive the small, trespassing shadows which invaded his vision from the left and made slow passage across the face of the moon to merge silently with the opposite blackness. At the instant of their exit, however, he pressed his hand tightly across his eyes, and, in an after-vision, he saw them again. He counted three separate silhouettes this time, moving in leisured, phantom flight like interstellar couriers intent on a mission. He decided the three silhouettes were herons and reached for his pad and pencil. This was the third time, he noted, that the after-image had been successful, and he knew Professor Brooks would like to hear about it.

Ralph had first seen Professor Brooks one evening at sunset when he looked up from his bait cage and saw a stranger step out on the dock. He wondered how the stranger found the rut road through the palmettos and how he got his heavy car through the sand. And when the man asked for a rowboat Ralph had wondered why anybody without any fishing gear wanted to rent a boat, particularly if he had to have someone else to row it.

"Let's just drift, son," the professor had said when they reached midstream. So they drifted down the cool trough between the trees, and as the sky deepened the stranger began to talk about the birds which flew overhead or made their roosting cries back in the swamp. Ralph regarded the stranger with new respect after he had identified a limpkin by its mewling cry and caused a kingfisher to circle them twice as he mimicked its call.

"You know more about birds than I do, mister," Ralph said.

The stranger laughed. "That's my job; that's why I came out here. I'm an ornithologist; ever hear of it?"

"Maybe you ain't never seen the nest of a flamingo?"

The professor laughed again. "Few people have, son; you have to penetrate the everglades, and have a lot of luck as well, before you can ever see a flamingo."

"I'll show you one," Ralph said.

He butted the rowboat against Highbanks and led the way along the ridge that marked the old river bank through the swamp. Suddenly Ralph pointed, but the professor had already seen the flash of pink sail off the nest, exposing a single white egg.

They moved forward, and Ralph smiled at the way the professor kept cleaning his glasses and squatting all around the mud nest muttering, "It is, son. It is, son. It really is," like a man who had discovered something too precious to touch.

"I seen her up close," Ralph said, "and she's got a band on her leg. I figured she escaped from some place to come raise her family. I knowed her wings been clipped from the way she works herself when she flies."

"I have to leave for the North, tomorrow," the professor said, when they returned to the boat, "but I'm coming out in the morning to take some pictures of this flamingo. And I'm bringing you a box of stationery so you can send the society regular reports on the nesting habits. You'll watch the nest, won't you, son?"

"I been watching it right along."

"And you won't let anybody molest it?"

"Nobody ever comes out here 'cept fishing parties renting my boats on week ends. I don't aim to tell them about my pink lady."

The next morning after the professor took his pictures, he asked Ralph if he had seen any other rare birds.

"I wouldn't know about 'em being rare," Ralph said, "but one day I seen a fish hawk that drops grasshoppers on the water so he can dive on the fish what comes up to feed."

"That's just what I want," the professor said, recording Ralph's comments in a notebook. "Anything else?"

"I reckon that's all I recall, unless you ain't ever heard of ospreys flying eleven thousand feet high."

The professor stopped writing and glanced skeptically at Ralph. "Now that would be pretty hard to tell, wouldn't it, son?"

"I seen 'em up close," Ralph said, "during wartime. I was a steward in the Air Transport Command and one day I looked out the window, and there they were, two of 'em. I knowed it was eleven thousand 'cause I checked it on the altimeter up front."

"You'll make a good naturalist, my boy," the professor

smiled as he started his car. "Don't forget to send me your reports. The society will send you a regular check."

Each week after the professor left, Ralph rowed the eight miles into Curlew to mail his report. On the fourth trip, when he wrote that the flamingo egg had successfully hatched, he found a twenty-dollar check and a long letter from Professor Brooks asking him to send in reports on bird migrations for the society. He wanted to send Ralph a spotting telescope and forms to fill out, and he was to count the birds as they passed in front of the moon. Ralph pondered the letter all the way home.

"It may seem strange to you," the professor wrote, "but this is the only way we've found to count the birds at night when most of them fly. You pick out a good high place, watch the moon four hours a night, and from your count the society can estimate the number of birds migrating down the St. Johns River."

It had taken him less than a week to hoist up the lumber and nail his shack together at the top of the cypress. The first night after the telescope arrived, he counted forty-seven birds migrating in front of the moon, then fifty-four, and now he reached for his pad and pencil and made his first entry for the third night: "Number, 3; Time, 11:15; Direction, south; Flight, high and slow."

From time to time he made other entries or re-aimed the telescope as the moon traversed, but, for the most part, he gazed steadily upward. He grew drowsy occasionally, but his right eye never left the telescope for more than an instant.

He did not know how long he had gazed thus, only partially hearing the singsong of the tree frogs beneath him and an occasional hoot of an owl off in the swamp, when he first became aware of the odd sensation of staring, not up, but down at the moon. He was startled, at first, and consciously exerted his will to overcome the strange inversion. It was exactly as if he were floating dizzily above the moon and gazing down upon its splendor from some tenuously arrested position in space. Then, quite gradually, he felt himself to be slowly falling. He could even imagine the faint rush of air past his ears and feel the languorous tumbling of his body through space. It was a pleasant fall, luxurious and mesmeric, and he watched in fascination as the moon grew larger and slowly darker, becoming, finally, a purplish-brown in color. There were shifting forms on its surface which settled, after a moment, into a vaguely familiar shape.

Puzzled and somewhat disappointed, he identified the shape, finally, as the geographic form of North America. The glistening rivulet which rose from the Gulf of Mexico to intricately divide into tiny capillaries of silver, he knew to be the Mississippi River system, and in the wan, greenish light he could easily recognize the tangled ridges of the Rocky Mountains and the distant, serene arc of the Pacific.

With a sudden sickening fear at his stomach, he glanced directly beneath him and realized that, should his fall continue, he would strike the earth near the Mississippi River, somewhere in the vicinity of Memphis. Instantly, however, almost as if he had willed it, his fall was broken.

As the rush of wind faded, he hung motionless above the land, too awed by the vast and silent panorama below to remember his terror. With the exception of a curious bank of clouds which lay like sullied snow over the northwest, he could see the entire United States and could even make out the dim electric glow above the larger cities. To his amazement, he found he could move at will in any direction he chose. Tremulously, he flew over the New England area, trying to summon the courage to descend to the earth.

"I'll do it now or never!" he told himself, finally. But as he tried to fall, his arms and legs suddenly felt weighted with fatigue, and the galaxy of cities grew milky and indistinct. He felt himself rising swiftly through the night skies, and when he next blinked his eyes he was again looking up at the bright, round face of the moon.

As Ralph stepped out on the platform, he had to brace himself against the shack and blink his eyes to shake away the tiny moons which dogged his vision. After a moment he let himself over the side, feeling clumsily with his feet for the narrow planks. When he reached the bottom, he sank to the ground with his back to the trunk, squinting up only once at the usually absorbing spectacle of Whiteface swinging down by his tail from rung to rung. A few moments later his chin fell forward against his chest.

He awoke at dawn and pushed Whiteface from his lap. As he made his way along the path to his hut by the river, he paused from time to time and glanced up curiously. The pale dawn sky was cloudless. There was no sign of the moon.

Later, after he had washed his face in the river and was squatting over his breakfast fire, he continued to cast thoughtful glances at the sky and his loft in the cypress, struggling to recollect the details of the previous night. After he had eaten, he placed a can of tar on the fire, and when it had heated he began to paint the bottom of an upturned rowboat. As he worked the sticky tar into the boat bottom, he tried to account for his strange flight above the earth.

He remembered that as a boy on his father's farm in Georgia he had often watched the hawks and wished he could look down like the birds and see a whole county at one look. Then, one day after the war broke out, he remembered he had actually flown above the earth. It had happened about four months after he had been drafted and he had just been assigned to work on the gas trucks at MacDill Field. He was refueling a newly arrived transport named The Brown Dragon when he overheard the pilots as they stepped down from the plane. One of them, a captain who needed a shave, was exclaiming over a rainbow they had just seen below them as they flew over the Gulf of Mexico.

As Ralph watched them saunter away, he wondered if there were sights in the sky more marvelous even than a rainbow curving down to the sea. He wondered if it might even be possible to fly through a rainbow and become drenched in all the colors.

That evening after dark, he hid himself behind the cargo in the slender portion of the tail of The Brown Dragon. Sometime the next morning he heard the engines cough and start, and after a while he heard their roar and felt the lift and then the dip of the tail. And he knew he had left the earth. Twenty minutes passed before he dared to crawl forward and press his face against the nearest window. He closed his eyes for a moment, opened them, then caught his breath.

For the next two hours, his eyes never left the miniature world of still lakes and streams and the caterpillar trains beneath him. It was just as he had imagined it from his father's farm in Georgia, except he could see even more than a single county.

Some time later, there was a slight bump like a small wave under the bow of a rowboat, and a chill, gray light closed about the windows. He decided they had flown into a cloud and started to return to his hiding place. Suddenly the door to the pilots' compartment opened. A captain entered, the same one who still needed a shave. Ralph stiffened. He watched the captain open a bag hanging on the wall and remove a pint bottle of whisky. As the bottle came down from the captain's lips, two black, sober eyes looked directly into Ralph's.

"Who the hell are you?"

Ralph struggled to his feet and had difficulty standing in the moving plane.

"I come from—I mean—I put gas in this airplane yesterday. I just wanted to see how it is to fly. I mean——"

"What's your name?"

"Ralph Teeler."

The captain looked him over slowly and carefully, then put the bottle back in his bag.

"Well, we're not going to hurt you, Teeler," he said. "We're landing at Mitchell Field, and tomorrow you can get a courier back to MacDill. So you like to fly, do you?"

"Yes, sir."

After the captain closed the door, Ralph sank back on the bucket seat and stared into the gray cloud. After a moment there was another bump as they left the cloud, and he pressed his face to the window again. He did not look up till almost an hour later when he felt a hand on his shoulder.

"You had anything to eat?" the captain asked. "Now that you're here, you may as well ride up front with us. You can see more up there."

Obediently, Ralph followed him through the plane till they stood behind the pilots' seats.

"Chick," the captain said to the copilot, "let the boy sit there a moment, will you? He looks like he's getting the wild blue fever."

Ralph eased into the seat and looked across at the captain gratefully.

"Well, what is it like?" the captain grinned after a moment.

"It's good," Ralph said, "except in them clouds. Then it's like being shut up, like in a closet. But it's good now, like being in a church."

The captain laughed. "Hear that, Chick? Like being in a church. That's pretty good, Teeler. Go ahead; what's it look like to you down there?"

Ralph pressed his face against the window. "It's all good," he said, after a moment. "If a farmer knowed what a pretty thing he was fixin' when he plowed under a green field, he'd be wanting to come up here and look at it."

Ralph gulped down his sandwich without taking his eyes from the earth. From time to time, Captain Pollard called his attention to objects below, then Ralph, growing bolder, began to point out things to the captain. It was after they crossed the Virginia line that Captain Pollard suddenly turned to Ralph and asked him how he'd like to be the regular flight steward.

"Sure, I can fix it," he said. "You like to fly, don't you? A man who likes to fly shouldn't be a gas monkey on the ground."

During the next few weeks, Ralph discovered The Brown Dragon was a sort of gypsy airplane that hauled spare parts and light freight to airfields all over the country. Then, one day when they flew into Amarillo to get their pay, Captain Pollard received transfer orders. From then on, The Brown Dragon was flown by a series of strangers. Ralph began to ride regularly in the back of the plane, sitting long hours by the window. The only pilot he disliked and whose name he remembered was a Lieutenant Statler, a short man with a thick mustache. They were flying over New England one day when Lieutenant Statler made one of his infrequent trips to the back of the plane.

"What's the matter with you, corporal?" he said. "Why don't you give us a little company occasionally? What do you do back here all the time?"

"I just look out the window," Ralph said, "and watch the ground and think about things down there."

"What the hell do you find to think about?"

"I think about lots of things, lieutenant. I like it back here."

Lieutenant Statler had frowned and slammed the door; and until there was another transfer and he got a new pilot, Ralph had worried about being sent back to the gas trucks.

He remembered he decided, finally, to sleep in The Brown Dragon to avoid the noisy transient barracks at the various fields, and during the day he spent his free time sitting under the wing, waiting for the plane to fly. Sometimes an officer or guard asked him who he was. "I belong to The Brown Dragon," he answered, and they didn't ask any more questions.

He didn't actually mind the loneliness, Ralph recalled, as he finished tarring the bottom of the rowboat; what was most important was that he got to fly. He figured that, during his two years in the A.T.C., he flew over every state in the union except those four or five which were hidden last night by the curious cloud bank.

Ralph tossed the empty tar bucket far out into the river. Then he glanced up at the sky and smiled; the sun was already starting downhill. He turned over another rowboat and began to scrape the bottom. Perhaps, if he kept busy, it would soon be dark and the time of the moon.

That evening, after he climbed to the loft with Whiteface, he took his place quickly beneath the telescope and immediately tried to fall toward the moon, but it was not until nearly midnight when he had almost despaired of trying and was lying with his hands behind his head, picking out pictures on the moon, that the descent began.

After a few seconds, he found himself hanging above the earth in the same position he had occupied the previous night. Again, he found the United States incredibly still and beautiful. "Why, it's better'n the first time I ever climbed a tree!" he told himself. "And now I got real maneuvering power. I aim to go all the way down this time."

He drifted easily downward over the New York area, settling, finally, on the corner of a building above Times Square. He sat on the cold stone and gazed down in fascination at the theater crowds spreading out along the sidewalk, jostling one another to get into the taxis.

After the crowds had thinned to little knots of hurrying people, he stood up, steadied himself in the night breeze and gave a slight upward dive, with his arms still relaxed at his sides. Almost instantly, he zoomed high enough to see the entire Atlantic coast line; he paused, trying to decide where he would next land. Then he saw Florida, with its three large lakes and the St. Johns River tracking down from Jacksonville.

"That's it!" he decided suddenly. "I'll go down there to my river. I'll drop down near Curlew and find my place on the river!"

Then, just as it was on his first flight, he felt the fatigue begin to spread through his arms and legs. Quickly he tried to fall, but the earth began to waver as though it were under moving water. And he was rising instead of falling, and Florida became lost in the dazzling light of the moon.

The next morning, as Ralph rowed up the river to collect the channel cats and bass from his trotlines, he worried about the clouds in the sky for fear he wouldn't be able to see the moon that night and take his flight down to Florida. But he felt that somehow the clouds would go away.

"But I ought to have me a good name," he told himself. "Ralph don't sound like an angel name. I got it; I'll call myself Raphael. That's a pretty name, kinda like an angel in the Bible."

Several times during the day he said the name aloud, smiling at the nice way it came off his tongue.

About five o'clock that evening some men came down to rent a boat. While the party was up the river, Ralph sat on the bank, wondering why flying down to his own place had not occurred to him sooner. The first time, he recalled, that he had seen this spot on the river was from the rain-streaked window of The Brown Dragon, but he knew it would look different now, with his tree house and seven rows of corn. He was proud of the changes he had made since the day, just after the end of the war, when The Brown Dragon got lost in a storm. They had been flying down to Atlanta, and a solid overcast settled down near the Georgia line. Before the radio went out, he inquired up front and learned that Florida had reported clear weather. As they flew steadily south and the overcast grew darker, he watched the gas gauges flicker downward and the sweat soak up the back of the new pilot's shirt.

Later, when the air became really rough and threatening, he remembered he went back to his window in the rear and stared at the rain beading over the wing. He wondered, if he got out alive, where he would go when he was discharged. He thought of the last letter he received from his father, sent from a little town in Arkansas.

"It ain't fitten, Ralph," he had read, "to be grubbing in the land when there's good living in building Army camps. I ain't regretting selling the farm. Why, I got me a automobile, son, and a shiny trailer house, and I'm going up as a union man. When you get out, I aim to get you a hammer-and-saw job with me. I don't aim for us ever to go back to plowing. The land don't pay no more."

It was then that the window began to brighten and Ralph saw the beads on the wing spread farther apart. As they broke into the clear, he could see the ground just a few hundred feet below and the brilliant sunshine pouring down on the green trees which were still wet and misting. There was a river below, and white herons were soaring over a diamond-shaped island. He leaned far forward, imagining how a shack and a patch of corn would look. Then, as the plane banked sharply, he saw a sandy rut road winding through the trees to the river bank.

A few minutes later, he heard the flaps grinding down, and he ran up front, his heart beating in wild fear of a crash. To his surprise, The Brown Dragon kicked up mud and water on a short dirt runway, then skidded to a halt in a patch of palmettos. When the pilot started to taxi, the starboard engine ran out of gas.

Later, over coffee in the roadside hangar, the copilot tried to keep his hand from shaking as he held out a navigation chart.

"There's the little gift from God that saved our necks, corporal—that sweet little ace of diamonds sitting in the middle of the river. If I hadn't recognized that island and seen this flivver field on the chart, we'd be feeding the fishes by now."

Ralph took the map and looked at the red circle drawn around the island which was shaped like a diamond.

It was not long after his discharge that he remembered looking up, one day, from his corn planting and wondering if he ever had been up in the sky, wishing he had a place on the river. Ever since he had traded his mustering-out pay for the property, with six rowboats thrown in, he had the odd feeling of having become exactly what he had dreamed.

When the fishing party returned his rowboat, Ralph was still musing on the river bank. After he had bidden them a cheerful good night, he turned the boat over on the bank so the early morning sun could dry it out for the tar. Then he looked up and saw that the clouds were thinning out.

"It'll be a clear sky for Raphael tonight," he said. "I bet my place will look real good from up there."

Some time after dark, when he reached the base of the tall cypress, he started to clap his hands for Whiteface; then he remembered seeing him in the persimmon tree near the corn patch. "I'll just let him be," he decided. He stretched up his arms and began the long climb to the top of the tree.

Again, he had to stare at the moon for almost two hours

before he felt himself released in space. As he fell toward the United States, he searched the moonlit bends in the St. Johns for the island which was shaped like a diamond. When he reached the mounded treetops, he leveled off just above the river, slowing his flight to the pace of a downstream canoe. He knew he was not far from his tree house, and he wanted to prolong the sensations of coming home.

He heard a black bass smack a floating island of hyacinths, and spotted a night ibis perched like a swamp ghost in the foliage; he could even catch the subtle, horizontal fragrance of the bay trees mingled, occasionally, with an oversweet cloud of jasmine. From the banks came the constant serenade of the green frogs, their wet eyes, he knew, glistening like yellow fire in the moonlight. It was the most vivid flight of them all.

He was delighted to notice that he was not in the least tired, despite the fact that his present flight was already longer than either of the two others. He realized, with a sense of confidence and power, that he had mastered the strange fatigue that had brought the previous flights to an end; it would not bother him tonight. He could zoom in the heavens to his heart's content.

Then, just as he expected it to be, he saw his loft ahead of him, sitting like a boxy nest in the dead cypress.

Raphael dipped briefly toward the water, picked up speed, then as he coasted upward in a slowing arc toward the loft he brought his feet forward and landed with a slight jar upon the platform.

Ralph pulled back from the telescope and rubbed his eyes. Then he rose and opened the door. Outside, he stretched his arms and squatted to loosen the stiffness in his knees. When he looked up he saw several small moons gliding across the heavens. He blinked, but the moons jerked back to a new starting position and glided again. He looked down the long, gray column of the cypress and gave a slight chuckle as the moons swam along with his glance, brighter than ever against the dark foliage.

It was the time of morning when a moist haze hovered above the trees, catching and holding the moonlight in a gauzy, luminous veil. It always came with such gradualness that he was never able to mark its transition at all. He just looked out and it was there, like a blanket, he thought, that finally covers the trees, quieting them even beyond their usual quietness, and hushing all the green frogs and all the night birds, and calming the fish in the river, grown tired of their nocturnal feeding.

Ralph knew the veil was not very thick. It was like the morning fogs he remembered around the airports before the sun burned them off. He knew he could rise through it easily in a matter of seconds, and could soar on up to where he could see the Mississippi River and the Gulf of Mexico and, finally, the Pacific Ocean itself.

He placed his toes over the edge of the platform and gave a slight upward dive, with his arms still relaxed at his sides. For a brief instant, his body was serenely poised above the swamp in attitude of expected flight.

A few seconds later, the nesting flamingo on the far side of the river suddenly extended her long neck in alarm. After a moment when the noise was not repeated, she drew her neck back down upon her breast and resumed her wary sleep. And on the near side of the river, Whiteface, startled by the jarring thump against the ground, scurried swiftly to the top of the persimmon tree, where he sat sniffing the air with his whiskered nose and blinking his round eyes in the moonlight.

The Little Terror
by Will F. Jenkins

"The Little Terror" is a pure horror-fantasy story. Absolute power in the hands of a young child is a cornerstone of the fantastic literature of the last three decades: from the realism of William March's "The Bad Seed" to the pure science fiction of John Windham's "Midwitch Cuckoos," which was filmed as "Children of the Damned." The latest rage in this type of tale, the demonic child, portrayed in such works as David Seltzer's "The Omen," Ira Levin's "Rosemary's Baby" and Tom Tryon's "The Other," is exemplified as pure malevolence. Jenkins' tale in its innocence is far more frightening—no disguised evil, no aliens from the depths of space, but the horror of an uncontrolled elemental force.

The Little Terror

by Will F. Jenkins

There was no crashing roll of thunder when the principles of psychological acosmistic idealism became practicalities in the world inhabited by Nancy. Her mother had no twinge of uneasiness, and her father was reading his newspaper. There was no breathless hush over the earth at the bloodcurdling instant, though possibly Bishop Berkeley (1685-1753), up in heaven, was pleasantly interested. Joe Holt, who was a practicing psychiatrist and might be presumed to have a feeling for such things, hadn't the trace of an intuition of it. The skies did not darken suddenly, nor were there deep rumblings underground. There was not even an unnatural gray twilight in which birds chirped faintly and cattle affrightedly rolled their eyes. There was no sign whatever that the most alarming moment in history was at hand. But still—

Nancy went to the gate with her grandfather. She was six and he was sixty, and they were very congenial. Nancy skipped, because she never walked when she could skip or, preferably, run. It was nearing dusk, but there was still a ruddy sunshine in the air, yet the sky was perceptibly darkening.

At the gate Nancy permitted her grandfather to kiss her good-by, in the benign, smug condescension of little girls who know they are irresistible.

Then she said, "Make a penny go away, granddaddy."

Her grandfather obediently took a copper penny from his pocket. He put it between his thumb and middle finger and offered it gravely for Nancy's inspection. She held her breath. Her grandfather snapped his fingers. The penny vanished.

Nancy beamed. "Do it again, granddaddy!"

Her grandfather prepared to repeat. Nancy put her eyes within inches of the coin. She watched with rapt fascination.

The penny vanished a second time.

"It's real magic?" asked Nancy hopefully. She was beginning to discover that one could not count on fairy godmothers—not confidently, at any rate—in moments of despair. But still she hoped.

"It's real magic," agreed her grandfather.

"Show me how!" begged Nancy. "Please!"

Her grandfather whispered confidentially in her ear, "I say 'oogledeboo' and it vanishes. Can you say that?"

Nancy whispered, "Oogledeboo."

"Splendid!" said her grandfather. He straightened up. "Now you say 'oogledeboo' at this penny, and see what happens!" He held the penny as before, between thumb and middle finger.

Nancy giggled at it. She said, "Oogledeboo!"

Her grandfather's fingers snapped. The penny vanished.

Nancy beamed. "Again, granddaddy?"

"Once more," conceded her grandfather. He proffered the penny. It was the same one, but Nancy did not reflect upon that. He took it in his fingers. Her eyes sparkled. She said, "Oogledeboo!"

The penny vanished. Her grandfather looked slightly surprised. But it was natural. He had never heard of Bishop Berkeley's dictum that *esse* is *percipi,* nor drawn inferences from the statement. However, he beamed at Nancy.

"Now I have to go, Nancy. Good night."

Nancy waved cheerfully as he walked down the street. When he was out of sight, she skipped back to where she had been playing. She did not notice that her grandfather was shaking his coat sleeve absently, as if to make something come out of it—something that did not come.

Nancy settled down placidly to play alone. There was a caterpillar on the doll she had neglected for her grandfather. Nancy regarded it with disfavor. She said sternly, "Oogledeboo!"

The caterpillar vanished. Nancy played with her doll. The sunset proceeded. Twilight fell. Nancy's mother called her, and she went in cheerfully, dragging the doll by one arm. She ate her supper with excellent appetite and beamed at her father and mother. There was only one alarming incident, and it happened to pass unnoticed. Nancy did not want to finish her milk. Her mother said firmly that she must. Then the telephone rang, and her mother got up to answer it.

Nancy looked confidently at the milk in her glass and said, "Oogledeboo."

The milk vanished.

Nancy went happily to bed later, after kissing her father and mother with extravagant affection. She went dreamlessly and placidly to sleep. She slept blissfully all night long.

All was serene through all the cosmos. There was no hint of the appalling thing that had happened. Nobody cringed in nameless horror. Nobody trembled in justified apprehension. Nobody, it appears, happened to be thinking of the Right Reverend George Berkeley, of the Anglican Church, who wrote books of philosophy and died in 1753.

Nancy woke next morning in her customary ebullient mood. She sang lustily as she was dressed, and there was no hint of disturbance until breakfast was served. Then there was a slight collision of wills over Nancy's reluctance to eat her cereal. But just then the milkman came to collect, and her mother went to pay him. When her mother came back, the cereal bowl was quite empty. Nancy's mother praised her warmly. Nancy giggled.

It was a charming morning. Nancy, scrubbed to radiance and wearing a playsuit of healthful brevity, went out to play in her sand box behind the house. She sang as she played. She was a delightfully happy child. Presently Charles, the little boy next door, came over to play with her. She greeted him with that cordial suspicion with which little girls regard little boys. He stepped on a sand house she had decorated with small stray sticks and cherished bottle caps. She scolded.

"Huh!" said Charles scornfully. "That's no fun! Let's play going to the moon. Let's fight the cat men. Rnnnnn-nnh! Bang-bang!"

Nancy demurred.

"Let's play space ship," insisted Charles. He began to hop excitedly. He shouted, "Whoooooooom! Three gravs! Four! Turn on the stern rockets! Whoooooooooom! There come the space pirates! Warm up the disintegrators! Shoot the space warp! Bang! Bang! Rnnnnnnnnnnh! Bang!"

He rushed about madly, fighting a splendid space battle with space pirates from the rings of Saturn, while Nancy placidly practiced interior decoration in her sand pile. She set a wilted buttercup on a dab of sand which to her represented a sideboard—undoubtedly Sheraton. She reflectively arranged another dab of sand into a luxurious sofa. She began to smooth out wall-to-wall carpeting, with the intent to add a grandfather's clock next to her sand-pile scheme for gracious living.

Charles got into difficulties. A fleet of black space ships from Sirius winked into existence from the fourth dimension over by the back-porch steps. They sped toward him, disintegrator rays flaming. He flashed into faster-than-light attack, throwing out atomic bombs and with tractor and pressor beams busy. Then came a despairing call from an Earth passenger space liner under attack by pirates near the hydrangea bush.

"Whoooooooom!" shouted Charles ferociously. "Coming, Earthship, with all jets firing! Rnnnnnnnnh! Take that! And that! Bang! Bang! Here's an H-bomb for you! Boom!"

Disaster struck. Charles, rushing to the defense of the helpless passenger craft, cut across the sand pile. One sandaled foot landed in the kitchen of Nancy's ranch-type sand house. Kitchen sink, dishwasher and breakfast nook —they were marked by rather wobbly lines of pebbles—were obliterated as if by collision with a giant meteor in space. Sand sprayed on Nancy.

"Bang, bang!" roared Charles in his high treble. "Rnnnnnnnh! Take that, you old pirates! Calling Earth! Space-patrol ship reporting pirates wiped out! I'm taking off for Pluto!"

Nancy trembled with indignation. She said sternly, "You go home!"

"Huh?" said Charles. He stopped short. "I'm Captain Space! I've got to fight space pirates and things, haven't I?"

"You go home!" said Nancy sternly. "You stepped on my house! You go home or I'll say something at you!"

If she had threatened to tell her mother on him, it might have been effective. But this threat had no meaning to Charles. He shouted, "Whoooooooom! Taking off for Pluto! Invaders from space! Coming, Earth garrison! Hold on, I'm coming with all jets firing! Whoooooom!"

He started for Pluto. Unfortunately, it appeared that Pluto lay somewhere in the general direction of a yellow tea-rose bush at the edge of the lawn. Charles' orbit would coincide with the sand pile again.

Nancy said vengefully, "Oogledeboo!"

Charles vanished.

Silence fell, and Nancy returned to the building of a sand-pile ranch house. Presently she sang happily as she worked. Presently, again, she went into the house and asked for cookies. Having skipped her breakfast cereal, she was hungry.

Her mother said, "Where's Charles? Didn't I hear him playing with you?"

Nancy bit into a cooky and said placidly, "I said 'oogledeboo' at him and he went away."

Nancy's mother smiled absently and went about what she thought were more important affairs. Which was a mistake. There were no more important affairs. According to the principles laid down by Bishop Berkeley between 1685 and 1753, things exist because a mind thinks of them as existing. Nancy had acquired the ability to think confidently of things as ceasing to exist—a gift no adult can acquire. So—by a natural extrapolation of Bishop Berkeley's principle—when she thought of something as ceasing to exist, it did. All of us have wished for such a talent at some time or another, but Nancy had it.

When she was at lunch, the voice of Charles' mother could be heard, calling him. He did not answer, and presently she was at the door. Nancy had arrived at the custard-with-strawberry-jam stage of her lunch then, and she worked zestfully with a spoon. Her mother went to confer with Charles' mother about his whereabouts.

"Why, no," Nancy heard her say. "He was playing with Nancy, but he left." She called, "Nancy! Do you know where Charles went?"

"No, mother-r!" Nancy sang out happily. She worked further on the custard. She was absorbed.

There was talk at the door. Nancy got some strawberry jam on the large napkin her mother spread over her at mealtime. She was enjoyably licking it off when her mother returned.

"Charles' mother is worried," said Nancy's mother. She frowned a little. "He doesn't usually wander away. You're sure you didn't notice which way he went?" Nancy shook her head. "He didn't go with anybody?" her mother asked uneasily.

Nancy got a big spoonful of custard. "No," she said placidly. "I said 'oogledeboo' at him and he went away."

Her mother did not inquire further. But she looked unhappy. A parent of a small child always shares the anguish of another parent when a small child can't be found. But it didn't occur to Nancy's mother that she might have heard a complete and accurate description of Charles' disappearance.

Immediately after lunch, Nancy's mother dressed her up to go downtown. There was to be a parade, and Nancy's mother was making the sacrifice of an afternoon to Nancy's pleasure. Of course Nancy loathed being dragged through stores, but since her mother was devoting an entire afternoon to her, it was only reasonable that they should start early, to do some shopping, and do more shopping later. This is what is called thinking only of one's children.

Nancy had no forebodings. She adored being dressed up, and wriggled with pleasure as her mother attired her in a very frilly dress, a very frilly hat, a smart little coat and tiny white gloves which to Nancy were the ultimate of bliss. She sang and paraded before a mirror as her mother prepared for the outing.

She sang, also, as her mother drove downtown. When the traffic grew thick and they stopped at traffic lights, Nancy continued to sing lustily and without self-consciousness. People looked at her and smiled, thinking of innocent and happy childhood.

There were mobs in every store. Other self-sacrificing mothers were out to show their children the parade. They constituted an outrageous crush by a ladies'-purse counter. A fat woman jammed Nancy against a counter. She was enraged. Somebody protested, and the fat woman turned indignantly, and in pivoting, that protruding part of her body which was at the height of Nancy's six-year-old head sent Nancy reeling.

Nancy said wrathfully, "Oogledeboo!"

There was no fat woman.

Somebody screamed in a stifled fashion. But nobody believed it. There was a surging of bodies to fill the space where a fat woman had been, and Nancy was banged again and wailed, and grabbed her mother hysterically by the legs.

Her mother completed the purchase of a handbag and harassedly got Nancy out of the crowd. Nancy's frilly hat was dangling and she was very unhappy.

"There, darling!" said her mother penitently. "I shouldn't have brought you into such a crowded place! We'll go upstairs where there won't be so many people."

They got into an elevator. Then a mob charged it. A horde of women resolutely thrust and pushed and shoved, while small children howled. Women are less than ladylike when there are no men around. The elevator operator tried to stem the flood, to no avail.

Nancy was crushed ruthlessly. She became terrified. She gasped, "Oogledeboo!"

There were only five people in the elevator. There was not even a crowd trying to push in.

Nancy's mother trembled for a considerable time after that. Of course it could not possibly be true. Even the elevator operator merely stammered unintelligibly when a floorwalker questioned him. There was nothing to tell. The elevator had been crowded, and suddenly it wasn't. There had been no outcry. The crowd hadn't even visibly faded. It just was—and then it wasn't. So the elevator operator, completely overwrought, was relieved of duty and the floorwalker apologized to the few passengers remaining. They were all remarkably pale, and they all went quickly out of the store. But of course they didn't believe it either. Not even Nancy's mother.

But Nancy felt much better. More confident. Now, she knew placidly, she could always get room around her if people pushed. Her mother drank a cup of tea in the nearest tea room, and tried tremblingly to remember the psychiatric meaning of the delusion that people vanished before one's eyes. But while her mother trembled, Nancy ate a small plate of vanilla ice cream, with relish.

Nancy's mother really wanted to go straight home then. Already she had made up her mind to ask Joe Holt about the experience. He was the only psychiatrist she knew personally, but he and his wife were fairly close friends. She could mention it in an offhand manner, perhaps. But Nancy had been promised the parade. So they saw it.

It began appropriately with motorcycle policemen, at whom Nancy waved enthusiastically. Her mother had been able to get a place at the very curb, so nothing would interfere with Nancy's view. There came a high-school band, with drum-majorettes strutting in costumes which would have caused their great-grandmothers to die of heart failure. There came a cadet corps. And then the floats.

Nancy was thrilled by a float in the shape of a swan, decorated by young girls in tinsel dresses and fixed smiles. There was a float showing embarrassed Boy Scouts about a campfire. A float resembling a battleship. A Girl Scout float.

There came a traveling squealing down the street. Children's shrill voices shrieked and shouted. Nancy squirmed to look. Her mother held her tightly. But Nancy's mother was thinking desperately that she'd never expected to call on Joe Holt professionally, but, after all, he was a psychiatrist and he played golf with——

Nancy squealed in pure excitement. Her mother looked numbly at the float which caused all the high-pitched tumult. It represented a dragon. It was a very ambitious job. The body of the beast completely hid the truck on which it was built, and a long and ungainly hooped-canvas tail trailed three car lengths behind. But it was what went on before that caused the excitement.

The dragon had a twenty-foot movable neck of hooped canvas painted red, with a five-foot head at the end of it. The head had short, blunt horns. It had eyes the size of saucers, and an expression of imbecilic amiability, and smoke came lavishly out of its nostrils. And its head moved from side to side on the movable neck, and it turned coquettishly and seemed to gaze at the spectators wherever it turned with an admirable look of benign imbecility.

Children squealed and shrieked and cheered as the dragon proceeded down the main street. Those at whom it seemed to look shrank back in delighted terror. Those from whom it looked away yelled in sheer excitement.

Nancy trembled in delicious thrill. She jumped up and down. She squealed.

Opposite her, the long, articulated neck swung in her direction. The dragon's head turned toward her. It seemed to look directly at her, in a sort of wall-eyed cordiality. Smoke welled from its nostrils. It swung still closer, as if to take an even closer and even more admiring look.

Nancy said zestfully, "Oogledeboo!"

A smoke pot fell to the pavement and smashed. It scattered strangling, smoldering stuff over five yards of asphalt. A man fell with a clank, landing astride the hood of a battered motor truck which had been hidden by the dragon's body. His expression was that of stunned bewilderment, and he stared at his hands. They had held ropes by which he moved the dragon's neck and head. Now they were empty. There were four men in their undershirts, riding in the truck, and they regarded their public incredulously, because there was no longer a dragon to hide them.

There was, though, an impressive smoldering conflagration on the street. It called for fire engines. They came.

Nancy's mother was in a chaotic state of mind when she

managed to fight her way, with Nancy, to where her car was parked. Her expression tended to be on the wild-eyed side, but she got Nancy into the car and herself behind the wheel. Then she doubted frenziedly whether she was in a fit state to drive. She started off, finally, on the dubious premise that somebody who is really crazy never suspects it.

They were late getting home, and Nancy's father was beginning to be worried. He'd been informed of the disappearance of Charles, next door, and of the feverish hunt for him by police and all the neighbors.

He was relieved when Nancy and her mother turned up, but Nancy's mother got out of the car and said tautly, "Get Joe Holt to come here at once." Nancy's mother spoke in the level, tense tone of one who is likely to scream in another split second. "He's a psychiatrist. I have to see a psychiatrist. Everything's happened today! Charles disappeared. An elevatorful of people vanished before my eyes and a dragon faded to nothingness while I was looking at it. Things like that don't happen! I'm going crazy, but maybe Joe Holt can do something! Get him, quick!"

Then she collapsed, blubbering. She was thinking of Nancy. Already she envisioned a broken home, herself a madwoman and divorced, Nancy's father remarried to someone who would be cruel to Nancy, and Nancy haunted by the specter of madness looming ever before her. Nancy's mother did not worry about her husband. Perhaps that was significant.

But Nancy's father knew when not to try to be reasonable. Also, he was frightened. He grabbed the telephone and spoke with such desperate urgency that in five minutes Joe Holt, that rising young psychiatrist, had got into his car, raced the necessary five blocks, and was looking anxiously at Nancy's mother, in his house slippers and without a necktie.

"What the hell?" asked Joe Holt unprofessionally.

Nobody noticed Nancy. Her mother began to tell her wholly incredible story. Her tone was pure desperation. She suddenly remembered the fat woman. She told about it, shrilly.

Nancy said reassuringly, "But that was all right, mother-r! I said 'oogledeboo' at her!"

Her mother paid no heed. Nancy's father moved to take her out of the room. She clung convulsively to her mother, and her mother to her. Nancy's father was in an unenviable spot for a moment, there.

"Don't take her away!" panted her mother despairingly. "Not yet! Wait! . . . And five minutes later an elevatorful of people vanished before my eyes!"

She sobbed suddenly. Nancy's father ran his hands through his hair.

Nancy's voice said consolingly, "But mother-r, they were crowding us! That's why I said 'oogledeboo' at them. Like Charles was bothering me and I said 'oogledeboo' at him and made him go away."

Her mother's whole body jerked. She stared at Nancy. And then her anguished face smoothed out suddenly. She said in a quiet and interested tone, "Did you, darling?" But she turned tragic eyes upon Joe Holt. "You see, Joe? Listen to her! The things that've happened have turned her little brain too! Don't bother about me, Joe! Do something for Nancy!"

Joe breathed a small sigh of professional relief. All this business was completely bewildering, but he did know that sometimes a woman will do anything for her child—even stay sane, if necessary.

So he said cheerfully to Nancy, "So you made things go away? That's interesting, Nancy. Tell us about it."

Nancy beamed at him. She liked people. They found her irresistible. So she told how her granddaddy had told her how to do magic. One said "oogledeboo" at things and they went away.

"I said it to the penny," she finished happily, "and to a caterpillar on my doll, and my milk last night, and my cereal this morning, and Charles, and a fat woman, and the people in the elevator, and the dragon. It's easy," she finished generously. "Want me to show you?"

Her mother gasped. But Joe Holt noticed that she wasn't thinking of herself any longer but of Nancy. And as a practical matter, nobody is neurotic who sincerely cares about anybody else. Joe didn't understand anything, but he began to have hope.

"Why, yes, Nancy!" he said blithely. "Make this—h'm—this vase of flowers go away, will you?"

Nancy's mother said involuntarily, "That's my best vase." But then she said calmly, "Yes, darling, make that go away."

So Nancy, blithe and beaming and six years old, looked at her mother's most-prized almost-Ming vase and said happily, "Oogledeboo."

And of course the vase went away.

It was two o'clock in the morning and raining heavily when they got Nancy's grandfather out of bed to answer the bell. Then Nancy's father and Joe Holt crowded inside the door to talk desperately to him with rain-wet, disheveled faces. He stared.

"You've got to come to the house, sir!" said Nancy's father feverishly. "Nancy's got a psychological acosmistic idea from you, and it's got to be cured!"

Joe Holt said reprovingly, if harassedly, "Not idea. Ability. It's a psychokinetic ability."

Nancy's grandfather said in a rising tone, "Nancy's sick? Sick? And you talk? Come on!"

He grabbed an overcoat and flung out of the house, pulling the coat on over his pajamas. Rain poured down. Lightning glinted on it as it fell. They piled into Joe's convertible and he started it off at frantic speed.

Nancy's grandfather snapped, "How's she sick? When did it start?"

"She says 'oogledeboo' at things!" panted Nancy's father. "And they vanish! We've got her to bed now, but she's got to be cured! Think what she may do next! She says 'oogledeboo'!"

Nancy's grandfather barked, "Oogledeboo? What's the matter with saying 'oogledeboo'? I say 'oogledeboo' if I feel like it! I taught her to say it!"

"That's just it," said Joe Holt, swallowing. He turned to gesticulate. "You showed her that a penny vanished when she said it. She believed it! It's—idealistic immaterialism! . . . Oops!"

He yanked at the wheel and pulled the car out of a skid as it headed for a telephone pole aglitter with wetness.

"It was Bishop Berkeley," panted Nancy's father. "Joe just showed me! In a book! Bishop Berkeley said that matter cannot exist without mind. A mind has to perceive something in order for it to exist. It's been a big argument for years. Locke, Hume, Kant, Hegel and all the rest."

The car plunged through a black puddle on the pavement, pockmarked with falling rain under an arc light. Sheets of water, like shining wings, rose on either side of the car.

"*Esse,*" said Joe Holt, gulping, "is *percipi*. If a thing isn't perceived by some mind somewhere, it isn't. But when we know something is, we have to let it go at that. Nancy doesn't. You fixed it so she doesn't. When she says 'oogledeboo' at something, she's able to think of it as ceasing to exist. So it does cease to exist. Nobody else in the world, thank God, can do that! But Nancy can!"

In the racing, leaking car, Nancy's grandfather stared suspiciously at the water-soaked and nerve-racked individuals beside him. His pajama collar rose out of his overcoat. His white hair bristled.

"And you're telling me Nancy's sick!" he roared. "You two lunatics!"

They babbled further details. Preposterous details. They explained what he had to do. Then, suddenly, Joe Holt swung into the driveway of the house Nancy lived in. As if on signal, the rain stopped. The two younger men piled out of the car and raced into the house. Nancy's grandfather plodded after them. He entered to hear the chattered query, "She's—still asleep?"

"Yes, the darling!" said Nancy's mother in a warm, throaty voice. She hugged Nancy's grandfather. "Daddy! I'm so glad——"

The living room looked like a shambles. The piano was gone. The almost-Ming vase—of course. The picture over the mantel. Two chairs. A scatter rug.

"We experimented!" babbled Joe Holt desperately. "She made the vase vanish. We couldn't believe it. So she said 'oogledeboo' at the piano. It wasn't there. The picture over the fireplace! It got to be a happy game! She stood there beaming and saying 'oogledeboo.' She looked at me once——" He shuddered violently.

Nancy's grandfather could not believe. Naturally! But Nancy's mother pleaded with him. The three of them—Nancy's parents and the psychiatrist—argued hysterically. Their voices rose.

Then there was a delighted giggle from the doorway. Nancy stood there, smiling brightly at her grandfather. She wore her very favorite blue pajamas with Mickey Mouse figures printed on them.

She was sleepy-eyed, but very glad to see her grandfather.

"Hello, granddaddy!" she said happily. "You waked me up. I can do magic like you told me. Want to see?"

Her grandfather gulped suddenly. He had a moment of dreadful doubt. His daughter had turned wholly pale. Nancy's father was speechless. Joe Holt wrung his hands.

"Wait, now," said Nancy's grandfather shakily. "Just try it on a little thing, Nancy. Just a little thing."

With the sure instinct of a grandfather, he remembered that his overcoat was wet. He put it down on a remaining chair before he took Nancy in his arms. Stout elderly man and beaming six-year-old, they made a pleasant picture in their pajamas.

"There, there," said Nancy's grandfather fondly.

"Su-su-suppose," said Joe Holt, "you make your granddaddy's overcoat go away, Nancy?"

Nancy giggled. Her soft, happy voice pronounced the fateful syllables. Her grandfather's overcoat abruptly was not. Her grandfather sat down suddenly. Nancy slipped from his arms to his knee.

She said benignly, "Are you cold, granddaddy? You're shivering!"

Nancy's grandfather swallowed, loudly. Then he said with infinite care, "Why, yes, Nancy. I am cold. I shouldn't have taken off my overcoat. I need it back. Will you get it back for me, Nancy?"

Nancy said fondly, "But I don't know how, granddaddy!"

"Why—er—you say 'oogledeboo' backwards, Nancy. But you have to say it. You made my overcoat go away, so you have to make it come back. 'Oogledeboo' backwards is—ah—is——"

"'Oobedelgoo,'" said Nancy's father hoarsely. "'Oogledeboo' spelled backwards is 'oobedelgoo.' Oobedelgoo!"

Nancy considered, and snuggled against her grandfather. "You say it, granddaddy!"

"It's no good when I say it," said her grandfather, with false heartiness. "See? Oobedelgoo! But it will work for you! And—now—— Wait a moment, Nancy! When you say it, don't say it at just my overcoat. You say it at all the things you said 'oogledeboo' at, all at the same time, and they'll all come back at once. Won't that be nice?"

"No," said Nancy. "Charles bothers me."

Joe Holt moaned.

Nancy's mother said softly, "But he won't any more, darling! Just say 'oobe—oobedelgoo' nicely, darling, for mother, at all the things you said the other word to!"

Nancy considered again. Her mother stroked her hand. And presently Nancy said, without enthusiasm, without verve, but with a sort of resigned acquiescence, "Oobedelgoo."

The almost-Ming vase came back, and her grandfather's overcoat, and the piano, and the picture over the mantelpiece and a scatter rug and two chairs. Out on the lawn there was suddenly the howling wail of a scared small boy, "Wa-a-a-ah!" That was Charles, who found himself suddenly in the dark on a rain-wet lawn. He howled. Those in Nancy's house heard doors open next door and shrieks of joy. Nancy's mother closed her eyes and imagined other screams: A fat woman suddenly finding herself alone in the ladies'-purse department of a closed-up department store. An elevatorful of people finding themselves parked in the cellar of the same store, to wait for morning. The night watchman of that store would have a busy half hour.

The policeman who suddenly found a dragon in the middle of the street would be upset, too, as would the hard-working detectives now busily hunting for a small boy who would insist frantically that he hadn't been anywhere. And he hadn't. He'd been nowhere.

Even a caterpillar, which had been crawling on Nancy's doll until she said "oogledeboo" at it, would have a difficult time finding a proper place to hide from the rain. It happened to be a diurnal caterpillar, not used to being out at night.

Then Nancy's grandfather spoke with very great care and painstaking charm.

"I forgot to tell you, Nancy," he said with seeming ruefulness, "that now you've said 'oobedelgoo,' saying 'oogledeboo' won't work for you any longer. That's why I can't work that magic any more myself. But you won't mind things not going away when you say 'oogledeboo,' will you?"

"Won't they?" asked Nancy disappointedly. She said loudly, "Oogledeboo!"

Her father and mother and Joe Holt jumped a foot.

But nothing happened. The four grownups sat still, weak with relief. Nancy cuddled against her grandfather. She sighed. Presently her eyelids drooped sleepily.

There had been no rolling of thunder or flashing of lightning, or earthquakes when the most bloodcurdling instant in history began. But, now that everything was all over, there was a blinding flash of lightning and a reverberating roar of thunder, and the rain began to pour down again.

The Answer
by Philip Wylie

Philip Wylie was one of the best-known writers of the fantastic novel. With science fiction novels The Disappearance *and* Tomorrow, *along with works of social criticism like* Generation of Vipers *and a rich and varied career as a film writer (among others he scripted* The Island of Lost Souls *from H.G. Wells'* The Island of Dr. Moreau), *Wylie guaranteed a place for himself in American letters. "The Answer" is one of his best stories. Within a mood of despair he creates a gleam of hope and a touching tale indeed.*

The Answer

by Philip Wylie

"Fifteen minutes!" . . . The loud-speakers blared on the flight deck, boomed below, and murmured on the bridge where the brass was assembling. The length of the carrier was great. Consonants from distant horns came belatedly to every ear, and metal fabric set up echoes besides. So the phrase stuttered through the ship and over the sea. Fifteen minutes to the bomb test.

Maj. Gen. Marcus Scott walked to the cable railing around the deck and looked at the very blue morning. The ship's engines had stopped and she lay still, aimed west toward the target island like an arrow in a drawn bow.

Men passing saluted. The general returned the salutes, bringing a weathered hand to a lofty forehead, to straight, coal-black hair above gray eyes and the hawk nose of an Indian.

His thoughts veered to the weather. The far surface of the Pacific was lavender; the nearby water, seen deeper, a lucent violet. White clouds passed gradually—clouds much of a size and shape—with cobalt avenues between. The general, to whom the sky was more familiar than the sea, marveled at that mechanized appearance. It was as if some cosmic weather engine—east, and below the Equator—puffed clouds from Brobdingnagian stacks and sent them rolling over the earth, as regular and even-spaced as the white snorts of a climbing locomotive.

He put away the image. Such fantasy belonged in another era, when he had been a young man at West Point, a brilliant young man, more literary than military, a young man fascinated by the "soldier poets" of the first World War. The second, which he had helped to command in the air, produced no romanticists. Here a third war was in the making, perhaps, a third that might put an end to poetry forever.

"Ten minutes! All personnel complete checks, take assigned stations for test!"

General Scott went across the iron deck on scissoring legs that seemed to hurry the tall man without themselves hurrying. Sailors had finished stringing the temporary cables which, should a freak buffet from the H-bomb reach the area, would prevent them from being tossed overboard. They were gathering, now, to watch. Marc Scott entered the carrier's island and hastened to the bridge on turning steps of metal, not using the shined brass rail.

Admiral Stanforth was there—anvil shoulders, marble hair, feldspar complexion. Pouring coffee for Senator Blaine with a good-host chuckle and that tiger look in the corners of his eyes. "Morning, Marc! Get any sleep at all?" He gave the general no time to answer. "This is General Scott, gentlemen. In charge of today's drop. Commands base on Sangre Islands. Senator Blaine—"

The senator had the trappings of office: the *embonpoint* and shrewd eyes, the pince-nez on a ribbon, the hat with the wide brim that meant a Western or Southern senator. He had the William Jennings Bryan voice. But these were for his constituents.

The man who used the voice said genuinely, "General, I'm honored. Your record in the Eighth Air Force is one we're almost too proud of to mention in front of you."

"Thank you, sir."

"You know Doctor Trumbul?"

Trumbul was thin and thirty, an all-brown scholar whose brown eyes were so vivid the rest seemed but a background for his eyes. His hand clasped Scott's. "All too well! I flew with Marc Scott when we dropped Thermonuclear Number Eleven—on a parachute!"

There was some laughter; they knew about that near-disastrous test.

"How's everybody at Los Alamos?" the general asked.

The physicist shrugged. "Same. They'll feel better later today—if this one comes up to expectations."

The admiral was introducing again. "Doctor Antheim, general. Antheim's from MIT. He's also the best amateur magician I ever saw perform. Too bad you came aboard so late last night."

Antheim was as quietly composed as a family physician —a big man in a gray suit.

"Five minutes!" the loud-speaker proclaimed.

You could see the lonely open ocean, the sky, the cumulus clouds. But the target island—five miles long and jungle-painted—lay over the horizon. An island created by volcanic cataclysm millions of years ago and destined this day to vanish in a man-patented calamity. Somewhere a hundred thousand feet above, his own ship, a B-111, was moving at more than seven hundred miles an hour, closing on an imaginary point from which, along an imaginary line, a big bomb would curve earthward, never to hit, but utterly to devastate. You could not see his B-111 and you would probably not even see the high, far-off tornadoes of smoke when, the bomb away, she let go with her rockets to hurtle off even faster from the expanding sphere of blast.

"Personally," Antheim, the MIT scientist, was saying to General Larsen, "it's my feeling that whether or not your cocker is a fawning type depends on your attitude as a dog owner. I agree, all cockers have Saint Bernard appetites. Nevertheless, I'm sold on spaniels. In field trials last autumn——"

Talking about dogs. Well, why not? Random talk was the best antidote for tension, for the electrically counted minutes that stretched unbearably because of their measurement. He had a dog—his kids had one, rather: Pompey, the mutt, whose field trials took place in the yards and playgrounds of Baltimore, Maryland, in the vicinity of Millbrook Road. He wondered what would be happening at home—where Ellen would be at—he calculated time belts, the hour-wide, orange-peel-shaped sections into which man had carved his planet. Be evening on Millbrook Road——

John Farrier arrived—Farrier, of the great Farrier Corporation. His pale blue eyes looked out over the ship's flat deck toward the west, the target. But he was saying to somebody, in his crisp yet not uncourteous voice, "I consider myself something of a connoisseur in the matter of honey. We have our own apiary at Hobe Sound. Did you ever taste antidesma honey? Or the honey gathered from palmetto flowers?"

"Two minutes!"

The count-down was the hardest part of a weapons test. What went before was work—sheer work, detailed, exhausting. But what came after had excitements, real and potential, like hazardous exploring, the general thought; you never knew precisely what would ensue. Not precisely.

Tension, he repeated to himself. And he thought, *Why do I feel sad? Is it prescience of failure? Will we finally manage to produce a dud?*

Fatigue, he answered himself. Setting up this one had been a colossal chore. They called it Bugaboo—Operation Bugaboo in Test Series Avalanche. Suddenly he wished Bugaboo wouldn't go off.

"One minute! All goggles in place! Exposed personnel

without goggles, sit down, turn backs toward west, cover eyes with hands!"

Before he blacked out the world, he took a last look at the sky, the sea—and the sailors, wheeling, sitting, covering their eyes. Then he put on the goggles. The obsidian lenses brought absolute dark. From habit, he cut his eyes back and forth to make certain there was no leak of light—light that could damage the retina.

"Ten seconds!"

The ship drew a last deep breath and held it. In an incredibly long silence, the general mused on thousands upon thousands of other men in other ships, ashore and in the air, who now were also holding back breathing.

"Five!"

An imbecile notion flickered in the general's brain and expired: He could leap up and cry "Stop!" He still could. A word from Stanforth. A button pressed. The whole shebang would chute on down, unexploded. And umpteen million dollars' worth of taxpayers' money would be wasted by that solitary syllable of his.

"Four!"

Still, the general thought, his lips smiling, his heart frozen, why should they—or anybody—*be doing this?*

"Three seconds . . . two . . . one . . . zero!"

Slowly, the sky blew up.

On the horizon, a supersun grabbed up degrees of diameter and rose degrees. The sea, ship, praying sailors became as plain as they had been bare-eyed in full sun, then plainer still. Eyes, looking through the inky glass, saw the universe stark white. A hundred-times-sun-sized sun mottled itself with lesser whiteness, bulked up, became the perfect sphere, ascending hideously and setting forth on the Pacific a molten track from ship to livid self. Tumors of light more brilliant than the sun sprang up on the mathematical sphere; yet these, less blazing than the fireball, appeared as blacknesses.

The thing swelled and swelled and rose; nonetheless, instant miles of upthrust were diminished by the expansion. Abruptly, it exploded around itself a white lewd ring, a halo.

For a time there was no air beneath it, only the rays and neutrons in vacuum. The atmosphere beyond—incandescent, compressed harder than steel—moved toward the spectators. No sound.

The fireball burned within itself and around itself, burnt the sea away—a hole in it—and a hole in the planet. It melted part way, lopsided, threw out a cubic mile of fire this way—a scarlet asteroid, that.

To greet the birthing of a new, brief star, the regimental sky hung a bunting on every cloud. The mushroom formed quietly, immensely and in haste; it towered, spread, and the incandescent air hurtled at the watchers on the circumferences. In the mushroom new fire burst forth, cubic miles of phosphor-pale flame. The general heard Antheim sigh. That would be the "igniter effect," the new thing, to set fire, infinitely, in the wake of the fire blown out by the miles-out blast. A hellish bit of physics.

Again, again, again the thorium-lithium pulse! Each time—had it been other than jungle and sea; had it been a city, Baltimore—the urban tinder, and the people, would have hair-fired in the debris.

The mushroom climbed on its stalk, the ten-mile circle of what had been part of earth. It split the atmospheric layers and reached for the purple dark, that the flying general knew, where the real sun was also unbearably bright.

Mouths agape, goggles now dangling, the men on the bridge of the *Ticonderoga* could look naked-eyed at the sky's exploded rainbows and seething prismatics.

"Stand by for the blast wave!"

It came like the shadow of eclipse. The carrier shuddered. Men sagged, spun on their bottoms. The general felt the familiar compression, a thousand boxing gloves, padded but hitting squarely every part of his body at once.

Then Antheim and Trumbul were shaking hands.

"Congratulations! That ought to be—about it!"

It for what? The enemy? A city? Humanity?

"Magnificent," said Senator Blaine. He added, "We seem O.K."

"Good thing too," a voice laughed. "A dozen of the best sets of brains in America, right in this one spot."

The general thought about that. Two of the world's leading nuclear physicists, the ablest member of the Joint Chiefs of Staff, a senator wise for all his vaudeville appearance, an unbelievably versatile industrialist, the Navy's best tactician. Good brains. But what an occupation for human brains!

Unobtrusively he moved to the iron stairs—the "ladder." Let the good brains and the sight-seers gape at the kaleidoscope aloft. He hurried to his assigned office.

An hour later he had received the important reports. His B-111 was back on the field, "hot," but not dangerous; damaged, but not severely; the crew in good shape. Celebrating, Major Stokely had bothered to add.

Two drones lost; three more landed in unapproachable condition. One photo recon plane had been hit by a flying chunk of something eighteen miles from ground zero and eight minutes—if the time was right—after the blast. Something that had been thrown mighty high or somehow remained aloft a long while. Wing damage and radioactivity; but, again, no personnel injured.

Phones rang. Messengers came—sailors—quick, quiet, polite. The *Ticonderoga* was moving, moving swiftly, in toward the place where nothing was, in under the colored bomb clouds.

He had a sensation that something was missing, that more was to be done, that news awaited—which he attributed again to tiredness. Tiredness: what a general was supposed never to feel—and the burden that settled on every pair of starred shoulders. He sighed and picked up the book he had read in empty spaces of the preceding night: Thoreau's Walden Pond.

Why had he taken Thoreau on this trip? He knew the answer. To be as far as possible, in one way, from the torrent of technology in mid-Pacific; to be as close as possible to a proper view of Atomic-Age Man, in a different way. But now he closed the book as if it had blank pages. After all, Thoreau couldn't take straight Nature, himself; a couple of years beside his pond and he went back to town and lived in Emerson's back yard. For the general that was an aggrieved and aggrieving thought.

Lieutenant Tobey hurried in from the next office. "Something special on TLS. Shall I switch it?"

His nerves tightened. He had expected "Something special" on his most restricted wire, without a reason for the expectation. He picked up the instrument when the light went red. "Scott here."

"Rawson. Point L 15."

"Right." That would be instrument site near the mission school on Tempest Island.

"Matter of Import Z." Which meant an emergency.

"I see." General Scott felt almost relieved. Something was wrong; to know even that was better than to have a merely mystifying sense of wrongness.

Rawson—Maj. Dudley Rawson, the general's cleverest Intelligence officer, simply said, "Import Z, and, I'd say, general, the Z Grade."

"Can't clarify?"

"No, sir."

General Scott marveled for a moment at the tone of Rawson's voice: it was high and the syllables shook. He said, "Right, Raw. Be over." He leaned back in his chair and spoke to the lieutenant, "Would you get me Captain Elverson? I'd like a whirlybird ride."

The helicopter deposited the general in the center of the

playing field where the natives at the mission school learned American games. Rawson and two others were waiting. The general gave the customary grateful good-by to his naval escort; then waited for the racket of the departing helicopter to diminish.

He observed that Major Rawson, a lieutenant he did not know and a technical sergeant were soaked with perspiration. But that scarcely surprised him; the sun was now high and the island steamed formidably.

Rawson said, "I put it through Banjo, direct to you, sir. Took the liberty. There's been a casualty."

"Lord!" The general shook his head. "Who?"

"I'd rather show you, sir." The major's eyes traveled to the road that led from the field, through banyan trees, toward the mission. Corrugated-metal roofs sparkled behind the trees, and on the road in the shade a jeep waited.

The general started for the vehicle. "Just give me what particulars you can——"

"I'd rather you saw—it—for yourself."

General Scott climbed into the car, sat, looked closely at the major.

He'd seen funk, seen panic. This was that—and more. They sweated like horses, yet they were pallid. They shook —and made no pretense of hiding or controlling it. A "casualty"—and they were soldiers! No casualty could——

"You said 'it,'" the general said. "Just what——"

"For the love of God, don't ask me to explain! It's just behind the mission buildings." Major Rawson tapped the sergeant's shoulder, "Can you drive O.K., Sam?"

The man jerked his head and started the motor. The jeep moved.

The general had impressions of buildings, of brown boys working in a banana grove, and native girls flapping along in such clothes as missionaries consider moral. Then they entered a colonnade of tree trunks which upheld the jungle canopy.

He was afraid in some new way. He must not show it. He concentrated on seeming not to concentrate.

The jeep stopped. Panting slightly, Rawson stepped out, pushed aside the fronds of a large fern tree and hurried along a leafy tunnel. "Little glade up here. That's where the casualty dropped."

"Who found—it?"

"The missionary's youngest boy. Kid named Ted. His dad too. The padre—or whatever the Devoted Brethren call 'em."

The glade appeared—a clear pool of water bordered by terrestrial orchids. A man lay in their way, face down, his clerical collar unbuttoned, his arms extended, hands clasped, breath issuing in hoarse groans.

From maps, memoranda, somewhere, the general remembered the man's name. "You mean Reverend Simms is the victim?" he asked in amazement.

"No," said Rawson; "up ahead." He led the general around the bole of a jacaranda tree. "There."

For a speechless minute the general stood still. On the ground, almost at his feet, in the full sunshine, lay the casualty.

"Agnostic," the general had been called by many; "mystic," by more; "Natural philosopher," by devoted chaplains who had served with him. But he was not a man of orthodox religion.

What lay on the fringe of purple flowers was recognizable. He could not, would not, identify it aloud.

Behind him, the major, the lieutenant and the sergeant were waiting shakily for him to name it. Near them, prostrate on the earth, was the missionary—who had already named it and commenced to worship.

It was motionless. The beautiful human face slept in death; the alabastrine body was relaxed in death; the unimaginable eyes were closed and the immense white wings were folded. It was an angel.

The general could bring himself to say, in a soft voice, only, "It looks like one."

The three faces behind him were distracted. "It's an angel," Rawson said in a frantic tone. "And everything we've done, and thought, and believed is nuts! Science is nuts! Who knows, now, what the next move will be?"

The sergeant had knelt and was crossing himself. A babble of repentance issued from his lips—as if he were at confessional. Seeing the general's eyes on him, he interrupted himself to murmur, "I was brought up Catholic." Then, turning back to the figure, with the utmost fright, he crossed himself and went on in a compulsive listing of his sad misdemeanors.

The lieutenant, a buck-toothed young man, was now laughing in a morbid way. A way that was the sure prelude to hysteria.

"Shut up!" the general said; then strode to the figure among the flowers and reached down for its pulse.

At that, Reverend Simms made a sound near to a scream and leaped to his feet. His garments were stained with the black humus in which he had lain; his clerical collar flapped loosely at his neck.

"Don't you even touch it! Heretic! You are not fit to be here! You—and your martial kind—your scientists! Do you not yet see what you have done? Your last infernal bomb has shot down Gabriel, angel of the Lord! This is the end of the world!" His voice tore his throat. "And you are responsible! You are the destroyers!"

The general could not say but that every word the missionary had spoken was true. The beautiful being might indeed be Gabriel. Certainly it was an unearthly creature. The general felt a tendency, if not to panic, at least to take seriously the idea that he was now dreaming or had gone mad. Human hysteria, however, was a known field, and one with which he was equipped to deal.

He spoke sharply, authoritatively, somehow keeping his

thoughts a few syllables ahead of his ringing voice, "Reverend Simms, I am a soldier in charge here. If your surmise is correct, God will be my judge. But you have not examined this pathetic victim. That is neither human nor Christian. Suppose it is only hurt, and needs medical attention? What sort of Samaritans would we be, then, to let it perish here in the heat? You may also be mistaken, and that would be a greater cruelty. Suppose it is not what you so logically assume? Suppose it merely happens to be a creature like ourselves, from some real but different planet—thrown, say, from its space-voyaging vehicle by the violence of the morning test?"

The thought, rushing into the general's mind from nowhere, encouraged him. He was at that time willing to concede the likelihood that he stood in the presence of a miracle—and a miracle of the most horrifying sort, since the angel was seemingly dead. But to deal with men, with their minds, and even his own thought process, he needed a less appalling possibility to set alongside apparent fact. If he were to accept the miracle, he would be obliged first to alter his own deep and hard-won faith, along with its corollaries—and that would mean a change in the general's very personality. It would take pain, and time. Meanwhile there were men to deal with—men in mortal frenzy.

The missionary heard him vaguely, caught the suggestion that the general might doubt the being on the ground to be Gabriel, and burst into grotesque, astounding laughter. He rushed from the glade.

After his antic departure, the general said grimly, "That man has about lost his mind! A stupid way to behave, if what he believes is the case!" Then, in drill-sergeant tones, he barked, "Sergeant! Take a leg. . . . Lieutenant, the other. . . . Rawson, help me here."

He took gentle hold. The flesh, if it was flesh, felt cool, but not yet cold. When he lifted, the shoulder turned easily; it was less heavy than he had expected. The other men, slowly, dubiously, took stations and drew nerving breaths.

"See to it, men," the general ordered—as if it were mere routine and likely to be overlooked by second-rate soldiers—"that those wings don't drag on the ground! Let's go!"

He could observe and think a little more analytically as they carried the being toward the jeep. The single garment worn by the angel was snow-white and exquisitely pleated. The back and shoulder muscles were obviously of great power, and constructed to beat the great wings. They were, he gathered, operational wings, not vestigial. Perhaps the creature came from a small planet where gravity was so slight that these wings sufficed for flying about. That was at least thinkable.

A different theory which he entertained briefly—because he was a soldier—seemed impossible on close scrutiny. The creature they carried from the glade was not a fake—not some biological device of the enemy fabricated to startle the Free World. What they were carrying could not have been man-made, unless the Reds had moved centuries ahead of everyone else in the science of biology. This was no hybrid. The angel had lived, grown, moved its wings and been of one substance.

It filled the back seat of the jeep. The general said, "I'll drive. . . . Lieutenant . . . sergeant, meet me at the field. . . . Raw, you get HQ again on a Z line and have them send a helicopter. Two extra passengers for the trip out, tell them. Have General Budford fly in now, if possible. Give no information except that these suggestions are from me."

"Yes, sir."

"Then black out all communications from this island."

"Yes, sir."

"If the Devoted Brethren Mission won't shut its radio off, see that it stops working."

The major nodded, waited a moment, and walked down the jungle track in haunted obedience.

"I'll drive it," the general repeated.

He felt long and carefully for a pulse. Nothing. The body was growing rigid. He started the jeep. Once he glanced back at his incredible companion. The face was perfectly serene; the lurching of the vehicle, for all his care in driving, had parted the lips.

He reached the shade at the edge of the playing field where the jeep had first been parked. He cut the motor. The school compound had been empty of persons when he passed this time. There had been no one on the road; not even any children. Presently the mission bell began to toll slowly. Reverend Simms, he thought, would be holding services. That probably explained the absence of people, the hush in the heat of midday, the jade quietude.

He pulled out a cigarette, hesitated to smoke it. He wondered if there were any further steps which he should take. For his own sake, he again carefully examined the angel, and he was certain afterward only that it was like nothing earthly, that it could be an angel and that it had died, without any external trace of the cause. Concussion, doubtless.

He went over his rationalizations. If men with wings like this did exist on some small, remote planet; if any of them had visited Earth in rocket ships in antiquity, it would explain a great deal about what he had thitherto called "superstitious" beliefs. Fiery chariots, old prophets being taken to heaven by angels, and much else.

If the Russian had "made" it and dropped it to confuse the Free World, then it was all over; they were already too far ahead scientifically.

He lighted the cigarette. Deep in the banyans, behind the screens of thick, aerial roots and oval leaves, a twig snapped. His head swung fearfully. He half expected another form—winged, clothed in light—to step forth and demand the body of its fallen colleague.

A boy emerged—a boy of about nine, sun-tanned, big-eyed and muscular in the stringy way of boys. He wore only a T-shirt and shorts; both bore marks of his green progress through the jungle.

"You have it," he said. Not accusatively. Not even very emotionally. "Where's father?"

"Are you—"

"I'm Ted Simms." The brown gaze was suddenly excited. "And you're a general!"

The man nodded. "General Scott." He smiled. "You've seen"—he moved his head gently toward the rear seat—"my passenger before?"

"I saw him fall. I was there, getting Aunt Cora a bunch of flowers."

The general remained casual, in tone of voice, "Tell me about it."

"Can I sit in the jeep? I never rode in one yet."

"Sure."

The boy climbed in, looked intently at the angel, and sat beside the general. He sighed. "Sure is handsome, an angel," said the boy. "I was just up there at the spring, picking flowers, because Aunt Cora likes flowers quite a lot, and she was mad because I didn't do my arithmetic well. We had seen the old test shot, earlier, and we're sick and tired of them, anyhow! They scare the natives and make them go back to their old, heathen customs. Well, I heard this whizzing up in the air, and down it came, wings out, trying to fly, but only spiraling, sort of. Like a bird with an arrow through it. You've seen that kind of wobbly flying?"

"Yes."

"It came down. It stood there a second and then it sat."

"Sat?" The general's lips felt dry. He licked them. "Did it—see you?"

"See me? I was right beside it."

The boy hesitated and the general was on the dubious

verge of prodding when the larklike voice continued, "It sat there crying for a while."

"Crying!"

"Of course. The H-bomb must of hurt it something awful. It was crying. You could hear it sobbing and trying to get its breath even before it touched the ground. It cried, and then it looked at me and it stopped crying and it smiled. It had a real wonderful smile when it smiled."

The boy paused. He had begun to look with fascination at the dashboard instruments.

"Then what?" the general murmured.

"Can I switch on the lights?" He responded eagerly to the nod and talked as he switched the lights, tried the horn. "Then not much. It smiled and I didn't know what to do. I never saw an angel before. Father says he knows people who have, though. So I said, 'Hello,' and it said, 'Hello,' and it said, after a minute or so, 'I was a little too late,' and tears got in its eyes again and it leaned back and kind of tucked in its wings and, after a while, it died."

"You mean the—angel—spoke to you—in English?"

"Don't they know all languages?" the boy asked, smiling.

"I couldn't say," the general replied. "I suppose they do."

He framed another question, and heard a sharp "Look out!" There was a thwack in the foliage. Feet ran. A man grunted. He threw himself in front of the boy.

Reverend Simms had crept from the banyan, carrying a shotgun, intent, undoubtedly, on preventing the removal of the unearthly being from his island. The lieutenant and sergeant, rounding a turn in the road, had seen him, thrown a stone to divert him, and rushed him. There was almost no scuffle.

The general jumped down from the jeep, took the gun, looked into the missionary's eyes and saw no sanity there—just fury and bafflement.

"You've had a terrible shock, dominie," he said, putting the gun in the front of the jeep. "We all have. But this is a thing for the whole world, if it's what you believe it to be. Not just for here and now and you. We shall have to take it away and ascertain—"

"Ye of little faith!" the missionary intoned.

The general pitied the man and suddenly envied him; it was comforting to be so sure about anything.

Comforting. But was such comfort valid or was it specious? He looked toward the jeep. Who could doubt now?

He could. It was his way of being—to doubt at first. It was also his duty, as he saw duty.

Rawson, looking old and deathly ill, came down the cart track in the green shadows. But he had regained something of his manner. "All set, Marc. No word will leave here. Plane's on the way; General Budford's flying in himself. Old Bloodshed said it better be Z priority." The major eyed the white, folded wings. "I judge he'll be satisfied."

General Scott grinned slightly. "Have a cigarette, Raw." He sat beside the praying missionary with some hope of trying to bring the man's mind from dread and ecstasy back to the human problems—the awesome, unpredictable human enigmas—which would be involved by this "casualty."

One thing was sure. The people who had felt for years that man didn't yet know enough to experiment with the elemental forces of Nature were going to feel entirely justified when this story rocked the planet.

If, the general thought on with a sudden, icy feeling, it wasn't labeled Top Secret and concealed forever.

That could be. The possibility appalled him. He looked up angrily at the hot sky. No bomb effects were visible here; only the clouds' cyclorama toiling across the blue firmament. Plenty of Top Secrets up there still, he thought.

The President of the United States was awakened after a conference. When they told him, he reached for his dressing gown, started to get up and then sat on the edge of his bed. "Say that again."

They said it again.

The President's white hair was awry, his eyes had the sleep-hung look of a man in need of more rest. His brain, however, came wide awake.

"Let me have that in the right sequence. The Bugaboo test brought down, on Tempest Island, above Salandra Strait, an angel—or something that looked human and had wings, anyhow. Who's outside and who brought that over?"

His aide, Smith, said, "Weatherby, Colton and Dwane."

The Secretary of State. The chairman of the Joint Chiefs of Staff. The chairman of the Atomic Energy Commission.

"Sure of communications? Could be a terrific propaganda gag. The Reds could monkey with our wave lengths——" The President gestured, put on the dressing gown.

"Quadruple-checked. Budford talked on the scrambler. Also Marc Scott, who made the first investigation of the—er—casualty." Smith's peaceful, professorish face was composed, still, but his eyes were wrong.

"Good men."

"None better. Admiral Stanforth sent independent verification. Green, of AEC, reported in on Navy and Air Force channels. Captain Wilmot, ranking Navy chaplain out there, swore it was a genuine angel. It must be—something, Mr. President! Something all right!"

"Where is it now?"

"On the way, naturally. Scott put it aboard a B-111. Due in here by three o'clock. Coffee waiting in the office."

"I'll go out, Clem. Get the rest of the Cabinet up and here. The rest of the JCS. Get Ames at CIA. This thing has got to stay absolutely restricted till we know more."

"Of course."

"Scott with it?"

"Budford." Smith smiled. "Ranked Scott. Some mission, hunh? An angel. Imagine!"

"All my life I've been a God-fearing man," the President

replied. "But I can't imagine. We'll wait till it's here." He started toward the door where other men waited tensely. He paused. "Whatever it is, it's the end to—what has been, these last fifteen years. And that's a good thing." The President smiled.

It was, perhaps, the longest morning in the history of the capital. Arrangements had been made for the transportation of the cargo secretly but swiftly from the airfield to the White House. A select but celebrated group of men had been chosen to examine the cargo. They kept flying in to Washington and arriving in limousines all morning. But they did not know why they had been summoned. Reporters could not reach a single Cabinet member. No one available at State or the Pentagon, at AEC or CIA could give any information at all. So there were merely conjectures, which led to rumors:

Something had gone wrong with an H-bomb.

The President had been assassinated.

Russia had sent an ultimatum.

Hitler had reappeared.

Toward the end of that morning, a call came which the President took in person. About thirty men watched his face, and all of them became afraid.

When he hung up he said unsteadily, "Gentlemen, the B-111 flying it in is overdue at San Francisco and presumed down at sea. All agencies have commenced a search. I have asked, meantime, that those officers and scientists who saw, examined or had any contact with the—strange being be flown here immediately. Unless they find the plane and recover what it carried, that's all we can do."

"The whole business," Dwane said, after a long silence, "could be a hoax. If the entire work party engaged in Test Series Avalanche formed a conspiracy——"

"Why should they?" asked Weatherby.

"Because, Mr. Secretary," Dwane answered, "a good

many people on this globe think mankind has carried this atomic-weapons business too far."

General Colton smiled. "I can see a few frightened men conspiring against the world and their own government, with some half-baked idealistic motive. But not a fleet and an army. Not, for that matter, Stanforth or Scott. Not Scott. Not a hoax."

"They'll report here tonight, gentlemen, in any case." The President walked to a window and looked out at the spring green of a lawn and the budding trees above. "We'll know then what they learned, at least. Luncheon?"

On the evening of the third day afterward, Marc Scott greeted the President formally in his office. At the President's suggestion they went out together, in the warm April twilight, to a low-walled terrace.

"The reason I asked you to come to the White House again," the President began, "was to talk to you entirely alone. I gathered, not from your words, but from your manner at recent meetings, general, that you had some feelings about this matter."

"Feelings, Mr. President?" He had feelings. But would the statesman understand or regard them as naïve, as childish?

The President chuckled and ran his fingers through his thick white hair in a hesitant way that suggested he was uncertain of himself. "I have a fearful decision to make." He sighed and was silent for several seconds as he watched the toy silhouettes of three jet planes move across the lemon-yellow sky. "There are several courses I can take. I can order complete silence about the whole affair. Perhaps a hundred people know. If I put it on a Top Secret basis, rumors may creep out. But they could be scotched. The world would then be deprived of any real knowledge of your—angel.

"Next, I could take up the matter with the other heads

of state. The friendly ones." He paused and then nodded his head unsurely. "Yes. Even the Russians. And the satellite governments. With heaven knows what useful effect! Finally, I could simply announce to the world that you and a handful of others found the body of what appears to have been an angel, and that it was irretrievably lost while being flown to Washington."

Since the President stopped with those words, Marc said, "Yes, sir."

"Three equally poor possibilities. If it was an angel—a divine messenger—and our test destroyed it, I have, I feel, no moral right whatever to keep the world from knowing. Irrespective of any consequences."

"The consequences!" Marc Scott murmured.

"You can imagine them!" The President uncrossed his legs, stretched, felt for a cigarette, took a light from the general. "Tremendous, incalculable, dangerous consequences! All truly and decently religious people would be given a tremendous surge of hope, along with an equal despair over the angel's death and the subsequent loss of the —body. Fanatics would literally go mad. The news could produce panic, civil unrest, bloodshed. And we have nothing to show. No proof. Nothing tangible. The enemy could use the whole story for propaganda in a thousand evil ways. Being atheistic, they would proclaim it an American madness—what you will. Even clergymen, among themselves, are utterly unagreed, when they are told the situation."

"I can imagine."

The President smiled a little and went on, "I called half a dozen leaders to Washington. Cardinal Thrace. Bishop Neuermann. Father Bolder. Reverend Matthews. Every solitary man had a different reaction. When they became assured that I meant precisely what I said, they began a theological battle"—the President chuckled ruefully at the memory—"that went on until they left, and looked good for a thousand years. Whole denominations would split! Most of the clergy, however, agreed on one point: it was not an angel."

The general was startled. "Not an angel? Then, what——"

"Because it died. Because it was killed or destroyed. Angels, general, are immortal. They are not human flesh and blood. No. I think you can say that, by and large, the churches would never assent to the idea that the being you saw was Gabriel or any other angel."

"I hadn't thought of that."

"I had," the President replied. "You are not, general, among the orthodox believers, I take it."

"No, Mr. President."

"So I judged. Well, let me get to my reason for asking you to confer privately with me. The churchmen debated hotly—to use the politest possible phrase—over the subject. But the scientists—whom I also consulted"—he drew a breath and swallowed, like a man whose memory of hard-controlled temper is still painful—"the scientists were at scandalous loggerheads. Two of them actually came to blows! I've heard every theory you can conceive of, and a lot I couldn't. Every idea from the one that you, general, and all the rest of you out in the Pacific, were victims of mass hypnosis and the whole thing's an illusion, to a hundred versions of the 'little men from outer space' angle. In the meeting day before yesterday, however, I noticed you were rather quiet and reserved about expressing any opinion. I've since looked up your record. It's magnificent." The President hesitated.

Marc said nothing.

"You're a brave, brilliant, levelheaded, sensitive person, and a man's man. Your record makes a great deal too plain for you to deny out of modesty. You are an exceptional man. In short, you're the very sort of person I'd pick to look into a mere report of an incident of that sort. So what I want—why I asked you here—is your impression. Your feelings. Your reactions at the time. Your reflections since. Your man-to-man, down-to-earth, open-hearted emotions about it all—and not more theory, whether theological or allegedly scientific! Do you see?"

The appeal was forceful. Marc felt as if he were all the members of some audiences the President had swayed—all of them in one person, one American citizen—now asked—now all but commanded—to bare his soul. He felt the great, inner power of the President and understood why the people of the nation had chosen him for office.

"I'll tell you," he answered quietly. "For what it's worth. I'm afraid that it is mighty little." He pondered a moment. "First, when I suddenly saw it, I was shocked. Not frightened, Mr. President—though the rest were. Just—startled. When I really looked at the—casualty, I thought, first of all, that it was beautiful. I thought it had, in its dead face, great intelligence and other qualities."

The President rested his hand on the uniformed knee. "That's it, man! The 'other qualities'! What were they?"

Marc exhaled unevenly. "This is risky. It's all—remembered impression. I thought it looked kind. Noble too. Almost, but not exactly, sweet. I thought it had tremendous courage. The kind that—well, I thought of it as roaring through space and danger and unimagined risks to get here. Daring H-bombs. And I thought, Mr. President, one more thing: I thought it had determination—as if there was a gigantic feel about it of—mission."

There was a long silence. Then the President said in a low voice, "That all, Marc?"

"Yes. Yes, sir."

"So I thought." He stood up suddenly, not a man of reflection and unresolved responsibility, but an executive with work ahead. "Mission! We don't know what it was. If only there was something tangible!" He held out his hand and gripped the general with great strength. "I needed that word to decide. We'll wait. Keep it absolutely restricted.

There might be another. The message to us, from them, whoever they are, might come in some different way or by more of these messengers! After all, I cannot represent them to the world—expose this incredible incident—without knowing what the mission was. But to know there was a mission——" He sighed and went on firmly, "When I finally get to bed tonight, I'll sleep, Marc, as I haven't slept since I took office!"

"It's only my guess," the general responded. "I haven't any evidence to explain those feelings."

"You've said enough for me! Thank you, general." Then, to Marc Scott's honor and embarrassment, the President drew himself straight, executed a salute, held it a moment, turned from the terrace and marched alone into the White House.

During the months-long, single day of Northern Siberia's summertime, on a night that had no darkness, a fireball burst suddenly above the arctic rim. As it rose, it turned the tundra blood-red. For a radius of miles the permafrost was hammered down and a vast, charred basin was formed. In the adjacent polar seas ice melted. A mushroom cloud broke through the atmospheric layers with a speed and to a height that would have perplexed, if not horrified, the Free World's nuclear physicists.

In due course, counters the world around would begin to click and the information would be whispered about that the Russians were ahead in the H-bomb field. That information would be thereupon restricted so that the American public would never learn the truth.

In Siberia the next morning awed Soviet technicians—and the most detached nuclear physicists have been awed, even stupefied, by their creations—measured the effects of their new bomb carefully: area of absolute incineration, area of absolute destruction by blast, putative scope of fire storm, radius of penetrative radiation, kinds and concentrations of radioactive fall-out, half-lives, dispersion of same, kilos of pressure per square centimeter. Then, on maps of the United States of America, these technicians superimposed tinted circles of colored plastics, so that a glance would show exactly what such a bomb would destroy of Buffalo and environs, St. Paul, Seattle, Dallas, as well as New York, Chicago, Philadelphia, Los Angeles, and so on—the better targets. These maps, indicating the imaginary annihilation of millions, were identical with certain American maps, save for the fact that the latter bore such city names as Moscow, Leningrad, Stalingrad, Vladivostok, Ordzhonikidze, Dnepropetrovsk, and the like.

It was while the technicians were correlating their bomb data—and the sky over the test base was still lava—that coded word came in to the commanding officer of the base concerning a "casualty." The casualty had been found in dying condition by a peasant who had been ordered to evacuate his sod hut in that region weeks before. After the casualty, he had been summarily shot for disobedience.

The general went to the scene forthwith—and returned a silent, shaken man. Using communication channels intended only for war emergency, he got in touch with Moscow. The premier was not in his offices in the new, forty-six-story skyscraper; but his aides were persuaded to disturb him at one of his suburban villas. They were reluctant; he had retired to the country with Lamenula, the communist Italian actress.

The premier listened to the faint, agitated news from Siberia and said, "The garrison must be drunk."

"I assure you, comrade——"

"Put Vorshiv on."

Vorshiv said, uneasily, the same thing. Yes, he had seen it. . . . Yes, it had wings. . . . No, it could not be an enemy trick. . . . No, there were no interplanetary vehicles about; nothing on the radar in the nature of an unidentified flying object. . . . Certainly, they had been meticulous in the sky watch; this had been a new type of bomb, incorporating a new principle, and it would never have done to let an enemy reconnaissance plane observe the effects.

"I will come," said the premier.

He ordered a new Khalov-239 prepared for the flight. He was very angry. Lamenula had been coy—and the premier had enjoyed the novelty of that, until the call from Siberia had interrupted. Now he would have to make a long, uncomfortable journey in a jet—which always frightened him a little—and he would be obliged to postpone the furthering of his friendship with the talented, beautiful, honey-haired young Italian.

Night came to the Siberian flatlands and the sky clouded so that there was a semblance of darkness. A frigid wind swept from the Pole, freezing the vast area of mud created by the H-bomb. In the morning the premier came in at the base airfield, twelve jets streaming in the icy atmosphere, forward rockets blasting to brake the race of the great ship over the hard-packed terrain. It stopped only a few score rods short of the place where the "inadequate workers" lay buried—the more than ten thousand slaves who had died to make the field.

Curiously enough, it was an American jeep which took the premier out to the scrubby patch of firs. The angel lay untouched, but covered with a tarpaulin and prodigiously guarded round about by men and war machines.

"Take it off."

He stood a long time, simply looking, his silent generals and aides beside him.

Not a tall man, this Soviet premier, but broad, overweight, bearlike in fur clothing—a man with a Mongol face and eyes as dark, as inexpressive and unfeeling as prunes. A man whose face was always shiny, as if he exuded minutely a thin oil. A man highly educated by the standards of his land; a man ruthless by any standard in history.

What went through his head as he regarded the dazzling figure, he would not afterward have catalogued. Not in its entirety. He was afraid, of course. He was always afraid. But he had achieved that level of awareness which acknowledges, and uses, fear. In the angel he saw immediately a possible finish to the dreams of Engels, Marx, the rest. He saw a potential end of communism, and even of the human race. This milk-white cadaver, this impossible reality, this beauty Praxiteles could never have achieved even symbolically, could mean—anything.

Aloud, he said—his first remark—"Michelangelo would have appreciated this."

Some of the men around him, scared, breathing steam in the gray, purgatorial morning, smiled or chuckled at their chief's erudition and self-possession. Others agreed solemnly: Michelangelo—whoever he was or had been—would have appreciated this incredible carcass.

He then went up and kicked the foot of the angel with his own felted boot. It alarmed him to do so, but he felt, as premier, the duty. First, the noble comment; next, the boot.

He was aware of the fact that the men around him kept glancing from the frozen angel up toward the barely discernible gray clouds. They were wondering, of course, if it could be God-sent. Sounds came to him—bells of churches, litanies recited, chants—Gregorian music in Caucasian bass. To his nostrils came the smell of incense. He thought, as atheists must, what if they were right?

Against that thought he ranged another speedily enough; it was his custom. He wrenched the ears and eyes of his mind from the church pageantry of recollected boyhood, in the Czar's time, to other parts of his expanding domain. He made himself hear temple bells, watch sacred elephants parade, behold the imbecile sacrifices and rituals of the heathen. They, too, were believers, and they had no angels. Angels, he therefore reasoned, were myths.

It occurred to him—it had already been suggested to him by General Mornsk, of Intelligence—that some such being as this, come on a brief visit from an unknown small planet, had given rise to the whole notion of angels. He chuckled.

Vorshiv had the temerity to ask, "You have formed an opinion, comrade?"

The premier stared at the stringy, leathern man with his watery eyes and his record: eighteen million unworthy citizens "subdued." "Certainly." He looked once more at the casualty. "Autopsy it. Then destroy the remains."

"No," a voice murmured.

The premier whirled about. "Who said that?"

It was a young man, the youngest general, one born after 1917, one who had seen no world but the Soviet. Now, pale with horror and shame, the young man said, "I merely thought, sir, to preserve this for study."

"I detected sentiment. Credulity. Superstition. Your protest was a whimper."

The young officer showed a further brief flicker of dissent. "Perhaps—this being cannot be destroyed by our means."

The premier nodded at the body, and his thin, long lips became longer, thinner. A smile, perhaps. "Is not our second test planned for the very near future?"

"Tomorrow," Mornsk said. "But we are prepared to postpone it if you think the situation——"

"Postpone it?" The premier smiled. "On the contrary. Follow plans. Autopsy this animal. Attach what remains to the bomb. That should destroy it effectively." He glanced icily at the young general, made a daub at a salute and tramped over the ice-crisped tundra toward the jeeps.

On the way back to the base, Mornsk, of Intelligence, decided to mention his theory. Mornsk turned in his front seat. "One thing, comrade. Our American information is not, as you know, what it was. However, we had word this spring of what the British call a 'flap.' Many sudden, very secret conferences. Rumors. We never were able to determine the cause—and the brief state of near-panic among the leadership has abated. Could it be—the 'flap' followed one of their tests—that they, too, had a 'casualty'?"

"It could be," the premier replied. "What of it?"

"Nothing. I merely would have thought, comrade, that they would have announced it to the world."

The thin lips drew thinner again. "They are afraid. They would, today, keep secret a thousand things that, yesterday, they would have told one another freely. Freedom. Where is it now? We are driving it into limbo—their kind. To limbo." He shut his prune eyes, opened them, turned to the officer on his left. "Gromov, I hope the food's good here. I'm famished."

An old Russian proverb ran through his mind: "Where hangs the smoke of hate burns a fiercer fire called fear."

The trick, he reflected, was to keep that fire of fear alive, but to know at the same time it might consume you also. Then the trick was to make the fear invisible in the smokes of hatred. Having accomplished that, you would own men's souls and your power would be absolute, so long as you never allowed men to see how their hate was but fear, and so long as you, afraid, knowing it, hence more shrewd and cautious than the rest, did not become a corpse at the hands of the hating fearful.

There, in a nutshell, was the recipe for dictatorship. Over the proletariat. Over the godly believers. Over the heathen. Over all men, even those who imagined they were free and yet could be made to hate:

Frighten; then furnish the whipping boys. Then seize. Like governing children.

If more of these angels showed up, he reflected, it would simply be necessary to pretend they were demons, Lucifers, outer-space men bent on assassinating humanity. So simple.

The slate-hued buildings of the base rose over the tundra. From the frigid outdoors he entered rooms heated to a tropical temperature by the nearby reactors. There, too, the Soviets had somewhat surpassed the free peoples.

His secretary, Maximov, had thoughtfully forwarded Lamenula, to temper the hardships of the premier's Siberian hegira. He was amused, even somewhat stirred, to learn the young lady had objected to the trip, had fought, was even now in a state of alternate hysteria and coma—or simulated coma. A little communist discipline was evidently needed, and being applied; and he would take pleasure in administering the finishing touches.

Late that night he woke up with a feeling of uneasiness. A feeling, he decided, of fear. The room was quiet, the guards were in place, nothing menaced him in the immediate moment, and Lamenula was asleep. Her bruises were beginning to show, but she had learned how to avoid them in the future, which was the use of bruises.

What frightened him was the angel. Church music, which he had remembered, but refused to listen to in his mind, now came back to him. It did not cause him to believe that the visitor had given a new validity to an Old Testament. It had already caused him to speculate that what he, and a billion others, had thitherto regarded as pure myth might actually be founded on scientific fact.

What therefore frightened the premier as he lay on the great bed in the huge, gaudily decorated bedchamber, was an intuition of ignorance. Neither he nor his physicists, he nor his political philosophers—nor any men in the world that still, ludicrously, blindly, referred to itself as "free"—really knew anything fundamental about the universe. Nobody really knew, and could demonstrate scientifically, the "why" of time and space and energy—or matter. The angel—the very beautiful angel that had lain on the cold tundra—might possibly mean and be something that not he nor any living man, skeptic or believer, could even comprehend.

That idea wakened him thoroughly. Here was a brand-new dimension of the unknown to be faced. He sat up, switched on the light and put a cigarette in his thin mouth.

How, he asked himself, could this fear of the unknown be translated into a hatred of something known, and so employed to enhance power? His power. That was, invariably, the formulation; once made, it generally supplied its own answer.

You could not, however, set the people in the Soviets and the people in the rest of the world to hating angels. Not when, especially, their reality—or real counterpart—could never be exhibited and had become a military secret.

Mornsk's theory bemused him. Had the Americans also shot one down with an H-bomb? If so, they'd followed a procedure like his own, apparently. Saying nothing. Examining the victim, doubtless.

He realized he should go to sleep. He was to be roused early for the test of the next super-H-bomb, but he kept ruminating, as he smoked, on the people of the United States. *Whom,* he reflected, *we shall destroy in millions* in—— The number of months and days remaining before the blitz of the U.S.A. was so immense a secret that he did not let himself reckon it exactly. *Whom we shall slaughter in sudden millions, soon.*

But suppose something intervened? Angels?

He smiled again. Even if such creatures had visited the earth once before, it was long ago. They might be here again now. They would presumably go away again, for millenniums. Ample time to plant the Red flag everywhere in the world.

Still, he could not know, and not to know was alarming.

There was a phone beside his bed. He could astound telephone operators halfway around the world, and yet, doubtless, in ten minutes, fifteen—perhaps an hour—he could converse with the President of the United States.

"Seen any angels, Mr. President? . . . What do you make of it? . . . Perhaps we aren't as knowing as we imagine. . . . Possibly we should meet and talk things over—postpone any—plans we might have for the near future? At least, until this matter of invading angels is settled."

It wouldn't be that simple or that quick, but it might be done. And it might be that that was the only possible way to save the Soviet, because it might be the one way left to save man and his planet.

He thought about the abandonment of the communist philosophy, the scrapping of decades of horror and sacrifice, the relaxing of the steely discipline; he thought of the dreams of world domination gone glimmering—of "freedom" being equated with communism. There welled in him the avalanche of hatred which was his essence and the essence of his world. He ground out his cigarette and tried to sleep. . . .

In the morning, after the test shot—which was also very successful and, the premier thought, frightening—he requested the report on the autopsy of the casualty. He had to ask repeatedly, since it became clear that none of the nearby persons—generals, commissars, aides, technicians—wanted to answer. He commanded Mornsk.

The general sweated in the cold air, under a sky again clear and as palely blue as a turquoise. "We have no report, comrade. The autopsy was undertaken last night by Smidz. An ideal man, we felt—the great biologist, who happened to be here, working on radiation effects on pigs. He labored alone all night, and then—your orders, comrade—the—remains were fixed to the bomb." Mornsk's glance at the towering mushroom disposed of that matter. "It was then discovered that Smidz made no notes of whatever he learned."

"Get Smidz."

"This morning early, comrade, he killed himself."

General Scott did not return to the Pacific until nearly Christmastime. He had hoped not to go back at all, particularly since he had spent the autumn with his family in Baltimore, commuting weekdays to the Pentagon. In December, however, he received secret information of still another series of springtime nuclear-weapons tests and orders to fly again to the Sangre Islands, where he would prepare another of the group for total sacrifice. The death of islands was becoming commonplace to the weaponeers. In the unfinished span of his own military career, a suitable target had grown from a square of canvas stretched over a wooden frame to a building, and then to a city block, next a city's heart, and now, an island the size of Manhattan. This, moreover, was not holed, wrecked or merely set afire, but wiped off the earth's face, its roots burned away deep into the sea, its substance thrown, poisonous, across the skies.

He went reluctantly, but as a soldier must, aware that by now he had the broadest experience—among general officers—for the task at hand.

Work went ahead with no more than the usual quota of "bugs"—or what his orderly would have called "snafus." It was a matter of "multiple snafu," however, which finally led the general to order a light plane to fly him to Tempest Island. There had arisen an argument with the natives about property rights; there was some trouble with the placement of instruments; a problem about electric power had come up; and a continuing report of bad chow was being turned in from the island mess hall. Time for a high-echelon look-see.

As he flew in, General Scott noticed the changes which he had helped to devise. The mission playing field had been bulldozed big enough to accommodate fair-sized cargo planes on two x-angled strips. Here and there the green rug of jungle had been macheted open to contain new measuring devices of the scientists. The harbor had been deepened; dredged-up coral made a mole against the purple Pacific as well as the foundation for a sizable pier. Otherwise, Tempest was the same.

His mind, naturally, returned to his previous trip and to what had been found on the island. The general had observed a growing tendency, even in Admiral Stanforth and Rawson, now a colonel, to recall the angel more as a figure of a dream than as reality. Just before the landing gear came down he looked for, and saw, the very glade in which the angel had fallen. Its clear spring was an emerald eye and the Bletias were in violet bloom all around.

Then he was on the ground, busy with other officers, busy with the plans and problems of a great nation, scared, arming, ready these days for war at the notice of a moment or at no notice whatever. Even here, thousands upon thousands of miles from the nervous target areas of civilization, the fear and the desperate urgency of man had rolled up, parting the jungle and erecting grim engines associated with ruin.

He was on his way to the headquarters tent when he noticed, and recognized, the young boy.

Teddy Simms, he thought, was about ten now, the age of his own son. But Teddy looked older than ten, and very sad.

The general stepped away from his accompanying officers. "You go on," he said. "I'll soon catch up. This is an old friend of mine." He waved then. "Hi, Ted! Why you all dressed up? Remember me?"

The youngster stopped and did recognize the general, with a look of anxiousness. He nodded and glanced down at his clothes. "I'm gonna leave! Tonight. It'll be"—his face brightened slightly—"my very first airplane ride!"

"That's swell!" The general had been puzzled by signs

of apprehension in the boy. "How's your father? And your aunt? Cora, wasn't it?"

"She's O.K. But father——" His lip shook.

Marc Scott no longer smiled. "Your father——"

The boy answered stonily, "Went nuts."

"After——" the general asked, knew the answer and was unsurprised by the boy's increased anxiousness.

"I'm not allowed to say. I'd go to prison forever."

A jeepful of soldiers passed. The general moved to the boy's side and said, "With me, you are, Ted. Because I know all about it too. I'm—I'm mighty sorry your father—is ill. Maybe he'll recover, though."

"The board doesn't think so. They're giving up the mission. That's why I'm going away. To school, Stateside. Father"—he fell in step with the general, leaping slightly with each stride—"father never got any better—after that old day you were here."

"What say, we go back where—it happened? I'd like to see it once more, Ted."

"No." Teddy amended it, "No, sir. I'm not even allowed to talk about it. I don't ever go there!"

"It's too bad. I thought it was the most beautiful thing that ever happened to me in my life."

The boy stared at the man incredulously. "You did? Father thought it was the worst thing ever happened."

"I felt as if you, Ted—and I—all of us—were seeing something completely wonderful!"

The boy's face showed an agreement which changed, slowly, to a pitiable emotion—regret, or fear, perhaps shame. It was the general's intuition which bridged the moment: Teddy knew more than he had ever said about the angel; he had lied originally or omitted something.

"What is it, son?" The general's tone was fatherly. Eyes darted toward the jungle, back to the general and rested measuringly, then hopelessly. It was as if the youngster had considered aloud running away and had decided his adversary was too powerful to evade.

He stood silent a moment longer; then said almost incoherently, "I never meant to keep it! But it is gold! And we were always so mighty poor! I thought, for a while, if father sold it— But he couldn't even think of things like selling gold books. He had lost his reason."

If the general's heart surged, if his mind was stunned, he did not show it. "Gold books?" His eyes forgave in advance.

"Just one book, but heavy." The dismal boy looked at the ground. "I didn't steal it, really! That angel–dropped it."

The general's effort was tremendous. Not in battle had composure cost him as dear. "You–read it?"

"Huh!" the boy said. "It was in all kinds of other languages. 'Wisdom,' that angel said it was. 'Gathered from our whole galaxy–for Earth.' Did you ever know—" His voice intensified with the question, as if by asking it he might divert attention from his guilt. "Did you know there are other people on other planets of other suns, all around? Maybe Vega, or the North Star, or Rigel, or more likely old Sirius? That angel mentioned a few names. I forget which."

"No. I didn't realize it. And, you say, this book had a message for the people on Earth, written in all languages? Not English, though?"

"I didn't see any English. I saw–like Japanese and Arabian–and a lot of kinds of alphabets you never heard of–some, just dots."

"And you–threw it away?" He asked it easily too.

"Naw. You couldn't do that! It's gold–at least, it looks like gold. All metal pages. It's got hinges, kind of, for every page. I guess it's fireproof and even space-proof, at the least. I didn't throw it away. I hid it under an old rock. Come on. I'll show you."

They returned to the glade. The book lay beneath a flat

stone. There had been another the general was never to know about—a book buried beneath a sod hut in Siberia by a peasant who also had intended to sell it, for he, too, had been poor. But the other book, identical, along with the hovel above it, had been reduced to fractions of its atoms by a certain test weapon which had destroyed the body of its bearer.

This one the general picked up with shaking hands, opened and gazed upon with an ashen face.

The hot sun of noon illumined the violet orchids around his tailored legs. The boy stood looking up at him, awaiting judgment, accustomed to harshness; and about them was the black and white filigree of tropical forest. With inexpressible amazement, Marc searched page after page of inscriptions in languages unknown, unsuspected until then. It became apparent that there was one message only, very short, set again and again and again, but he did not know what it was until, toward the last pages, he found the tongues of Earth.

A sound was made by the man as he read them—a sound that began with murmurous despair and ended, as comprehension entered his brain, with a note of exultation. For the message of icy space and flaring stars was this: "Love one another."

Vincent Miranda *has been a photo journalist since 1968, working for newspaper and television. Having a strong interest in science fiction, he found himself assisting educators in setting up science fiction courses at the beginning of the present surge of interest in the field. He has been published in serious fan journals such as* The Rohmer Review *and such diverse magazines as* Eclectic *and* The Magazine of Fantasy and Science Fiction, *and is now preparing books on both the fantastic film and the history of science fiction. Mr. Miranda is the science fiction editor of* The Saturday Evening Post. *He is a member of the Science Fiction Research Association and a participant in the Annual Conference on Teaching Science Fiction.*